WILDER

WILDER

#1 *NEW YORK TIMES* BESTSELLING AUTHOR

REBECCA YARROS

Entangled Publishing, LLC
644 Shrewsbury Commons Ave., STE 181
Shrewsbury, PA 17361
rights@entangledpublishing.com

Amara is an imprint of Entangled Publishing, LLC.

Visit our website at www.entangledpublishing.com.

Edited by Karen Grove
Cover design by Elizabeth Turner Stokes
Cover photography by KOTOIMAGES/Shutterstock
Interior design by Britt Marczak

Trade ISBN 978-1-64937-733-3
Ebook ISBN 978-1-63375-713-4

Manufactured in the United States of America

First Printing March 2024

10 9 8 7 6 5 4 3 2 1

AMARA
an imprint of Entangled Publishing LLC

ALSO BY REBECCA YARROS

RENEGADES SERIES

Wilder
Nova
Rebel

FLIGHT & GLORY SERIES

Full Measures
Eyes Turned Skyward
Beyond What is Given
Hallowed Ground
The Reality of Everything

THE EMPYREAN SERIES

Fourth Wing
Iron Flame

STANDALONES

The Things We Leave Unfinished
Great and Precious Things
The Last Letter

To Emily "Leah" Byer.
I can't imagine a world where you're not my best friend.

At Entangled, we want our readers to be well-informed. If you would like to know if this book contains any elements that might be of concern for you, please check the back of the book for details.

CHAPTER ONE

LEAH

Port of Miami

The elevator was hot and humid despite the air conditioning, filled with four other students, their luggage, and the unmistakable taste of excitement and salt water.

With a *ding*, the doors opened on the tenth floor, and the bellboy got off with my luggage. Wait. Were they called bellboys on cruise ships? Cabin stewards? I should have probably known that, seeing as this ship was my home for the next nine months.

"Wait," I said, following him. "This isn't my floor."

"No mistake," he promised, tossing a cute grin over his white-uniformed shoulder. "Your room is right this way, Miss Baxter."

I flipped through my file folder while trying not to trip over my feet or the other students crowding the narrow hall during move-in day. "See?" I asked, waving the paper from my "room and board" section. "I'm supposed to be on the fourth floor."

In steerage. I laughed to myself, dodging a sweaty guy with frat letters on his sleeveless tee as he manhandled a suitcase into a room on my right.

"I have you on this deck," he answered, correcting my terminology. "Do you know if your roommate is here yet?"

"She came down with mono three days ago." And I already missed my best friend. Guilt sank my heart. Was her mom taking care of her? Was she getting enough rest? She'd taken such good care of me when I needed her the last two years, and I'd just *left* her. *She told you to.*

Considering I hadn't left the house without Rachel pushing me in the last two years—hell, at first getting out of bed had been nearly impossible—I could barely believe that I'd actually come without her.

But she'd been right—living my life didn't mean I loved him less, it just meant I loved myself, too.

"Oh, no. Did she get a refund?" he asked, waiting for another group to cross in front of us into their room.

"No, she'll be here at the start of next term." Thank God the Study at Sea program worked on the trimester system, otherwise Rachel would have had to wait until January to come. Instead, she could join us in Abu Dhabi in November.

Abu Dhabi. Being accepted to this program—a full academic year studying on a worldwide cruise—had been surreal. But now I was actually living it. I was really in Miami, saying good-bye to the U.S. for nine entire months. I just never imagined—or wanted—to do it on my own.

But that was why I'd agreed to this program, right? It was time to step out of the comfort zone I'd walled myself into the last two years, and it would look killer when I applied to graduate programs for International Relations.

Besides, Rachel couldn't hold my hand for the rest of my life.

"Here we are," the cabin steward said, fumbling with the

card key as we reached the back—*aft*, I corrected myself—corner of the ship.

Two girls in short dresses bumped into me, apologizing as they passed. They giggled with a lightness I slightly envied and entered the room on the opposite corner from mine.

"Sorry," the cabin steward apologized. "It's only my second day on the ship, and I don't have the hang of these locks yet." He sighed in relief when the door clicked open.

"It's okay," I said as he held the door for me. "Thank you, Hugo," I added after reading the green tag on his shirt.

"No problem," he said as I passed him, walking into the entry hall of the suite.

Holy. Shit.

"Yeah, that was my reaction, too," he said with a soft chuckle.

"Oh, I said that out loud?" I asked, more distracted by the marble floors and the sheer size of the suite.

His brown eyes danced with laughter. "It's your room. Feel free to swear as much as you want. Hall closet is here." He pointed to a door on the right.

Hall closet? My entire room should have fit in there.

I tuned him out and simply walked. There were two bedrooms off to the right, connected by a large bathroom with double sinks, a shower, and a jetted tub. Seriously?

I picked my jaw up off the floor as I made my way farther into the suite. There was a dining area set up with a table to seat six and a living room with supple, buttery leather couches and a big-screen TV. But it wasn't the space that had me speechless—it was the view from the floor-to-ceiling windows that lined the exquisite suite. What would it be like to wake up every day here for the next nine months? To walk through those huge doors to the balcony and bask in the sunlight?

To be the kind of person who could even think about affording this?

It was perfect, but it wasn't mine.

If this place was on my bill for even one week, I could kiss every dollar of my savings good-bye.

"Hugo, I'm not supposed to be here. I'm in the work-study program. I'm supposed to be on deck four."

He stopped inspecting how my mini-fridge was stocked and looked up at me. "Right. I know." He shook his head. "I mean that I know you're in the program. I am, too. But you're supposed to be here, I promise. You're a tutor, right?"

I nodded. That had been the offer that had woken me up, brought me back to life this year: if I tutored one student on the *Athena*, not only would my tuition, field-studies, and room and board be paid, but the program would do the same for Rachel. As soon as I'd made sure that it wasn't some cruel joke, I'd pinched myself and signed the papers. With my parents under a Hollywood-Hills-house amount of medical bills, and Rachel's uber-uptight parents declaring that she couldn't go if I didn't... well, everything had fallen into place perfectly.

"Well, then this is your room."

"No way," I protested, looking up at the chandelier. *Seriously? A freaking chandelier?* "Is every tutor in a suite? Even with a ship that caters to rich kids, I have a hard time thinking the program is this hard up for tutors."

He stood and smiled. "Nope, just you. Why don't you pick out a bedroom? Or check out the balcony? I'll give Mrs. Trenton a buzz if it makes you feel better."

"That would be awesome, thanks." I opted for the balcony. The afternoon was winding down—the air still heavy with sultry heat as I opened the heavy glass door and stepped onto the polished wooden surface. Miami in August was hot as hell, and wearing jeans wasn't helping. I pulled my thick hair into a messy topknot to get it off my neck and moved toward the smooth railing, testing my limits. After all, that's what this trip was for, right? But my chest constricted with every step, and as the water came into view stories below, the roaring that filled my ears sounded too similar to a California canyon wind and not enough like the Miami breeze. *Not now. God, not now.* I heeded my body's warning, backing away from the nauseating height. *Guess you're not quite ready.* But I had nine months on this ship, and maybe if I tried a little each day, by the end I could do it. Until then...well, I'd hang back here.

It was a gorgeous space with a fleet of cushioned lounge chairs and an unencumbered view down to the right— *starboard*—side of the ship.

Another student leaned against the railing about twenty feet away, his very tanned, toned, tattooed body on display in nothing but a pair of dark blue Hawaiian print board shorts that hung low on his hips.

I openly ogled the cut lines of his muscles, from his worship-worthy washboard abs to the way his biceps flexed, tattoos rippling as he pushed off the railing and sighed, running his hands over his midnight-black hair and lacing his fingers behind his neck.

He was *hot*. And not passingly hot, but more like *I-can-make-you-come-with-a-look* hot. Hell, I was halfway there, and he hadn't so much as glanced in my direction.

What the hell is wrong with you?

I shook my head and tore my eyes away. What was the point of looking, wanting, when he was so far out of my league that we were playing different sports? And besides, what kind of sport gave a guy a body like that? Where every muscle had a purpose?

My gaze drifted back to the stranger, appreciating the strong angles of his face that I could make out from here, the tattoos that moved with his skin.

Not for you. Yeah, obviously, but one more second of gawking wasn't going to hurt me. Hell, at least it reminded me that my sex drive still worked...and was currently in overdrive, apparently.

He looked pensive, like he carried some impossible, Atlas-worthy weight on his shoulders, and while part of me wondered what someone like him could possibly have to worry about, the other part instinctively wanted to soothe him.

Then he caught me staring.

I ignored my flight reflex and forced myself to hold his gaze across the distance. He cocked his head to the side, like he was trying to decide if he knew me, and smiled softly.

Yep. The old sex drive is definitely working again.

Damn it, he wasn't just hot, he was beautiful.

The door opened behind him and a goddess with long blond hair and longer legs floated onto the deck. He turned to her, his entire presence morphing into one word: cocky.

"You ready?" she asked. Even her voice was gorgeous.

I turned away from the obvious couple and was saved by Hugo opening the door. "Miss Baxter?"

"Leah," I corrected him.

"Leah, Mrs. Trenton is here." He held the door open, and I walked through, mentally kissing all this opulence—including the hot stranger—good-bye.

A middle-aged blond woman in a pencil skirt leaned over

a folder of paperwork at my dining room table. *The table, not yours. Don't get used to this.*

"Miss Baxter." She greeted me with a smile and an outstretched hand, which I shook. "I understand that you don't like your room?"

My cheeks heated instantly. "No, it's gorgeous. I love it, but I'm supposed to be in an inside cabin on the crew deck. Is there another Leah Baxter?"

"No, this wasn't a mistake. The student you're tutoring asked that you be put here so he could have easier access to you as his schedule is quite demanding."

"Who would do that?"

"Paxton Wilder," she replied, her smile still firmly affixed to her face.

"Miss Baxter, which bedroom did you want?" Hugo called from the entry hall, my luggage in hand.

"None!" I called out. Easier access? Did this guy think I was going to be at his beck and call? Hopefully not, because I was no one's beck-and-call girl.

"Nonsense, give her the bigger one since her roommate won't be joining her until November."

"Absolutely not. This is Rachel's dream and she would deserve the bigger one."

"Perfect. Give her the blue room with the bigger balcony," Mrs. Trenton answered.

Crap. Did I inadvertently accept the room? "I can't afford this," I said quietly.

"Well, I'll look into that with the bursar's office. Now, here's your ID. It doubles as your room key as well as access to all your VIP privileges such as early disembarkation for field-study days, so don't lose it. Hopefully the lanyard helps in that department."

VIP? Unless that stood for *very impoverished person*, there was no way. She handed me the card and, yep, there it was— Eleanor Baxter, VIP. It said so right next to the cringe-worthy picture I'd taken in the cruise terminal. Fabulous, my normally tame brown hair was pretty much the before picture on an intervention makeover show.

"Enjoy your year with us."

How was I going to enjoy it if I couldn't pay for it? Before I could sputter an intelligent response, Mrs. Trenton was leaving.

"Hugo, you'll take good care of her?"

"Yes, ma'am," he replied as the door shut behind her.

"What does she mean take good care of me?" I asked.

"Your work-study is to tutor Mr. Wilder. Mine is to be your butler. I'm here to help you."

Butler? That was it. I was in some kind of parallel universe. I tried to crank my jaw up off the floor and found some semblance of a coherent thought. "Which room is Mr. Wilder in?" I managed to ask.

"Ten thirty-two," he answered.

I was in the hallway, my ID around my neck, before he finished. "Ten thirty-two," I mumbled to myself as I walked two doors away to the other corner suite and knocked.

Loud rock music blared from inside, and I knocked again, this time harder.

"Hold on!" came a loud male voice.

A moment later, the door opened and a beefy, bald guy answered. "Can I help you?"

"Umm... I'm looking for Mr. Wilder?"

He looked me up and down and then smirked. "Not his type, honey. Sorry."

If my cheeks had warmed earlier, now they were on fucking fire. "I'm not looking to score him; I'm his tutor." I lifted the lanyard from my neck and dangled the attached ID.

His eyes widened. "Oh, Miss Baxter? He's getting ready, but come on in. Wilder!" he yelled as he shut the door behind me. "I'm Little John, by the way."

"Nice to meet you," I said, and bit my tongue when I wanted to ask where Robin Hood was hiding.

Wilder's suite was bigger than mine, which was absolutely mind-boggling. What would someone need with all this space? We cleared the hallway into the huge living area, and I snorted. There were at least a dozen bikini-clad girls lounged over his couches, drinking out of red Solo cups. I guess you needed that much room when you traveled with your own harem.

Don't get judgy.

Too late.

I couldn't help it. I was here for serious academics and travel, and he was, well…apparently not.

Looking up, I watched him come down the stairs. I might have been blown away by the fact that he had a two-story suite if I hadn't been stunned by Mr. Out of My League walking toward me with a grin. *No way. No. Fucking. Way.*

"Balcony girl?"

Oh God. He had seen me. And that *voice*. It was deep, slightly gravelly, and sexy as hell. Almost as sexy as the dragon tattoo that wound itself from his heart to where the tail dragged along the lickable line of his abs. *Not lickable. Nope. Not one bit.*

"Uhh, hi." Oh my God, that was up there with *I carried a watermelon.* "I didn't mean that."

His incredibly sexy grin widened. "You didn't mean to say hi?"

I blinked. "No, of course I did."

"Then I don't see an issue."

One of the partygoers knocked me off-balance—and right into Wilder. He caught me easily, his fingers flexing on my waist. I should have worn a thicker tank top—the silky material of this one let the heat from his hands right through to wake up every nerve ending in my skin.

"Are you okay?" he asked, turning the full force of his incredibly blue eyes on me. Magnetic. Glorious. Hypnotizing. Those were all better words to describe the wild variations of color there, or the way he pinned me in place without a single ounce of effort.

My first impression had been right. He could probably make me come with one look...and that exact look was trained on me with all the accuracy of a guided missile straight to my thighs.

I didn't believe in love at first sight. I wasn't that naive. But science? Chemistry? Pheromones? Yeah, lust at first encounter, I believed that all day long.

Words, Leah. Find them.

"Oh, you found your tutor," Little John said with a slap on Wilder's back. "We have to go soon, so get ready."

Wilder stiffened and carefully set me away from him. "You're Eleanor Baxter?"

"Leah," I corrected him automatically and dug my thumbs into the belt loops of my jeans.

"Holy shit." He closed his eyes.

"Are *you* okay?" I turned his words around on him.

He nodded, his eyes squeezed tight. "Just moving you out of the fuckable category in my brain. I'm going to need a minute."

Wait. He had categories? Scrap that. I'd barely met the guy

and he's already friend-zoned me? *Out of your league.*

"Leah," he said, opening his eyes with a slight smile, like he enjoyed saying it. "So what can I do for you?"

"You can explain why I'm in a ridiculously huge suite that I can't possibly afford and ask them to move me, since apparently you have the power over where I sleep." I crossed my arms under my breasts, well aware that I was fidgeting.

"Oh, do I?" he asked with a suggestive smile.

Apparently friend-zone was still flirt-zone to him.

I tried to look over his shoulder but, realizing he was too tall for that, I peeked around his side at the collection of girls who might have had an entire outfit if you strung their clothes together. "Unfortunately. Look, I don't mind tutoring you. I'm happy to do it to be in this program, but I can do it as effectively from deck four. I want my assigned room back. Now."

His eyes widened. "You're turning down the suite?"

My spine straightened. "I am."

"Wilder, we gotta go," Little John said, handing him a mess of black straps.

"That's not okay," Wilder said.

"Dude, we have a schedule, and the crew is already set up and ready."

He waved off Little John. "No, we're cool, I'm talking to Leah. You can't give back the suite. It's yours."

"No." I shook my head.

He stepped between the straps and twisted himself through the contraption until he had it on, clipping what was apparently a harness over his chest with a final snap. "Leah, it's paid for."

Wait. What?

I blinked rapidly, knowing that my anti-capitalist parents would be groaning if they heard my hesitation. "Mr. Wilder, that's...that's way too much. All I needed was my room and board; even the shore excursions were too much." What did he expect from me with that kind of "gift"? What kind of access was he looking for?

"It's Paxton to you, or Pax, whichever you prefer, and you're keeping the suite."

"Wilder, we have to go," Little John shouted over the music, the brunette next to him impatiently glaring our way.

"Right. Leah, if we can finish this later?"

I shook my head. I was only getting this courage up once. Anything more and I'd be basking in the glory of that room, the view, the bed, and the way that tub would soothe my sore muscles. "No. We're finishing this now."

He cocked his head to the side exactly like he had out on the deck, but the pensive guy wasn't here. No, this man was sure, confident, and oozed a blatant and obvious sexuality that made me glad I had my jeans on. "Are you ready for an adventure?"

"What? I came on the cruise, right? And what does that have to do with the mini-mansion my suitcase is currently camped in?"

He studied me carefully, and I shifted my weight. Being around this guy threw me off my hard-earned balance, and I couldn't afford that, not when I was barely back to standing on my own as it was.

"Okay, well, if you want to keep up this discussion, you'll have to come with me. Is that okay?"

"Fine," I answered.

"After you." He motioned toward the doors, and I walked in front of him through the party. Once we reached Little John and the brunette, who shot me snotty looks like it was her day job, Paxton stopped.

"Zoe, how about you sit this one out. I'll get you another time."

Her jaw dropped. "You have got to be kidding me."

"I'm not." He dismissed her without another look, calling out to his guests, "Let's continue this on deck, shall we? I'll meet you guys at the pool!"

They all cheered as we left the room. "International frat party," I mumbled as I followed Little John's massive back down the hallway.

"I'm not in a frat." Paxton laughed behind me as we dodged a couple of students moving into their rooms. "Now could you please tell me what it is you have against that room? It's nice. I checked it out to make sure."

I looked back over my shoulder. "Did you know that my scholarship includes my best friend, too? It's already too much."

He shook his head. "But you're earning it as part of your compensation. Trust me, you'll more than earn it."

Compensation? He'd better not think— I stopped dead in my tracks and he bumped into me, the metal on his chest strap hitting me in the head.

"Oh man, you okay?" he asked and reached for my head, but I stepped away before he could make contact. Once had been more than enough.

"I'm your tutor. You know that, right? Only your tutor. Just studying. There's no need for me to have a giant suite with a"—I swallowed—"separate bedroom."

"Is that what you think?" he asked with an incredulous laugh. "Leah, get in the elevator."

We moved into the small space, and Little John pretended to ignore us, fiddling with the straps of another harness in his hands to give us privacy.

"What am I supposed to think?" I asked as we descended. "I was already told that you'd need *easy access* to me. I just want to make sure we start out with a crystal-clear understanding of what we both expect." *I'm sure as hell not your beck-and-call girl.* Especially not the call-girl part.

"I can't escape people even in my own suite," he answered simply, watching the numbers light with each floor we passed. The doors dinged, and I followed him out through the crew deck to the exit ramp.

"What does that have to do with my suite? And why are we leaving the ship? We're supposed to sail"—I checked my watch—"in exactly fifteen minutes. I'd kind of like to be on board when that happens."

"Don't worry. The ship isn't leaving without me, and I'll get you on board." His smile deepened, revealing two dimples. *Damn.* I had to find a way to not be affected by this guy if I was going to successfully tutor him for the year. I wouldn't exactly be effective with mush brain, and then where would I be? He had to pass, or my scholarship was gone. Rachel's scholarship was gone. The amazing experience for grad school was gone. That was the deal. Besides, he was just a pretty face, and it took a lot more than that to turn my head.

Fine, then as of this moment, you are not attracted to Paxton Wilder. Nope. Not at all.

"Watch your step," he said, offering his hand as we moved onto the ramp.

Okay, well maybe a little attracted.

I took his hand, more worried about falling on my face than anything else. His skin was warm, his grip firm on mine as we moved down the ramp. He let go, and I realized that we'd reached the bottom.

I hadn't slipped or freaked about the height once. Miraculous.

"Thank you," I said quietly.

"No problem," he answered easily. "Look," he started as we walked through the nearly empty terminal in the opposite direction of where I'd entered earlier today. "I want you to keep the suite, and it's selfish, I know."

"How is that selfish?" I asked, walking next to him.

"School's never been easy for me. Ever. I need someplace quiet to study, and I'm hoping you'll lend me your living room—and your brain—at night, that's all. I made sure you were close to my room so I don't have to go far, and I can't exactly move you in with me without raising some eyebrows. I promise we'll work out a schedule. I don't expect you to be at my beck and call, but I'm going to need your help. A ton of your help."

Beck and call? *It's like he's in your brain.* "You're honestly that worried about your grades?"

"There is more than you could ever imagine riding on my grades right now. And, well, you have your work cut out for you."

Before I could question him, Little John opened the door to a stairwell and ushered us straight to another elevator while he whistled. The doors dinged open, where a tall, lean, hot, equally tattooed guy leaned against the wall, wearing the same kind of harness as Paxton.

"Cutting the timing a little close, aren't we, Wilder?" he called out, uncrossing his arms and openly glaring at me.

"Leah, this asshat is Landon, my best friend. Nova, meet Leah, my tutor." He emphasized the last two words.

"Oh." His eyebrows rose over crystal green eyes. "Nice to meet you, Leah. You ready for this?"

"I think so," I answered. "As ready as you can be for a cruise around the world, right?"

His eyes narrowed, and he shot his gaze toward Paxton. "Wilder..."

Paxton sighed as the light moved from floor to floor with our ascent. "Leah, remember that whole nondisclosure agreement you signed to get your scholarship?"

"Sure. I signed an NDA about whomever I would tutor for their privacy."

"Right. And the media release?"

My forehead puckered. There had been so many papers I'd signed. "The one that said I would release my image, video, that kind of thing for future promotion of the program as part of my scholarship agreement?"

Paxton winced. "Yeah, about that. We're kind of making a documentary, and being my tutor, you're probably going to show up in it a little."

"A documentary? For video class or something? And by a little, you mean..."

He scratched the back of his neck. "A lot. I mean a lot. I'll do my best to keep you out of the camera, but it's going to happen. I mean, as long as you want to stay as my tutor, it will."

I knew what he was saying: if I didn't agree, I couldn't be his tutor. Not being his tutor meant no scholarship, no cruise. No Mykonos. No Rachel.

Do it for her.

I pulled in a deep breath. "How long do I have to decide?"

"About twenty seconds," Landon answered.

"What?" I shouted.

Paxton hit the emergency stop on the elevator. "You have as long as you need. But your answer is kind of holding up the departure of the ship."

I rubbed the damp skin of my forehead and cursed my jeans for the thousandth time. It was only a little documentary. Who was possibly going to see it? The media club at whatever college he went to? "Okay, fine."

He relaxed next to me and gave me a relieved smile as the elevator started to move again. "Thank you."

"You're welcome." Besides, there wasn't much interesting about me, anyway. I'd mostly be in the background.

The doors opened, and the cameras that met us were anything but amateur. They looked like they cost more than my parents' cars. *Oh. Shit.*

"Pretend they're not there," Paxton whispered.

"Right. Because that's possible."

The cameras and crew moved out of our way as we walked onto what was obviously the top of the terminal's tower. Glass walls greeted us, as well as at least a dozen people holding cameras, microphones, and lights. "This isn't for your college media club, is it?" I asked quietly.

"No. It's not."

"Of course not," I mumbled.

"You ready for this?" Landon asked a camera like it was a real person. He'd transformed instantly, from sulky to star, making me wonder which one was more the real him. "We're about to kick off this worldwide spectacle."

"What about you, Wilder?" the cameraman asked.

"I was born ready," Paxton replied, his voice downright arrogant. He'd undergone the same transformation as Landon, oozing a cool, cocky persona that gave me whiplash.

"And who is your new flavor?" Someone in the crew laughed.

"Watch your mouth, Lance," Paxton fired back, pointing

his finger. "Leah is new to the Renegade family, and you might not realize it, but she's got your job in her hands."

The room fell to a hush, and all eyes swung toward me. I had zero clue what the hell Paxton was talking about, but I managed a shaky smile and wave for the camera. "Hi."

Smooth, Leah.

"Wilder, we're all set up for single on left, tandem on right," Little John said from across the room, where a single glass door was open to the balcony.

Paxton led me through the crowd until we stood on the grated metal balcony. *Holy shit.* How many stories up were we? How far apart were the metal slats? For the love of God, I could see the sidewalk through the space between my feet and the small crowd that had gathered there.

My vision narrowed, blackening at the edges, and what had been the grate seconds earlier now looked like a steep canyon wall with nothing between me and the ground hundreds of feet below. I blinked rapidly until the grate returned.

"I think I'll go inside," I whispered, backing up slowly until I bumped into Little John's belly, my breath accelerating.

"This is for you, Bambi," he said, handing me the harness he'd been carrying.

"What?" I squeaked. *Don't look down. Focus on him.*

"Bambi, you know...because you look like a deer in the headlights," he answered.

"Bambi is a boy, and what the hell would I need a harness for?"

"That." Landon pointed toward two thick wires Paxton was inspecting, which led from the top of the tower to—*no fucking way*—a wall at the end of the pool. On the ship. Our ship. The one in port at least six stories beneath us. "We're zip-lining into the set-sail party," he said with a grin, as if I'd been given some kind of gift.

"No. Nope. Not happening," I said, shaking my head, trying to back into the tower.

"Wilder, we've got a no-go," Little John called out.

Paxton looked over from where it appeared he was securing whatever contraption wanted to kill me. He took me gently by the arm to the side of the tower where the cameras weren't pointing and, for once, my thoughts weren't on how hot he was but rather how quickly I could kill him and bury the body.

"There's no chance I'm doing that." My words ran together. "I don't even know how to do that, nor would I ever *want* to. It's wild." *And dangerous. And so high.*

"It's fun," he promised and knelt in front of me. "Step here," he said, guiding my feet.

"It's not fun, it's death, and I want no part of it."

"It's perfectly safe. Step again."

My legs acted on autopilot, my eyes firmly focused on the zip line. "Why the hell would you even do something like this?"

"Because no one has," he answered, as if that was reason enough.

"Did you ever stop to think there's a reason no one has done it? Maybe it's dangerous? Or illegal?"

He laughed and stood, pulling something up my legs and fastening it around my waist. "It's actually safe, I promise. I've done it hundreds of times. Never onto a cruise ship, but through jungles, off a parasail, that kind of thing. Zip-lining is one of the tamer things that I do."

"You're unbelievable."

"So I've been told. Arm?"

I thrust it out. "Well, I'm saying no. I'm going to walk down this deathtrap tower and get on the ship."

"You can't."

"Excuse me?" I fired back as he snapped the clasp over my chest. Holy shit, I was in the harness. "I am a fully grown woman, I most certainly can say no."

"Oh, that you can. But they've already shut the doors and begun the launch, see?" He motioned behind him.

I leaned around his massive shoulders, my fingers digging into his taut, inked skin to avoid falling over the railing. He was telling the truth. The hatches had all shut, the ramps were down, and the engines were on.

"You have *got* to be kidding me."

"I'm not," he said, his nose wrinkled in apology. "Look, Leah, I made a wrong assumption. I never thought you wouldn't want to do this. I figured the minute you agreed to come with me, you knew what you were getting into."

"What?" My head snapped back. "Because I should automatically assume someone is going to zip-line onto our cruise ship?"

"Well, I'm not just anyone," he said. "Don't you know who I am?"

"Oh my God, could you be any more arrogant?"

"Yes."

I scoffed. "Hard to believe. What am I supposed to do?"

"Ride tandem with me," he answered with a dimple-deepened grin. *Asshole.* "It'll be fun. Plus, it's the only way to get on the ship, because it leaves the minute we land and they cut the line."

"Wilder, we've got to go!" Landon called out, already latched on to his wire.

"So my options are I slide down the death-wire with you, or

I go home?"

"You could always meet us at the next port. I think it's four days away, right?"

"I'd miss a whole week of class!"

"Well, there is that." He shrugged.

"I. Do. Not. Like. You." I spat out every word at Paxton as Little John came over with two helmets. *Hold on to the anger, it's safer than fear.*

"Well, I actually kinda like you, so that's enough for me. Then again, I've always liked firecrackers."

Unbelievable.

"Let's go, kids," Little John called.

"Come on, live a little."

"That seems more like a quick route to death. Unless you have some foolproof method of keeping me safe."

He took the helmet from Little John, slipped my hair tie free, and ran his fingers over my hair. "You have gorgeous hair, Leah."

"You have a huge ego, Paxton," I fired back.

He slid the helmet onto my head, adjusted the chin strap, and snapped it before doing the same to his own. "If there was one thing you wanted from this trip, what would it be?"

"Not to zip-line right now."

"Not an option. Tell me. What's the one thing you've been looking forward to?"

I swallowed and focused on what I'd been dreaming of for the last six months. "Mykonos. We have an optional shore excursion that week, and I want to go to Mykonos."

His eyes flashed with surprise, but he quickly masked it. "Really?"

"Really. My dad proposed to my mom on Kalafatis Beach."

She'd always been scared of marriage, commitment in general, but told me once that there was something about being there with Dad that made her abandon her fears and embrace her destiny. I knew it was stupid, but I couldn't let go of the hope that maybe if I stood there, I could do the same. But as of right now, that fear was holding my feet firmly on the ground and off that zip-line.

"Done. I will take you to Mykonos."

My breath caught, knowing how much that shore excursion cost, and that it wasn't included in my scholarship packet. "Why?"

"Because I need to get my tutor on that ship." He looked past me, and the cocky grin was back in place seconds before a lens came over my left shoulder. Our privacy was at an end. "It's up to you, Firecracker, but you've got about a minute to decide."

Wasn't that the theme of my day?

He walked me back through the crowd to where Landon stood on a platform, looking more than a little irritated.

My mind raced a million miles an hour, but it slowed the minute Paxton put his hands on my shoulders and demanded my attention. "If you do this, I'll take you to Mykonos. I will personally make sure that this is the trip of your life. But you have to accept the agreement. The tutoring, the suite, the cameras, all of it."

"And if I don't?"

His tongue swiped across his lower lip and, as sexy as it was, it seemed more like a nervous, subconscious motion. "Then I'll fly you home, first class, on me. You can think of this as that one day you were almost a daredevil."

"And what happens to you? Nothing, right? You pull the next name out of the tutor hat?"

He shook his head. "Every other tutor is assigned. And besides, you were hand-picked for me for your academic strengths. If I lose you, I probably fail. All these people"—he gestured to the crew around us and leaned in to whisper—"they all lose their jobs."

A heavy weight settled on my shoulders, and I wondered in that instant if that was what he'd been thinking of back on the ship, if that was what made him so pensive. "How long does it take?"

"Five seconds, max."

My heart started to pound, as if it already knew the decision I was coming to.

If I kept my eyes closed, it would be over before I knew it, right?

He gently tucked my hair behind my ears, clearing it of the helmet's ear straps. How could I tell him what he was putting me through without laying everything bare and looking foolish? Without going into that night...and the following morning? Without seeing the cocky way he looked at me change to the inevitable looks of pity and morbid curiosity?

How could I ever get past it if I didn't get on that damn ship? Was it better to stay safe, locked away in myself? *Yes*.

But the crew around us? The ones who would lose their jobs?

I looked up into Paxton's eyes, and we lingered there, wordlessly exchanging something I hadn't had in years: trust. He would keep me safe. I somehow knew it with every bone in my pieced-together body.

"What do you say, Leah? Are you ready for an adventure?" He questioned me softly this time, as if he had somehow realized what he was asking me to risk.

I gave the one word that I knew would change...everything.

"Yes."

CHAPTER TWO

PAXTON

She said yes. I didn't realize how much one word could mean until it slipped past her pursed, pissed-off lips. Lips that had my attention from the first second I saw her. I brought her up to the platform where Landon waited, subtly shaking his head at me.

I'd had easily a dozen girls beg me to tandem them on this, and he knew it. Instead, I'd told them all, including Zoe, to basically fuck off, and brought my uptight tutor in the hopes that it would win her over. Leah looked anything but won over.

She'd stiffened even more as I buckled her in.

Once John secured the rigs, he gave us the lowdown. "Okay, drop zone is marked. Pull the kill strap, and you'll fall. It's about ten feet and thickly padded, so don't worry."

"Wait, we're falling, too?" she squeaked, her hands white-knuckling the harness. "You didn't say fall. You said safe."

"It's into a huge pad, Leah. It's either that or we slam into the wall, right? We have brakes, I'll slow us down, don't worry."

"Don't worry, he says," she muttered. "Safe, he says. Asshole."

"Hey, I heard that," I sputtered. It usually took me dumping a girl the morning after I fucked her to get that kind of label. Not that I'd mind fucking Leah—hell, I was already itching to get my hands on her incredibly perfect ass—but that would ruin any chance of me getting through this year with the GPA I needed.

"Good," she spat back.

"Oh, I like her." Landon laughed.

"Shut up, Nova," I threw back with his stage name, knowing the cameras were on us, and reminded myself to warn Leah about how he got that "Casanova" nickname in the first place.

I buckled in behind Leah and pulled her tight little body back against mine by her harness. The minute she made contact, she nearly sagged against me, and I had the strangest instinct to wrap her in my arms and carry her back to the ship, fuck the stunt, the cameras, all of it. Something told me that all that anger thrown my way was masking another emotion—fear. "Are you sure?" I asked, my lips brushing the shell of her ear.

"Yeah, I'm okay," she whispered.

We moved forward to the edge of the platform the Renegade team had built, and she stiffened again. "I...I don't do heights."

Now she fucking tells me. God, I was an asshole. "Say the word, and I'll call it off, Leah. We'll find another way to get you onto the ship."

"No." Tremors ran down the length of her body, but her voice was sure and strong. "I'll do it. Just..." Her breathing picked up, and I wrapped my arms around her, nearly enveloping her tiny frame. "Just don't let me fall."

She trusted me. An almost unrecognizable feeling unfurled, stretching through my limbs, the need to protect her making me feel simultaneously like a prick for putting her through it and as strong as Superman with her in my arms.

But why did I suspect this slip of a woman was going to be my kryptonite?

I shook the thought out of my head. "I won't let anything happen to you. I swear it."

"Okay, then let's get this over with."

I gave the thumbs-up to Landon. "Nova?"

"Good to go! Wilder?"

"Let's rock this!"

A running leap and we were airborne, the exhilarating rush racing through my veins in a familiar hit of the only drug I was addicted to—adrenaline.

Leah's breath stuttered in her chest, and then she let out a gasp, her hands not reaching for her own tether, but my arms still wrapped securely around her waist. I should have let her go, given her the foot or so of space that safety dictated, but something told me she'd be safest closer to me.

Or maybe it was my own extreme need to get a little closer to her.

We passed over the bow of the ship, then the bridge, until we neared the top deck, the bass from the party reaching up to welcome us to our temporary home. The thousand or so students on board partied beneath us, cheering as we soared overhead, passing too quickly for any of them to come into focus.

The drop zone was before the pool, a huge air cushion with a giant *X*, as if there was any chance I was going to miss it. I reached up right around the same time as Landon to apply the brakes and slow us down.

I pulled, but nothing happened.

We flew past Landon, and I pulled harder. *Fuck.*

Don't panic. I reached forward for the separate braking

mechanism on Leah's harness, but it gave way with too much ease. If anything, we were moving faster.

The drop zone would be on us in one second, and we were going way too fast. *You promised her she'd be safe, that she wouldn't get hurt.* At this speed, she was in real danger of hitting the air cushion and flying straight off it into the crowd, or worse, off the boat.

"Can you swim?" I shouted, squeezing her ribs.

"Yes?" she responded.

"Good!" The drop zone sped underneath us in less time than it took to breathe. "Hold your breath!"

I felt her chest expand. Right before we reached the pool, I grabbed both of our kill straps and pulled with all my strength, saying a little prayer those worked. They gave way.

We fell.

I tucked her into me and raised my knees so I'd take the brunt of the impact.

Fuck, this is going to hurt.

We hit the water so hard I was astonished that we didn't bounce. My breath abandoned me and pain shot up my back, but I didn't let go of Leah, not until my ass hit the bottom of the pool. Then I pushed her up with all the strength I had so she popped to the surface.

I kicked my way to the sun, then filled my lungs with pure, sweet air. "Are you okay?" I asked Leah, who treaded water next to me. Her eyes were huge, her breaths choppy and verging on hyperventilation. "Leah?" I closed the distance between us and pulled her against me, moving us back to the shallows until I could touch the bottom.

Her mouth opened and closed, but no sound emerged.

"Dude, that was epic!" a student called out from the side

WILDER

of the pool, and I became aware that we were very much in the public eye.

"Renegades! Renegades!" A chant erupted.

For the first time in my life, I didn't give my wild Renegade grin to the camera, didn't throw my hands up in victory. Instead, I cupped Leah's face in my hands and tilted her chin so I could meet those whiskey-colored eyes. "Leah, I need you to say something. Anything."

She took a full breath, and her tremors stopped as she brought her hands to my chest. "You. Are. An. Asshole."

Well, I guess that was something.

Then she shoved me backward. My feet slipped and I went under, water shooting up my nose. I got my bearings and came back up to Leah walking out of the pool, her wet T-shirt clinging to every one of her petite curves, her jeans pasted to her thighs. Why the hell was she wearing jeans in the first place?

She was okay, right? She wasn't limping, and I thought I'd done a good job of cushioning the drop as much as possible, but still. She looked okay. Pissed, but okay.

"Wilder, you're on!" Bobby shouted from the side of the pool, his clipboard and earpiece fully in place.

I took off my helmet, raked my hair back from my face, and forced myself to walk in the opposite direction of Leah, toward the stage where Landon dwarfed Penna's slight frame next to the DJ. The music was drumming a deep beat, and usually this was the pinnacle of my high, reveling in another stunt accomplished. Girls, guys, they all touched me or slapped me on the back as I made my way to the stage.

I plastered my fake-ass Wilder smile on my face and took the stairs two at a time. "I want both those fucking rigs," I said quietly to Bobby as I passed him.

His eyes widened, but he nodded. "Sure thing, Wilder. I'll have the crew grab them."

I needed to rip those brake assemblies apart and find out why the hell they both failed. God, that stunt could have gone wrong so easily. I could be carrying Leah to get a broken bone set, or worse, scraping pieces of her skin off the wall where the end of the line was mounted.

Penna gave me a million-watt smile and raised her hand for a high five, but I saw the worry in her eyes. I pulled her into what looked like a celebration hug, keeping my hands way above her waist. Putting my hands on her while she was in a bikini was always weird. "Are you okay?" she whispered.

"Yeah. We need to meet up after. No cameras."

She nodded and pulled back with a huge smile, then brought the microphone up. "Talk about a wild ride, huh?" she asked with a contagious laugh.

The crowd of students cheered, and Landon raised his hands in victory, but he arched his eyebrows when he looked back over at me. "Later," I mouthed, and he nodded.

Penna passed me the mic, and I was on. "What's up, Renegades?"

The crowd went wild, and I shot them the grin I was famous for. "In case you hadn't caught on, I'm Wilder, this here is Nova"—I motioned to Landon who raised his fist—"this is Rebel"—Penna gave her signature wave—"and we're the Renegades." Another cheer went up from the crowd. "We figured since the Summer X Games are over, we'd take a break from winning medals and doing stupid shit you guys like to watch on YouTube and sail around the world with you. Luckily our sponsors agreed. What do you say?"

The crowd screamed.

Landon took the microphone. "Now don't go expecting any wild antics on board. We promised to be on our best behavior."

"As you can see, they're already obeying those rules," Penna said into Landon's mic, and the crowd laughed.

The ship moved away from the dock, and Landon handed me the mic. "This is it, guys. Are you ready for the adventure of a lifetime?" I asked, using our signature line.

"We're ready!"

"You little Renegades," Penna teased with a grin.

"Then let's get this party on!" I shouted and cued the DJ.

The music returned to full volume, and the students all started to dance, drinks waving in hands. I handed the mic to the DJ and motioned Penna and Landon to the side of the stage before the cameras could get there.

"What the fuck happened?" Landon asked, all business.

"The brakes failed. Both of them."

A knowing look passed between us. "Before you even ask, I double-checked the assemblies in my room before we left for the tower."

"Before or after you brought your new plaything into the picture?" Penna asked. "She wasn't part of the plan, and you know I hate it when you go off map."

"She's my tutor. Nothing more. And you both know if she isn't fully invested, I'm fucked. We all are. I was hoping to get on her good side."

"That plan kind of backfired on you there, brother," Landon added.

"Tell me about it. Look, I'm not going to get paranoid, but until I get my hands on those rigs and figure out what I missed, we all install our own gear. Deal?"

They both nodded. I hadn't messed up a rig, and they both

knew it, but the only other option was unmentionable, and I refused to think that someone had deliberately sabotaged the stunt, especially once I'd put Leah on there tandem with me. That was the least risky stunt we'd pulled in the last two years, but it easily could have had the worst ending.

"Eyes open, and let's try to meet up later to talk about the next site. And not a word about this in front of the cameras. Or Leah." I looked them both in the eye until they nodded.

"Wilder." Bobby jogged over, his forehead all puckered. He'd been producing our footage the last twelve months or so, and I'd never seen him stress.

"What's up?"

"The rigs are gone. I don't know who removed them, but there's just empty cord. Nova's is still swinging, but yours are both gone."

"Fuck," I swore.

"Eyes," Penna said, motioning behind me, where the camera crew had caught up.

"We're all done here guys; you can film the party and stuff, but I'm going to head back to my room and make sure everything is in order to start classes tomorrow," I said.

"Class...yay," Penna added with false clapping.

Landon rolled his eyes and walked away, no doubt headed to find the next girl to add to his Casanova legacy. I normally didn't give a shit about my friends' sex lives, but Landon's was borderline self-destructive. The guy he'd been slipped away a little more with each of his conquests, his eyes a little dimmer, more vacant. And, of course, I didn't get to say a fucking word about it, not until I could fix what I'd broken...if he was still fixable.

The camera crew took the invite to check out the bikini-clad co-eds and left me standing with Penna at the end of the stage.

I scanned the crowd, but it was stupid to think I'd be able to spot her in a crowd of a thousand students.

"She left," Penna said, smirking.

"I just need to make sure she's okay. I think I may have royally fucked up when I put her on that line. It never occurred to me that she'd be that terrified."

"Not everyone is built like we are, Pax. Most people are cool with watching us pull stunts, jump bikes, ski extreme slopes, but they'd never actually do it. Plus, from what I saw in the suite, she didn't exactly know who you were. Even the famous Paxton Wilder has his limits of reach."

I put my hands up in surrender. "Okay, point taken."

"Plus, if you want her to have some privacy, you might consider not putting her in the middle of a stunt, jackass."

"Yes, Mom."

She smacked my chest with the back of her hand. "Also, don't go to her suite through the front door. You'll start a rumor fire you can't put out, and she didn't exactly strike me as the kind of girl who wants the attention you bring, so go through the balcony."

"Good idea. What would I do without you?"

She leaned her head on my shoulder. "You'll never have to know. Now go. If you mingle with the crowd they can get some good shots, and you can sneak off by the bar to check on her."

I hugged my oldest friend. "Thanks."

"No problem," she said as we broke apart. "And yeah, the girl was terrified, but she's stronger than you think."

"What makes you say that?" She'd been shaking, hardly breathing, and I had white sheets with more color than her face when we'd splashed down.

"First off, she did the stunt. She could have said no and demanded you get her back on the ship, and you know you would have. But she didn't. She strapped up and trusted you."

"Yeah, well, look how that turned out."

"We'll figure out what happened to the rigs. We just have to find them. I bet one of the crew took them for storage before Bobby could get there. Don't stress about it."

I hoped that was all it was, an accident, a quickly cleaned-up site, but something nagged in the back of my head that this wasn't how it looked, and I couldn't put my finger on why. "Yeah, let's find the rigs. I'll catch you later." I faced the party and looked for the quickest route out.

"Pax, she didn't scream."

"What?" I asked, turning back around.

"That entire ride, even when you dropped her over the pool. When you fell, she didn't scream. She might have been scared, but she didn't let it show. Remember that when you go apologize."

"What makes you think I'm going to apologize?" I never apologized. Sorry wasn't a word I said. Why be sorry when everything you did brought you to where you were? Made you who you were? Even the most epic mistake was merely another thread that wove into whatever tapestry we were.

"I saw the way you looked at her. Believe me, you'll apologize, if not for this, then for something else."

The one thing I could hardly stand about Penna? She was almost always right.

· · ·

I looked down both hallways before I knocked on Leah's door. Penna was right, I didn't want her at the center of some kind of rumor storm, but I couldn't exactly barge into her room through the sliding door yet—not after she'd made those *easy access* comments.

The door swung open, and Leah glared up at me, her face shiny from a shower, wearing a white tank top and pajama pants. Holy shit, did she have to have such a killer body? Why couldn't she be average? Bitchy? This attraction was damn inconvenient.

"What do you want, Wilder?" she asked, crossing her arms under her perfect breasts. But I wasn't looking. Hell no. My eyes were firmly on her face, where they'd remain. She leaned to look behind me. "And where is your legion of cameras and adoring fans?"

I grimaced. "No cameras. No fans. Can I come in?"

She arched an eyebrow. "And if I say no?"

"I'll be forced to sit outside your door until said cameras and fans show up."

She snorted but backed up, letting me into her suite. The door shut behind us, and she led me to her sitting room, which was smaller yet more welcoming than mine. I ran my hands over my still-damp trunks to make sure I wouldn't leave a puddle of water she could slip on later. "I like this room."

"Good, since you insist on paying for it. How long do I have before the camera crews show up and demand entrance? Because I'm not letting them in here. I didn't sign up for that, Wilder."

"Paxton," I corrected her. "I'm Wilder to the rest of the world, but since we'll be spending an excessive amount of time together, I'd like to not have to keep that public face up around you, if that's okay." Damn, I bit that out harder than I intended. Something about this girl set every one of my nerves on edge, made me forget the cool, collected demeanor I'd worked so hard to perfect over the last few years. I could tell with a single glance at her crossed arms that this girl—this puzzle—had walls a mile thick. Walls that I desperately needed to breach if I wanted to keep her happy, wanted her to give a damn if I passed or failed. "And no cameras. They don't have the right to be in here. Your room is completely off-limits to filming and the crew."

Her shoulders relaxed in obvious relief. "Well, thank you for that consideration."

"And you can tell your roommate that there's nothing to worry about."

Leah shook her head, the wet strands sliding along her top. "Rachel can't make it until next term. She has mono."

Damn. Three whole months. How the hell was I going to keep Leah happy until Rachel got here? Penna's research showed they were basically inseparable. What if Leah hated me and left before the term was over? This definitely had the potential to fuck my carefully laid plans. "So you're all alone in here? Are you going to be lonely?"

She rubbed her hands down her arms. "I'm perfectly okay. Besides, if you need to study, you're right, you'll be doing it here, because I'm not going anywhere near those cameras unless I have to."

My muscles relaxed as I realized she wasn't going to renege on our deal and not tutor me. "I understand."

"Okay then. Do you have your schedule so I know what classes you have?"

"I have every class you do."

Her mouth dropped open. "How is that even possible?"

"I needed to know you could help me, or take notes if I had to miss class." *Because I engineered it that way.*

"Did you sleep with the registrar or something? How did

you make that happen? You know what? I don't even want to know. We have seminar at nine a.m. tomorrow. Do you think you can make it? Or were you planning on waterskiing behind the ship or something?"

"That's not even..." Huh. I wondered if it *was* possible. Maybe if the rope was long enough, and we launched from—

"Unbelievable. No wonder you need a tutor. You've killed off all your brain cells doing stupid crap. Tell me something— are you just here for the Renegade Channel?"

My eyes widened. "I thought you didn't know who I was?"

She rolled hers. "Come on. We're still close enough to port to have good internet, and there's not a lot of Paxton Wilders running around. Google is pretty nifty with the whole search thing."

I swallowed. How much did she know? "What did it tell you?"

"That you run a YouTube channel with a few friends who all have ridiculous stage names, you've won a couple X Game medals in motocross or snowmobiling or something."

"Both," I answered automatically.

"Great. You enjoy flinging yourself off mountains and buildings and generally see exactly what it would take to kill yourself, and I'm responsible for getting you through this academic year while you're doing it all over the world, right?"

Fuck. She put it together so quickly. "What makes you think that?"

"Well, I doubt those hugely expensive cameras are here to document some boring reality show featuring your academics center stage, so the only plausible explanation is that you're here to take your little channel international. Or is it bigger?"

"Bigger," I answered truthfully. "Some of the things we

have planned aren't exactly legal in the U.S., so it seemed to be a great time to shoot the documentary. What else did you learn?"

"That you prefer leggy blondes who have a disproportionate ratio of breast to waist. Which is fine with me; I'm sure there's a full treasure trove here to select from, and I'm safe since I don't fit any of that criteria."

"Whoa, when did I even hint—?"

She threw her palms out. "You didn't. I just figured I'd get ahead of you. Look, you almost killed me, dumped me into a huge pool, and now I'm stuck with you if I want to stay on this trip. I understand what I signed up for. But I will not be involved in anything you do—like I was today—ever again. You and I are business only, got it?"

I nodded slowly. "Got it." What the fuck just happened?

"Good. Now you can leave. I'll see you at seminar in the morning." She walked to the door and held it open until I left her room, closing the door behind me with a loud *click*.

I was halfway to my room before I started laughing. Little Eleanor Baxter had done the one thing no other girl had done in my lifetime—dismissed me outright.

I knew I liked her for a reason.

CHAPTER THREE

LEAH

AT SEA

Books, paper, pen, registration information...yep, I had it all. I sent another glare toward my espresso machine and headed out the door for seminar. Screw World Literature, I needed a course in how to use *that*.

Maybe it was good to kick my caffeine addiction. But morning coffee with Rachel was the one thing that had gotten me out of bed when I'd wanted the universe to swallow me whole freshman year, and now it was a habit I couldn't break. It wasn't even the drink itself as much as it was the routine, knowing that the world didn't care if I wanted it to stop turning—it was going to keep going, and so was I...whether or not I saw the purpose to it.

So I'd gotten up every morning, carefully masked the pain, the hopelessness, and the dread that took up residence in my soul every time the alarm clock went off and I realized I was still alive...still the *lucky* one. I showered off the sweat from the nightmares, put on my clothes, and poured a goddamned cup of coffee with Rachel, because that's what living people did. They...lived.

Sure, the time had passed, my memories of *him* softening enough to breathe, to move on. *Brian.* See? I could think his name now without crying. There was even a sweetness to it instead of the oppressive grief that had been my constant companion these last couple of years, but I still dreaded mornings.

Maybe this trip would change that.

Maybe my heart wasn't pristine. Maybe it was stitched together. Maybe the seams were even a little frayed over the parts that refused to knit—the parts I had a feeling never would—but it was whole again. I was living.

And if I didn't hurry, I was going to be late for seminar.

I glanced toward Paxton's room and debated knocking on his door. *Nope. He's a big boy.* There was zero chance in hell I was going to be his babysitter for the next nine months. I'd thought about it all night and came to the conclusion that the only way I was going to keep my sanity this year was to distance myself whenever possible.

But if he missed seminar, I'd be forced to fill him in.

His door opened, and I breathed a sigh of relief—until I realized that he wasn't the one walking out of it. A beautiful brunette in bright white shorts emerged, pulling her hair down around her sunglasses to frame her face until she saw me standing outside my door.

Then she raised those glasses and stalked toward me.

"So you're the one," she sang sweetly, her eyes nowhere near matching the saccharine tone of her voice.

"The one, what?" I asked. It was too early to deal with this.

"The one who wormed her way into my harness yesterday." Her eyes swept up and down my frame, her arched eyebrows making it fairly obvious that she found me lacking.

"Look, I don't know who you are—"

"I'm Zoe."

The girl from yesterday. "Well, hi, Zoe. I'm Leah, and despite what you may think, given that you came out of Paxton's room, I'm only his tutor. I had zero desire to be a part of that ridiculousness yesterday, so if you have an issue with what happened, you can take it up with your boyfriend." The worst part of it all was that I didn't even have a sense of pride that I'd gone through with the stunt—just a nauseating fear that I'd have to do something like that again.

Her mouth opened, but before she said anything else, the door between mine and Paxton's opened and a tall, willowy blonde walked out with her arms full of books. Was she the girl I'd seen yesterday on Paxton's balcony? She glanced between us and shook her head. "Don't be an asshole, Zo. If Wilder had wanted you on that line, he would have taken you."

Zoe's eyes narrowed, but she simply turned on her heel and dismissed me, as if she'd realized I wasn't worth talking to. I breathed a little easier with every step she took in the opposite direction, swaying her flawless figure.

A stab of irrational jealousy ripped through me. Of course that was the type of girl Paxton went for. He wasn't the guy to settle for anything less than perfection.

"Thank you," I said to the girl as she approached.

"Don't worry about it," she said, offering me a kind smile as we walked toward the elevator. "You're Leah, right? Wilder's tutor?"

I nodded. "That's me. How did you know?"

Her laugh was musical. "You're kind of the talk of our little town right now. I'm Brooke, Penna's sister." She must have seen the confused look on my face, because she took mercy and explained. "She goes by Rebel."

"Ahh, one of Paxton's Renegades."

"Yep, one of the Originals. Those guys are inseparable and inflicted with the same daredevil disease. Wilder's a magnet for those kind of people." The way her voice softened caught my attention.

"Oh, are you two...?"

She hit the button for the elevator. "No way. And he's not with Zoe, either, no matter how badly she wishes. She's full of shit and probably crawled out of Landon's bed, so don't let her get to you about Pax."

"I don't care who he dates," I protested as the doors *dinged* open. "I just need him to keep his grades up."

"Well, that makes a whole bunch of us," she said as we took the elevator to deck eight. "I know it's odd, the position he's put you in with the suite. Weird, but you're kind of his Obi Wan."

"Are you seriously telling me I'm his only hope?" I asked, unable to stifle my grin.

"A girl after my own heart." She laughed. "And yes. You were selected for him for a reason, not simply tossed into the tutor pool."

"Weirdest thing ever," I muttered as we walked through the doors onto the deck.

The auditorium, which had been the theater before the ship was remodeled for the program last year, was filling quickly. "There's Penna. Did you want to sit with us?" Brooke asked.

Without Rachel, who'd been my security blanket these last couple of years, I'd have to make new friends or sit in my room alone the next three months until she got here. "Sure, thanks."

"Oh, and Leah," she said, gently stopping me with her hand on my arm, "maybe the question isn't why it's weird that you're stuck with the Renegades, but why you're the one he chose."

She patted my arm and walked toward her sister, leaving me a bigger mass of confusion. *Chose?* He *chose* me? He was allowed the choice? None of the other tutors I'd met had been chosen, they'd all simply been assigned.

We took our seats next to another blonde, and I immediately recognized her as the girl I'd seen outside on Paxton's balcony. "Nice to meet you, Firecracker." Penna waved from the other side of her sister.

Apparently Paxton's nickname for me had traveled fast.

"You, too, Penna. Or do you prefer Rebel?" I asked, realizing my error.

She had a supermodel smile and matching legs. "Penna's fine for you, Leah." The genetics in that family were seriously enviable. "Of course Wilder is late. I barely got him up when I walked out the door."

"Oh, you room together?" That would explain the balcony.

"Yeah, it's a three bedroom, and they thought the team should be together."

I nodded, not knowing what to say. Conversation wasn't something I was particularly skilled at, and nodding usually saved me from whatever awkward comment was undoubtedly going to come out of my mouth.

My watch read 9:05 a.m. Of course he was late, but I saved the seat next to me anyway.

"Good morning, students, I'm Dr. Paul, Dean of Academics." A middle-aged man with salt and pepper hair appeared from behind the curtain center stage. "Welcome to the *Athena*. I trust that your first night went well?"

A cheer went through the auditorium.

"Good. Now it's time to buckle down. Today is your first full day of classes. The ship functions as a self-contained college campus. You'll have regular classes, exams, homework—all the fun. You should have registered for the relevant shore excursions, but if you find that you need extra credit, contact your professors to see if they're offering any extra field studies to boost your grades."

"Morning, Firecracker," Paxton whispered in my ear as he slid into the empty seat next to me.

"You're late," I chided, trying to ignore the way my stomach tightened at the sound of his voice.

He simply winked and slid a steaming cup of coffee my way. I took a tentative sip and nearly moaned in ecstasy. Where I'd had an outright battle with the huge espresso machine, he'd obviously had no issues with his.

"Thank you," I said with a soft smile, more than aware that I hadn't exactly been nice to him yesterday.

He winked.

My stomach nearly dropped to the floor. How was something so simple so incredibly sexy? *At least he has a shirt on today.* I called that a win for womankind. After all, we had to study somehow.

"All classes occur during at-sea days. When it comes to shore days, if we're in port, you're given free rein. You're adults, after all. But you'd better be on board when it's time to sail, or we will leave you behind. If you are so unfortunate as to be left, you'd better make it to the next port before we leave, or you're out of the program. No exceptions. That includes you, Mr. Wilder." He pointed up to Paxton, who grinned.

"Hey, I made it on before we left port."

"Uh-huh." Dean Paul didn't seem amused. I liked him already.

He went on to explain meal times, activities on the ship, locations of the bookstore and our classrooms. I took copious notes while Paxton sat with his arms folded across his chest, looking bored.

"Now this is the first excursion of its kind. I'm sure you're all familiar with the Semester at Sea program, and that is not what we're doing here. It's a full academic year on board the *Athena*. You'll go home for Christmas and return in the new year just like any other college. You're expected to keep up your grades, and you can be expelled like at any other school. This program is unique in its makeup, its opportunities in port, the freedom you're given, and its work-study program. Respect all the students aboard, stay out of my office, and we'll get along fine."

The differences in the programs were what made this one so much more expensive—hell, it catered to rich kids—but the work-study made it possible for people like me. The expense afforded the luxury for kids like Paxton.

"Ready for Lit?" Paxton asked as we exited the auditorium.

"No cameras?" I asked, looking both directions down the hall.

"I think the crew is still hungover. Besides, they're not that interested in the academic side of this. Hey," he said to Brooke as she started to pass us. "Little John said you had the Bermuda papers."

"I did," she answered. "Don't worry, I popped them into your safe after I faxed them over to the permit office."

"Sweet. Thank you," he said before she went ahead to her class.

"It must take a lot of coordination to do…whatever it is you do."

"It does. I'm lucky I've got some great friends to do it with."

As we walked down the narrow halls, I was acutely aware of the eyes on us, but I did my best to ignore them. If this was the cost for taking the trip, then so be it.

"So, I met Zoe this morning," I said, sneaking a sideways look at Paxton. "She's…um…"

"She's something else," he said, shaking his head. "Was she a bitch?"

"She was…unfriendly."

He flinched. "I'd apologize for her, but she wouldn't be sorry. When they opened up the reservations for the team first, I figured she'd skip out. College was never her thing, but then she signed up, and I couldn't tell her no. She's a Renegade."

He held the door for me into our classroom, and I buried my instinct to smile. This wasn't a date, for God's sake. He was just being a gentleman. "How many of you are there on the ship?"

"Three of the Originals who started the channel, and we do the majority of the stunts and all the larger ones, but the entire team is about fifteen of us, plus camera crew. Landon is another Original. Brooke and Penna handle a ton of our tech, but Penna's also a badass on a bike. Don't let her cute looks fool you."

"Noted," I said, taking an empty seat in the front. He surprised me by sliding into the one directly behind me instead of beside me.

"Some view," he said quietly into my hair, which I'd left down today.

I took in the floor-to-ceiling windows that ran the length of the room. For miles there was only blue Caribbean water. "Breathtaking."

"Yeah," he agreed, but I felt the slight movement of my hair, and when I glanced back, he dropped a few strands from between his fingers.

I snapped my head to face forward. *Not for you. That guy is not for you.*

"Good morning, class," our professor said as she sailed through the doors, headed for the podium. Her red hair was swept into a topknot, and she wore the same kind of linen pants I did. "I'm Dr. Mae, and I'll be your professor for World Literature in the first trimester. If that's not the class you signed up for, the door is behind you," she added with a friendly smile.

"We take on a ton of reading in this class, and I've found that students work better in pairs to discuss reading on their own time. First and third rows, turn around and meet your partner."

I turned to see Paxton grin, his blue eyes sparkling more than the water we were sailing through. "Hi."

"Go figure," I mumbled. There was no escaping him. *Why do you want to?*

I nearly scoffed at my own thoughts. There was wanting something you couldn't have, and then there was being shown fresh-baked chocolate chip cookies right out of the oven and being told not to touch—they'd burn you, and besides, they were for the prettier, whole girls, not the broken ones.

Broken girls got the stale, crumbled, oatmeal raisin ones.

"Now find out a few things about your partner, because you're going to give their introduction."

"You have to be kidding." If there hadn't been twenty eyes on me, I would have slammed my forehead into the desk. Like Paxton needed an introduction.

"Okay, what do you want the class to know, Mr. Wilder?"

I asked.

His eyes narrowed slightly, and he sucked his lower lip into his mouth, skimming his teeth over it. My stomach clenched in a way it had no business doing, imagining what he would do to *my* lower lip.

"I don't care about the class. What do *you* want to know?"

I blinked, tearing my eyes away from his before I couldn't think. "I want to know what's not on Google."

One of his dimples made an appearance, and I had the huge impulse to run my tongue along it. *Holy shit, get a grip.* "Ask anything you want."

"What's your major?"

"Physics. Come on, you can do better than that."

"Why even go to college, or do this program, if you're already a superstar?"

"I took last year off when we made it big. Graduating is part of the legal agreement to get my trust fund, among other things my father likes to bargain for."

Trust-fund baby. Of course. "So it's all about money?"

He shook his head. "It's about the movie, the stunts, the rush, doing something no one's ever done before. The money just makes it possible."

"I thought you were sponsored? You have that energy drink stuff all over your YouTube channel."

"Checking up on me again, eh, Firecracker?"

I felt my cheeks heat. "If I'd forced you onto a zip-line and into a documentary, scared the living crap out of you, and then nearly drowned you, you'd be checking up on me, too."

"No, I'd be saying thank you. Everything you said sounds pretty damn good. Well, except the cameras. They get old fast." He tapped his pencil on the desktop, and his eyes flickered toward the door, where there was, in fact, a camera with its lens against the glass panel. "Especially when they show up places they said they wouldn't."

"Then why keep them?"

"Because if no one sees the epic moments, did they ever really happen?"

Our eyes locked, and my breath became pure energy in my lungs, sending butterflies into my stomach while rushing a strange chill through my limbs. "I think it depends on who you define as no one. Not everything epic is meant for a worldwide audience."

The cocky camera grin replaced the one I was quickly becoming enamored with, transforming him from Paxton to Wilder right in front of my eyes. "Well, that depends on what your definition of epic is. I can definitely say there are some one-on-one moments that aren't meant for camera. Unless they're giving the documentary an X rating."

Well, if that didn't kill the butterflies. *Arrogant asshole.*

"We're going to get started," Dr. Mae said, and the people down the line from us began their intros.

"You don't know anything about me," I whispered at him.

"Not nearly enough, Firecracker, but I can get through this."

Why did I have the feeling that was going to be his entire attitude to schoolwork this year? Fine, if he wanted to skate by, I could do it, too.

Shit, it was already our turn.

"Begin when you're ready," Dr. Mae said from her desk at the front of the room.

"I'm Leah Baxter, and this is Wilder, but I'm sure you all know that," I said, taking in every awestruck look on the guys and every wistful look on the girls. I nearly smacked Paxton in the stomach when I saw him raise his eyebrows for a girl in the third row. "Wilder is a senior, majoring in physics, most likely because he likes to hurl his body at every obstacle he can." The class laughed. "He's stubborn, ambitious, and has two X Game medals."

"Five. I have five," he corrected me, looking like I'd killed his puppy.

"He's also a know-it-all. He's all about challenges, doesn't take no for an answer—"

"Except from you," he muttered.

"—and likes pushing people outside their comfort zones."

"I also speak fluent Spanish, German, and Greek, but that seems pretty trivial," Paxton added with a shrug.

Cocky, arrogant...ugh. I couldn't even think of a less-offensive word to describe him.

Dr. Mae cleared her throat, poorly stifling a laugh. "Wilder?"

He gave me a crooked grin, and I reminded myself not to melt into a puddle in front of the class. Hell, if he gave that grin out any more there would be a pile of panties in front of him in no time. Thank God I was wearing pants. They were an extra layer of protection.

Even your pants would join the pile if he really wanted. I was so screwed.

"Leah is a junior, majoring in international relations at Dartmouth. She wants to get her Masters in International Relations and is currently ranked second in her class, which means I think she'll get into whatever grad school she wants. She's an only child, raised in California, only a dozen miles away from my house, actually—"

"How?" I whispered.

He leaned to the side and whispered in my ear, "If someone actually agreed to strap into a zip-line when they were terrified, and they held your future in your hands, don't you think you'd Google them?"

I should have been flattered that he'd taken the time to research me, but I couldn't get past the giant knot in my throat, the crippling sensation of complete paralysis. He'd Googled. What else did he know? How deep had he dug? Did he see pictures? Would his cool, flirtatious condescension turn to pity? *God, I'd rather he ignore me completely than pity me.*

"She's had to work for everything she has, and that makes her proud, ambitious, which is a trait I recognize." He looked over and locked eyes with me. "And she's incredibly brave, which I respect above everything else."

I swallowed, my emotions so conflicted that I wasn't sure how to respond. Or breathe. Yeah. I was screwed.

Distance. That was it. *Remember the plan.* I needed to distance myself from Pax and the other Renegades when I wasn't in class or tutoring him. Find a different circle of friends, or even a guy I might be interested in. Yup, that was the answer.

I made it through World Lit and headed back to the room during our two-hour break. Paxton walked me to the door and then promised to meet me before physics.

I walked in to find Hugo in my room, hanging up clean towels. "You don't have to do that," I assured him.

"You don't have to tutor Wilder, either, but we both have jobs to do if we're going to stay on our little trip," he responded with a wide grin. "Besides, as people go, I lucked out when I got you. My friend Luke got Zoe."

"Oh God."

"See? I'll fetch your towels all day long."

I laughed. "Fine, but only if you show me how to work the freaking espresso machine."

"I could make it for you," he offered.

"Oh, no thank you. It's honestly part of my routine." The part that told me the day was coming for me whether or not I wanted it to, so I may as well hit the ground caffeinated.

He snapped his fingers and ran over to the machine, showing me with quick hands how to get my early morning caffeine fix.

"Perfect, now I'll feel right at home. Thank you."

"Speaking of at home, why haven't you unpacked?"

I sipped my coffee, reveling in the dark taste. "Because I wasn't certain I was going to keep the suite, honestly."

"And now?" he asked.

"Given the rather odd circumstances of my scholarship, I don't think I have a choice."

His shoulders sagged with obvious relief. "Phew. Okay. I was scared you'd quit and they'd move Zoe in here."

"You're safe," I promised him with a smile.

"In that case, I'll go work on getting you unpacked."

"No, I can—"

The doorbell rang.

"There's a doorbell? Seriously?" It must have been Paxton, but we weren't expected in class yet.

"Ah, how the other half lives." He grinned.

"I'll get it," I said, walking over to the door and opening it to find Penna standing on the other side, two giant bags in her hand.

"Thank you, God," she muttered, sliding in past me. "Which bedroom is empty?"

"The first one on the right," Hugo answered.

"What..." I followed her into Rachel's room, and she

dumped her bags onto the bed.

"Oh, nice, it has a private balcony, too. Does yours?"

"Yes," I answered. Benefits of a corner suite, I guessed. Not that I'd explored it. The huge one that ran between my room and Paxton's was quite enough, thank you.

"I couldn't stay in that room one more night, with the music, and the girls, and the fucking cameras. Pax said the cameras aren't allowed in here, right?"

"Right..."

"Well, then I'm your roommate until your other one arrives. God knows if I have to listen to one more girl cry out Landon's name I'm going to vomit. It's like hearing your brother's porn. Gross."

My power of speech failed me.

"Besides, as much as we're all adventurers, my parents had freaked about Brooke sharing with another girl, leaving me with the guys." She wandered into the hallway, looking at the rooms. "What about your parents?"

"Um. They told me to have a good time?"

She walked into my room, where Hugo had my suitcase open on the bed and was unpacking my stuff. Then she picked up a large box of condoms out of my bag. *Oh. My. Fucking. Lord. No.*

"Those aren't mine," I whispered, knowing how ridiculous that sounded.

Her laugh was bright when she turned over the box, then showed me the sticky note in my mom's handwriting. "Be safe. Have fun. Loosen up for crying out loud. There's a whole wide world waiting for you, Leah-bug. Love, Mom."

"That's what I get for being born to hippies."

Penna wrapped her arm around my shoulder and tossed

the condoms at Hugo, who was redder than the pair of cherry pumps he'd unpacked.

"I think we'll get along just fine."

After I kicked Hugo out and unpacked with Penna telling me hilarious stories while sitting on my bed, I realized that I hadn't distanced myself from the Renegades at all...

I'd moved in with one.

CHAPTER FOUR

PAXTON

BERMUDA

I stretched my legs out, trying to avoid the Flyboard parts scattered on the floor next to me. I'd watched every minute of film Bobby's crew had taken from the zip-line yesterday but still couldn't figure out what had gone wrong or where the rigs had disappeared to. I wanted to write it off as a fluke accident, but the nagging feeling that it had been something more wouldn't go away.

Penna and Landon had agreed that it was strange, but neither seemed too worried. After all, we'd done far more dangerous stunts and had way worse things go wrong. But just in case, no one else was touching these Flyboards.

"Seriously? Could you hurry up already? We have places to be," Leah exclaimed from the doorway of my bedroom.

I nearly dropped the buckle assembly I was examining. "Well, I think that might be the first time a woman has said that to me in here."

Her mouth dropped into a little *O* before she snapped it shut. "Well, you've only been sleeping in here a few days. Give it another week."

"You're assuming I've ever had a complaint. Usually the only requests I get in here are along the lines of *faster, harder, deeper.*"

She sputtered, and I couldn't stop the grin that transformed my features and my mood. After the last few days with Leah, I was realizing that she did that to me. Even when she told me to go to hell, I kinda wanted to go because it riled her up.

"Where is it you think we're supposed to be?" I asked, picking up the hose coupling and inspecting the seal.

"We're in Bermuda."

"And?"

"We have a mandatory field-study today. All day. And it starts in half an hour."

Was that a gap? I pulled it closer and ran my finger along the seam. Nope. Good to go.

"We have to leave, so get your butt off the floor."

I looked up. Damn, she looked good today. Her pants were skintight leggings, and her blue top was oversize to fall off one shoulder, revealing a black bra strap.

Maybe her panties matched, too.

Was she a thong kind of girl? In those pants she had to be.

"Paxton, it's time to go!" She crossed her arms and tapped her little sandaled foot at me.

"You go. I'm getting ready for tomorrow. Hell, add in a massage on me. Have them charge it to your room." I reached for another part, but she beat me to it, snatching the board.

"This isn't for fun, Paxton. It's for World Religion."

Fuck. I'd gotten through three of the flyboards, but there were seven left to examine. "Is it required?"

Her eyes narrowed dangerously. "Yes. That's what I just

said, which you would know if you'd put this down and pay attention."

"I have things I need to do," I argued, tugging on the hose.

"Yeah, like pass World Religion. Now stop whining and let's go." She pulled harder.

We locked eyes, and I read the determination in hers. "What will you give me if I go?" I asked. I could check the remaining gear tonight.

Her eyes rolled. "A pat on the back for being a good student. I'm your tutor, not your nanny. Now be a big boy and do the mature thing."

"Not good enough," I said, a smile tugging at my lips. She was so much fun to piss off. That's when her shell peeled back to reveal a fire I desperately wanted to feel, to witness her burning.

"What do you want?" she asked.

"I want your tomorrow."

"You have my next nine months. That should be sufficient." She turned her wrist to check her watch. "We're going to be late!"

"The world might end." Hell, I couldn't remember the last time I'd been on time for something.

Her lips pursed, but it wasn't the anger that got me moving, it was the spark of fear in her eyes. She was seriously worried about missing whatever fucking field trip we were supposed to be on. "I want your tomorrow. If I go where you say today, you go where I say tomorrow." Maybe if she saw the fun side of what we did, she'd start to understand.

She closed her eyes and sighed as if she was kissing her plans for tomorrow good-bye. "Fine."

"Okay, then let's go." *Victory!* I rose to my feet and moved toward where she stood tugging on that long braid she had running along the side of her face. Her eyes drifted down the line of my chest, following my tattoos to my abs, and then she squeezed her eyes shut. I could have crowed with satisfaction that she'd been looking and, by her reaction, liked what she saw. "Problem?"

"Nope. Just do the world a favor and put on a shirt." She spun, leaving me alone in my room.

"Chicken," I muttered under my breath, but I knew the truth. She was simply stronger than I was. There was zero chance I'd be able to back away if she was half dressed.

Twenty minutes later, after showing Leah the VIP disembarkation point on the ship, we barely made it to our excursion. There looked to be about sixty of us corralled together like cattle in front of two passenger buses.

"You owe me," I whispered to the top of her head.

Her smile was gorgeous. "You'll thank me later."

As we were ready to load the cattle cars—uh, buses—I heard my name called and turned to see Bobby and a cameraman sprinting toward us.

Shit. We'd almost made it without Big Brother tagging along. The see-everything cameras were getting old, and it was only our first port.

Two extras and a cranky professor later, we were off. "Aren't you going to be hot?" I asked Leah as she adjusted, looking for a seat belt.

She looked at her leggings and tilted her head. "Probably."

I waited for her to say something else, but she didn't, and I didn't push. I glanced around at the other girls on the bus, none of whom were in anything longer than their knees. *Huh.* Come to think of it, I hadn't seen Leah in anything but pants.

About thirty minutes later, we parked and all filed out of

the bus. "Where are we?"

"St. Peter's Church," Leah answered, leading me up the stone steps to the bright chapel with green shutters. "It's the oldest Protestant church still in continuous use in the western hemisphere."

We listened as the professor gave us the history of the church—from the front, which had been brought with the settlers, to the graveyards that had been segregated between the white Christians and enslaved Africans. Then he turned us loose to explore.

"Isn't it magnificent?" Leah asked, running her fingers across the dark wood of the boxed church pews. "Think of everything that's happened here. All the people who have been through these doors."

"Think of all the sins confessed," I whispered.

She smacked my stomach with her notebook. "No appreciation of history."

I shrugged. "I like history. I'd just rather be making it than observing it."

"There's something exquisite about this, though," she said, taking in every detail of the church. "Hurricanes came and went, and they simply rebuilt. They didn't tear it down and start new. They fixed what was broken because it meant something to them. It's beautiful."

Doesn't our marriage mean anything to you?

You can't fix what's irreparable.

I blinked. Where the hell had that come from? I hadn't thought about that fight—the one where I finally realized my parents were going to divorce—in the last ten years.

"Are you ready to go?" she asked, looking up at me with bright, honest eyes. How long had it been since I'd been around a girl who didn't have an agenda? Who wasn't looking for five minutes in the spotlight, or to say she'd fucked me?

But Leah, she was none of that. Hell, she barely wanted to be around me as it was. Instead, the tables had been flipped, and I was the one constantly angling for a minute of her time.

"Yeah, let's go."

She pointed to a white van in the parking lot. "That's our ride this time."

"We're not going back to the ship?" I asked, trying to keep the disappointment out of my voice. I needed to inspect those rigs, make sure that nothing went wrong tomorrow.

"Not yet. Don't worry, Cinderella, I'll get you home by midnight." She led me over to the van and gave our names to the driver.

"Where are we going?"

She laughed, scooting over so I could sit next to her as another half-dozen students filed in behind us. "Didn't you bother to look at your itinerary?"

"Nope. I saw your excursion list and had the registrar match it."

"You're entirely too trusting."

If you only knew the truth. "I didn't do it until after I'd met you. I decided you weren't half bad to be around and, given that you'd agreed to stay on as my tutor, you had good taste."

"Unbelievable."

The van started to roll, and when I looked in the rearview mirror, I started to laugh.

"What?"

I pointed behind us. "Bobby didn't make it."

She turned to see and then she giggled. Fucking giggled. It was the most entrancing sound I'd ever heard, light, playful, and sexy as hell.

"Oh my God, now he's running." She laughed full-out, and I joined her, watching him try his best to catch the van. "Want to stop for him?" She arched an eyebrow, and I recognized the challenge when I saw it.

"Nope. It's just you, me, and these other fine seagoers."

Her smile was well worth what I knew would be a shitstorm later. Wherever we were going, it had to be somewhere worthwhile, and I'd cut out the documentary team. Too damn bad.

The water was a spectacular sight as we wound our way down the island. It was hard to believe that we had nine whole months of this ahead of us—that as amazing as it was here, there was so much more amazing waiting to happen.

When we hit a pothole, Leah bumped against my shoulder, and then inched toward the window, as if touching me wasn't acceptable. I swallowed, knowing that my stupid physical craving to get my hands on her would only screw over my trip, my GPA, and her life. Hell, my life, too. She was too important to even think about that way.

Besides, I'd always wanted what I couldn't have, and that had to be it. She was in the center of my radar because I already knew she was untouchable.

Ten minutes later we stood outside next to a large sign that read PEDESTRIAN PATH TO THE CRYSTAL CAVES OF BERMUDA.

"Spelunking?" I asked hopefully.

"Sightseeing. Come on." She smiled over her shoulder, and I followed after her, enjoying the slight sway of her curved hips ahead of me.

We passed rows of palm trees, a botanical garden, and finally made it to a curved archway that started a ramped descent. The stone walls rose around us, becoming a tunnel and, though the walkway wasn't steep, I didn't miss the way Leah's fingers tightened on the banister.

"Why don't you let me go first?" I asked, sliding to the side. She shot me a curious look, and I shrugged. "That way if you stumble, I'll catch you."

"Catch me?"

"Well, it would be more like you catching yourself on my back, but you can use me."

Her eyebrows shot sky-high.

"My back. You can use my back." *And any other part of me you want.* "You know what? I'm going first just to make this conversation stop."

I took the lead behind the tour guide, shaking my head as he rambled on about the history of the cave. Where the hell was my game? Not that I was trying to hook up with Leah, but it would have been nice to put two words together correctly.

We made it out of the tunnel, and I sucked in a breath. "Whoa." Stalactites hung from every square foot of the ceiling, all pointing to the clearest, bluest water I'd ever seen.

Leah's cheek brushed my shoulder as she leaned around to see. "Told you it would be worth it."

I turned to her, my lips brushing across the crown of her head. Her hair smelled like oranges, and damn if I didn't like it. "It's beautiful."

She pulled back enough to look into my eyes. "And you're thinking of how fast you could skateboard down the ramp, aren't you?"

Actually, it hadn't even occurred to me. I'd been too focused on her. *You're slipping.* I glanced back up the ramp, past the remainder of our tour. "I could probably get a ton of speed, but

I'd need something to bank me through this turn."

The two girls behind us giggled, and the hot blond one gave me the smile I'd become accustomed to in the last three years I'd made a name for myself. The one that usually ended with a phone number I didn't use because I'd already moved on.

"Do you ever stop to think that you're moving too fast to savor anything around you before it's gone?" Leah asked.

I jolted, my entire body snapping to face hers. Had she been in my head? No. She was leaned over the railing of the outcropping, absorbing everything around us, experiencing it in a way I didn't, because she was right—I was always moving too fast.

I leaned next to her, her bare shoulder rubbing against mine, and simply watched, not only the incredible scene around us but the play of emotion on her face, as she did the same. "This was worth slowing down for," I admitted.

She turned those eyes on me, and I realized that I meant that in more than one way. It would be so easy to run my fingers into her hair, tip her face to mine, and kiss her, to see if she tasted as sweet as she looked. Maybe then I could be satisfied, the challenge over, the curiosity appeased.

You know better.

"Hey...um...aren't you Wilder?" a guy asked from behind me, and I could have hit him for cock-blocking me and thanked him at the same time.

I turned around, but Leah didn't. "Yeah," I answered.

"Whoa!" The guy high fived his Abercrombie-styled buddy, the hot blonde tucked under his arm. "I knew you were on board but didn't expect to get to meet you!"

"Well, hi." I gave them a nod.

"Hi," his girl said with a smile and a once-over that let me know she'd be all too happy to take a private tour of my room later.

Oddly enough, that didn't sound too appealing.

"Dude, we saw you at the Summer X Games year before last. The Big Air finals were awesome! You nailed it!"

A sliver of apprehension cracked the peaceful veneer I'd had since we left the ship. "Thanks. It was...a night." *What would you give to have changed it?*

"How did it feel?" Abercrombie asked.

"Winning?" I clarified, reaching for the railing behind me. *Don't do it. Don't ask.*

"Beating your best friend. Everyone figured Nitro was going to take gold that year, and then you owned it!"

My fingers dug into the railing. Beating Nick had never been in the plans and had sucked almost every ounce of joy from the moment they hung that medal around my neck. It had been the start of a spiral I hadn't been able to stop.

No one had.

"Where is he, anyway?" the other one asked before it got too apparent that I wasn't going to answer the first question. "I haven't seen him on the Renegade Channel in forever."

"He's taking some time off," I said easily, the way I'd been coached by my publicist. "Working on some new tricks."

"So he can beat your ass, huh? The guy has to be dying to get back on top now that you've been there the last couple years."

I forced a tight smile.

Fingers tentatively brushed over my knuckles. *Leah.*

"Hey, Paxton, we'd better catch up with the guide. I know you want to get back to the ship," she said quietly.

The blonde narrowed her eyes at who she obviously viewed

as competition. I almost laughed. If Leah had shown one ounce of actual, actionable interest, there would be no contest.

Hell, the idea of getting Leah's curves under me was miles ahead of a nameless fuck. *Take it back. Right now. You're not interested in sleeping with Leah.*

Liar.

"I'm Elyse," the blonde said to Leah. "Who are you?"

"No one you have to worry about," Leah answered with a laugh in her voice. "Pax, you ready?"

She tugged on my fingers, prying them loose from the railing. Then she slipped her hand into mine, and my stomach flipped like a thirteen-year-old.

"Yeah," I answered. "Nice to meet you guys. See you on board sometime."

She led me away from the other students, down the railway over the fifty-foot-deep lake beneath us, her thumb rubbing circles into my palm, taking away a piece of my stress with each motion.

"Are you going to ask me?"

"About what?" she asked over her shoulder, her thick, loose braid sliding against her skin.

"The X Games? Nitro? Any of it?"

She paused, then turned until we faced each other, as alone as we'd been since we met. "Do you want to tell me?"

"No. Not yet."

Her eyes were soft and deep as the corner of her mouth turned up. "Then I'm not going to pry. It's not any of my business, anyway."

She turned away, dropping her hand, and I couldn't help but feel off, like I'd pulled a half when I meant to turn a full—as if I'd just fallen short of whatever the possibility could have been.

...

"You busy?" I asked Landon from his doorway.

"What does it look like?" he said from behind a book.

"Looks like you need to be distracted."

He lowered the book and snorted. "Some of us enjoy reading, Pax. You should try it sometime. Then maybe you wouldn't have to harass your timid little tutor so much."

"She's not timid." I crossed my arms over my chest and leaned against his doorframe.

"Compared to your normal scores, she's a church mouse." He put his hands up when I stepped into the room. "Look, I honestly think she's great. She's really nice, and she might pull you through this year, but I see the way you look at her."

"I'm not fucking looking at her," I argued.

"Au contraire. You're looking like you'd love to fuck her."

My eyes narrowed. If he wasn't some heartbroken sap, I'd have laid into him about his own self-destructive sexual habits—there was a reason we called him Casanova—but that only would have made me more of an asshole than I already was. It wasn't like I didn't play a role in that heartbreak...and the way he'd changed afterward. "I'm not going to touch her."

"Good." He picked up the book again.

"Wait. Aren't you my friend? Aren't you supposed to be my wingman if I wanted to actually be with Leah?"

He sighed and put the book down on his stomach. "First, I'll wingman you through anything you want. Say the word. Even if it's the worst decision you've ever made, you know I'll have your back. Second, do you realize what you just said?"

I rubbed my fingers over my forehead. "My head hurts from studying all evening. Enlighten me."

"You said *be with Leah*. Not hook up, or score, or fuck, like you have ever *been with* anyone. And I can tell you that as your best friend, she's not the kind of girl you screw, drop for the next hot piece of ass, and expect her to tutor you after. Keep your hands in your pockets and your dick in your pants, because if you fuck this up we're all screwed." He raised the book and waved me off. "If you need to get laid, call Zoe. Leave the tutor alone."

"So I guess this means you don't approve of me bringing her out with us tomorrow."

His sigh was hard enough to move the pages, but he didn't put the book down. "If you're hell-bent on screwing this up, I won't stop you. Hell, I'll find her a wetsuit."

"Thank you, she'll need one. And for the record, I'm not screwing this up, or screwing Leah. I'm more than capable of controlling my dick, and I know my grades are more important than any *hookup*." The word tasted like shit in my mouth.

I closed his door and found Penna leaning against the wall. "He's right," she said with a shrug.

"Not you, too." I passed her, shaking my head as she followed me down the stairs in the suite. Thank God the camera crews weren't here right now. "What the hell have I done to deserve you two launching into me?"

She tilted her head. "Do you honestly want me to list every female we've had to replace because you don't specialize in morning afters? What, two camera women? Your physical therapist? My twenty-first birthday party planner?"

Way to drive it home. "I get the fucking point. Don't touch Leah. Don't risk my tutor, my grades, our future. Got it. I've known the girl for a week. She's not under my skin or anything, so chill the hell out. It's an infatuation."

Penna arched a perfectly sculpted eyebrow. "Don't get an attitude with me. I'm well aware that you have control over your"—her hands pointed to my general groin area—"manly parts. But you know what I've realized over the last week?"

"What?"

"This is a small ship, Pax. There's nowhere to go, and that makes everything just a little more intense, a little more... intimate, especially when you're spending almost every waking minute with her. That's more than enough time for her to get under your skin. This girl is at the center of your universe because you need her, which is fine, but remember that you're at the center of hers, too, because your grades keep her on board."

"Right?" I didn't see the fucking problem. Leah and I had already come to terms with our symbiotic relationship.

Penna sighed, and her shoulders drooped. "Just... I really like her. She's funny, honest, smart...but there's some damage there, too. She's in your orbit because she has to be, but you've got some ridiculously strong gravity. Be careful around her."

"I'm only trying to keep her happy. She's got three months until her roommate shows up, and I don't want her to be lonely. What if she hates me and quits? Leaves? Everything we spent the last year setting up will be down the drain."

"I think there's a line between keeping her happy and making her fall for you. You're so used to doing the second with every potential hookup, I'm not sure you'd even recognize it."

But everything with Leah felt...different, and I didn't know how to explain that to Penna without looking ridiculous. Not just the way my hands gravitated to Leah's skin, or the way I admired her bravery...it was her loyalty, the way she'd calmed me in the caves with a simple touch, the way she hadn't pressed for more information.

"She heard some guys talking about Nick today."

Penna blinked at the subject change. "What did you tell her?"

"I didn't." I opened the sliding glass door to the balcony and was rewarded with a mild breeze and the setting sun over Bermuda.

She followed, leaned against the railing, and examined me, her familiar blue eyes skimming over my features while she passed judgment. "Well, I guess she's not the only one with some damage." She looked past me and waved.

I followed her line of sight to see Leah lounging on her deck chair, the light breeze blowing her shirt against the line of her waist, her eyes covered in huge sunglasses. She waved back to Penna, her smile instant and bright.

"See what I mean? Small ship. Small universe."

She skipped off to sit with Leah, but I kept my distance. Maybe I did need to call Zoe, fuck myself into a clear head, but the last thing I wanted were her fake moans and faker breasts.

Maybe I wanted soft curves and softer eyes. Maybe I wanted a conversation and understanding. Or maybe I was fucked up and only wanted to land the trick I knew I shouldn't, because it was too dangerous.

But what I wanted wasn't an option.

I walked into my suite, slamming the sliding glass door behind me.

Wanting what I couldn't have was a bitch.

CHAPTER FIVE

LEAH

BERMUDA

The Bermuda sun soaked into my shoulders as I rubbed on another coat of sunscreen, avoiding the straps of my halter top. The beach was crowded with students enjoying our last day on shore before the trek across the Atlantic.

A shadow came over me, and I lowered my sunglasses to see Brooke standing above me in a bikini and sarong. "Wilder said I could find you here," she said with an open smile.

"Hey, Brooke." I checked my watch. "I'm supposed to meet him in fifteen minutes."

"I think he was scared you wouldn't show," she admitted, taking the lounge chair next to me and dropping an enormous beach bag. "He still feels pretty guilty about the stunt with the zip-line."

"I already told Penna, I'm okay. Seriously. He didn't know that I'm scared of heights." He didn't know what it took for me to climb onto that platform, either, or that I'd taken the entire ride with my eyes shut until he asked if I could swim.

"You okay with water?"

"Yeah. I grew up in southern California. The ocean and I are well acquainted." In fact, the lack of Pacific blue was the only drawback to living in New Hampshire. Well, besides the cold, and snow, and generally dismal springs.

"Good, because we're supposed meet Wilder on the dock."

Dock. Water. Swimming suit? I swallowed the momentary blast of panic that tightened in my throat and gathered up my things. "Then let's get to him."

It was a short walk down the beach to the picturesque dock where a large yacht was tied. My jaw dropped when Paxton jumped from the boat to the dock, wearing only a pair of dark blue board shorts and a smile.

Damn, his abs just... *Eyes up, Leah.*

"How did you get a yacht?" I asked when he met us halfway down the pier.

"Borrowed it," he said with a grin.

"It's his dad's," Brooke answered.

Paxton shot her a disgruntled look.

"What? It is," she repeated.

Close your mouth, you must look like a fish. My lips clamped together with a smack. "Oh, that's nice," I managed. That thing would have paid for my college tuition, grad school, hell, probably my entire life.

"He owns bigger ones," Brooke said with a shrug.

"Bigger? Like what? The *QE2*?" I knew Paxton had money, how else was he paying for his suite—and mine—but there was money and there was...*this.*

"Actually—"

Paxton shot Brooke another look. "Let's get you on board," he said to me, and then took us to the stairs that connected the dock to the yacht. *Stairs. Seriously.*

"Are you ready, Mr. Wilder?" A uniformed captain walked from the bridge area.

"We are, Mac. Is everything else in order?"

"We're ready to go, but if you could keep the camera crews off the bridge?"

Right on cue, Bobby came onto the deck, clipboard and all, followed by two cameras and more crew. Fantastic.

"Bobby, keep the cameras off the bridge and out of the crew's hair," Paxton ordered as the captain smiled his thanks and headed back to the bridge.

"Firecracker!" Little John said with a giant smile as he came from belowdeck. "You lived! I'm glad to see you've made it this far."

"Hey! How did you…?" The last time I'd seen him was on the tower before Paxton had zipped me on board.

"I'm the advance party. I'm always one step behind, cleaning up the stunt, and then I fly one step ahead to set up the next one."

"Well, it's good to see you."

"You probably want to sit," Paxton said to me, pointing to one of the oversized chairs that looked like they belonged more in a Pottery Barn catalog than a boat.

I took the seat, and he lounged in the one next to mine, pulling his sunglasses over his eyes as the boat began to move away from shore.

"Okay, what are we doing?" I asked, unable to hold it in one more minute, despite a camera being two feet off my shoulder.

"You didn't tell her?" Brooke asked from Paxton's other side.

His grin was slow and incredibly sexy. "Don't worry, Firecracker. It'll be worth your while."

Heat flamed in my cheeks, and I ducked my head, knowing

my face was probably as red as Brooke's bikini top.

"Are we swimming?" I asked, running my hands down my white linen pants, brushing off imaginary sand. They were my favorite pair, light and airy, and I wasn't in a hurry to remove them.

"In a way," Paxton answered and pointed over his shoulder. "We're almost there."

I looked over the starboard side and my breath abandoned me. "What are they doing?" I asked.

"Flyboards," he said in my ear. I felt his warmth against my back and called on every piece of my self-control to keep from leaning in to him. Paxton might not be able to help that he was naturally seductive, but I could sure as hell not help him along. "The water is sucked in through the WaveRunner, and then forced out through the hoses under the board. See Nova?"

Landon's Renegade name was enough to remind me that we were on camera, and I moved away from Paxton as the boat slowed to a stop outside a circle of WaveRunners. "How high is he?"

"About fifty feet."

"Holy shit."

"We're going to get them higher."

I walked to the deck railing. "Why would you want to?"

"Because it's never been done." His face was set in determined lines, but his eyes were bright with excitement. "At least not how we're going to do it."

"Who is this 'we'?" My stomach dropped at the same rate Landon did as he dove under the water, only to pop back up like a dolphin twenty feet away.

"You don't even want to try?" He had the nerve to look wounded.

"Did you forget the part where I told you I don't do heights?" I asked, a knot already forming in my chest, tightening with each breath at the thought of doing...that.

"Yeah, but you did the zip-line, so I thought maybe..."

"No." I shook my head so hard my scalp hurt from where my bun tugged. "There's zero chance in hell."

"Oh, come on. I went down into your cave."

Bobby snorted behind me, and I knew exactly what meaning he was taking out of that...what the cameras just heard.

"Crystal Cave. Bermuda, jackass," Paxton immediately corrected his production manager, as if he couldn't stand to have them thinking he'd...well...explored *me*. I couldn't decide if I was flattered or pissed off.

Pissed won. "There was nothing dangerous about that."

"I'll teach you. It'll be fun. I brought you a wet suit and everything."

Great, now he sounded like I'd Grinched his Christmas presents. "Well, I'm sure it will fit Brooke."

"Oh hell no, I'm not going out there," she said from her lounge chair, already relaxed with a Kindle in her hand.

"She has the right idea."

"Don't you want to conquer your fears?" Paxton asked me, undeterred. He turned me around to face him, pops of electricity rushing from where his hands held my upper arms to stutter my heart.

My eyes darted to the cameras, and he sighed but got the point. He took my hand and led me through a door to go below the deck and into a sumptuous bedroom. I wasn't done gawking at the ornate woodwork or luscious fabrics before he lit into me. "Are you going to be afraid your whole life? You're about to pass on a once-in-a-lifetime experience over what? A little anxiety about height? You control the height; you don't have to do what we're doing."

A *little* anxiety? God, just the thought of being that high had me ready to vomit on this pristine carpet. There wasn't even anything to hold on to.

"Afraid my whole life? Newsflash, Paxton, you don't fucking know me. You have no clue what I think or feel, but you might if you so much as asked before you tried to shove me at reckless things I would never consider." *Can't consider.*

"Forgive me for trying to bring you out of your shell a little, Leah."

Wait. How did he get off looking hurt?

"You're not bringing me out, you're breaking me. If you had any idea—" My throat closed as the images broke past my carefully constructed walls and assaulted me. The sight of the canyon beneath me, the steady drip of blood, the nauseating sound of metal against rock...it was all there, as fresh as it had been two years ago. When I looked up, Paxton's blue eyes had somehow morphed into Brian's brown ones, my own hallucination more punishing to my soul than the zip-line had ever dreamed of being. My eyes slammed shut, and I forced air into my lungs with a gross sucking sound.

"Leah." Paxton's whisper sounded strangled, and he pulled me against his chest, wrapping his arms around me.

For a second, I almost gave in and let him hold me. It felt so good, his heartbeat so steady...so alive.

No. I had not come this far to suddenly become one of those girls who needed a guy to prop her up. Using both hands, I shoved off his chest, breaking his hold on me. "You can't fix something you don't understand. I'm not one of your stunts, Pax. I'm not your project." I said it as gently as I could without wavering.

His shoulders fell, and his tongue swiped across his lower lip. "You know, you're right." He grasped the back of his neck. "This is totally up to you, but I at least hope you'll stay and watch. I want to take you somewhere after, if you'll trust me not to force you into something you don't want."

I rubbed my upper arms, concentrating on the friction to force my neat little compartmentalized walls back up. "I can leave if I want?"

He cupped my face, those blue eyes of his wide and earnest. "Of course. I'll have someone take you back to the beach if you want. I meant it, I won't force you into anything ever again. Not like I did with the zip-line, and I won't ambush you again. It was a bad choice on my part, but I'm glad we're having this conversation."

His hand was warm on my cheek, thrumming with life, scented with sand and ocean and Paxton.

Maybe I couldn't get onto one of those things and catapult myself into the air, but I could watch him do what he loved. "Okay," I said quietly.

His smile was soft and mine followed. "Thank you."

We stood there for a moment, absorbed in each other, something intangible passing between us. My heart sparked to life, reminding me that I wasn't just a patient, a student, a daughter, a tutor—I was a woman, who was stupidly, ridiculously, unavoidably attracted to the man standing in front of me.

Shit.

Was I even allowed to feel that? It had been two years. Surely he wouldn't have wanted—

A knock sounded on the door, saving me from doing something entirely foolish. *Like finding out if Paxton's lips are as soft as they look.*

"Hey, Wilder?" Zoe's voice slapped some sense into me,

and I stepped out of Paxton's reach.

"Zoe," he said, his tone resigned as I retreated.

"If she doesn't want to go, I'm suited up and ready," she sang.

"Noted." His eyebrows rose in my direction.

I shook my head, unable to fathom going out there, putting myself in a position to fall. I'd probably lock up the minute I went ten feet in the air, and then what the hell would I do. "I can't."

"Okay," he said softly. "Zoe, we need a tenth, anyway, so go wave Landon over and have him get you to a Flyboard."

Her squeal grated on every exposed nerve—and there were a lot of them right now—but I managed a nod of my head. "Good choice."

He swallowed. "Yeah, well, your wet suit is hanging there in the closet. You can change here. You are down with swimming, right?"

"Yeah, of course." Water I could handle. Water you could swim in, control your movements, propel yourself up. Air was the traitorous bitch that let you go without a moment of consideration.

"I'll see you up there," he said, and left.

I opened the closet to see the wet suit Paxton had left for me. Maybe if I got into the water quickly he wouldn't see—

Whoa.

My heart jumped sweetly, and my smile was immediate. He'd gotten me a full-length wet suit. Either it was a stroke of luck…or he actually paid attention to me—noticed that I only wore pants.

Either way, it meant I could swim without an ounce of self-consciousness.

About ten minutes later, I'd wiggled into the wet suit and headed up to the deck. "I told him that the water was eighty degrees, and you wouldn't need a wet suit to swim, but he insisted," Brooke said as she zipped me up.

"Did he say why?"

"He said if you're so modest that he's never seen you in a pair of shorts, he doubted you'd willingly strut around in a swimsuit."

He'd noticed. "Oh," I said, trying to sound casual. "That's thoughtful of him."

"Uncharacteristic, is what it is, but I like this side of him." She mirrored me, leaning against the railing at my side. "Thank God they took the cameras with them." She pointed to a speedboat that lingered near the WaveRunners.

"It's nice," I agreed.

"Don't relax too much, the helicopter will be here in a minute. That's all they're waiting on."

"Helicopter?" As if on cue, the sound of rotors reached us, and as the helicopter came from the island, Paxton and the others took to the sky.

They were giants rising from the water, their legs long and powerful as they flexed. Paxton rose a little higher than the others, then dipped back to the water only to skyrocket again. Then they all started to experiment, the water-powered hoverboards allowing them to flip, turn, and even dive beneath the water as Landon had earlier.

I held my breath as Paxton soared again, then pulled a double backflip as he fell to the water, catching himself right before impact. He'd broken his fifty-foot goal. Then he did it again, and again, just because he could.

I found myself grinning, enjoying the show as I'm sure

Paxton was loving putting it on. He raised his arm, and they all dropped back down to the water. "What are they doing?" I asked.

"Running over the game plan before they perform."

"There are a lot of them."

"Yeah, there's Penna." She pointed to the left. "Then Landon and Paxton, then a few regulars, and the CTDs."

"CTDs?" I asked. I hadn't realized the Renegade crew was this big.

"Crash Test Dummies," she answered. "Groupies who hang around hoping that the four Originals will make them regulars on the Renegade Channel."

"Like Zoe."

"She's the worst of them. I've never minded the ones who are here for the stunts, or even the fame. They're as reckless as Penna or Pax. But Zoe? She's trying to sleep her way in, and it annoys the shit out of me."

"Which ones are Originals?" I asked, trying to make out the faces I didn't recognize and wishing I'd spent more time in Paxton's suite this last week.

"Paxton, of course. He's the Pied Piper of daredevils, I swear. Then Penna, Landon, and N—" Her voice died suddenly, and she rubbed her hand across the bridge of her nose, moving her sunglasses, but not enough to reveal her eyes.

"Nick?" I guessed.

"Did your research, huh?" she asked with a wry smile.

"No, he kind of came up in discussion yesterday, and Paxton clammed right up."

"Yeah, he doesn't talk about Nick. Ever. No one does. Oh, look!"

All ten of them rose again, but this time they squared off,

five against five. Paxton backed away, then raised something over his head.

"You have got to be kidding me," I muttered as he tossed the football.

I laughed at the sheer absurdity of it, and then watched the wildest football game I'd ever seen play out fifty feet above the water.

"This is much more my speed," I said, treading the crystal blue water next to Paxton. "How did you manage to get away from the cameras?"

"I may have insinuated that we'd be naked."

"You did not!"

"No, I didn't. Then they really would have insisted they come with." He pulled his snorkel mask down over his eyes and nose. "Shall we?" he asked in a nasal tone before popping in his mouthpiece.

I did the same and nodded. Then I took a deep breath, and we descended into paradise. The water was perfect, the color, the clarity, the temperature—everything. Colorful fish swam in schools along the reef, lingering on the shipwreck Paxton had brought us here to see.

My lungs subtly protested their lack of oxygen, and I swam back up, taking a breath before heading back down. Paxton kept pace with me, pointing to certain pieces of the wreckage, lingering when I did, breathing when I needed to.

This was incredible.

I'd always loved the water. Even…after, when it had become more of a prescription than an enjoyment, it had always welcomed me home with open arms. There was something about being infinitely weightless, of living in a world without walls, that was simply blissful.

We swam through the fish, across the wreck, explored the shallower shorelines, and seemed to find a perfect harmony together without uttering a word.

After over an hour, when we broke the surface for the last time, we both removed our mouthpieces and masks, facing each other as we treaded water about thirty feet from the boat.

"Worth it?" Paxton asked.

"Every second. This is amazing—seriously one of the coolest things I've ever done. Thank you."

The smile he gave me was more beautiful than the scenery around us and more intimate than a kiss. It was soft, open, with a touch of vulnerability that was sexier than any of his performances. "I'm glad that you enjoyed it. You know, if you're stuck with me the next nine months, you may as well get perks. If there's something you want that's not on the excursion list in any port we come to, just tell me. I know it's going to suck for you at times, and that you got yanked into my world without having a fair choice, but I swear I won't let you regret it."

"And what about you?" I asked. "I'm your tutor. You're stuck with me for study sessions and test prep and papers. None of this was what you agreed to. You don't have to spend your free shore time entertaining me. I know there are a lot of... demands on you."

The brief internet search I'd done on him hadn't only turned up his X Games medals, but pages of party pictures with tons of different women. Add that to the mug shots from the few times he'd been arrested for jumping off things he shouldn't have, and it painted a different picture of Paxton from the one swimming in front of me.

He tilted his head, making the tattoo along his neck flex and ripple. "No bullshit?"

My chest tightened in a way I knew had nothing to do with the workout I'd just had. "No bullshit."

He moved closer, until only a couple of feet separated us, until I could imagine crossing the distance and finding out how a saltwater kiss tasted. He took a deep breath, like he was trying to decide how much to say. "I like being around you. I can't explain it any better than that."

As much as I wanted to analyze that comment, decipher what he meant, the immediate fear that slid into my peaceful afternoon stole the show. "Don't play games with me, Paxton."

"No games," he promised. "Just my...friendship. Nine months is a long time not to get to know someone."

That pause meant nothing, right? *That pause is everything.*

"Right." I silenced the joyful thirteen-year-old girl who was dancing around in my stomach with the reminder that Zoe had come out of his room a few days ago. "I'd like to be friends," I admitted. But no further. No deeper. No chance for him to rip through my scars.

Then he led me back to our ride, helping me up the ladder onto the smaller ski boat. As we headed toward the dock, he gave me that smile again—the one that felt like it was only for me—and those damn butterflies were back. Why did he have to have such different sides to him?

Wilder I could shut out. He was a pompous, reckless ass who would no doubt get me hurt in more ways than one.

But Paxton? Yeah. I was defenseless against him, and that was even more dangerous.

CHAPTER SIX

LEAH

AT SEA

I glanced at the door as Dr. Westwick droned on about the principals of inertia. Physics had to be the most frustrating class I'd ever taken, and honestly, I didn't care when the ball I'd rolled would stop rolling.

Unless that rolling ball would explain to me where the hell Paxton was.

We'd been at sea four straight days, and he had already missed two of our World Lit classes, one of World Religion, and now all of our Physics. How the hell was I supposed to keep his grades up if he didn't come to class?

My eyes drifted to the window, where the waves of the Atlantic were currently affecting the pitch of my stomach.

"Make sure you turn in your answers via eCampus by midnight tomorrow, and look over the guide for the quiz on Monday. Don't slack off just because you have a couple days in Barcelona," Dr. Westwick warned, ending our class.

I gathered my things to leave, shoving my binder into my bag a little harder than necessary.

"Miss Baxter?" Dr. Westwick called from the podium.

I plastered a tight-lipped smile onto my face before turning to him. "Dr. Westwick?"

His fingers trailed down a list I couldn't see. "You're Mr. Wilder's tutor, aren't you?"

Shit. "I am."

He pushed his square-rimmed glasses up his nose. "Well, if you could persuade him to attend, that might help his participation grade a little. Tell him that watching from his room isn't quite the same."

I'm going to kill him. Dead. Then I'll throw the body overboard where no one will find it. "I'll tell him, Professor."

He nodded his thanks, and I took off to my room—our room. Sharing with Penna was actually pretty enjoyable. She wasn't around much, and when she was, she respected my space but was still easy to talk to.

"That asshole!" I shouted as I slammed our door behind me, throwing my bag into the hall closet.

"Who?" Penna called from the living room, where I found her painting her toenails. Her perfect legs stretched out in front of her, all tan and smooth, and I tried to ignore the stab of sheer envy that lanced through my heart. *You are grateful for the life you've been given. These scars are a beautiful reminder of your second chance. The second chance he would have wanted you to have.* I repeated the mantra in my head until the pain faded into a sense of peace. Dr. Scott would have been proud. *Because that only took two years of therapy.*

But even with therapy and two years, there were moments when everything hurt like hell, where the pain was still so rough that it scraped my soul until it bled. Those were the scars only I saw, the ones I picked at every once in a while so

I didn't forget him.

"Leah, who's the asshole?" Penna repeated, jarring me.

"Oh." I shook my head and collapsed into the armchair. "Paxton."

"Well, that's not the first time I've heard that word associated with his name," she said. "What did he do?"

"He's skipping classes. I'm about to do some experiments with inertia and my fist to his freaking face."

She snorted. "Pax hasn't ever been one to do what he's supposed to. That's why he has you." She lifted the brush as the ship pitched slightly. "This is impossible in these waves."

"Well, I guess I'm failing that one."

She lifted the construction-cone orange polish and raised her eyebrows. "Want to do yours?"

I shook my head. Toes, I could handle, but if something slipped... "No, thank you. I may as well go kick Zoe out of his bed or whatever. He's blown off all of today, but I'll be damned if he misses anything tomorrow."

"Zoe isn't sleeping with him. She hasn't in the last six months or so. It doesn't stop her from trying, but that ship sailed a while ago, and Paxton isn't one to climb the same mountain twice, if you know what I mean." She closed up the polish.

"Yeah, of course, right," I rushed. "Why would he be? Half the women on this ship would jump at the chance to...well, jump *him*, and the other half are lying to themselves. Why would he want someone twice?"

Penna flinched. "Shit, that's not what I meant. I don't want you to think he's a man-whore or anything."

I raised my eyebrows at her, and she looked around the room briefly before finally nodding. "Okay, so maybe he's a little man-whorish, but his heart, that's solid, untouched...for the most part, at least."

I never understood people who could differentiate the two. Where my heart went, there my body did, and so forth. *But if Paxton offered...* I shut down that line of thinking and locked the door on it. "Why are you telling me this?"

She leaned forward. "Because he's my oldest friend, and I care what you think about him. And I know he cares what you think about him, too."

I swallowed. "Well, right now I think that he doesn't know what an alarm clock is."

She smiled. "How about I take you to him?"

"He's not in his room?"

"Nope. And besides, I'd like to see what happens when he gets a load of how pissed you are. If you want to wait a few minutes, I'll make popcorn."

"Penna!"

She threw out her hands. "Just kidding. Give my piggies a chance to dry, and we'll track him down."

We didn't have to wait long before Landon came in through the sliding door, dripping sweat. "Hey, asshat, knock!" Penna chastised, throwing a pillow at him.

"What? It's not like I haven't already seen you naked," he shot back.

Penna snapped her gaze to me. "He didn't mean it that way. We've been friends since we were kids, all of us."

"Chill out, Penna. I don't think Firecracker cares." Landon laughed and sank into the couch across from me. "Damn, I'm wiped out. Pax is a fucking machine these last couple of days."

Penna's hand popped up. "He didn't mean that, either. Pax hasn't been fucking anyone, especially not Landon."

"That's none of my business," I said, smoothing the lines of my leggings. As if leggings could have wrinkles.

"Yeah, anyway, he sent me to get you, Penna." Landon lifted his shirt to wipe the sweat off his face, and my eyebrows shot skyward. In some parallel universe, the Hemsworths were searching for their lost brother, because he was here. Landon was hot. Not in the walking sex-dream kind of hot that Paxton was, but a broodier hot.

"I want nothing to do with that damn trick." She crossed her arms.

"It's not like he has his bike out, Penna. He's working on the BMX for Barcelona, and he's going to need your advice before he gets himself killed."

Killed? I sat up. "What is he doing?"

"Trying to nail a Five-forty Double Tailwhip in these waves," Landon answered. "He's going to break his damn neck."

"Show me."

"How the hell did he...?" I shook my head as I stared at the monstrosity onstage. "You know, I'm not sure I even want to know."

"Yeah, that's a question for Wilder," Landon answered.

"He looks a little busy at the moment."

Little was an understatement. Paxton was currently riding his BMX bike on a monstrous half-pipe that consumed the entire stage of the auditorium. My breath caught every time he rose over one end, flying through the air, the bike twisting while he turned above it, only to gracefully fall back to the pipe and glide to the other end so it could all begin again.

He was magnificent.

"How tall is that thing?" I asked Landon.

"About six meters. A little under twenty feet."

"Isn't this a little dangerous on a ship?"

"Yeah, it's pretty dense," Landon agreed. "But he's as stubborn as they come."

"He's a reckless fool," I whispered in equal parts awe and fear. I knew reckless guys, knew what happened when they mistakenly thought they were in control. *He's not Brian. Pax might be worse.*

"That, he is."

At least the fool wore a helmet.

But he was a driven fool. His movements were hypnotizing as we walked down the aisle toward the stage.

The ship pitched slightly. I caught myself on the back of a chair and gasped as Paxton hit the side of the ramp, sliding down in a heap of limbs. "Paxton!" I yelled.

He sat up and blocked the stage lights from his eyes. "Firecracker?"

Shit. Was I supposed to be using his real name in front of the cameras? Well, too late.

"What the hell are you doing?"

He stood, holding his handlebars. "Watching a *Gilmore Girls* marathon. What does it look like I'm doing?"

"It looks like you're being an absolute bonehead. Have you seen the waves out there?"

"What? No." He walked the few feet between the ramp and the edge of the stage. It was only ten or so feet from the base of the stage to the bottom of the orchestra pit, but my stomach tightened all the same.

"He hasn't left the theater during daylight hours in the last two days," Landon said quietly.

"You've missed six classes," I called up as we came closer,

my neck craning to keep him in eyesight.

"What? I can't hear you," he said with a grin, putting his hand to his ear.

"You can hear me just fine, Paxton Wilder," I shouted.

"Come on up. I don't want to have to yell back at you." He motioned to the ladder that led to the stage. "Or there's a ramp right there."

I opted for the second, heading for the side of the theater.

"Hey!" Brooke said from a seat at the edge, her notebooks perched on her lap. "Did you come to watch?"

"More to yell at Paxton for missing class," I said, passing behind her.

"Nothing better than a nagging woman hanging around," Zoe bit back, kicking her feet from the edge of the stage.

"I'm getting tired of telling you to stop being a bitch, Zoe," Brooke snapped. "I'll walk you up, Leah."

"How is Wilder juggling schoolwork and practice?" Bobby asked, a camera not far behind him.

I stole Landon's line. "That's a question for Wilder, don't you think?"

He tipped his hat with a smile. "You're a fast learner."

"You're always in my face," I said with an overly sweet smile.

Brooke tugged me past the crew and up the ramp.

"Come on," Pax said with a grin, now at the top of the half-pipe.

"Would you stop going higher?" I asked, my heart jumping.

"How much do you want to yell at me for missing class?" he responded, motioning to the ladder that led to the platform at the top of the half-pipe.

My hands grasped both sides of the ladder in a death grip.

The landing had a railing at the back of it, no doubt to keep his reckless ass from falling off when a trick went wrong. I could easily make it up there. It was only twenty feet, and by God, he was not killing my scholarship because he couldn't get his ass to class.

Rung by rung, I climbed the ladder, humming Katy Perry's "Firework" to distract me from the distance to the ground.

My head popped over the rim of the half-pipe, and Paxton offered his hand, his eyes shining with a kind of victory.

"What are you so happy about?" I mumbled as he pulled me onto the platform, which was wider than I'd expected. My hand immediately sought and found the railing, and I loosened my death grip on Paxton.

"Look at you, up on my pipe."

My eyebrow arched. "Your pipe is distracting you from class."

He smirked. "It always does."

"Oh my God, you two." Brooke laughed, climbing up behind me. "I'll give you some space," she said as she skirted around us, heading to the other end.

The camera was on the opposite side, giving us a tiny bit of privacy. "It's good to see you," Paxton said, his eyes skimming my features.

"That's because you haven't been to class in about two and a half days. You've missed every single Physics class since Bermuda."

"I'm studying physics right now," he joked. "Shouldn't that count as extra credit?"

"No."

All traces of joking left his face, and he absentmindedly rubbed the tattoo on the side of his neck with his empty hand. "Look, I get kind of in the zone and forget that things outside this exist."

"You can't do that," I snapped, keeping my voice quiet to avoid the microphones on the opposite side. "You're losing participation points, and your homework—"

"I turned it in on eCampus," he interjected.

"And the discussion in Lit?" He was not getting off the hook that easily.

"Did you take notes?" He lifted his arms behind his neck, his biceps flexing.

Don't get distracted. "Of course I did."

He shrugged. "Then what's the issue?"

My mouth hung for a second before I managed to close it. "What's the issue? You're not in class!"

"But you are."

"And?"

"And you're my tutor. So you have notes and can catch me up, right?"

Do not smack him. Don't do it. I sucked in a deep breath through my nose. "I am your tutor, not your teacher. You have to be there! Damn it, Paxton, there's more than yourself to think about. My scholarship rides on your grades, too!"

"So do all of their jobs," he said quietly, his hand sweeping to encompass everyone on the pipe. "Leah, if I don't make grades, the documentary is canceled."

"Wait. What? What kind of producer would tie a movie to your academics?"

"The kind who shares my last name." He wiped away his sweat the same way Landon had, by lifting his shirt, and I kept my eyes locked on his face. I knew one look at those cut lines and I'd be a puddle of hormones, which wouldn't do either of us any good.

"Your last..." His dad owned the boat on Bermuda, but how much money did he really come from? "Is your dad the producer?"

He nodded. "Yeah, and he agreed to the movie as long as my grades held. It's his way of getting me to finish college."

The ship pitched again, and my hand tightened on the railing as Paxton's gripped my waist. He inhaled with a hiss and then dropped his hand like I'd burned him. I knew my waist was thicker than the athletic goddesses he hung out with, but really? "Well, you can't finish college without making grades, so maybe you should get your ass to class."

"Well, I make the tricks, or the studio exec pulls the movie," he snapped, then closed his eyes for a moment before he opened them. "Leah, I'm damned if I do and damned if I don't. That's why I need you."

Those blue eyes cut straight through my anger, or maybe it was the damnable situation he was in.

"Half this camera crew has families they need to support, and...well, there're more people involved than just you and me, so you tell me what I'm supposed to do."

"I don't know," I whispered.

"I don't, either. I know I have to study. I also have to practice, keep in shape, plan the next stunt, check on the one after that, and keep my sanity with a camera in my face every five seconds. I told you this wasn't going to be easy."

"Why would you sign up for all of this?" I found my hand on the skin of his bicep before I realized I'd even reached for him, as if the physical connection of our skin could make me understand something utterly ridiculous to me. "Not famous enough already? Not rich enough?"

"Sure, partly. This will set our careers for years, and the

opportunities are incredible, but more than that"—his eyes flickered to the camera—"look, I have my reasons. I should have come to class. I should have studied. I made a choice, and it might have been the wrong one."

"That's some apology," I huffed.

He slowly reached for my face but dropped his hand before he connected. "I'm not apologizing. If skipping class was what it took to get you up here, then I'm okay with it."

"Of course you are," I said with a sarcastic twinge, but the sting had left my voice.

"Well, since you came all the way up here, do you want to see some cool stuff?" he asked, his Wilder grin plastered on his face.

"Are you asking if I'm ready for an adventure?" I tossed his catch phrase at him.

"I'm asking if you're ready to witness one," he answered. "Landon, toss up a helmet?"

"Oh, hell no, I'm not getting on anything that slides down this ramp. You've lost your fool mind."

He caught the helmet easily and slipped it onto my head, his fingers ghosting across the skin of my throat before he snapped it under my chin. "This is just in case. I'm not forcing you into anything, but sometimes bikes or boards go flying up here. I want to protect that beautiful brain of yours so you can get me through this term, okay?"

"Fine," I answered, letting a smile slip. "Go do whatever it is you do. I'm giving you ten minutes before I haul you to my room."

One of the crew whistled. "To study!" I yelled out in correction. "Taking him to my room to study! For the love—!" Why did *everything* have a double meaning around here?

Paxton's laugh anchored my heart to my dipping stomach as he jumped onto his bike and took off down the pipe. He began his series of turns and dips, keeping clear of the section where I stood with Brooke next to me.

Up close, it felt more like art than sport, the way he moved, flying then falling, over and over again in a rhythm he created. He fell too often for my peace of mind, each time climbing up to the pipe to talk with Landon and then hitting the ramp again. He was 100 percent focused, never once looking my way or checking the cameras. It was as if nothing existed outside the bike, the ramp, and his own abilities.

The longer I watched him, the more I realized it was the same for me, holding my breath when he did a trick, releasing only when I saw him land it. My hands tightened when he gripped the handlebars of his spinning bike, my heart caught the higher he took to the air. Just as his world had narrowed to training, mine had narrowed to him.

"Amazing, isn't it?" Brooke asked.

"Incredible."

"I've been watching them since we were kids, always amazed that they could all do these things, like gravity is some kind of game to them."

"You never wanted to try?"

She scoffed. "Oh, no. Penna's the rebel in the family. The things she can do...well, that's not me. I don't mind the tamer stuff—skiing, snowboarding, motorcycles—but the minute they take to the air, my butt usually hits the bench. I realized a long time ago that there's a difference between admiring and actually being a part of it."

"Agreed." Paxton did another trick where he flipped around, and my breath froze in my chest until he landed...

backward. *Show-off.* "I get it now," I said quietly. "Why all the girls chase him. That kind of intensity is captivating." Even the thought of him applying that same focus, drive, and passion to sex was enough to send a flash of pure want through me.

I shifted my weight, inconveniently aware that I was a little more than turned on.

What would it be like to have his complete attention on me? *You'll never know.*

Paxton came to a stop on the other side of the ramp and pulled off his helmet. "It's still not right," he called over to me.

"You're amazing," I said, my mouth going dry as he wiped the sweat with his shirt. This time I didn't look away from the carved lines of his stomach, the muscles that roped around his body. What the hell? Did the guy do sit-ups in his sleep or something? How was that kind of body even possible?

"Oh good, Colin is up," Brooke said, coming to attention next to me. "Have you seen him? He's gorgeous. If you're looking for a little ship-fling, I can totally hook you up there."

"I haven't met him yet." Plus, if I was looking for a ship-fling, I had a feeling it wouldn't be Colin. Was I even capable of a fling? Or ready for any kind of relationship? Man, I was picking at scabs left and right today.

A guy hauled a bike up next to where Paxton stood, and they talked for a moment before Paxton gave him the go-ahead, motioning to the ramp. Colin strapped the helmet over his curly brown hair and mounted his bike.

The guy was good, I'd give him that, but not as good as Paxton. The bike turned and flipped at his direction, skimming along the pipe's edge just to slide back down.

"What do you think, Firecracker?" Paxton called over to me.

"Incredible," I answered truthfully as Colin headed back toward us, aimed about ten feet to the right.

The boat pitched, and Paxton's eyes widened with a fear I'd never seen. "Leah!" he shouted.

Colin's bike flew my way.

Everything slowed.

Huh, where's Colin?

The metal frame hurtled toward me, racing faster than I could move. *This is going to hurt.*

I accepted the impending injury the way I'd calmly accepted the foregone conclusion of my death that night. Some things were simply unavoidable.

Just before impact, my right side was shoved. Brooke.

She sent me skidding out of the path of the bike, my feet flying from under me.

"No!" Paxton's voice sounded so far away.

I looked down as I fell, watched the wood of the ramp rushing up to meet me, morphing into the barren landscape of a California ravine.

It's not real. It's not real.

But it was all I saw—the burning, the blood...Brian.

Then I saw nothing.

CHAPTER SEVEN

PAXTON

AT SEA

"Leah!" Her name ripped from my throat, the sound almost inhuman, animalistic, as she fell. She'd gone limp before impact, the angle working in her favor as she slid to the bottom, but she wasn't moving.

Just like *he* hadn't.

I used the ramp as a slide, barely noticing the friction burns on my calves.

Skidding to a stop next to her, I gathered her limp body into my arms and pressed the side of her face to my heart, stroking her other cheek with my hand. She was cold, clammy, but her chest rose and fell, her pulse strong.

She was also unconscious.

I'd seen enough falls to know she hadn't hurt her neck, and she still had her helmet on, so why wouldn't she wake up?

"Is she okay?" Brooke asked next to me, her voice shaking.

"I don't know," I answered, my thumb stroking her cheekbone, then down her nose, over her lips. "Leah. Eleanor. You have to wake up. Show me those eyes, come on, baby."

"Oh God. If she's not okay... I'm so sorry, Pax," Brooke babbled.

"Why won't she wake up?" Panic like I'd never known tore through me. I'd fallen while mountain climbing, dangled over a sheer cliff face, snowboarded from a helicopter, but I'd never been this scared in my life. I unsnapped her helmet, in case the strap was putting pressure somewhere, and leaned down, pressing my forehead to hers. "Leah, please. Please."

She gasped, the sound of air rushing past her lips breathing life into me, and I nearly crumbled with relief. "Leah?"

I pulled back enough to see her eyes flutter open, the whiskey color vague instead of bright, but she was here. "I've got you. You're okay."

"I'm not dead," she whispered.

"No." I shook my head, unable to stop the smile of relief from spreading across my face. "You're not dead. You're okay. I have you."

"Paxton?" she asked, her voice soft, weak.

"Yeah?" I couldn't stop my fingers from tracing the soft lines of her face, more than aware of how bad it could have been.

"I don't do heights."

I pulled her tight against me, tucking her into my neck, my shakes of laughter bordering on hysterical—bordering on uncontrolled.

"I'm so glad you woke up." I was always in control, it was how I survived, how I thrived and excelled, but this girl—this woman—had the power to shred that control if I wasn't careful.

"I heard you calling me."

Then I lost it.

• • •

I jumped to my feet when Penna walked into their living room. "How is she?"

"Ready to sleep," she answered, slumping onto the couch next to Brooke. "Doc gave her something to help her sleep, but she doesn't have any major damage. Well, physically, at least. He said it was a panic attack."

I don't do heights.

"I'm so sorry," Brooke said, her voice small.

"It wasn't your fault," I said to her. She'd already been through so much this last year. "I saw the angle; Colin's bike would have hit her. It was a snap decision, and no one blames you."

"She knows you were trying to help her," Penna assured her, putting her arm around Brooke's shoulder.

"Some help. Should I go apologize?"

"If you want to. She's pretty out of it, but it might make you feel better."

Brooke nodded slowly and stood. "Yeah. That sounds good. I'll see you guys tomorrow?"

"Absolutely," I said, forcing a smile. Brooke said her goodbyes and headed back to Leah's room as Landon came in through the sliding door.

"Bobby said he'd kill the footage. It won't go in the documentary." He took Brooke's vacated seat.

"Do you trust him?" Penna asked.

"I don't think we have much of a choice," I answered, pacing the length of the area rug. "She won't want it in there, but she signed a release, so we don't have much recourse if he chooses to."

Landon shook his head. "Sometimes I wonder what the fuck we were thinking, letting them film our entire lives this year."

"We were thinking that this was the only way to give Nick a future where he could stand on his own. If we can't pull this off, then it was all for nothing. You guys know what this means to him. It's all he has," I said.

"I wish we could tell people that," Penna added softly.

"Yeah, well, we can't," Landon said. "So this is what we're stuck with."

The silence that descended was thick with memories and regret, yet hollow, knowing we were missing him, that he, of all people, should be on this trip.

"When she fell…" I said softly.

"Flashbacks?" Penna asked.

I nodded. I'd never flown across a half-pipe faster in my life.

"Me, too," Landon said, rubbing his hands over his face. "She's going to be okay?"

"Yeah," Penna answered.

"She's still awake," Brooke said as she came back in. "Not sure for how long, though, so if you want to see her, you'd better be quick. I'll catch you guys tomorrow." She waved before walking out through the back door.

"Go on," Penna urged me.

My hands itched, nearly tingling with the need to put my arms around Leah, to feel her breathing. "I'm not sure that's a good idea."

"You like her," Landon said, as if it could be that simple.

"I like her," I admitted, wishing that saying it would somehow free me.

"Fuck," he muttered. "Pax, I love you, but you destroy just about every girl you touch. I know it's not intentional, but it happens, and this girl…"

"I know," I said louder than I'd intended. "But as much as I love you guys, I'm not asking your permission."

"Well, I'd give it," Penna said, curling her legs under her. "She's a great girl, and exactly what you need."

"Sure, but for how long?" Landon argued. "Until he gets bored with her and then he's lost his tutor? Then what do we do? Find another one who isn't already booked and is willing to sign all the media releases and the NDA?"

A couple of years ago, Landon would have agreed with Penna, championed a new relationship. But this new jaded version of my best friend was what I was stuck with—what I'd created.

"This isn't up for debate," I snapped. "And besides, I said I like her, I didn't say I was going to act on it."

"Well, if it was up for a vote, Leah has mine," Penna said. "We're a family, and we always have been, but I think we all know that there's more to life outside the Renegades."

Landon looked from her to me and then sighed. "Right. Okay. Just...be careful."

After what happened today, how could I not be? "Penna, you ran the background check when I chose her, right?"

"I know what you're about to ask, and it's not for me to tell." Her eyes took that fierce glint I knew meant she wasn't budging.

"So something did happen to her?" I asked. "Is that why she's so scared of heights?"

She crossed her arms and glared. "Ask her yourself."

"You're supposed to be on my side here."

She thrust her fist into the air. "Team Leah."

"Nice." I gathered up every ounce of self-control I had and walked down the hall, gently knocking on Leah's door.

"Come in," she said, her voice groggy.

I opened the door and saw her curled on her side, her mass of brown hair wrapped around her shoulder. "Hey."

"Hi." Her smile was unbelievably beautiful, and incredibly drug-induced.

The bed sagged under my weight as I sat next to her. "How are you feeling?"

"Sleepy."

I tucked her hair behind her ear, lingering only long enough to feel the silken strands slip through my fingers. "Then you should sleep."

Her forehead puckered. "Sometimes I have nightmares."

"About what happened?" I asked, blatantly fishing.

She nodded.

"Do you want to tell me about them?"

"No. I don't want to think about it."

"Okay. Maybe someday?" Someday when she wasn't drugged, when she knew what she was telling me, when she was ready to open up to me.

"Maybe." She took my hand and put it on her cheek, then turned and placed a kiss on the palm.

I felt it in my soul.

"What was that for?" I asked, wishing for so many things that I had no right to.

"Because I wanted to."

My thumb stroked over her cheek, unable to stay motionless against her skin. I loved how soft she was. Her curves, her eyes, her kindness. In my world everything was hard—the stunts, the bodies, even the women—but the only sharp parts of Leah were those that I loved best, her brain and her mouth.

"I was so scared," she mumbled, her eyes half closing. "I looked down and...I shut down. I'm sorry I was so weak."

"No, no. That's not weakness. Don't think that."

"It wasn't all bad. I woke up with you holding me. I knew you'd come." Her trust made me feel invincible while simultaneously scaring the shit out of me.

"Of course I came," I whispered. "I damn near flew to get there."

She forced her eyes open, her blinks becoming longer and longer. "No one came that night."

Every muscle in my body locked. "Leah…"

"I waited, but no one came. All night. Then the next day. No one came." She leaned deeper into my palm.

"I'm here," I promised.

"I don't want to be scared anymore, Pax. Will you help me? You're never scared." Her eyes closed. How much of this would she remember in the morning?

"Yeah, Firecracker. We'll get you past it." We would. No matter what she needed, I could do it. It was the least I could do after I was the one who dared her onto the half-pipe in the first place. Yet another person my ego injured.

Her breathing evened out, and I let myself run my hand over her hair before standing to leave. I had the door open when she called my name.

"Pax?"

"Leah?"

"Class is at ten a.m. tomorrow," she slurred. "If you're late, I'm telling everyone that tattoo on your neck is from you chickening out on a dare."

"Got it." I laughed as I shut her bedroom door.

I went to every single class until we docked in Barcelona three days later.

CHAPTER EIGHT

LEAH

BARCELONA

"Come on. We have three days in Barcelona. The least you can do is spend one with me." Paxton leaned against my doorframe, looking good enough to send my heartbeat—and hormones—into overdrive. I swore, when that guy came within fifteen feet of me, my panties knew before I did.

I rolled my eyes and slipped my money and ID into my travel wallet. "I am. Tomorrow. Today, I'm touring the churches for extra credit, which is what *you* should be doing."

"I'll go with you tomorrow, and what the hell is that?" he asked, pointing to my wallet.

"It's a wallet," I answered.

"It's the weirdest wallet I've ever seen."

"It hooks on my belt and goes inside my clothes to protect me from pickpockets. Stop changing the subject." Where was my sunscreen?

"I went to every class."

"Do you want a gold star?" I asked, putting my sunglasses

on top of my head. My tank top straps slid down my shoulders.

"That should get me something," he damn near whined.

"Yeah, like a good grade," I threw back.

"You're impossible. Turn around." He made the circle motion with his fingers, and I did as he asked.

"Why? And what is so freaking important about today?"

I jumped when his fingers brushed against the bare skin of my back, and my breath hitched as he manipulated the strap, tightening it for me. God, if he could do that with one touch, what would it be like if he actually ever meant to turn me on? I'd probably spontaneously combust.

"I'm doing something really cool, and I selfishly want you to watch. And then I may have planned something for us."

I froze. Planned something? Like a date? No. There was no way he would ever consider that. "Like what?" I turned slowly, bringing me super close to him—so close that all it would take was a push onto my toes and I could actually kiss him. But I couldn't kiss him. I was his tutor, and he'd moved me off his *fuckable list* within minutes of meeting me. That look on his face, though...that didn't say that the attraction was one-sided.

"You only get to know if you come with me," he said, his smile slow and incredibly sexy. "Come on, Firecracker. Trust me."

It was his eyes that made me waver, made me forget damn near every thought in my brain besides Paxton, and sex...and Paxton. His hands, lips, smile, body, intensity—everything I wasn't supposed to want. Mush-brain, indeed. "Fine, but I promised Rachel I'd call her today, so you have to have me back before midnight. Did you just fist pump?"

"Hell yes, Cinderella, I'll have you home by midnight. Now take your fanny pack and let's go."

"It's a wallet!" I called after him as he practically skipped out of my room. "You asked him to help you," I muttered to myself. No matter what he had planned, I was going to give it a try. I had to find a way to push past this fear, as debilitating as it was. The way my body had shut down... It was a miracle I hadn't hurt more than my pride in that fall.

Two hours later I walked up to Brooke, who leaned against a tiled wall on a hilltop in Barcelona overlooking the Park Guell, Gaudi's exquisite creation that looked like Dr. Seuss had dabbled in architecture.

"Leah!" She hugged me, squeezing a little too tight.

"If you say that you're sorry again, I'm going to walk away," I said with a smile. She'd been apologizing nonstop for three days.

"I can't help it. I'm just..."

I narrowed my eyes at her.

"I'm just so excited to see them pull this off."

"That's better," I said, leaning cautiously over the wall of our ten-foot-high overlook to see the majority of the park that had been emptied for production. Beautiful tile mosaics decorated the walls that rose against the blue sky, a gorgeous cacophony of color and light that somehow reminded me of Paxton—pieced together in a way that shouldn't make sense yet was hypnotic to the eye.

However, I highly doubted the half-pipe that rested at the bottom of the iconic steps in the courtyard before us was part of Gaudi's plan. Or the mini ramps situated around the park leading up to it.

Most of the camera crew was locally hired for this one;

there were too many places they needed to catch shots, and I watched them scurry into position.

"Here they come," I said, watching the first riders—these ones on BMX bikes—make the park their personal playground.

"Are you ready for an adventure?" Brooke asked, laying on her best Paxton impression.

"That was scary close." I laughed.

"There's Penna!" she said, leaning farther to see her sister pull a 360 off one of the rails. It was hard to believe that the girl with the supermodel looks rode like one of the guys.

"I can't believe they let them shut down the park for this," I said, watching another wave of riders, this one with Paxton in the lead and Landon on his heels.

"They had to agree to extreme protective measures of the art, hire locally, and you know Paxton's father throwing money at it didn't hurt."

"It never does, right? Are they all like that? The Originals?"

She shook her head. "No. Paxton and Landon come from money. Big money. Penna and I, well, our parents aren't hurting, that's for sure, but Nick—" She rubbed her forehead and forced a fake smile. "Sorry."

"No, don't be," I said. "I shouldn't have asked."

The park was quiet for a moment, resetting the course for the real shots now that the riders had navigated it once.

"You have as much right to know as anyone, seeing as you're a part of this now."

I scoffed. "Falling off a half-pipe does not a Renegade make."

She tilted her head, watching the cameramen adjust their angles. "No, but carrying Paxton does. Where he goes, they follow. What he does, they emulate. If he fails, they all do, and you're more a part of that than you know."

"Why do you follow?" *Holy shit, foot in mouth much?* "Crap, that wasn't how I meant that to sound. I mean if you don't get into all of this"—I gestured to the scrambling crew and Renegades hauling their bikes back up to the top of the park—"why would you spend your life around it?"

"You haven't researched their little Renegade troop much, have you?" she asked with a wry smile.

I shook my head. "No. Once I knew who he was, what he did, I decided it was best to let him show me who he was as opposed to judging him based off what everyone else assumed. I'm kind of stuck with the guy for the next nine months."

"You're good for him," she said quietly.

"I'm nothing to him," I replied. "Just his tutor."

"If you believe that, maybe you're the one who needs the tutoring. I'd give you the cliché of 'he's different around you,' but you don't know what he's like normally."

Before I could ask her what she meant, the second wave started. We watched, entranced by the different tricks they pulled on the pipe, cringing when they didn't quite make it, and cheering for the ones who did.

"I didn't realize how many there were," I said.

"There's probably close to twenty CTDs on board, all with different ways they're willing to put their bodies on the line to worship at Paxton's altar."

The tone in her voice brought me up short. "Have you ever...worshipped at his altar?" *Why the hell does it matter? Why would you care?*

She laughed. "Hell, no. Paxton's pretty much a brother to Penna and me. And even if I could manage some level of attraction to him, I have personally witnessed the revolving door that doubles as his bed. He's not as bad as Landon, but at least Landon has his reasons."

Something precious inside—that I hadn't even realized had been growing until this moment—withered and died. "Right. He does enjoy the chase."

She gently covered my hand with hers. "I wasn't talking about you, Leah. He's careful with you—around you."

"It doesn't matter." I waved her off, slipping my hand free and trying to find my composure when I had no freaking reason to lose it in the first place. Paxton wasn't mine. He was free to sleep with whomever he wanted, whenever he wanted.

Oh, speaking of whomever, that was Zoe on rollerblades.

Brooke followed my line of sight. "He hasn't slept with anyone since we left Miami."

Damn it, that pesky feeling was back. "I don't—"

"Care, I know. But you should know that, just in case you do. I've never seen him as scared as he was when you fell from the pipe. The way he held you after..."

My attention snapped to her, despite Landon's turn on the pipe. "He held me after?" Oh God, was that my voice sounding so lovesick?

She nodded, her eyes slightly watering as she looked back to the park. "I wish someone held me like that."

This time I covered her hand as Paxton took to the pipe on his BMX. He glided like he was part of the bike, his speed, agility, and acrobatics simply...beautiful, there was no other word for it. The way he moved his body, the confidence in his abilities, it all drew me in when I knew I should be backing away.

Then he flew higher than I'd ever seen, twisting in the air in a move that left me breathless. "Whoa."

"Five-Forty Double Tailwhip. That practice paid off," Penna called up, cheering when he dismounted the ramp. "And if you think that's great, wait until you see him on a motocross bike."

I was too stunned to move.

Paxton looked up at me with a wide grin and bowed as if he'd performed only for my pleasure. My smile was impossible to contain as I clapped for him.

The rest of his crew then did the same, all bowing up to where Brooke and I watched, and my laughter was instant.

I'd known who he was since Miami, but it had never hit home until this moment. He wasn't just any extreme athlete, he was one of the best in the world.

"We have to do another set, is that okay?" he asked.

"Of course," I called down. "I'm having fun watching you."

You sound like one of his groupies.

"Wanna try?" He wiggled his eyebrows under his helmet and GoPro camera.

"Not in a million years. Now go start the wild rumpus."

"What?" he asked.

"Well, let's face it, you're pretty much king of all the wild things around here." Even his name, Pax, was too close to Max to not draw the comparison to my favorite children's book.

"I'll go find my wolf suit," he said, laughing as he walked off.

Knowing he'd gotten my little joke made me smile even wider.

The trees to the left of the staircase rustled, and three preteen boys popped their heads over the concrete barrier only high enough to see the pipe. "We have an audience," I told Brooke.

"Always do," she said. "They all want to be just like the

Renegades. Well, until they realize what it costs."

"What's that?" King of all the wild things, indeed.

"Time, tears, broken bones, and broken hearts."

The next set began, and while the others were good—Landon the best, even—none of them held my attention like Paxton. Only Pax made me hold my breath with his tricks and made my pulse pound.

Then one of the CTDs lost his board mid-trick. His arms and legs flailed as gravity pulled him back to the ground. The cracking sound sickened my stomach.

Paxton and Landon ran to the ramp while the staff huddled around the rider. "Who is that?" I asked.

"Not sure," Brooke said. "But my guess would be that arm is broken."

A few minutes later, the guy stood, supporting the injured arm, and Paxton walked him off to a nearby waiting ambulance as the others went back to the pipe. "They're not going to stop?"

Brooke laughed. "None of them would ever have gotten this far if a broken arm stopped them. Hell, Penna had broken both her arms at least three times before our parents stopped trying to talk her out of this career choice." Her smile faded. "Nothing stops them, even when it should."

On his way back to the pipe, Paxton paused at the concrete barrier and leaned over. *He's seen the boys.*

All three of the boys stood, but instead of kicking them out, Pax signed their skateboards and took selfies. Warmth bloomed in my chest, tight and freeing all in the same breath.

I ignored it and concentrated on the tricks in front of us until it was time to call it quits, but damn if it didn't keep coming back every time I watched Paxton.

• • •

"You're kidding me, right? This is some kind of bad joke?" I asked as he handed me a harness on the beach of Barcelona later that afternoon.

"It's your choice," he assured me, his eyes as blue as the water behind him and just as distracting. *Maybe he could talk with his eyes closed.*

"If I say no?"

"Then we take a nice boat ride along the coast."

"If I say yes?"

"Then we parasail. That's where the boat pulls the towline and we float up under the parachute."

"I know what parasailing is," I snapped. My shoulders slumped. "I'm sorry. I just didn't think this was what you had in mind."

"Don't ever be sorry for telling me how you feel. I'd rather know than have you fake it. You asked me to help you get past the fear, right?"

"Sure, when I was drugged," I mumbled, looking at the sand between my toes. It had been a ridiculous thought that I could even try to conquer the terror, but I couldn't afford to pass out every time I was put in a risky situation. But seriously, how many times was I ever going to be put in that position?

Depends. Are you planning on hanging around Paxton much?

"Then let me help you."

"Maybe we could start with something a little lower first," I suggested.

"What did you have in mind?"

"Something where my feet stay on the ground?" I smiled.

"That's not going to help you. I promise this is safe, and there's already a parachute. And the minute you say you're done, we come down."

"We?" I blinked. "You're not sending me up there alone?"

His forehead puckered. "No. I was going to take you up tandem. I mean, if you want to go solo, I won't stand in your way."

"No!" I shouted. "I mean, if we're doing this, I'd rather have you with me. You seem like you're pretty handy in these situations."

"Then you're in?"

"If you're with me, then I'm in."

The crew strapped us in side-by-side, and I thanked God I'd worn leggings today. They slid easily through the harness. "So this is safe, right?"

"Absolutely," Paxton answered.

"Are you sure? I saw this show where the line snapped, and this father and son, well, stepson, went flying into the jungle and crashed into a tree and then the stepdad *died*." One of the techs stifled his laughter as he snapped my harness in place.

Paxton's eyes narrowed. "Wasn't that one of the Jurassic Park movies?"

"Yeah? So? It's still parasailing."

"Well, if I remember correctly, the line was snapped because a dinosaur bit it."

"So?"

He cupped my chin, and I about melted. "There are no dinosaurs in Barcelona. We'll be okay, Leah." His eyes dropped to my lips, and they automatically parted, more than ready for everything my head stubbornly refused.

What would happen if he kissed me? If we crossed the line—and he broke my already pieced-together heart? I didn't know if I'd be able to tutor him if I became just another one of his notches. But the closer he came, the louder my heart cried out that it was healed enough to try.

That was the thing about hearts, though—they jumped and then it was always up to the brain to put them back together, and Paxton had the power to shred me if I wasn't careful.

"Ready, Wilder?" Bobby asked, the cameras aimed in our direction. I hated that we hadn't been able to shake them, but there hadn't been a good enough reason to ditch them.

"Are you ready for an adventure, Leah?" Pax asked me softly, where the cameras couldn't hear.

"Don't let me get hurt."

All trace of kidding fell from his face. "I will never hurt you, and I won't let anything else, either. Understand?"

I nodded, wishing he'd answered the question I was too chicken to ask. We listened to the instructions from the boat crew, and thanks to my Paxton distraction, before I knew it, we launched into the air.

I closed my eyes as a shriek ripped from my throat, and I bit my lower lip to silence the sound. Paxton took my hand from the harness, lacing our fingers. There was nothing but wind beneath my feet, just air that would be only too happy to let me fall.

But Paxton…he wouldn't.

"You can close your eyes the whole time, but you'll never see this view again." His thumb stroked the palm of my hand.

I slowly opened my lids and gasped. "How high are we?" *High enough to feel surreal, which is oddly more comforting.*

"Don't think about it," he urged. "Look, you can see La Sagrada Familia."

"What?" My eyes darted to the cityscape and found the world-renowned church. "That's amazing!"

"I wonder if we could get extra credit in World Religion for this," he joked. "And there's the Park Guell." He pointed with his empty hand. "Where we were riding earlier today."

The city was beautiful from here, divided from the Mediterranean by a strip of beach. "This is...I don't have words," I said.

He squeezed my hands. "I know."

"Is this how you feel when you're doing a trick?" It was exhilarating, pure joy flooding my bloodstream, infusing every cell in my body with an incomparable high.

"Not usually."

I looked over at him. "Why?"

"Because tricks I have to work for, practice on. They take every ounce of my concentration, my body, my mind, all of me is in it."

"And this is just fun," I guessed.

"Usually."

That pressure was back in my chest. "But not this time."

He shook his head. "This time I used everything, my concentration, my body, my mind, all of me, to get you up here, and seeing you smile feels better than landing any trick."

Up here there was nothing to distract me from his words, his eyes, or the tenderness in either of them. "Thank you," I said.

"You're so welcome," he answered with a soft smile.

I kept my eyes on the city to the side of us, or the shoreline ahead of us, never looking down, never letting go of the wonder in my heart just in case the fear crept in and stole this moment from me.

It was over too quickly and not soon enough, my fear escalating the closer we came to the ground, until Paxton took the brunt of our landing on the soft beach.

You did it! I wanted to shout to the sky that I was victorious—that I'd won this one battle, and it was more than enough. It was a taste of what I'd been before that night, before I knew what it was to watch love die right in front of me. It was freedom, joy, exhilaration, and the ability to simply breathe. And it was all because of Paxton.

He unclipped our parachute and unsnapped our harnesses from the towline, his hands moving quickly with supreme focus. Focus, that for once, I needed on me. My stomach tightened, my heart jumping like it did right before I zip-lined, already knowing that it might be the wrong choice, but I'd made my decision.

"How are you feeling?" he asked when he saw that I stood there, simply watching him.

I didn't have words, only this overwhelming need buzzing through me, demanding to take another, more dangerous leap. Paxton had given me something priceless, and I didn't know how to communicate everything that meant to me, what he was starting to mean to me, but I knew I had to.

I'd never wanted something—someone—so badly in my life.

Damn the consequences.

"Leah?" he asked, leaning down slightly to cup my cheeks in his hands, then swiping his tongue across his lower lip—his nervous tell.

My fingers found the warm skin of his biceps, and before I could find the words I wanted to say, I surged on my toes, pressing my mouth to his and kissing him. Our lips clung, the simple pressure lasting far longer than I meant it to.

I hadn't meant for it to happen at all. Not really.

Oh God. I kissed Paxton. I'm kissing Paxton.

But then I realized he wasn't kissing me back.

I broke the contact, that pressure in my chest turning nearly sour, my heart pounding not in exhilaration but embarrassment.

"Leah," he leaned down and whispered against my lips, the sound equal parts discovery and plea. Then he kissed me. His mouth moved gently over mine, his hands cradling my face as if I was something precious and rare, each new caress stripping away another hardened layer of my soul. He didn't press deeper, even though I was ready to beg him to, just gave me that soft kiss that lingered, made me burn for more.

His tongue caressed my lower lip, and I leaned in to him. It was perfect. *He* was perfect.

Then he suddenly stopped, stepping back like I'd burned him, his chest heaving.

"Paxton?" I asked, my voice shaking from everything I'd risked, everything I'd ridiculously thought I could have.

He met my eyes, and the desire I saw there soothed the raw edges of my nerves. He licked his lips, not in nervousness this time, but as if he could still taste me, and I seriously debated attacking him a second time.

With the simple touch of his lips, he'd awoken something in me I'd thought long dead, and I wanted more.

He shook his head, as if he knew what I was thinking, and that's when I heard them running toward us, their footsteps heavy in the sand.

"We got some amazing shots!" Bobby said, his breath even where his cameraman was damn near hyperventilating.

"Good," Paxton said, his voice rough but his touch light as he unbuckled the snaps on my harness so I could step out. How could he function perfectly when I could barely breathe?

"How was your ride?" Bobby asked me, but putting two words together proved impossible.

"Enlightening," Paxton answered, sparing me.

"What do you think, Leah? You going to do it again?"

I locked eyes with Paxton, and he raised an eyebrow, both of us sensing a second meaning to that question. "I'm not sure."

A corner of his mouth tilted up into an incredibly sexy smirk. "Yeah, you are. I'm sure enough for the both of us."

Before I could respond, Paxton looked over my shoulder and swore under his breath.

"What?" I asked, turning to see what upset him.

Standing about fifteen feet away in a well-tailored suit was a man who might have been a clean-cut version of Paxton if he'd had any spark of life in his judgmental eyes. I felt like I was standing there naked or something else equally exposing.

"Paxton. If I could maybe have some of your time?" the man asked, his voice the same deep timbre of Pax's.

"Who is that?" I asked quietly.

"The angel of death," he responded as the man walked toward us.

"Very funny," the man replied, his eyes traveling the length of Paxton's body before he rolled his eyes. "For fuck's sake, Paxton, you're in Barcelona, one of the foremost centers for culture and architecture, and you'd still rather concentrate on stupid antics and getting laid than go to a museum."

I stepped back, stopping when I came into contact with Paxton's chest.

"Leah, meet my brother, Brandon. Brandon, this is Leah. Do you want to tell me why the hell you flew halfway around the world?"

"Sure," Brandon answered, his smirk nearly identical to Paxton's but for the edge of malice. "I'm here to shut you down."

CHAPTER NINE

PAXTON

BARCELONA

"You have zero authority to shut me down," I growled at my asshole brother as he put ice cubes into one of the glasses on my bar.

We'd successfully completed three of the stunts, and we hadn't had a repeat of the zip-line incident. There were zero grounds for him to pull this shit. Hell, I was even beginning to relax.

"So this is what four hundred million dollars will buy you," he drawled. "You don't even have a decent bottle of liquor."

"Settle for a Corona," I said, pulling one out of the mini-fridge and handing it to him without opening it. He could slice his hand open for all I cared. "Now tell me what the fuck you're really doing here."

"Besides attempting to talk you out of your lunacy?" he asked, sitting in the largest armchair like it was his living room...his ship.

"Make your point or get the hell out of my room, Brandon. If you're interested in seeing the Mediterranean, you can do it from one of Dad's yachts. There's one parked in St. Tropez, or I don't know, maybe visit Mom."

His eyes hardened. "Unlike you, I work for a living. I'm not off gallivanting, chasing a naive dream like I'm five years old on the dirt pile."

I smirked, letting his comments roll off as always. "Funny, seems like that's exactly what you're doing."

"If you answered emails I wouldn't have to fly around the world to track you down."

"Bullshit, you'd fly across the world if you had the craving for gelato."

He tapped his fingers rhythmically on the glass, the perfect picture of control. "What you're doing is ludicrous. I'm not going to approve funding this."

"Well, let me know when you're in charge of Wilder Enterprises, and then we can have this conversation again. Until then, I have a contract with Dad."

His eyes widened.

"You didn't know?" A childish thrill of victory brought a smirk to my face. "I assumed that was how you discovered what we were up to."

"Your asinine zip-line got posted to YouTube. Once I saw that, all I had to do was inquire as to Bobby's whereabouts to find you."

"How many hits do we have?" I asked. *Please be over a million.* We needed the boost to market the film.

He shook his head. "That's all you've ever cared about. Your stupid fucking tricks, and medals, and video games, and the Renegades."

"Sorry you don't have your own video game yet. I'll let you know when they come up with Corporate Asshole Three, okay?

I know a couple guys who will slip you in."

"Grow the fuck up. Dad indulged you with every stupid thing you thought would be fun, and he looked the other way with the tattoos, the piercings, the women, even dropping out last year—"

"Hey, it was only one piercing, and I took it out."

"But now you're blowing how much money on this project? Risking how many lives? For Christ's sake, Dad had to buy the *ship*. You couldn't finish college like a man, you had to make a movie out of it?"

My fingers dug into the upholstery on the chair, wishing just once I could beat the shit out of my straightlaced, clean-cut, Wharton-Business-graduating older brother. But I loved the asshole, so I kept my shit in check. "Why are you really here, Brandon?"

He leaned back. "Dad is passing the company to me."

"Bullshit. There's no way he's stepping down. He's given up way too much for that company to walk away." *Things like his marriage.*

"The signs are there. He's shifting assets, buying property."

I rolled my eyes at him. "You came all the way over here to tell me that there are signs he's passing the company to you?"

"No, I came because I was already in London," he said with a slow smile. "And you may be a jackass, but I miss you."

"You're not going to fight to shut me down?"

He shook his head. "Not if you have a contract with Dad. That's beyond even my control. Want to share the terms?"

"A little annoyed that you don't already know them?" I guessed.

"Yes." He sighed and loosened his tie, then ran his fingers over his hair, jacking up the professional gel job. Now he looked more like my brother and less the corporate stooge he'd turned into these last few years.

"The boat, getting UCLA to sponsor the Study at Sea program…we had different goals."

"Dad's is to get you through college."

I flinched. "Yeah, I know, and I used that against him to get what I wanted. I'm not proud, but it was the only way I could get the movie made. So we both gave what we didn't want to get what we needed."

"So you *have* learned the art of business," Brandon said with a salute of his glass. "Why is this movie so important to you? It's not like you're hurting for money or fame."

"Nick is. And it's not about the fame or the money. It's about the team, and Nick still being crucial to it."

Brandon's breath left in a hiss, and he took a long pull of the beer. "That's not your fault. It wasn't your fault when it happened, and it's not your fault now."

"Fault and responsibility are two different things."

He stared at me the same way Dad did when he was making an assessment. "Okay. And your grades?"

"If I fail my classes, he pulls the plug."

"Harsh."

"It's harsher for my tutor. If I fail my classes, her scholarship is yanked."

"Now there's responsibility for you. Anyone I know?"

I hesitated. Leah was mine. Not in the possessive sense, but in simply knowing about her. What we had—whatever it was— was ours. The minute I told him who she was, Brandon had something to use against me.

Trust him.

"The girl on the beach," I answered. "Leah."

I had to applaud his poker face; he didn't even blink. "The one I saw you kissing? Do you think it's smart to fu—"

"Watch it," I warned softly. *Damn it, that's why you should have kept your lips to yourself.* But she'd kissed me, all soft and happy, and that first touch was enough to break me. I'd almost succeeded in keeping that wall between us, but she'd tasted so damn good.

His head tilted slightly. "Okay. Well, is she qualified? I mean to tutor you, not the other stuff."

"Very. She goes to Dartmouth, and she's brilliant, stubborn, and driven." *And mine.* Damn, that was the second time my brain had gone all primal about Leah in the last five minutes. When had that instinct kicked in?

When you decided to say fuck the consequences and kiss her back. Or maybe when you protected her from the cameras, or when she first agreed to the zip-line.

The only thing I knew for certain was that it didn't matter when—it only mattered how I was going to convince her to take a chance on us. *Us.* Yeah, I'd just thought that. *Us.* I thought it again to try it on for size.

Shit, I was ignoring Brandon.

"—back in Los Angeles until you graduate."

The door to the suite clicked open, saving me. "Pax?"

"In here," I called out.

Penna walked in, her gaze darting between Brandon and me. "Oh, hey, Brandon. I didn't realize you were in Barcelona."

"I was just leaving," he said, redoing his tie and standing. "Good to see you, Penelope. Pax, try to stay out of jail, okay? Not all the shit you guys like to pull is legal."

We said our good-byes and he walked out, my blood pressure immediately dropping with the sound of the door closing behind him.

"Why the hell is he here?" she asked.

I loved Brandon, but he didn't do anything that didn't suit his immediate needs. "I don't know, but it can't be good. Knowing him, he honestly flew over here to find out what kind of deal I struck with Dad and how to manipulate it."

"Agreed. Just don't give him anything he can use against you."

And now he knew about Leah.

Fuck.

"I'll expect your papers filed in eCampus no later than midnight on Friday," our World Religion professor said into the bus microphone as we parked at the cruise terminal the next day. We'd seen enough churches that they'd all started to blend in by the afternoon. All except La Sagrada Familia, which might have been the coolest church I'd ever seen in my life.

"Ready?" I asked Leah as I stood in the aisle. She clutched her bag with both hands.

"Yes," she said, scooting out from the seat.

"One word again? You're so talkative today. Everything okay?" I asked, ready to poke her in the side to get her to talk to me.

"Yep," she answered with a fake smile, standing in front of me.

I didn't know whether to shake her or kiss the shit out of her. My entire body screamed for the second option, especially after spending all day next to her, watching her smile at architecture when I wanted her to smile at me, catching the scent of her perfume and the orange shampoo she used, listening to her laugh at something Hugo said.

I may as well have not existed.

We filed off the bus and headed for the ship. "Hey, Leah, we're over here," I said, pointing to the quicker entrance. She looked up at me, those eyes so full of conflict that I couldn't get a read on her emotions.

Welcome to the club, Leah.

"You know, Hugo and I were going to grab dinner, so I think I'll just go in the normal way," she said, her lips pressing together in a flat line.

Fucking ouch.

"Okay, well, then you two kids have fun," I said, forcing a smile that probably looked more like a gremlin. "Study tonight?"

She wavered. Hell if I was going to let her cancel our plans because she was freaked over what had happened yesterday. "We have that Lit assignment for *Epic of Gilgamesh*, remember?"

Her eyes closed briefly. "Of course I remember. Yeah, that's great. Tonight."

She turned and walked away, and not that I didn't enjoy the view of her ass in those jeans, but for once I'd love to see her walking toward me.

"I liked it better when she was kissing me," I mumbled.

"Tell me you didn't," Landon said.

I swore under my breath and turned, ignoring his disapproving look. "I did."

He looked up like he was praying for patience. "Worth the potential of fucking up everything that we've worked for?"

"Every second." My answer was instant.

"And you're going to let her walk away?" he asked.

When did he switch to Team Leah?

"I don't have much of a choice."

He started laughing, and I had the urge to toss him into the water instead of walking up the ramp with him.

"What the fuck is so funny?"

"You, my friend. You."

We gave our IDs to security for scanning, and then headed on board. "And how the hell am I amusing?"

He turned, clapping me on the shoulder. "You've never had to work for a woman that you wanted. They've been falling into your lap since you were fifteen."

"That's not true!"

"Name one girl you had to work for. And by work for, I mean, say more than, "I'm Paxton Wilder and I have a big pipe.""

"Hey, that was one time, and it was to another skateboarder. She totally got the meaning."

"Pax."

I tried to run through my mental Rolodex of women and found that I couldn't think of any, or remember most of their names. "Okay, point taken."

"You have two choices. You back away now, ignore whatever happened, and preserve your working relationship—"

"Not an option." Not when I could still feel her lips moving with mine, hear the tiny rush of air she released when we parted. My hands still itched to feel her skin under my fingertips, my head wouldn't stop running through things to say, and my dick wouldn't stop making his opinion known, either.

"Well, time to work, brother." He gave me a somewhat sympathetic half smile, laced with a flash of pain that sliced through me because I knew I'd helped put it there.

"I don't know what to do. She's not like the others."

"The good ones never are, and they don't usually give second chances, either, so don't fuck it up if you're serious."

He was right, and he knew from experience. I only had one shot at this, and the fate of our working relationship, my grades, the documentary, and whatever was happening with Leah and me was hanging on my ability to not screw it up, because I was incapable of staying away from her.

No pressure, or anything.

Holy shit, I hadn't been this nervous to lose my virginity. I knocked four times on her glass door and slid it open when she waved me in.

"Sorry, I wanted to be comfortable," she said dismissively from the bar, putting lemon into a glass of ice water and shrugging.

Translated: I didn't dress up for you. I don't care about impressing you.

No, she'd dressed down, and the result had my mouth watering. Her pajama pants were plaid, loose, and looked soft to the touch as they hung off her hips, showing a strip of smooth skin before her ribbed tank top started, hugging every lush line of her body to the bare skin of her shoulders. Her hair was up in a messy knot on the top of her head, the loose pieces ghosting the arch of her neck.

Instead of dressing up to look beautiful, she'd accidentally made herself fuckable.

It would be so easy to come up behind her, slip my fingers into the elastic of those pants, and slide them down to finally see that ass I couldn't get out of my dreams. I'd spin her back to the bar, lift her to the counter, and settle myself between her soft thighs while I devoured her.

"Paxton?" she asked, interrupting my fantasy. "Did you want to sit down?"

"Absolutely," I said, turning abruptly so she didn't see my raging hard-on. *Get yourself under control. What are you, fifteen?*

Once we were settled, me in the armchair and Leah on the couch, she started. "Okay, so we're dealing with the themes of love here, of how it changes you."

"I'll take your word for it," I said, thumbing through my notes.

"You don't think love changes you?" she asked.

"I wouldn't know, I've never been in love," I answered.

"Oh," she said, blinking quickly. "Well, in my limited experience, it has the ability to change you, break you, for good or for worse, depending on the person you foolishly fall for."

Warning bells went off in my head as we locked eyes. "You think all love is foolish?"

She blushed. "No, but maybe my choices have been in the past...or currently, I guess. But back to Gilgamesh—"

I ignored her subtle dig and went for the crack in her armor. "What about those choices is foolish?"

"We're not talking about me." She flipped open her laptop.

"I am."

"Well, I need you to concentrate on Gilgamesh and his transformation from a tyrant." She bit a pencil between her teeth.

"Sure, after you tell me what was foolish," I dared.

The pencil fell to her lap. "Seriously? This isn't tit for tat. I don't need to study; I already know the thematic arcs in the book."

Oh good, that wall she loved to hide behind was back up. *Too late, Leah, I already know what's behind it.*

I put my books on the coffee table and leaned forward, resting my forearms on my knees. "Doesn't matter what you know. Both of our trips depend on what *I* know."

"You'd screw yourself to get in my head?" She crossed her arms under her breasts, pushing the creamy globes higher above the neckline of her tank top.

"I'd use every weapon in my arsenal to get in your head." Landon was right. I was going to have to work for Leah like I did every single stunt, with a plan and a ton of balls. Half-assed got you hurt. It was all-in or watch from the sidelines.

I was all-in.

"Or maybe just my pants," she said quietly.

My eyebrows shot to the ceiling. "Is that what you think this is? Me just trying to fuck you?"

"I—I don't know." If her blush deepened any more she'd match the throw pillows.

I swallowed the ball of rage that tried to climb up my throat. I had a shit reputation when it came to women, and that was all she'd seen when she'd researched me. *But she should know better.* I hadn't touched another girl since we boarded. Since I met her. "If all I wanted was to get laid, I could walk downstairs to the lounge and bring at least one—if not two—girls back up with me. Problem solved."

"And that's supposed to make me think what?" she shot at me.

"That you're not one of those girls!"

"Exactly!" She slammed her laptop closed, tossed her books on the floor, and stood up. "I'm not like that, and if that's what you're looking for, then you have the wrong woman."

I stood, careful to keep the table between us since I was back to my urges from this afternoon, wanting to shake or kiss some sense into her. "Leah, you kissed *me*. Right? I didn't put a move on you, didn't push you for more, didn't strip you naked on that beach."

"Exactly," she muttered.

"What? For being the smartest person I know, you're making zero sense."

She rubbed her hands over her face, and I wanted to pull her hands away, to see those gorgeous, expressive eyes that never managed to hide whatever she was feeling no matter how hard she tried. "I'm sorry," she said.

"For what?" I asked. This girl had me spinning circles and dodging landmines.

"For doing this to us," she answered, her eyes wide and scared. "For ruining something that was so easy and so good by kissing you."

"You're sorry for kissing me?"

She tugged her lip between her teeth and nodded quickly. "I didn't give you a choice, or a chance to think about what it could change between us."

"It was a kiss, not a contract," I said, trying to get a hint of where she was coming from. "Why do you think it changes things?"

"Because I took advantage of you," she whispered.

Bullshit. I walked around the coffee table until we stood inches apart. "No. That's not what happened on that beach."

"It is. What were you supposed to do? When you didn't kiss me back at first... God, I was mortified, and then when you did..." She sighed, looking anywhere but at me. "I'm your tutor, and I put you in a shitty position."

"Did you ever stop to think that maybe I liked my position? That maybe I wanted to kiss you just as badly?"

She shook her head.

I tipped her chin so she'd meet my eyes. "There were cameras coming at us, and then my brother showed up. Trust me, if that moment had happened here, the outcome wouldn't have left you wondering if I wanted to kiss you."

"It was only a moment," she whispered. "We can take it back."

Not fucking happening. "Why would you want to?"

"Maybe we need to think about what we're risking."

I ordered my nerves to settle. She was skittish—one wrong move and I'd be back to square one, and now that I knew where I wanted to be...well, square one wasn't it. "There's no pressure. I'm not in a rush. If you need to think, that's okay with me, but I already know what I want."

"I need a minute," she whispered, the plea desperate.

It went against every instinct I had, but I could do this.

"Okay," I said, and backed away from her slowly. "This assignment isn't due for a couple of days. Let's pick this up tomorrow?"

"Paxton, I'm sorry," she said, a slight note of panic slipping in.

I gave her my best smile. "I'm not. Not about any of it."

Then I did something I'd never done—conceded the battle and walked away.

But the war would be worth it.

CHAPTER TEN

LEAH

"Oh God, Rachel, I kissed him. I don't know what I was thinking, but I kissed him!" I didn't even say hello, just word vomited from another continent on my best friend.

"Leah?" Rachel's voice came through the phone, and for a second, it felt like I was home, safe. "You kissed who? The hot guy you're tutoring?"

"Yeah." I sighed. "But we were on a beach, and we'd just gone parasailing, and he's so beautiful and has this edge that makes me feel alive."

"Back up. You went parasailing? Is this Eleanor Baxter?"

"Right? He makes me do ridiculous things!"

"Well, I'm all for he-who-cannot-be-named," she cheered.

"I'm so sorry that I can't tell you his name." Damn NDA. All I wanted to do was spew my guts to my best friend, and I was legally bound to keep it all to myself.

"It's okay. Makes it more of a mystery for when I get there."

I laid my head on the back of the couch. "I can't wait. Seriously. These people, the things they do—the things I do around them..." I trailed off, unable to explain what it was about Paxton that had me zip-lining, and parasailing, and kissing him on the beach. There were no words for the effect he had on me, the way my skin flushed the minute he walked into the room, every nerve waking up and coming to life.

"It's not drugs, is it? Oh God. Leah, you're not getting mixed up with that, are you?" Her worry was palpable from 3,600 miles away.

"What? No. Nothing like that."

"Okay, well, then I say enjoy yourself. Kiss the guy!"

"But I'm his tutor! And I've only known him for a little over two weeks!"

She full-out laughed, and I rolled my eyes while I waited for her to stop.

"It took Romeo and Juliet one night," she argued.

"Yeah, and look how that turned out."

She sighed. "What made you go on this trip?"

"You, duh," I scoffed.

"Yeah, I know we applied together, and I know that I was a huge factor in the choice when the acceptance came in—when the scholarship was offered—but what made you go when I couldn't make it?"

"Besides the experience for grad school? I wanted to live." Not just fake it like I had been since that night. Not in the routine monotony I'd used as my safety net, but to breathe free where my chest didn't hurt when I took in too much air—too much light. The grief, the healing, the fear...it had ruled me for so long, and I was desperate for a change. Instead I got a complete revolution.

"Then live. Kiss the guy. Or kiss a different guy if you want. Go on a trip. Sleep in, or get up early and watch the sun rise.

Stop thinking about what you *should* be doing and for once in your damned life do what you *want* to do."

"When did you get so smart?" I asked, my eyes prickling.

"I'm not. I just know a thing or two about liking reckless boys. A lot of reckless boys."

"I wish you were here," I said, repeating myself because I couldn't help it.

"Yeah, me too, but maybe this is good for you. I've let you hide for two years too long, missy."

I rubbed my forehead. "I didn't think about Brian. When I was kissing...him, I didn't think about Brian. Is that good? Does it make me awful?"

She paused, and I knew she was thinking of what to say. Rachel was impulsive with everyone in her life except me, but that was because we'd had to put each other back together before. "That's good. You deserve great things, new things, untainted feelings. Don't feel guilty."

Impossible.

A knock sounded at my door. "Hey, Rachel, I'll call you at the next port, okay? There's someone at the door. Oh God, what if it's him? He never said what he wanted, just that he knew. What if he's ditching me as his tutor?"

"Kiss the guy, Leah!" she shouted, smacking me a kiss through the phone line and disconnecting.

My stomach hung suspended as I opened the door. "Well, you're not the Wilder I was expecting," I said to Paxton's brother. "Brandon, right?"

He nodded, his cursory sweep of my pajamas making me wish I'd put on a robe or something. "And you're Paxton's tutor. Mind if I come in?"

"My mother taught me never to invite strange men into my

room after eleven p.m., Mr. Wilder."

His eyebrows rose. "Fair enough." He glanced down the hall toward Paxton's room before handing me a card. "This is for when he fucks up."

"I'm sorry?" I backed away from the card.

"Take it," he urged. "Paxton fucks up. It's what he does. He's going to break a bone, break a law, or break you. When he needs to be bailed out, call me. I've been cleaning up after him his entire life."

If I'd had hackles, they would have raised. "He might surprise you," I said softly.

"He already did. You're not the type of girl he usually pursues."

Oh yeah, hackles up, and now my teeth were ready to bare. "And why is that?"

"Because you're smart. Let's hope that you're smart enough not to get involved with my little brother. Only the strong survive in his little troop of lost boys. The weak ones leave mangled." He shook the card at me. "Take it."

"No." I stepped back, ready to slam the door in his face, but he thrust his other arm out, holding the door open.

"Miss Baxter, one day something will happen that you won't know how to handle. Maybe he'll end up in jail, maybe his parachute won't open, maybe someone will have gotten sick of his shit and pushed him before he was ready to jump. One day you will need this. Please take it. I don't have anyone else with eyes on him."

It was the plea in his eyes—so similar to Paxton's—that made me finally reach for the card. "I won't call you. He has an entire team of producers and a group of friends here with him."

"Yes, you will," he promised. "Because I'm telling you right now that there are few people who are loyal to Paxton. They're there as long as the getting is good, but when the shit hits the fan, they'll scatter in the fallout. And he may be a selfish, arrogant little shit, but there's nothing I wouldn't do for him. That's why you'll call me. Understand?"

I nodded slowly. "What will it cost him if I do?"

An ironic smile lifted the corner of his mouth. "That's between us brothers. Always has been."

"I'd like you to leave now," I said, unable to mince words.

"I like you," he said with a nod. "It's a shame he's not a one-girl kind of guy, because you'd be good for him."

"Good-bye, Brandon," I said, shutting the door as soon as he removed his hand.

The card was black with his name and phone number engraved with his title of Vice President of Operations at Wilder Enterprises. It felt heavy in my hand, but then again, it wasn't just a piece of paper. It was a promise, a reassurance, a warning, and a threat all in one.

Maybe Paxton was a daredevil because he'd grown up swimming with sharks.

I tucked the card into my bedside table and debated sleeping, but I wasn't tired enough. The suite felt empty without Penna, so I walked onto the back balcony. The railing was smooth under my hands as I looked out over the lights of Barcelona, careful not to look down.

Two weeks. I'd only been gone two weeks, and yet it felt like months—as if I was already changing. Even Hugo had noticed that I was stepping outside my shell when we met up for dinner with some of his friends. It had been nice, getting out with someone who wasn't a part of the Renegades, who saw life outside Paxton's vortex of chaos.

I knew why everyone got sucked in.

He was magnetic, hypnotizing. It wasn't just the body, the face, or the tattoos. He made me feel anything was possible, like there was a whole shiny world waiting for me to step inside and explore.

He was everything I wasn't, but he made me feel like I could be.

He was...standing on his balcony, too, staring up at the stars as if they held some kind of answer he was searching for. The same weight I saw him carrying that first day was back on his shoulders, and damn if that didn't draw me to him even more, because now I knew some of the burdens he bore. The documentary, his grades, his Renegades...what more could he possibly hold together?

As if he could read my thoughts, he turned and saw me. The tension between us was palpable, holding us together from dozens of feet away.

But he crossed the distance, and the tension didn't dissipate, just grew until I thought my chest might burst.

"Leah." He said my name like a prayer, a plea for something I didn't know if I was capable of giving. And, after that exchange with his brother, I wasn't sure I was even worthy of the tone, not when I'd accepted the card.

"Hey," I answered, turning my back to the railing as he stood in front of me. "Look, I just had—"

"Wait," he interrupted. "Can I go first? You got to talk last time."

I nodded.

He stepped forward and caged me in his arms with one hand on either side of my body. "I told you that I know what I want, and that I'd let you think. But it's not fair for you to make choices without knowing all the facts."

"Okay," I answered, my voice barely a whisper. God, did he have to smell so good? All saltwater and sand, and sandalwood and Paxton. *They should bottle it and sell it.* Scratch that. The female population would have been way too disadvantaged.

His eyes locked on mine, the moon reflecting in the blue depths, the intensity there as fierce as on the half-pipe, or when I'd seen him above me after I fell. "You said you took advantage of me, that you forced me into kissing you back because you're my tutor, like that puts you in a position of power."

"Maybe," I answered, my cheeks heating.

"Well, I'm here on my own feet, chasing you, pursuing *you*. Not vice versa. I don't know what's happening between us, but I'm also not stupid enough to dismiss it without exploration." One of his hands palmed my cheek, both soothing and electrifying me in one motion. "If we'd been alone on that beach when you kissed me, I wouldn't have held back, wouldn't have had to think about what you wouldn't want in the public eye."

He dragged his thumb across my lower lip, and I kissed it lightly, unable to stop myself.

He sucked in a breath. "I would have kissed you exactly as I've been fantasizing about since the first second I saw you standing on this balcony, all wide-eyed and beautiful."

"Paxton," I whispered, leaning in to him. His words melted me, made me want things like his mouth, his hands—things I couldn't have, like his heart.

"I would have kissed you like this." His mouth took mine, open and hungry, his tongue—sweet mercy, his *tongue*—slipping past my lips to stroke, explore, and savor, igniting a fire within me. I pressed at the same time he pulled, bringing our bodies flush against each other, and the fit was electrifying.

He tasted better than I imagined, all dark chocolate and mint.

His empty hand tunneled through my hair to the back of my head while mine wound around his neck, desperate to get closer, to take this one chance I had to not only taste but experience him. Over and over, he brought our mouths together, one moment gently sucking on my lower lip and the next sliding his tongue along mine. He'd caress my mouth gently, then plunge in possession, a blatant ownership that made my thighs clench, my stomach burn.

The man kissed like he rode—with a single-minded focus that made everything else in the world pale in comparison— and I could only go along for the ride.

He made me feel consumed yet empty, desperate yet sated all in one moment. Screw the sports documentary, he should make one on how to properly kiss a woman and save millions of clueless men.

My fingers dug into the muscles of his shoulders as his hands moved to my ass, squeezing and lifting me against his impossibly hard stomach with a groan. "Fuck, Leah. You have the most incredible ass," he groaned against my mouth, sending bolts of pure, dizzying lust spiraling through me. "All soft curves and perfect in my hands."

I whimpered when our mouths met again, the kiss taking on an edge that had me arching against him, exploring the ridges of his teeth with my tongue before he sucked it in. In that moment I was Paxton's, and it was glorious.

He broke the kiss, leaning his forehead against mine as his breath came in hot blasts against my swollen lips. My breathing was just as ragged. He lowered me to the ground, my belly grazing his erection. He hissed and put a few precious inches between our bodies.

Paxton Wilder wanted me.

That fact was just as consuming as his kiss. *Imagine sleeping with him.* Or don't. No. Not yet.

His hands were gentle on my face as he kissed me sweetly. "That's how I wanted to kiss you, Firecracker. That's how I plan on kissing you from now on if you tell me yes. I want this. I want you—us."

Say yes! Yes! Yes! My sex-starved body screamed at me, demanding I acknowledge that basic need I'd slammed in a box and shoved under my bed two years ago.

But starting a relationship meant letting him see…everything, exposing myself in a way I wasn't sure I was ready for.

"I need…" Time? To think? To jump him and test the thickness of the walls in my bedroom?

"Okay." He answered the demand I hadn't made. "I can give you that. I just wanted to make sure *that* was the kiss keeping you company in that head of yours. I'll see you tomorrow."

He kissed me one last time and left me standing on the balcony, wondering what price I would pay for stealing whatever time I could with him. I knew he was a shooting star—too hot, too intense, too reckless for me.

He'd burn me alive, then consume the ashes—the kiss had shown me that.

But it didn't stop me from wanting him.

And that was the scariest part of being around him. Not what he did to me, or how he made me feel, but the way I abandoned all sense of the caution that had kept me functioning these last couple of years.

He made me think there was a possibility I could live again outside the carefully constructed walls I'd built.

I just wasn't sure I could survive when he inevitably left.

CHAPTER ELEVEN

LEAH

ROME

The cameras flashed in every direction, Paxton's name called out like a rock star over the crowd. He tucked me under his arm and guided me through the crush with Landon and Penna in the lead. We had another twenty feet before we made it into the motocross park.

"Damn it," he seethed, but when I glanced at his face, he wore his Wilder grin, complete with putting his fist into the air.

"Wilder!" one reporter called out.

"He's not taking questions," Little John answered behind us.

"What are you doing in Rome? Is it true you're taking this year off? Is this in preparation for the live event you have scheduled in Abu Dhabi?" The questions fired from both aisles, conflicting with what they thought they knew.

Live event in Abu Dhabi? What?

If it wasn't the questions assaulting us, it was screaming fans.

"I thought this was supposed to be secret?" I asked.

"Me, too," he said, pressing a kiss into my hair.

"Who's your new girl?" another reporter asked.

Not his girl, my head protested.

Ahead of us, one of the male fans reached out and grabbed Penna. "Pax." I motioned toward them, but before I even finished saying his name, Penna had the guy's arm twisted behind his back.

"Didn't your mama ever teach you that it's not nice to touch a woman without her permission?" she said.

Holy shit.

Paxton grabbed the guy and shoved him toward Little John. "Get this fucker out of here before I start an international incident."

We made it to the steps, where the double doors had been thrown open. Little John and the security team kept the fans off the steps, and I sucked in my first full breath since getting out of the car.

"You okay?" Paxton asked, putting himself between me and the crowd and pressing his lips against my forehead.

"Yeah. I guess I didn't realize you were quite this popular."

"Depends on where we are," he answered. "Wait here, okay?"

I nodded, and he turned around to stand between Penna and Landon.

"Nice to meet you, Rome!" Paxton called out. I knew without looking that he was wearing that devil-may-care grin.

The crowd exploded.

"I think we have time for a couple questions, but not much more than that. You guys have a beautiful city, and we're anxious to get out and explore it."

Bobby stepped forward and pointed to one reporter. "Go."

"What are you doing here in Rome?"

"Broadening our horizons," Paxton said. "Plus Rebel here was craving pizza."

The reporters laughed when Penna nodded. "And we heard you guys had a sick super ramp, so we figured we'd stop by and give it a go."

Bobby pointed to another reporter.

"Any truth to this rumor of a live show in Abu Dhabi?"

"Maybe," Paxton answered.

"Will you be competing at the Winter X Games?"

Paxton tensed. "That isn't on our schedule at the moment."

"Does this mean the Renegades won't be contenders? Are you walking away? Have you given up on the quest for the triple front?" The questions fired rapidly.

"One more." Bobby pointed to another reporter on the side.

"Does this have anything to do with the rumors circulating around Nitro? We can't help but notice you've been one member short for a while now."

"We're fucking done here," Paxton said, spinning on his heel and walking inside, pulling me in his wake, his fingers in gentle contrast to his voice.

"The Renegades are more than just the Originals. And you can be assured that Nitro is as much a Renegade now as he was when we started this journey. Thanks for coming out, folks!" Landon's voice carried through into the hallway.

"Ah! Mr. Wilder! We're so happy to have you visiting our little track! I'm Renzo, and I manage things here," a middle-aged man said with a thick Italian accent.

"Who the fuck let the itinerary slip?" Penna asked, crossing her arms over her bright pink tank top.

"I'll find out," Bobby promised. "For now can we get our

team set up, please? Little John already has your bikes ready."

"I can assure you that our staff kept this as quiet as possible, and of course we can lead you to your setup." Renzo nodded, and three men stepped forward from behind him.

"Can you take me to the stands first? I need to get Miss Baxter comfortable," Paxton said.

"I can find it," I protested.

"I'm sure you could, Firecracker, but I'd like to know where you are."

Bobby's mouth opened, and Landon stepped in. "Our schedule's not that tight. I'm sure we're good, right, Bobby?"

"Right," Bobby answered, his mouth tense.

"Pick a good place, Leah. Brooke's on her way," Penna said with a smile. Then they headed off with a few of the track workers.

Renzo led us past the snack bar and up a set of stairs until we emerged on the bleachers. "What is that?" I asked Paxton as I pointed to a giant wooden…monstrosity.

"It's a super ramp. We're filming some shots here, and let's face it, we need the practice if we're going to pull off a live show in Abu Dhabi. It's not like we have one of these on board." He winked. "Relax, Firecracker, I'll take you all the places you want to see tomorrow. I'll even keep my sarcastic comments to myself while we listen to our prof on the Vatican tour."

I shook my head and pointed to the giant deathtrap in front of me. "Um…is that *safe*?"

Renzo quietly excused himself.

Paxton took my hands and lifted one to his mouth, pressing a kiss into my palm. "Nothing I do is really *safe*. That's why it's extraordinary."

You knew what he did. "Okay, well, I'll pick a spot in the shade up there and study some physics. I got my ass handed to me on that quiz yesterday."

"I'd hardly call a B getting your ass handed to you."

"Well, that's where we differ, Mr. Wilder. Besides, you never told me what you got. Do I need to be worried?"

He shook his head. "No, I'm pretty well versed in all the matters of physics…and physical matters, for what that's worth."

Heat rushed my cheeks, and it wasn't the sun. It had been three days since Barcelona, since he'd asked me to make a choice, and I still hadn't.

"Okay, well…go do whatever it is you do," I said, waving him off toward the ramp of death.

"Do I get a good-luck kiss?" he asked after checking for cameras, his hands framing my waist.

"Paxton." I tried to make it sound like a warning, but it came out too breathy, too wanting. For crying out loud, I couldn't even control my own voice against this guy.

He squeezed lightly and then groaned. "Did I ever tell you that I love this dress?"

I shook my head. The spaghetti-strap maxi dress had been a last-minute choice, but Penna said she was going to burn all my pants if she saw me in them for the twenty-first day in a row.

He leaned down, his mouth against the shell of my ear. "I can feel every curve under my hands, which makes me pretty damn desperate to slide this up your legs and really get my hands on you. But I won't. You know why?"

I shook my head.

"Because you haven't said yes—yet—and I'm a goddamned gentleman."

My fingers traced the lines of the tattoos that ran up his neck, simply unable not to touch him. "Do I have to say yes to everything to get to kiss you?" I asked.

His breath stuttered. "Do you want to say yes?"

Our eyes met, and it would have been so easy to say it, to throw my hesitation overboard and jump. But that wasn't me, and it didn't matter that I was in a breezy dress under the Italian sun with the hottest extreme athlete on the planet, I was still... me. "I'm thinking about it."

His forehead puckered for a millisecond before he relaxed and smoothed the line of my waist. "Then I think we can take yeses on a case-by-case basis."

My heart pounded in anticipation.

"Leah, would you like me to kiss you?"

"Yes," I answered instantly.

Our hips met first as he drew me in. My hands slipped down the edges of his T-shirt to grasp the inked lines of his biceps. *Arms like his should be modeled, sculpted, revered...or maybe just outlawed.*

"Do you want to kiss me?" I asked.

"Hell yes," he answered, then brushed his mouth against mine once before settling over me.

I opened for him, and he dove in, his tongue filling my mouth while my ass filled his hands. *Gentleman, indeed.*

Kissing him was addictive—the world around us faded into nothingness, and all that existed was Paxton and the way he made me feel. I kissed him back with everything I had, reveling in his groan when I gently bit his lower lip.

He attacked again, this time taking full control of the kiss, cradling my head and angling me where he wanted, taking me off-balance so that he supported my weight. I moaned when he kissed me deeper, our tongues tangling, our breath ragged, the taste of him overwhelming every one of my senses.

"Leah, that sound will get you fucked," he promised, his lips skimming my jawline.

"What happened to being a gentleman?" I asked, trying to remember where we were, or hell, even my last name.

"Being a gentleman, I'll make sure you'll come first, second, even third, if you're up for it. After that, all bets are off as to gentlemanly behavior in my bed."

Oh shit. Were those my panties walking away? Yup. "If *I'm* up for it?" I challenged, running my hands lightly through his thick hair. "You sure you could keep up?"

He laughed, the sound incredibly sexy. "I guess it's good for you that I keep my body at peak physical condition, isn't it?"

"Mmmm," I agreed, as he nipped my earlobe.

"Paxton! We're waiting on you, buddy!" Bobby called up.

Paxton groaned in my ear, and even though it was pure frustration, I couldn't help but save the sound for a little mental playback later. "Fine!" he shouted over his shoulder.

He kissed me softly, sucking gently on my lip before releasing it. "God, I love being able to do that. You should say yes more often."

Yeah, I really should. "You should go...be Wilder."

His eyes turned serious. "Leah, we're trying some new stuff today. People fall. A lot of people fall. Unless you see everyone rushing the ramp, don't let it bother you. This is what I do, what I've done since I was old enough to swing my leg over a Power Wheel. Don't let the fact that it's a motorcycle worry you, okay?"

I swallowed. "Okay."

He kissed me one last time and skipped down a few steps. "Oh, and if at any time you decide it turns you on, just like... wave a red flag or something." The way he wiggled his eyebrows had me laughing.

"What, are you two together now?" Zoe asked, her voice dripping with equal parts sarcasm and venom. I'd been so consumed by kissing Paxton that I hadn't even realized she'd been standing next to Bobby.

"Yes," Paxton answered.

"No," I responded at the same time.

Paxton just grinned and ran his hands over the hair that I'd thoroughly mussed. "Well, I'm with *her*. She hasn't quite decided if she's with me yet. But I have some pretty convincing powers of persuasion."

"Oh my God. Just go," I said, laughing again. I couldn't remember the last time I'd kissed and laughed and felt...normal. A tiny stab of guilt marred the feeling but didn't take it away completely. That was progress.

He winked at me once and then disappeared beneath the stands. I headed for the shade of the awning near the center front row. I tucked my legs under me as I sat and opened my physics book, trying to find the correct answers for what I missed in class. I wasn't fucking up my 4.0 on a stupid physics course.

"It won't last, you know," Zoe said, taking the seat next to me and stretching her long legs out on the bar in front of us.

I tapped my pen on the paper, debating my options on how to handle this wench, and then went for it. "How the hell do you know? And besides, I said we weren't together."

She lowered her sunglasses to roll her eyes at me. "Right. First, Wilder tends to get what he wants, and given that he just publicly pawed you to mark his territory, it's a matter of time until you fall. Second, you should know that this is as good as it's going to get."

"Because it's as good as you ever got?" I fired back, done with her intruding on everything.

Her shoulders drooped, and all trace of bullshit cleared from her expression. "Do you see the way he goes after a new trick? He practices so hard that nothing else matters. Everything else doesn't exist to him until he gets it."

"So? I think that drive is admirable. And I'm not the type of girl to focus my life on what my boyfriend is doing." *Did you call him your boyfriend? For fuck's sake, focus.*

A wry smile twisted her lips. "You're missing the point. That's how he goes after women, with that same drive. But once he nails the trick, gets the girl, the thrill is gone for him, and he's on to his next trick, the bigger air, the faster bike...the better woman. I'm not saying this because I want to hurt your little feelings. I'm actually telling you because you don't seem like the kind of girl who would take that well—being fucked and dumped."

Despite my best efforts to keep her words from touching me, my heart sank, knowing some of what she said was true. If I was going to give in to Paxton, then I had to be prepared for him to walk away...probably sooner rather than later.

Zoe stood. "Look what you're doing. For someone who wouldn't focus her life on her boyfriend, you're sitting at practice while the entire city of Rome is just over that hill." She shrugged. "Food for thought."

She walked off without another glance, passing Brooke on her way.

"Everything okay?" Brooke asked, taking Zoe's empty seat.

"Yeah," I lied, nodding a little too enthusiastically.

She narrowed her eyes. "Uh-huh."

"Can I ask you something personal?"

"Thirty-four D, usually 3.1 when my grades are decent, and eighteen months."

I blinked.

She laughed. "Bra size, GPA, and how long since I've had sex."

"Oh, I was going in a different direction."

"Shoot."

"Why do you watch the practices? Follow Penna? Why not go into Rome, or something else that you want to do?"

She studied me for a moment. "I was there the first time Penna broke her arm on the makeshift ramp at the back of Paxton's house. I put my arm around her and carried her home. I come because there's honestly no place else I'd rather be. These guys are my family. Plus"—she motioned to the ramp—"the show is amazing. I love to see her fly. That's her."

The motorcycle revved at the end of the course, and Penna came flying, hitting the ramp, and then going airborne. My breath held as she flipped the bike mid-air, coming down and landing smoothly on the dirt landing ramp.

"Holy. Shit."

Brooke smiled. "She's stunning. One of her medals is in an all-guy category, too."

I watched a series of jumpers, twisting, turning, flipping in the air. They were amazing, powerful, brave, and ridiculously talented.

When Paxton's turn came, I watched white-knuckled as he took the ramp, flipping mid-air and then letting the bike go momentarily. My heart stopped, my chest constricting until he put his hands back on the bars and landed gracefully.

"Whoa! Go, Wilder!" Brooke yelled, her hands cupped around her mouth.

I was barely breathing. "He let go of it."

"Yeah! Wait for Penna to go. She's even better. They all know it."

"He let go. Mid-air."

She turned slowly. "It's okay, Leah. He does it all the time. They all do. They practice over giant foam pits to start with until they get good enough. They're okay."

"He's ridiculous."

She shrugged. "Yeah, they all kind of are, honestly."

Another round of riders went by, not all landing, some spinning to the end of the dirt, or sliding on their asses. Brooke told me when each one was okay, her voice calm and even. "You'll be able to tell when something serious happens," she promised.

The day wore on, but the riders didn't stop. The motors revved as they sped toward the ramp, only to go nearly silent along with my heartbeat as they took to the air. Hearing the engine purr as riders hit the gas after the landing became my favorite sound in the world. It was noisy and dirty, but being under the awning made everything feel slightly separated, like the Renegades were in their own little world. Penna did a trick I couldn't even describe, where she unseated herself and then pulled back on while the bike was mid-flip. Landon brought his entire bike vertical.

Paxton did a double backflip.

"He's over-rotating," Brooke whispered, leaning forward.

My books fell from my lap as Paxton neared the landing, nearly vertical to the ramp. "Oh my God."

His back tire slammed into the dirt.

The bike flew from under him as he made impact.

Then the bike made impact...with him.

The engine stayed silent.

"Paxton!" I screamed, the sound ripping from my throat without thought.

His head bounced off the ramp, and then both he and the bike slid to the bottom.

"This…this isn't okay," Brooke whispered from behind me. I was already jumping down from the bleachers, uncaring of the six-foot drop to the track. I flew across the distance to the ramp as the crew flocked to him.

"You can't go in there," one of the guards said, catching me around the waist.

"Let me go!" I fought, but he had about six inches and a hundred pounds on me. I stomped, kicked, and flailed, but I may as well have been a gnat to the guy.

I couldn't see Paxton, but I did make out the mangled back tire of the bike.

Oh God. Is he…?

"He's not dead," Penna said, breaking through the crowd, dressed in all of her protective gear but helmetless. "Get off her, Mike."

The guard let me go, and I rushed toward her. "How hurt is he?"

The arriving ambulance answered that question for me.

"Oh, no."

"Get Brooke. We'll meet the guys at the hospital."

CHAPTER TWELVE

Paxton

ROME

I swatted away the light shining in my eyes. "I'm fine," I said, having assured the hundredth doctor in the last twenty minutes.

How long had it been since the crash? An hour? More?

"Well, you look like shit," Landon said, leaning back in the chair next to my bed.

"Thanks." I flipped him off. "I over-rotated."

"Yeah," he agreed and leaned forward. "Your chest protector saved your life. You cracked it clean down the middle."

"Damn. That must have been some crash. You still have it for the wall?"

Landon nodded. "I snaked it once they cut the straps off you. You can hang it next to the protector you destroyed that year you were going for the long-distance jump."

I grunted my approval. "Where are we?"

"Hospital in Rome. What do you remember?"

I thought back. "I knew I over-rotated, so I tried to push the bike back, but we came down vertical. I don't remember anything after impact." *After hearing Leah scream my name.* "Where's Leah?"

Landon smirked. "In the waiting room. You want her?"

"Yeah," I answered. "She's got to be scared shitless."

"She's tougher than you give her credit for, your little firecracker. She actually broke one of the guard's toes trying to get to you."

My chest swelled with pride. "She's something else."

"She is," he agreed, then left the room, closing the door behind him. I took a moment and soaked in the quiet of the private room, testing my limb function. Everything wiggled and moved, but it hurt to breathe too deeply.

"You're okay!" Leah exclaimed right after she burst through the door. Her braid had come undone at the sides, giving her a slightly frazzled look that made her all the more beautiful to me.

"I'm okay," I promised, moving to sit up.

"Don't you dare!" she snapped, rushing to the side of my bed. "You're really okay?"

"Yeah." She was worried, and not only worried about how long I'd be out if I was hurt, but genuinely concerned for me. Damn, I liked that a little too much. "Do you want to kiss me?" I offered.

"Yes," she said softly, bending to caress my lips with her own. That glow was back in my heart, shiny and warm.

"Do I get a sympathy yes, now?"

She arched an eyebrow. "No."

"A guy has to try," I said as the door opened. Apparently Italian doctors weren't too big on knocking.

"Mr. Wilder," the doc said in accented English, lifting a chest X-ray to the light board and flipping it on. "You are lucky.

Nothing is broken. No concussion."

I did a mini fist-pump. "Yes," I hissed.

He gave me a look of pure disdain that was echoed by Leah. "But your ninth and tenth ribs are bruised, probably where you impacted with your motorbike."

"But not broken," I reiterated. Broken was a pain in the ass, but I could still function, still perform with bruised.

"No. Not broken. You'll need to rest until the ribs heal, but other than the scrapes on your torso, you're fine."

Score one for protective gear. At least this accident had been of my own making. Hell, if I could screw up something like this, maybe I had overlooked something in the rigs. Besides, nothing bad had happened since Miami. Maybe I'd been stressed out over nothing—or worse—over my own ignorance.

"We'd like to keep you overnight for observation—"

"No thanks," I interrupted, yanking the IV out of my arm. "I never did like hospitals much, so if I can sign a release, I'll be out of your hair."

Oh yeah, this doc was not impressed with me. "Of course. I'll have a nurse bring you the papers."

"I'll tell Little John to fire up the cars so we can get back to the ship," Landon said, following the doctor out.

"You sure you don't want to stay overnight?" Leah asked, her eyes imploring.

"I'm okay. Trust me, I've bruised a couple ribs in my life. I'll do better at home. I probably need a couple days of rest and I'll be fine."

"More like a couple weeks," she rebutted.

"Weeks will kill me. Days are all I'm giving myself. I've trained with way worse."

"Okay," she replied, but her eyes said something else

entirely. They shone with disappointment, and that *hurt*.

It was an odd revelation considering I'd never given a fuck what anyone thought of me, except maybe Mom. "I'm fine. I promise."

"I said okay," she rebutted softly. "You know the limits of your body way better than I do."

Before we could get further into it, the Renegades arrived with a ball-busting wheelchair, ready to take me home.

Leah stayed with us until they tucked me in like a five-year-old, but some of the light had faded from her eyes, and I hated knowing that I was responsible.

I hated thinking it wouldn't be the last time.

"Rise and shine," Leah said as I was coming out of my bathroom the next morning. Mixed with the aroma of the coffee she was holding, it was pretty damn perfect.

"Good morning, gorgeous," I said, wincing when I leaned over to grab the shirt I dropped on the floor.

Leah put the coffee on my nightstand and then raced over to help. "You're not supposed to be up." She grabbed the shirt but got a little distracted when she stood to hand it over.

"Leah."

"Uh-huh?" she asked, her eyes raking over my chest, examining my tattoos, gnawing on her lower lip.

Fuck, the way the woman looked at me got me instantly hard. I thought about flexing just for fun, to see if those eyes would dilate any further. My head swam with visions of stripping that long, strappy shirt off her, taking those gorgeous breasts in my mouth, and watching her eyes roll back.

I wanted to fuck her senseless and make love to her at the

same time, which wasn't a combination I was familiar with. Sex had never been emotional, merely a physical release, a challenge to see how many times I could get a girl to come before she was begging for me.

But I wanted to worship Leah.

"Paxton?" she asked, and I blinked. Now I was the distracted one. "Does it hurt?" She motioned to the dark purple bruising along my ribs.

"It's not too bad," I lied. It hurt like a bitch whenever I moved.

She thrust the shirt at me, her cheeks deliciously pink. I quickly pulled it over my head and shoved my arms through the sleeves, wincing again when the material brushed the scrape that took up a full seven inches on my side.

"You're not supposed to be up," she repeated her earlier comment.

"Well, I kind of had to use the bathroom, and my mouth tasted like something furry curled up and died in there, so I figured I should do something about that."

"Oh. Right. Of course."

I walked over to the bed and got in without making ugly "I hurt" faces, but she knew and propped three pillows behind my back. "Better?"

"Yeah. Thank you."

"Sure," she said, handing me coffee. Then she grabbed her backpack from the doorway where she'd dropped it. "Ready?"

"For what?" I asked, taking a sip of the nectar of the gods. "And shouldn't you be gone by now? The schedule said the excursion is leaving soon."

She rolled her eyes. "The excursion left an hour ago."

My mouth dropped open. "But the Vatican? The Pantheon?

What about the lab grade?"

She walked around to the opposite side of my bed and then—fuck my self-control—the woman got into bed with me. *She didn't say yes yet, so calm down.*

"Remote me," she ordered, her hand outstretched.

I passed her the TV remote, and she flipped through until she found what she was looking for, a shitty documentary with nauseatingly bad cinematography.

"There we go," she said.

I glanced between her and the TV. "I'm all for indie flicks, but this feels like the *Blair Witch Project*."

Her smile was sexy as hell. *And apparently you have one thing on your mind.* "It's a GoPro with sound, and Landon is wearing it," she answered. "He's on our excursion so you don't lose points. I gave our prof the note from the doc yesterday, and he's giving you an excuse."

That glow in my chest cranked up to nuclear level. This girl was amazing in ways I'd never be worthy of. "What about your grade?"

She shrugged. "I told him I'd guarantee that you'd watch, so he gave me the points, too."

"But this is *Rome*, and you're missing it." For me. Because of me.

"It's not going anywhere, is it? I can come back. Besides, logically speaking, if you fail, I miss the rest of my trip, so you can think of this as the payment for the next ports if you want to."

I didn't want to think about it at all. Liking her was one thing. Wanting her was a base, sexual need that I fully understood. But this feeling? I didn't know what the hell to do with this.

She leaned over me to get to her coffee, and I stopped

her mid-lean, putting my cup down next to hers. "You are incredible," I told her.

"Same goes for you, Mr. X Games."

I shook my head. "No, what I do is for me. For the fun, the victory, the hits, the records. But you...you're...incredible," I said again, my brain too fried to think of another word. "Can I—?"

"Yes," she answered before I could finish.

Then my mouth was on hers, and all words were gone.

She tasted like her toothpaste and coffee, earth and mint and...mine. My fingers tightened at the base of her skull, woven into the thick strands of her hair. I kissed her with every ounce of skill I had, wanting—needing—this kiss to brand her the same way she was branding me, setting the standard way too high for anyone who tried to come along next.

No next. Just this one. Just now.

I slammed the door on those thoughts and concentrated on kissing Leah, on the tiny gasps she made after I kissed her deeply, licked every line inside her mouth. I wanted to mark all of her recesses and curves, make her feel as owned as she made me feel.

I used my other arm to guide her on top of me, and she straddled my lap, the thin material of her leggings nearly no barrier between my dick and her hot center. She rubbed against me, and a groan rumbled through my chest.

"Did I hurt you?" she asked, her voice raspy.

"Fuck, no," I answered, pulling her back into my kiss.

She broke away. "Your ribs have to be killing you."

I did a mental check. Ribs? No pain. Dick? Throbbing. "You'll kill me if you stop."

She gave me a slow smile and then lowered her mouth

tantalizingly slow, first licking my lower lip and then gently tugging it with her teeth. "Leah," I growled.

Then she gave me her mouth, and I fucking took it.

Every stroke of her tongue drove me higher; every time she moaned it shook me to the core. I'd never gotten so wound up from kissing someone before, especially someone who probably wasn't ready for everything my body begged for. My hands gripped her waist, then her ass, loving the way she filled my hands, the way she moved against me when I squeezed gently.

She rubbed her breasts against my chest and suddenly I didn't just *want* to get my mouth on her, I *needed* to. I needed to give her something for staying with me today when everyone else usually walked away when I was hurt.

I needed her to feel as good as she made me feel.

My hands worked their way up her ribs until my thumbs grazed the underwire of her bra. "Firecracker?" I asked.

She leaned up, crossed her arms in front of her and removed her top. "Yes."

I nearly swallowed my tongue. I knew the shape of her breasts, hell, I'd caught myself looking way too often to be considered a good guy, but *fuuuuuck*. They were perfection, cupped in pink lace that was an equal mix of innocence and sexy that had my mouth watering.

I locked gazes with her, and she arched toward me. I closed my mouth over one hardened nipple, running my tongue over the lace. "Pax," she gasped, her hands flying to my hair.

That was all it took for my control to unravel. I didn't look away from her as I unclipped her bra, watching for the first sign of "no," or even hesitation. Instead, she slipped the straps down her arms, and the bra joined her shirt on the floor.

"You are exquisite," I said even before I glanced. I didn't

need eyes on her to know that she was sheer perfection.

"Quid pro quo?" she asked, tugging on my shirt.

I lifted my arms, and she slid it over my head, her breath catching in a way that made me feel like a god.

"May I?" she asked.

"Yes," I said enthusiastically. This yes game was fucking awesome.

Her fingertips skimmed my chest, pausing on my various tats and leaving a trail of fire in their wake. "How many do you have?" she asked.

"I don't know," I answered truthfully. "Some pieces grew into others, some morphed into different ones."

"Do they have meanings?"

"Some. Others I thought were beautiful, or were representative of what I was feeling at the time."

She lingered on the dragon that wrapped around my heart and trailed down my abs. "This is beautiful."

"So are you," I said, counting in my head to keep my hands off her until she was ready. I didn't know what was holding her back, but I sure as hell wasn't going to push her.

"I haven't...been with anyone in a really long time," she admitted.

"Okay. How long?" I gently tipped her chin so she'd meet my eyes. I would sit here all fucking day with our shirts off and not touch her if it meant she unlocked just one of those doors in her head and let me in. I might gnaw off my own hands, but it'd be worth it.

"A...a while." Her eyes were wide, tinged with fear and something else I couldn't name.

"Okay. Do you want to talk about it?" I asked, knowing there was a reason. There was zero chance she wasn't being chased by half the population of Dartmouth.

She shook her head. "No. I don't know if I can… I don't want to be a tease, or disappoint you."

I sat up higher, ignoring the near-crippling pain in my ribs. Then I kissed her gently, keeping it chaste despite the sheer electricity shooting through me where her breasts pressed against my chest. "You couldn't tease me because I have no expectations. I'm not a little boy, Leah. I can more than control myself, and if all we do is kiss, then that's more than I could ask for. Do you understand?"

She nodded.

I brought my hands up her rib cage, reveling in how silky soft her skin was, until I rested beneath her breasts. "And there's no chance of you ever disappointing me. You're perfect just sitting here, so I can't imagine how amazing you would be if I ever got my mouth on you."

Her lips parted and her eyes darkened. She liked it when I talked to her. *Noted.* I was going to learn every single secret there was to turning her on, and then I was going to systematically use them until she didn't know fear or doubt, just felt as sexy as she was.

"We're only going as far as you say, Leah. You're in control." *For now,* I promised myself. Once she said yes, I would make her forget her own name.

She leaned down slowly and kissed me, pressing me back onto the bed. I lost myself in her taste, the feel of her perfect mouth, the way she fit against me like she was meant to be there.

I kissed her until she started to grind, and then my fingers dug into her hips as the pleasure ripped through me. *You will not come in your pants like you're in high school. Didn't you promise that you could control yourself?*

WILDER

I focused on her, finally letting myself run my hands up her sides until I cupped her flawless breasts in my hands. She moaned and leaned forward, pushing them farther into my hands.

"Perfection," I murmured against her neck, lightly sucking a sensitive patch of skin as I thumbed her hard nipples. Now that I knew what was under her shirt, was I going to be able to keep my eyes above her shoulders?

Yeah, because her eyes are even better.

I pushed her forward gently and then lowered my head to take one peak into my mouth.

"Paxton!" she gasped, her fingers tightening in my hair in a nearly painful grip. Fuck, it felt amazing.

She rocked forward on my dick, and I angled her hips so she'd rub against her clit if she did it again. Then I tried to picture the most unsexy thing I could think of to keep from rolling her over, and went back to work on her other breast.

She rocked. She moaned. I nearly died, harder than the fucking steel this ship was made of. I couldn't remember a single time I'd been so turned on before my pants had even come off.

"Hey guys, have you seen Landon's backpack?" Penna's voice came from the other side of the door right before she opened it. "He left his wallet in it."

"Shit," I hissed, and rolled us off the bed, landing with a thump on the floor.

"Oh... Oh!" Penna said from the doorway.

I sat up, careful to keep Leah blocked from her sight. "You were saying?"

"I should have knocked."

"That would have been nice," I nearly growled at her, agony shooting through my ribs.

"Hey, Penna," Leah said, waving her hand above the bed but showing no other skin.

"Good to see you there, Leah!" Penna's eyes darted from wall to wall. "You know, I think I'll just wait downstairs."

"Backpack is under his bed," I suggested as she shut the door.

I turned to Leah, ready for the embarrassment, but she was doubled over in laughter. "Seriously? The first time I get to second base in *years*, and that happens? It's like living at home with my parents again."

I grinned. "There are no words for you, my little Firecracker."

She shook her head and crawled on hands and knees to find her clothes. *That ass. There are no words for* that.

"Get dressed," she said, tossing the shirt at me, her hair looking like she'd been thoroughly fucked. *You wish.*

I wanted to stomp my foot like an angry toddler who'd been denied a candy bar, because what I'd missed out on was so much sweeter.

"Relax," she said, leaning over the bed to kiss me quickly. "If you're a good boy, that might happen again."

I was ready to sit up and beg like a puppy.

"Shirt, Pax."

I grumbled but put the damn thing on before we wandered down the stairs to see Penna on her hands and knees under Landon's bed.

I spotted my chest protector on his dresser and picked it up, frowning at the break line.

"He kept it?" Leah asked.

"We always do," I answered, running my finger along the line. "We have a room at home full of gear we've busted in pursuit of whatever trick we were trying to pull."

"Oh," she answered. "Penna, do you need some help?"

"Sure," Penna answered under the blankets. "How much shit does he have down here?"

Leah took the other side, sticking that deliciously round ass in the air. Apparently my dick hadn't forgotten where she'd been a few minutes ago. I blinked and looked back at the breast plate.

The break was too straight. Too clean. Strange.

"He's got a ton of shit under here," Leah agreed, throwing some of the stuff onto the bed.

"Got it!" Penna lifted her hands in victory. She slung the pack over her shoulder. "Okay, I'll be back later. You two...you know...um...study or something."

"Nice, Penna." I rolled my eyes at her.

She blew me a sarcastic kiss and ran out the door.

"Everything okay?" Leah asked as she walked over to me.

"The chest plate. They never crack in a straight line. It's always along the ridges, or the point of impact. Never straight. It's strange."

"Huh," she said. "Maybe it's the handlebars or something?"

"Maybe," I answered.

"Let me get this stuff put away," she said, motioning to the bed.

The girls were right. Landon was a freaking pack rat. Harnesses, protective gear, a helmet— "No fucking way," I whispered.

"Okay, I won't put it away," Leah grumbled.

"No, that's not it." I dropped the chest plate and sat on the only clear spot on his bed, reaching for the two black rigs I'd been missing since we zip-lined onto the ship. "These are mine. They're the ones we used that first day."

"Oh," she said, not understanding. How could she? Even I couldn't put everything together.

I took the rigs back to my room and, while she sat on my bed sipping the latte that had gone nearly cold, I disassembled the rigs, looking up every now and then to watch the tour of the Vatican.

Landon's voice was in my head at every age. When we were kids jumping off the roof to the trampoline, to the first time I'd strapped a snowboard on my feet, to the night he'd chosen the team over love and broken his own heart, to right...now as he took the tour for me so I could heal.

Did he hate me so much for forcing him to choose? *No way. Don't even fucking think it.*

He'd been my best friend since grade school.

It didn't compute.

I picked up the braking mechanisms one at a time, my heart sinking, then shattering.

I looked at them twice, then a third time.

"What's wrong?" Leah asked.

"They were under Landon's bed."

"Yeah? It looks like half the gear for your team was under his bed."

I looked at her, and anger swelled through my limbs. She could have been hurt, or worse, killed that day. So many things could have gone wrong, all because I hadn't kept my gear on me at all times. I'd been too trusting.

"The brakes were tampered with."

CHAPTER THIRTEEN

LEAH

ISTANBUL

"To your right you can see the area in which the Holy Roman Emperors were crowned when the Hagia Sophia was a Christian church." Dr. Williams pointed to the Arabic symbols hung high above the floor. "As you can see, this served as a mosque before it was declared a museum."

"Everything changes, doesn't it?" Paxton said next to me as we walked around the massive structure.

"You could…you know, talk to Landon," I suggested.

"No point," he said.

"Okay." I exhaled slowly, counting to ten. We'd gone rounds for the last few days about what he was going to do, which was a big fat nothing.

"I told you, Landon didn't do this. There's zero chance. It had to have been an accident during assembly, or if someone opened it up to check it…or anything but Landon."

"Right," I said. *Keep quiet.* But of course I couldn't. "Because that's what happened to your chest protector, too, right?"

He shot me a go-to-hell look, which I shot right back. "Let's just look at some history, okay?"

He'd been this sour the whole damn time. On board, in class, during study sessions, all week. The worst? He hadn't so much as kissed me again. The minute I suggested that he look into Landon, he shut me out like I was a direct threat to his best friend.

For God's sake, I suggested he talk to him, not practice waterboarding.

"How's that going for you?" Hugo asked as Paxton walked ahead of me.

"He's an ass."

"He sure likes you, though," he answered, stopping to snap a picture on our way out.

"What makes you say that?" The treatment I'd gotten the last few days definitely didn't support that theory.

"We may have run out of that French roast you like while we were at sea."

"No!" I gasped. "My lifeblood!"

He laughed. "Yeah, well, Paxton knew and made sure that you got all of his." He watched for my reaction.

"Really?" I glanced forward to where Paxton walked, his thumbs tucked into the pockets of his jeans. Jeans that hung on nice hips and were accented with an incredible ass. Ugh.

"Really. I'm just saying that he's been a jerk since he got hurt, but if there's something there, give it a shot." He shrugged.

"Yes, wise one." I bowed my head.

"Hey, admit it, you're glad you kept the suite," he said as we boarded the bus.

I couldn't believe there had been a time when I almost said no to everything...to Paxton. "You're right. I'm glad."

"Firecracker?" Paxton asked as I approached where he sat. He pointed to the empty seat next to him and I took it after Hugo shot me a knowing look.

"Feel like talking now?" I asked.

"No."

I leaned out of my seat to move. I might be a little nonsensical over the guy, but I wasn't a martyr. He stopped me, his fingers gentle on my wrist as he pulled.

"I just want to be near you, if that's okay."

I sat down. How the hell could I turn that down? "Okay," I said, and settled in for a silent trip to the market. I looked past Paxton to where the Blue Mosque waited in quiet repose. The inside had stolen my breath, reminded me how much work it was to build something worth standing, worth marveling at.

"What are you thinking?" he asked as the bus rolled into Istanbul traffic.

"How beautiful things last when they're built well and loved."

He nodded but didn't say anything.

The drive over had me holding my breath more than once. I'd seen aggressive drivers, but even that trip to New York City couldn't hold a candle to this.

The entire ride, I wanted to touch him, to put my hand on his and tell him that we'd figure out what was going on, or I'd let him figure it out on his own if he needed to. His eyes tracked everything as we drove by, his foot tapping. I'd seen that look before as he was planning a trick. I knew that he was thinking, but I didn't quite expect it to hurt so much to be shut out.

But what the hell did I expect? We'd been together all of what, two weeks? Were we together? He said so, but I never did. What was worse than craving Paxton from an unattainable distance? Being in relationship gray area with him.

Maybe it was better to have a clean break now before I du
myself any deeper, though. Right? Cutting losses and all.

The bus stopped on the side of the street, and Dr. Willia
gave us the lecture about staying together, and safety, and h
easy it was to get lost. I tried to pay attention, but all my fo
was on the tiny crack in my heart that was growing by
minute.

Better to feel that now than to wait around for hi
pulverize me. And besides, you couldn't miss what you
had.

Except those tiny slivers of time where he'd been
those shone brighter than the rest of, well...everything.

We filed out of the bus and moved as a herd thro
pedestrian-only street, passing under a stone arch t
GRAND BAZAAR.

As we entered the covered market, I moved my s
to the top of my head. It was stunning, a kaleidoscope
sounds, and the scent of fruit and spices. The st
stretched above us for what seemed to be miles.
atmosphere was alive, raucous, and slightly overwhe

"Okay, take note, you have one hour," Dr. W
over the noise. "Do not be late. Ship pulls out at fiv
and I'd like to be on it." He waved us free.

"Want to shop with us?" Hugo asked, pointing

My gaze darted to where Paxton browsed in t
to us, picking up a ceramic crocodile. "I'd be
Paxton."

"You take those tutor duties seriously." He

"Always," I answered with a flat smile.

"How about I bring up some ice cream fo

later?" he offered.

"Only if you indulge with us."

"Deal." He looked in Paxton's direction. "Remember the coffee." Then he met up with his group of friends, and they took off in the opposite direction.

I kept Paxton in my peripheral vision while I looked at the intricate jewelry boxes in the booth. The blue one was gorgeous, but way outside my price range, so I set it down.

"How much do they want for it?" Paxton asked, picking it up.

"Too much," I answered.

"So? Get it. I haven't seen you buy yourself a single thing on this trip besides sunscreen." He opened and shut the lid.

"I need to be careful with my money. I budgeted everything before I came, and I can buy myself one thing for the whole trip." I turned away from him, running my fingers over the other boxes. They were all so detailed.

There was a vendor with teapots across the walkway. "I'll be right over there," I said as Paxton picked up something else within a glass case.

The teapots were as ornate as the boxes, the lines graceful but functional. I flipped one over and nearly swallowed my tongue at the price.

"I like that, too," Paxton said, leaning over my shoulder.

"Rachel and I have a thing for teapots," I answered.

"Rachel?" he asked.

"My roommate who isn't here yet." I turned the pot over in. "She's supposed to meet up with us at second trimester."

"Right." Paxton nodded. "I'm glad to hear she's still ing."

"Yeah, she's chomping at the bit."

"So the teapots?" he said, taking it from me to check it out.

"She loves that quote by Eleanor Roosevelt, the one that says women are like tea bags, because you never know how strong we are until we're in hot water. We both had rough freshman years, and it kind of became our thing."

Rachel would love that teapot. It could be my Paxton pot. The time I got in way over my head and let yet another reckless asshole break my heart. *At least this one won't break your body.*

I took it out of Paxton's hands and headed to the owner of the booth. This was definitely my Paxton pot. It could sit next to Rachel's "I failed my chem final" pot and right above my "doc said one more surgery" pot.

As I took my money out of my wallet, Paxton rolled his eyes. "Put your fanny pack away," he said with a smile.

It was the closest to a joke he'd made since we left Rome.

"I can pay for it," I argued. There was zero chance I was taking anything else from him. Not when he already had way too much of me.

We locked eyes, a battle raging along the tension that connected us. "Fine," he acquiesced. "But you're not paying full price."

"It's on the sticker, Pax," I said as we arrived to the booth.

"Haggling is half the fun," he said. "Besides, they expect you to."

I rolled my eyes and let him get to it. By the time it was over, we'd lost a ton of time, but he'd gotten my teapot more than half off.

"Thank you," I said, tucking it into my small backpack.

"No problem," he answered.

We walked side by side along the main walkways, then turned down a few alleys with smaller booths, tangling ourselves in the web of the market. With every step, the tension between us became something palpable, almost as if I could reach out and pluck it like a guitar string.

What if this was how it would be from now on?

Maybe he was done with me.

That thought hurt more than it should have.

"It feels good to get out," he said, breaking our awkward silence.

"I bet," I answered.

"It sucks that we blew the opportunity for the stunt, but I guess resting up before we head for more ramp practice is a safer bet."

I paused in the middle of the walkway, and Paxton turned around.

"What's wrong?"

"You're getting on another ramp?"

He nodded. "Of course."

"What the hell do you mean, of course? Like it's a given? Like there's not even the possibility that you might take a look at what almost happened to you and rethink that choice?"

"Leah, nothing happened." He took a step toward me, and I moved backward.

"Really? Because I was there. I saw you come down. I saw the bike hit, and you hit, and then the bike come down on you."

"I take risks every single day of my life. It's what I do. It's who I am. It's how I made my name."

"Even if it kills you?"

He shook his head. "It hasn't."

"Yet! You're not even healed and you're ready to jump back on a bike and flip it backward."

"Forward," he corrected. "We were going backward in Rome, but I'll actually be working on flipping it forward. Three times, which has never been done. We just didn't have the right kicker in Rome."

My mouth hung open for a second until I snapped it shut. "You nearly got yourself killed going backward, which—forgive my physics—should be easier than forward, and now you're going to take it up a notch?"

"If you think that's almost killing myself, then we should probably talk about your definition of death."

That carefully constructed wall I kept lost a brick.

"I am more acquainted with that concept than you have ever been!" I yelled.

Okay, maybe it lost an entire row of bricks.

"What? Because our brakes didn't work on the zip-line? That was a baby accident compared to what I've seen—what I've done."

My fingernails dug into my palms. "Like what happened in Rome? You can't tell me nothing happened when you're sitting on two tampered brake assemblies and a cracked chest plate. You're not that stupid."

His eyes narrowed. "Is that what you call trusting your friends? Stupid?"

"Is that seriously how you define trust?"

"Yes." He walked forward, and I retreated until I felt a stone wall at my back. "That's when you hand someone your faith."

"Blindly?"

His eyes narrowed. "I've known some of them my entire life. I would take a bullet for any of them."

"Would they take one for you?"

"Yes," he answered instantly.

"How the hell can you be so sure when you're sitting on evidence like that? You'd hop back up there and wait for someone to do something that kills you?"

"I don't expect you to understand." His eyes went glacial, which only fueled the anger controlling me.

"Why? Because I don't want to hurl my body through space? Because I think you don't have to do extraordinary things to be extraordinary? I can't understand because I'd rather curl up with Netflix than drive as fast as I can just to see if I can beat the score of the guy next to me?"

"What? I don't race." He shook his head. "You wouldn't understand because you live in a bubble of your own making. You can see the amazing things happening around you, but you'd rather watch from the inside because you think it's safer."

"It is safer!" I shouted. *Too close. He's too close.*

"There's a difference between being alive and living. I live. Every day. I challenge everything, even the law of gravity."

"Because you like people screaming your name," I hurled.

"You nailed it. It's all about the fame, isn't it?" he said, his voice dripping sarcasm. "It's about landing the trick, about doing something that's never been done before. About breaking every limit set, even the ones of my own body, because I make the rules. I decide what can and cannot be done. And it's honestly a hell of a lot of fun."

"Fun."

He leaned in closer. "Fun. You know, what happens when you let go just a little, step outside your bubble, maybe put on a pair of shorts."

I flinched. "You're an asshole."

He smirked. "I've been called worse."

"Given the trail of women you leave in your wake, I don't doubt that."

"Every woman I fuck knows what she's getting into."

I tried to swallow past the giant ball of pain that lodged in my throat. "And you wonder why it's hard to trust you."

His shoulders dropped, and he backed up a step. "So that's where we're at?"

"Is there a *we*?" I asked, my voice losing almost all of its fight.

"I thought so. But you see, there's the difference between us. I saw you and I wanted you. I talked to you and I liked you. I felt this connection between us and I jumped. You're the one on the fucking fence, as usual."

I would have snapped back, but damn it...he was right.

"Everything about you scares the shit out of me," I said honestly.

His hand cupped my face. "When are you going to understand that's where life begins? Right at the edge of that fear."

I looked away, unable to hold his gaze for one more second before I crumbled. I flipped my wrist and gasped. "Oh my God. Paxton, we were supposed to meet up with the class ten minutes ago."

He straightened. "They won't leave us. Let's go."

We backtracked our steps through the alleys, but they all looked the same. The arches looked the same, the roofline, too. When we came to the crowded main walkway, he grasped my hand. "Stay with me."

"Yes," I answered.

His smile did little to conquer the fear racing down my spine, but he was with me...what could happen?

"There's the door," he said, and we raced toward the arched exit. *Thank God.*

I blinked and pulled my sunglasses down as sunlight

assaulted my eyes. "Wait," I said, spinning. "This isn't the way we came in."

"But that's the exit," he said.

I looked at the door. "It's door four. We came in door nine."

He swore under his breath. "The whole layout is like a wagon wheel. We just need to get to door nine," he said, and pulled me back into the market. We ran the outside path of the market, counting the numbers of the doors as we passed them.

"Nine!" I said, but my heart sank and then pounded. "They left us."

He looked at his watch. "We're a half hour late. Damn it. What I wouldn't give for my fucking cell phone right about now."

I looked at my watch. "Oh God. Pax, it's four thirty."

He nodded like he'd made a decision. "Okay, we need to find a cab and get to the port."

My hand clasped tightly in his, we made our way through the crowded path until we reached the street. Paxton tried for five minutes to hail a cab and finally stepped into traffic.

A cab stopped right before hitting him.

I was too scared of missing the ship to chastise him, just got in the backseat. Paxton slid in next to me and, over the course of another five minutes, managed to convey our destination to the cabbie. We jolted into traffic, and I bolted forward when the driver hit the brakes.

Paxton leaned over me and fastened a seat belt that looked like it had been installed during the disco era. We hit gridlock traffic, and I broke into a sweat.

"They're going to leave us," I said as I looked at my watch. 4:55.

"They'd better not," he muttered. Then he glanced over

at me and sighed, wrapping his arm around my shoulders and pressing a kiss to my temple. "I'll take care of you."

I scoffed. "Who is going to take care of *you*?"

He laughed. "There's my Firecracker."

We were stopped on the bridge when I looked past him and lost all hope.

"Hey, Pax?"

"Yeah?"

"They left us."

"How are you sure?" he asked into my hair.

I pointed to the window. "Because that's the ship."

Paxton's attention snapped to the gorgeous white cruise ship with ATHENA painted across the bow that was currently sailing out of Istanbul.

"Well, fuck."

CHAPTER FOURTEEN

PAXTON

ISTANBUL

"What are we going to do?" Leah asked me, her voice pitching higher with every word.

My brain raced. It wasn't like we could land a helicopter on the ship...or could we?

"Whatever you're thinking, try bringing a little reality into it," she suggested, her eyes wide. "We're not strapping ourselves to the backs of dolphins or trying out a jet pack—"

I covered her mouth with mine, quieting her the only way I knew how—the only way I wanted to. I kissed her breathless, losing myself, groaning at the way she responded to every stroke of my tongue, every soft bite at her lower lip. I kissed her to put a Band-Aid over the gaping wound we'd ripped open in that market.

The cab lurched forward as traffic moved, and I broke the kiss. "It's going to be okay," I promised her. "No matter what just happened, we're going to be okay. Trust me, Firecracker." I meant more than being left behind, and by the timid smile she gave me, she knew it.

"Okay," she said.

Never had one word meant so damn much to me.

I tucked her under my arm and leaned toward the cabbie. "Can you change directions?"

"Where to?" he asked.

We needed a hotel for the night, and there was no way I was taking Leah anywhere she wasn't 100 percent comfortable. "The Ritz-Carlton," I answered.

"Pax, I don't have that much money on me," Leah whispered.

"Lucky for us, I do," I answered. She looked down, so I tipped her chin up to look into her eyes. "The money is nothing. Let me take care of you."

She nodded, and I kissed her puckered forehead.

An hour later, we were checked in to a terrace suite at the Ritz-Carlton, and I had never been so thankful that I'd brought my credit card. We'd devoured some room service and calmed down enough to think rationally.

"Okay, let's see what we have," Leah said, leaning toward the coffee table and emptying the contents of her travel wallet thing. "I have our passports—"

"Wait. You what?" I picked mine up and verified the goofy smile picture. "Why?"

"Because we're required to have them in Turkey. I knew you'd probably jump into the river or get yourself blown up, so Hugo gave me yours before we disembarked, thank God. Your middle name is Iskander? What's the origin of that?"

"Greek," I answered. "Have you been snooping, Firecracker?"

Her cheeks flushed pink. "It's only fair. I bet you have an

entire file on me, right?"

"Actually, Penna does," I answered honestly, then tossed the contents of my pocket into her pile. "And she won't tell me a damn thing that's in it."

She sighed in relief, piquing my curiosity.

"Okay, let's see." She picked through our pile, then included the teapot she'd stored in her little backpack with a tube of sunscreen. We had two passports, enough Turkish lira for lunch, breath mints, lip balm, a folded itinerary for today's plans, my credit card, our empty wallets, and a condom.

"Seriously?" She raised her eyebrows at me.

"I keep it in my wallet," I answered with a shrug. "I guess it's a good thing since we got fucked over by the ship."

She rolled her eyes. "We knew the rules. This is our fault."

"Okay, let's make a plan," I suggested, trying to focus my frustration.

"Right. Okay, we have to meet up with the ship by the next port or we're kicked out of the program." She opened the laptop I'd had the hotel deliver and slid it between us on the coffee table. As she logged on to the internet, she leaned forward, showing a strip of delicious skin right above her— Holy shit. She was wearing a thong. A pink one. A tiny pink string that led from the little triangle peeking above her jeans to slip between the globes of her perfect ass.

"Paxton?"

I snapped forward. "Sorry. I was shamelessly checking out your ass."

Her mouth opened and shut a couple times, but she didn't pull her shirt down in the back, just shook her head and half smiled in a way I couldn't interpret.

"Okay. Well, the next actual port is Athens, and that's in

five days. Well, five days from tomorrow."

Perfection. I had five days with her to work this shit out between us, figure out what the hell we were doing before we got slammed with cameras again. And I knew just the place to take her.

She sighed.

"What's wrong?" I asked. "Other than the obvious?"

Her shoulders dropped. "We're going to miss Mykonos. This is the week with the optional shore excursions." She clicked through the ship's itinerary. "Damn it."

Out of this entire experience, Mykonos was the one thing she'd wanted. "What day is the Mykonos one?"

"Thursday."

I could work with that. I put the computer on my lap and started to make arrangements.

Four days with her. Four days to show her who I really was, why I did the things I did. Fate had given me one opportunity, and I was taking it.

"What are you doing?" She looked over my shoulder.

"Buying plane tickets."

If I turned my head, I could kiss her again. I could set the computer down, flip her to her back, slide over her, and find out what my name sounded like when she was screaming it.

My fingers flew faster, booking us on the nine thirty a.m. flight.

"Mykonos?" she asked, looking at the screen.

"I figured we could spend four days there, then hop back with the shore excursion on the fifth day. We wouldn't even have to wait until Athens."

"You're...you're taking me to Mykonos?" Her eyes were huge pools of disbelief and wonder.

I clicked the purchase button before I gave her my full attention. "I promised you I would. I know a great house we can stay in, and I know we're missing classes, but it will give you a chance to re—"

This time she stopped me with a kiss. She didn't push it further, just a simple press of our lips, but when I felt her smile, it went down in my book as the third best kiss of my life.

And she already owned the top two.

"Thank you," she said.

This girl was tying me in some serious knots. "I had them bring up pajamas for you, if you wanted to hop in the shower."

"Thank you. That sounds like heaven." She pushed off the couch and stood, her stretch revealing another tantalizing strip of skin, this time of her stomach. "I'll take the couch tonight. Your ribs need that bed."

Hell no. "Absolutely not. My ribs are fine. You're in the bed." When she cocked her head at me, I almost laughed. "I never said chivalry was dead. I'll sleep on the floor before you're out here on the couch." After the day we'd had, the last thing I was going to do was put her to bed on the couch.

The few feet that separated us felt like a mile, the words we'd thrown at each other in the market coming back to wedge their way between us.

She nervously chewed on her lower lip before meeting my eyes. "You know what? We're adults. We'll both take the bed."

My mouth went dry, every possible scenario running through my oversexed brain. Could I sleep next to her and keep my hands to myself? *Yes, because you're not a fucking animal. Don't be an ass.* "Okay."

Her smile was tentative. "Okay. Then I'll be right back."

She disappeared into the bathroom, and my eyes locked

onto the door like I was suddenly going to develop X-ray vision. She was getting naked. Twenty feet away from me. I groaned, rubbing one hand over my eyes and the other adjusting the growing issue in my pants.

The draw I felt toward her was incredible, indescribable. Stronger than magnets, than chemistry, it was a primal, clawing need in me—not necessarily for her to be mine, but for me to be hers. To be worthy of being hers after all the shit I'd done, the fuckups of epic proportions that never went away.

And once she realized what I'd done...why I'd really chosen her...

I was so fucked.

This wasn't how I planned it.

She was nothing like I assumed she would be. She was strong yet unsure, smart yet naïve. Innocent, yet so sexy that my hands literally tingled whenever I thought of getting them on her skin.

Skin she wouldn't show anyone.

She turned on the water. Now she was naked *and* wet.

"Knock it off. It's not like she invited us," I said to my overly excited dick.

I fired off an email to Penna and Landon to explain our current situation, making sure they knew we were fine, had funds and a plan. The last thing I needed was them calling in the cavalry. I had zero doubt that if I wanted to, I could get us onto the *Athena* tomorrow. But then I would lose out on the private time I had with Leah, this precious chance to simply be with her. No school. No cameras. No distractions.

I left them with instructions not to rescue us and hit send.

Now I had to find a way to get us on the same page, to take down whatever walls she'd constructed.

The shower still ran. I debated all of five seconds and fired up Google.

This is wrong. Don't do it.

I brushed the angel off my shoulder. If I didn't know what had happened to her, I couldn't help her, and obviously she wasn't opening that door on her own. I didn't need to throw it wide open, just enough to get a peek.

Eleanor Baxter, California.

I typed three words into the search engine and sold my soul to the devil as I hit enter.

The screen filled with links, and I clicked the first one, my heart sinking at the title of the article. "Granada Hills Senior Survives Fatal Canyon Car Accident."

The article loaded, and the picture of a crumpled car at the bottom of a ravine came into focus. *Holy shit.*

How the hell did she walk away from that?

Maybe she didn't.

I devoured the article.

EIGHTEEN-YEAR-OLD ELEANOR BAXTER WAS FOUND LATE LAST NIGHT, SEVERELY INJURED, CLINGING TO THE TOPANGA CANYON WALL, OVER ONE HUNDRED FEET ABOVE WHERE THE CAR SHE HAD BEEN A PASSENGER IN BURNED INTO THE MORNING. THE DRIVER, IDENTIFIED AS NINETEEN-YEAR-OLD BRIAN NEWCOMB, WAS KILLED IN THE CRASH.

REPORTS INDICATE THAT NEWCOMB LOST CONTROL OF THE VEHICLE, A LATE-MODEL HONDA CIVIC, WHICH WENT OFF HIGHWAY 23 A LITTLE OVER TWENTY-FOUR HOURS BEFORE SANTA MONICA FIRE AND RESCUE DISCOVERED THE SCENE, USING A HELICOPTER RESCUE TEAM TO BRING MS. BAXTER FROM THE RAVINE.

INITIALLY, THE VEHICLE HAD RESTED ALONG THE CANYON

WALL, BUT EVENTUALLY FELL TO THE BOTTOM OF THE RAVINE.

"I DON'T KNOW HOW SHE HUNG THERE SO LONG," CAPTAIN DELMONICO, WITH SMFD TOLD US. "IT LOOKS LIKE SHE WAS IN THE CAR ALMOST EIGHTEEN HOURS BEFORE SHE MANAGED TO GET OUT. WITH THE CONDITION SHE WAS IN, IT'S A MIRACLE SHE HELD ON FOR ANOTHER SIX HOURS. STRONG YOUNG LADY, THAT ONE IS."

STRONG INDEED. WHAT IS EVEN MORE MIRACULOUS IS THAT SHE WASN'T KILLED DURING THE INITIAL CRASH, AS THE DRIVER WAS.

"ELEANOR TOLD US THAT BRIAN DIED INSTANTLY. SHE SAID HE WENT QUICKLY AND WITHOUT PAIN, AND THAT'S ALL WE COULD ASK FOR OUR SWEET BOY," CLAUDIA NEWCOMB, THE DECEASED DRIVER'S MOTHER, TOLD US. "WE KNOW HE WOULD HAVE DONE ANYTHING TO KEEP HER SAFE, AND WE'RE SO THANKFUL THAT SHE MADE IT OUT."

MS. BAXTER HAS DECLINED TO COMMENT.

My chest tightened, my vision swimming, until I remembered to suck in a breath. I'd held it the entire time I'd read the article. I closed out all the windows on the laptop and slammed the lid shut, wishing I didn't know. Wishing I hadn't invaded her privacy.

Wishing she'd told me herself.

My fingers raked down my face, and I rocked forward, bracing my elbows on my knees.

I'd made her zip-line.

I'd made her parasail.

She'd hung over a hundred feet in the air for twenty-four hours, and I'd made her strap up and face her devil while I laughingly told her it would be okay.

I was a fucking, flaming asshole.

We both had rough freshman years. That's what she'd told me about her and Rachel. She'd been recovering. God, how bad had it been? I thought back to Bermuda, the way she'd gripped the railing going into the caves. Hell, even boarding the ship, she kept both hands on the banister and barely spoke until we were off the ramp.

No wonder she'd passed out when she fell down the ramp.

And the guy she was with...Newcomb...the way his mom had spoken, they had to have been dating, right? Had she loved him? Did she still love him?

Was I competing with a ghost?

I closed my eyes, but I couldn't get the crumpled car out of my mind, the pile of mangled metal still smoking like a tiny piece of hell.

I don't do heights. That's what she'd said at the zip-line... and I'd forced her hand.

The fight in the market started to make sense—when she told me that she was more acquainted with the concept of death than I ever would be.

How much more could I have possibly fucked up with her?

Just don't let me fall.

Her words crashed through me, shredding every last defense I'd had against her. She trusted me. Despite whatever nightmare she'd lived through, she'd put her hand in mine and trusted me with her life. That instant connection I'd felt with her, first on the balcony and then when I found her in my suite— it hadn't been one-sided. She'd felt it, too, enough to trust me less than an hour later.

I was the luckiest and the stupidest bastard on the planet.

"Pax? You ready?" Leah asked, startling me.

I'd been so lost in my thoughts that I hadn't noticed she'd

turned off the shower, let alone had time to get dressed. She stood in the doorway to the bedroom, wearing a tank top and pajama pants, her hair still wet and hanging to frame her breasts.

I stood and walked over to her, cradling her face between my hands. "You look beautiful."

She snorted. "Whatever makeup I had with me went down the shower drain."

Her eyes were still wide, the color like the tiger's-eye bracelet my mother loved, her skin flushed and soft. "You're all the more beautiful for it." I meant it. She wasn't a high-maintenance girl who took an hour to get ready to go to the store.

I kissed her gently, sipping at her lips. "Look, about the marketplace..."

She shook her head slightly, sliding her eyes shut. "Don't. We both said things. Maybe they were things that needed to be said, but we probably could have been a little nicer about it."

"Just a little," I agreed. "I'm going to hop in the shower."

She nodded, and I stole one more kiss before leaving her.

I washed quickly, steadying my nerves and doing my best to fortify my self-control to spend the night next to Leah and not make a move.

By the time I got to the bed, she was curled on her side, facing away from me. "I sleep in boxers; I hope you don't mind," I told her.

When she didn't respond, I watched the even rise of her rib cage, realizing she'd fallen asleep. Well, that made tonight a shit-ton easier.

I slid between the sheets and faced her, but kept my hands to myself. The king-size monstrosity we slept in left me plenty of room. The moonlight played off her skin, and she looked so damn touchable.

Problem was, I didn't only want to touch her. Scratch that, I spent more than a decent amount of time fantasizing about her under me, her soft thighs wrapped around my hips, back arching, lips screaming my name as I stroked us both to phenomenal orgasms. Hell, I didn't think I'd ever be able to look at her without that being on my brain somewhere.

But I wanted to touch her mind, too, to know what made her strong enough to put the harness on. To know what had kept her holding on to that canyon wall long after the car had fallen. And that wasn't even the scary part.

I wanted to touch her heart, to claim a piece for my own, and that was something I'd never wanted from another woman. I'd never wanted to stake a real claim or to feel something more than affectionate responsibility. But Leah? I wanted to strip away her defenses like she'd obliterated mine. It wasn't enough to take the piece, to own it by force. No, I wanted it freely given, wanted her to look at me, see me, and then deem me worthy.

Considering I hadn't asked for anyone's validation in the last decade, that was fucking terrifying.

She was more complicated than any woman I'd ever been with, or around, for that matter. But if I could win five gold medals at the X Games, I could sure as hell set my mind to winning Leah.

You commit, or you quit, but half-assed gets you hurt. My father's words slammed through my brain.

When I headed for a stunt, there was a moment where I pushed the throttle, committed to the ramp, threw my body into the flip, and that's exactly what this felt like as I stared at the curl that stretched across her pillow toward me.

I had to treat our relationship like I did everything else:

with full dedication and concentration. As of this moment, I was committed, and I'd never failed at something I worked for.

Eleanor Baxter wouldn't know what hit her.

CHAPTER FIFTEEN

LEAH

ISTANBUL

"You're going too fast!" I screamed. Why did I even bother? He never listened to me.

"Loosen up, Leah," Brian said, shooting me a side-eye as we approached the curve. "I want to see how the new tires hold."

"Stop! I know how this ends. Please don't!"

But he didn't slow.

I closed my eyes against the sound of the tires on the pavement, and my body detached from the motion of the car, but my mind knew it all vividly.

We destroyed the guardrail and plummeted.

The scream I heard was my own but not.

I blessedly missed the fall, even the impact when we hit the first tree. As I opened my eyes, my stomach dropped.

Yes, here—this was where the nightmare always started.

I turned my head and saw Brian, his head slumped forward, blood pouring from his abdomen where part of the tree that braced us skewered him. I knew what I had to do—what I always had to do when I found myself here, what took me eighteen hours to find the courage to do the first time.

I didn't need to try my door handle to know that it was jammed, or turn in my seat to know I couldn't make it up to the rear window without upsetting the balance of the car.

Maybe if I'd realized that it wouldn't work, that I'd have to crawl over Brian's body, I would have spared my legs.

Brian turned toward me, his head at a macabre angle, blood dripping from his dead, opaque eyes and ruined mouth, and I screamed, raw and painfully.

"You know what you have to do," he rasped.

And I did. The nightmare never ended until I actually did it.

"Leah!" he yelled...but it sounded all wrong.

"Leah, baby, it's okay." His voice broke through the nightmare. *Paxton.* "Wake up, Firecracker."

I sucked in a lungful of air, lurching forward and farther into Paxton's arms. They wrapped around me, strong and secure, while I buried my face in his neck, breathing in his scent, feeling his heartbeat with my hand against his naked chest.

"It's okay," he repeated, stroking one hand down my hair while the other cupped the base of my neck.

"Nightmare," I mumbled into his neck, trying to calm my breathing to match his.

"I figured," he answered, his chin resting on the top of my head. He'd wrapped one of his legs over my hips, cocooning me in safety and warmth, like he'd known exactly what I needed.

"Want to talk about it?" he offered.

I shook my head. There was no need to let him witness my traumatic past. "I have them sometimes," I admitted, wanting to give him something. "Especially when I'm stressed out."

"Okay," he said, still stroking my hair, my back, in wide,

soothing motions. "Just know that if you ever want to talk about it, I'm here."

I nodded, but there was zero chance in hell I was going there. Paxton flung himself off ramps, snowboarded down avalanche-prone mountains, skydived for fun. He was reckless, fearless, and not only knew the limits of his body but pushed it there every single day. There was no way he'd understand the fear from that night—or the next day—the moments that I'd nearly chosen to give in to gravity and simply let go.

My heart pounded like I was still in that ravine, scared to move in case I fell farther. I breathed deep, taking in the scent of Paxton's warm skin to erase the metallic memory of blood.

Then I pressed a kiss to his neck.

He inhaled sharply. "Leah."

"Paxton," I answered, pressing another openmouthed kiss to his neck.

His fingers tightened in my hair, but he didn't pull me away. I moved up, tasting under his jaw and savoring the low groan that came from his chest but radiated through my thighs.

My fingers slipped down the outside line of his abs until I reached the waistband of his boxers, where I ran them along the inside of the band.

"Leah," he said again, capturing my hand. "Do you know what you're doing?"

"If you're asking if I'm awake, the answer is yes." I kissed his ear.

He pulled back to lock his lust-glazed eyes with mine. "That's not what I'm asking."

"Yes," I answered, my voice shakier than I intended. I wanted him, wanted to feel his mouth on my skin, his lips on mine. But how far did I want it to go? Was I prepared to let him see all of me? "No. I don't know."

His forehead puckered. "I'm not the guy who takes a maybe as a yes."

God, why did he want an answer? Why did I have to make a choice? "I don't want to think." I didn't want to remember, or sleep again to fall into that nightmare. I just wanted to *feel*. My eyes pleaded with his to understand.

His softened. "Okay. Do you trust me?"

"With my life," I answered honestly. How could I not? We were alone in a foreign country, almost seven thousand miles from home, and I was in his bed.

"Good." With that word, he flipped me to my back, the movement so quick that I could only blink. His massive frame rose above me. "You're the one in control. You say stop, I stop. Got it?" he asked, his voice steady and sure despite the slight tremor in his hand as he brushed my hair off my cheek.

I nodded.

"Good. Then as of this moment, the only thought I want in your head is how many different ways I can make you come."

If I'd had a response it would have been swallowed by his mouth, inhaled by his kiss. He took my mouth completely, his kiss deep, thorough, and delicious. Our tongues rubbed and danced, and I gave myself over to the perfection of finally being in his arms.

I explored his back, the yards of smooth, warm skin that draped over his roped muscles. He felt exactly the way he looked—toned, strong, and sinful.

Jolts of pure want rocketed through me as he set his mouth to my neck, working his way down to my collarbone as his hands shaped the curve of my waist. "You taste so damn good," he said against my skin. "Like strawberries and summer rain."

He pulled down a strap of my tank top enough to free one of my breasts, and I arched, the tip already hard, wanting his mouth, his fingers—anything. "Perfect," he said reverently, then swirled his tongue around my nipple.

I cried out, my hands flying to his head to hold him to me.

"You like that, don't you?" he asked, lightly blowing over the skin.

Chills raced up my arms. "Yes," I answered shamelessly. If all I ever had was this one night with Paxton, then I wasn't going to waste it being coy.

"Good," he replied, then took my nipple into his mouth completely. He licked and sucked, drawing every ounce of response from one breast before freeing the other to do the same.

His mouth was magical, sending sensations through me I'd long since forgotten—the rush of desire, the restlessness I knew instinctively that he could quell. But this need building within me, this primal demand to feel him deep within me—that was on a level I'd never experienced.

He tugged at the bottom of my tank top, and I lifted my arms as he pulled it off, leaving me bare to him. He studied me for a moment, his eyes dark with desire, and for the first time in the last couple of years, I felt beautiful, desirable, wanted—all because I felt like his.

He brought his mouth back to mine, kissing me with a hunger that had me whimpering with each deep, skilled thrust of his tongue against mine. He never stilled against my breasts, rolling my nipples between his fingers, caressing me in ways that fueled the deep ache that grew stronger inside me.

When I draped my leg over his hip, he settled between my thighs. His weight was exquisite, holding my body to the earth while he gave my soul the freedom to fly. As he rocked forward, I felt his erection hard between us, and instead of shrinking, I rocked back, reveling in the friction against my center.

He thrust forward again, sending sparks through me as he hit my clit, the fabric between us only heightening the sensation. "Is that what you want, Leah?" he asked, his breath hot against my ear, his breathing bordering on ragged.

I whimpered again, answering him with another push of my hips.

He drew back, denying me the pressure I was desperate for. "It's what I want. Except I want you naked, so I can feel all of your skin against me, taste the tiny beads of sweat I'll work you into."

I tried to roll up again, but he brought his hands to my hips, pinning me to the bed. "Paxton," I whined, trying to reach to kiss him, to get any part of him I could.

"Tell me, I want to hear you say it."

"Why? You know I want you. Isn't that enough?" I asked.

His thumbs caressed my hip bones, but I wanted more. Needed more.

"No. I want the words." He leaned down, dragging his tongue across my lower lip. When I tried to get more, he pulled back, no trace of teasing on his face. "I want to know that I have you on the same fucking edge you've had me dangling on for weeks now, desperate to know how you feel, taste, sound when you're coming apart."

His words—those sweet, seductive, dirty freaking words turned me up another notch, deepened the pulsing ache I had right where his hips were pressed. How the hell could I keep up with this man?

"Words give you power over me," I admitted. I tried to

roll my hips again, but he held me pinned, immobile. "You're already the one in control."

He lowered his head, dragging his tongue from the line of my pajama bottoms, past my belly button, through the valley of my breasts and ending at my neck before he kissed me. There was an edge of desperation to his kiss that hadn't been there before, like he could kiss my compliance from me.

He damn near did. I would have done almost anything to keep him kissing me like that, but it wasn't enough. My body was on fire, demanding a release I'd denied it for way too long.

"Control?" he questioned as he pulled away, those blue eyes digging into my soul in a way nothing else could. "Okay, I like being in control, especially when I have you underneath me. But the power is all yours. You just have to realize that I will do whatever you ask, whatever you need. I might control your body, but you control every...part...of...me." He punctuated each word with a slight thrust against me, the pressure enough to send tendrils of pleasure through my limbs as if he'd caressed my entire body. "Now tell me what you want. I am yours to command."

"I want your hands on me," I answered. Then, before he could ask me where, I showed him, taking one of his hands and sliding it under the waistband of my drawstring pants.

He groaned, his forehead leaning on mine, his eyes closed tight while his fingers slipped under the pink lace underwear the hotel had brought with my change of clothes for tomorrow.

His hand stilled, covering me completely for a moment, like he was savoring it. I arched my hips up, and he gave in, his fingers sliding through me. His breath left in a rush against my lips. "Fuck, you're so wet. I could slide inside you so easily right now."

"Then why don't you?" I challenged him, needing him inside me, a part of me.

He kissed my mouth softly as his thumb drew a lazy circle around my clit. "Because the first time I'm inside you, it will be because you're running toward me, to us, not away from something else."

I gasped as he lightly stroked me, dragging his thumb at the most sublime pressure. "Paxton," I begged. I just wished I knew exactly what for.

He switched his angle and slid one finger within me. "Tight. So damn tight. How long has it been?" he asked, stroking my inner walls.

"Years," I answered truthfully.

"God, I can't wait to be here." He stroked me again, sending spirals of fire through every nerve in my body. "You have no idea how good it's going to be between us."

"And you do?" I asked, gasping as he pressed on my clit.

"The way you respond to me? How wet you are? Your body is practically begging for mine, Leah. Here?" He inserted another finger, and my back bowed off the bed. It felt so damn good. "You're going to squeeze me perfectly, and I'm going to make you so glad that you said yes."

I rocked my hips against his hand, moving his fingers within me. "And you?" I asked with what brain power I had left.

He took my other hand and placed it on his erection. I squeezed his length gently, my eyes widening at the size of him.

"I've never been this hard for a woman. This desperate. I've never had to hold myself back and not take exactly what I wanted, and I've never wanted anyone the way I crave you. That's how I know we'll be good together. Because what we have right here is better than anything I've ever had."

Then he kissed me, his tongue moving in rhythm with his fingers below, stroking, teasing, giving me just enough to keep me on edge, but not enough to tip me over.

"What do you want?" he whispered again. "I'll give you whatever you want."

"Paxton," I begged.

"Say it."

"Let me come," I pleaded, knowing he held it back on purpose, loving that he had that control over my body as much as I hated it.

"God, yes," he groaned. Then he rubbed my clit, giving me the perfect amount of pressure and friction to curl my toes. When he stroked his fingers upward inside me, that blessed pressure tightened in my belly, so sweet I could taste it with his tongue moving with mine.

He worked me expertly, keeping the pressure steady, the rhythm perfect until that tightening grew unbearable and my body took over, riding back against him, my hands in his hair, desperate to hold on to whatever of him I could.

"Paxton!" I cried out his name as the tension broke in beautiful waves over me, releasing parts of my heart into his keeping with the same breath.

"You're exquisite," he said as he stroked me back down, kicking back the orgasm with skilled motions.

My heartbeat slowed along with my breathing, a peaceful lethargy stealing over my limbs. "You," I said, my hands moving down the rigid muscles of his abdomen.

He trapped my hands. "Nope. My control is one touch away from snapping."

It was ridiculously selfish, but the gesture made me feel separate from his conquests, like I was special—like we had something special.

He brushed a damp tendril of hair from my forehead. "Don't look at me like that. I'm not a martyr."

"Really?" I teased, rubbing my hips gently against his hard-on.

He eased off me and then turned my body in his arms, spooning against my back. *OMG, and he spoons? Paxton Wilder spoons.*

"Really. I have devious plans for you, Miss Baxter. They just won't happen here. But trust me. Very devious. I'd be bold enough to say nefarious."

I groaned. "Talk vocabulary to me, baby."

He laughed, the sound warming me even more than his raging body heat. "Downright diabolical, my little Firecracker."

Through the sliding glass door next to our bed, I watched a shooting star streak across the sky.

I wish that I could always feel like this.

Had there ever been a more romantic, perfect setting?

Sure, back on the ship...where you're supposed to be.

"What did you wish for?" he asked.

I turned in his arms and traced the lines of his face. "I wished I could be as fearless as you," I said, my hand absently stroking the head of his dragon tattoo.

"I'm not fearless. There are plenty of things that scare me."

I looked up at him, his features softened by moonlight. "Like what?"

"Snakes," he answered with a self-deprecating half smile. "They're slimy little fuckers who move without feet. It's unnatural."

My lips turned up. "What else?"

His forehead puckered. "The first time I bungee jumped. I didn't like that someone else had measured the line, decided how far I'd go. It wasn't fun, putting my life in someone's hands like that."

"But you did it."

"Yeah."

"Why?" My fingers slid along the dragon's spine that curved outside his pec, and down the tail that outlined his abs. I stopped short of the spiked ending that led to his incredible fuck-me lines, remembering not to torture him more.

He sucked in his breath as my fingers moved back up. "Because I knew it would haunt me if I didn't. Because I knew there was something exquisite waiting just past the fear if I could get there."

"And now that you're a daredevil extraordinaire?"

"There are still plenty of things that scare me."

"What scares you the most?"

His fingers threaded through the hair at the base of my skull and then tugged, guiding me to look up at him. He looked into my eyes for what seemed like an eternity. "You. You scare the shit out of me."

My heart lurched, instinctively reaching for his. "I'm not scary."

"No, you're terrifying. On paper you're everything I shouldn't mesh with, but I look at you, touch you, or get my mouth on you, and you're the only thing I see, the only one I want, and that's by far the scariest thought I've ever had."

"I'm just me."

His hand slid until his thumb stroked my cheekbones. "You are everything and don't even see it. You're smart, and strong, and so beautiful that you make me ache when I look at you."

"Don't say things like that," I whispered, my brain scrambling to build any wall around my heart while it did its best to reach for Paxton.

"Things like the truth?"

"Things that make me want what I can't have."

"You can have me, Leah. I'm yours for the asking."

There was nothing but honesty in his eyes—and God, I wanted to believe it. I wanted to be his, even if it was only for this moment, and not just physically.

He lifted his chin over my head, tucking me in. "Get some sleep, Firecracker. We have an early flight."

Despite the overpowering exhaustion I knew was the result of stress, our day, the nightmare, and a spectacular orgasm, I had to know. "What did you wish for?"

He sighed. "For you to give me a second chance."

My eyebrows puckered, but my limbs felt too heavy to move. "You haven't done anything wrong."

"It's not for now. It's for later."

"That's not necessary," I slurred as I drifted off, but just before I was pulled under, I heard the faintest whisper against my forehead.

"It will be."

CHAPTER SIXTEEN

LEAH

Istanbul

"First class?" I asked as we took our seats in the front row of the airplane.

"It's not hard to do when the plane is this small," Paxton answered, buckling his seat belt as I did the same.

The plane was tiny, with only about sixteen of us on board. "It's cozy."

"It's a sardine can with propellers," he muttered, looking past me at the window.

"You don't like flying," I said, a smile tugging at my lips.

"Not too fond of it," he answered, cracking his neck. The lines of his tattoos flexed with the movement.

The middle-aged man across the aisle noticed, too, frowning his disapproval.

"How can you, of all people, not like flying?"

"It's a control thing. I like having it."

"I noticed," I said as the flight attendant raised the door and sealed it for takeoff.

He rolled his eyes but didn't take the bait. Instead, he let out a huge, jaw-cracking yawn. We'd slept in this morning and barely made the flight, but hey, it wasn't like we could lose luggage we didn't have. I fingered the beautiful white skinny jeans that must have set him back a fortune to have delivered, especially with the blue silk top I'd found when we woke up this morning. He'd shrugged and said it was only money, but to me it was so much more.

It was the thought he'd put into it, the fact that he'd cared enough to get the right sizes, that he'd bought me pants instead of shorts or a skirt.

What I wouldn't give for a short, flirty skirt. Something that swirled a little when I turned, that left my legs bare to the sun.

But bare to his eyes, too.

"What are you thinking about?" he asked as we rolled toward the runway, another yawn distorting his last word.

"That you look awfully tired this morning."

"That's because you kept me up all night with your demands," he answered, closing his eyes and leaning back in his seat.

The gentleman across the aisle sputtered in his coffee.

"I most certainly did *not,*" I fired back in a stage whisper.

He cracked one eyelid as we barreled down the runway. "I'm sorry, was that not you under me last night? Asking me to put my hands on you, begging me to let you come?"

Now the guy was actually coughing, his wife slapping him on the back.

I glared at Paxton. "Seriously?" Not only was it hugely embarrassing to hear him say that, but I wasn't comfortable with the way it immediately flipped my sex switch to "go for launch."

He gave me a hot-as-hell grin as his hand worked its way

up my thigh. I promptly returned it to his own lap. "Relax," he whispered in my ear. "We'll never see these people again."

"I'm never going to see *you* again," I muttered, flipping open the emergency procedures booklet. What I wouldn't have given for my Kindle.

Paxton's grip tightened on the armrest between us. I'd never imagined that he wouldn't like something as simple as flying, but it was oddly endearing to see one tiny flaw in his impenetrable armor. I covered his hand with mine and gave him a reassuring squeeze as we launched into the air.

His breaths were even and steady, but his eyes stayed closed until we finished our climb to altitude. "You okay?" I asked.

His eyes finally opened, and he nodded. "Yeah. I'm just not a fan of takeoffs and landings."

"Yeah, I can understand that. Has it always been that way?"

He shook his head, focused on the space directly ahead of us. "I was flying with my mom once when an engine caught fire."

"Oh. That must have been terrifying. How old were you?"

"Nine. And yeah, it was scary, but I knew she'd keep me safe." A slight smile touched his lips.

"Did she hold your hand?" I tried to imagine a little Paxton, without tattoos, slightly needy.

"Hell no. She had both hands on the controls."

"She was the pilot," I guessed.

He nodded. "She's always had one foot on the ground and the other climbing for the sky."

She sounded just like her son. "So have you been nervous ever since then?"

He shrugged. "It's gotten a lot better. For the first years after it was hard to get in a plane, but I managed. What about you?"

"Oddly enough, flying doesn't bother me." I reached for the *Visit Istanbul* pamphlet in the pocket in front of us and started to flip through.

"No, I meant with cars?"

My fingers locked on the page showing the Cistern, my stomach dropping thousands of feet to the earth below. *He didn't mean it. He's talking about something else.*

I gave him a sideways glance and saw his eyes blown wide, then squeezing shut with a long breath.

He fucking knew.

I might as well have been sitting there naked with how exposed I felt. Even his inappropriate little comment earlier hadn't done this to me. My hands shook, but I turned the page, looking over the intricate details of the Blue Mosque. "How long have you known?" I asked, my voice a hell of a lot calmer than I was right now.

"Known what?" he tried.

"Cut the bullshit."

"Last night." He looked at me, but I stayed locked in my safe little booklet.

"Well then, you certainly can't keep a secret for long, can you?" I flipped another page. Why the hell were we on a plane? My knee started to bounce with restless energy, with the need to get away from him. Every single seat on this plane was taken, so it was either sit here or parachute.

"I didn't mean to say anything. It just slipped." He reached for my hand, and I jerked farther toward the window. *Parachuting looks like a great option.*

"Like your fingers slipped on the keyboard while you googled me?" I threw back.

His eyes closed briefly. "No, I deliberately did that."

No apology. What a first-class asshole. "Is this because I googled you?"

"No. God, no, Leah. I wanted to know how to help you, and I couldn't do that without knowing what you'd gone through. It was obvious that you'd had some kind of trauma."

My head snapped like he'd struck me. I wasn't proud of much, but I'd done a damn good job of recovering. Or at least faking it. "I told you that I wasn't ready to talk about it, that I wasn't your project to fix. When the hell did you find time last night to invade my privacy?"

"It's on the internet. Not exactly private," he pleaded for understanding.

Fuck. That. "When?"

"While you were in the shower. Please look at me."

I snapped the booklet closed and looked at him, only to immediately look away. Those eyes of his were an unfair advantage in an argument. *Wait. In the shower...before. Oh God.* I flicked the booklet back open and let anger take the place of mortification. "So was that a pity orgasm last night? Or were you just hoping to see if I'd show you where the damage is?"

Paxton's mouth dropped open before he snapped it shut, mirroring the guy across the aisle. "Eyes forward," his wife ordered him in English. Good woman.

"Hey," Paxton said, his voice deceptively soft. "What happened last night was because I wanted you, plain and simple."

"Right, and that's why you didn't fuck me when I asked you to, right? Because you wanted me soooo badly," I sang. God, I was going to throw up, or throw something at him. Either choice was reasonable.

The guy across the aisle started to whistle.

"Fuck," Paxton muttered under his breath before raking his hands over his hair. "You have no idea how hard it was for me not to—"

"Oh, I remember how hard it was. I was there."

Now the guy behind us started coughing.

"Leah."

"Oh, don't worry. We'll never see these people again, right?" I tore the page I was turning. "Fuck. Well, that's broken now, so no use trying to read it. Or maybe I should try the next page...you know, to make it feel not so broken."

"Look, if you want, I'll take you to the bathroom and show you how badly I want you. You're right, we won't see these people again, so I don't give a fuck if they hear you screaming my name."

That brought me up short. Everyone could hear us. I lowered my voice to a hiss. "Whatever. So did you get your curiosity appeased? Read the details? The speculation? Of course you did. You all do. Then the questions start."

"It's not like that."

"Go ahead and ask. Let's get it all done now. After all, your fingers have been inside me, may as well rip apart my head, too."

I kept rolling, embracing the anger that burned my veins like acid, eating away the glimpse of happiness I'd had in his arms. "You all want to know the same thing. Why was he in such a hurry to get home after our date? Didn't I ask him to slow down? How long was it before I decided I had to climb out over Brian's body? Was he still alive when we hit the first time? Why did I unbuckle? Why did I wait so long? How many times did the car fall? Was it hard to use my dead boyfriend as a step stool to get out? How long did I hang there on the cliff face? Did my fingers go numb? Did they bleed? Did I think about letting go? Did I want to die?"

"Leah!" Paxton snapped, forcibly turning my head to meet his eyes. "Stop."

"Why?" I asked, my voice breaking as tears pooled, stinging me with my own weakness. "Don't you want to know? You all do. You all want to dig inside, to know every detail like you were there, like it's your story. Like by knowing my tragedy you can somehow touch it. Well you can't, it's mine. I was alone then, and I'm alone now."

He flinched before his eyes narrowed in focus. "Stop assuming I'm everyone. I've lived my life making sure that no one is like me, so don't lump me in with those assholes."

"But you looked," I whispered, a tear slipping down my face.

He wiped it away with his thumb. "I can't say that I'm sorry I looked. Because I looked, because I fucked up and slipped, we're having this conversation now. Yes, it was a violation of your privacy. Yes, you did it to me, but this was not payback. I knew you guarded your legs. I'm not clueless. I can't imagine what you would have done had I tried to take off your pants, and believe me, getting in your pants has been at the top of my list since I saw you on that balcony."

Some of the fight drained from me. I hated that he was right, that I would have freaked out on him and ran the minute he tried to slip my jeans down my hips, but that didn't excuse what he'd done. How he made me feel.

"I'm not sorry that I know," he continued, his expression softening. "But I wish you'd been the one to tell me. That you would have trusted me."

"It's not about trust. It's about ripping open scabs I've barely let heal. That accident, losing Brian that way...it was the worst thing that has ever happened to me. It is something that changed who I am, what I'm capable of, and how I view my future. You had no right to cut open my scars. Just because you live your life in some transparent, camera-ridden world doesn't mean that the rest of us believe in cellophane for our bedroom walls. Some of us need to block out the light. Some of us need to lick our wounds in private."

"You're right," he said, wiping another tear that I hadn't realized had fallen. "My life is a public spectacle. But please don't think that you can find everything about me on Google."

"Okay. Then what is the worst thing that has ever happened to you? And I'm not talking about broken bones or failed stunts." I wanted him as raw as he'd scraped me, as vulnerable.

He swallowed, looking up to the cabin ceiling before he took a deep breath. "What's the one quality you have to see in someone you care about?"

My forehead puckered. "Honesty. You don't lie to someone you care about."

He nodded, like he was accepting my answer. "Mine is loyalty. With what we do, I have to know that I can trust my friends with my life. Hell, with more than my life."

"Okay?" Where was he going with this?

"My best friend betrayed me."

"What? How?"

He exhaled. "He slept with the only girl I'd ever called my girlfriend."

I couldn't decide if I was more offended that he thought that was even in the same league, or more surprised Paxton was anyone's second choice.

"I know it's an anthill next to your mountain. I'm not trying to compare the two. But yeah, I liked a girl. Liked her enough that I didn't even try to sleep with her. I dated her by the book, and the book got me fucked. Or rather, got *him* fucked. And the funny thing was that it wasn't even the girl who broke me, it was him. It was my notion of who and what I trusted about my life. For months he looked me in the eye and called me his best friend while he stuck a knife in my back. The same guy who helped me tune my bike and pack the chutes that kept me alive..." He sighed. "It ripped the ground from under me, took my gravity, spun the world backward, you name it. She didn't break my heart—he did."

"What happened with him?" I asked, trying to imagine what I'd do had it been Rachel. He was right. The loss of the friendship would destroy me.

"I couldn't stand to be around them, and once they were over, he and I hated being around each other, looking at what we'd cost the other. We seriously couldn't manage being in the same room, so we went our separate ways until we could."

Nick. That must have been where the fourth Original Renegade was. Banished for taking his girlfriend. That's why they kept him out of the media. Paxton was embarrassed. "How long ago was it?"

"A while," he answered, giving me the same answer I'd initially given him about my own heartbreak.

We sat in a tense silence for a few minutes while the normal noise of the plane came back to life. At least we weren't the in-flight entertainment anymore.

I looked out of the window, over the bluest water I'd ever seen. *Mediterranean blue.* It was its own unique color, deep and bright all in the same breath. Just like Paxton's eyes.

What was going to change between us now? Would I be off his radar since he knew how damaged I was? I rested my head against the seat and sighed. Maybe it was better this way, that I hadn't stressed about how to tell him, that he hadn't taken one look at my legs and blanched. Yeah. Maybe this was better. And maybe if I said that enough, I'd believe it.

He was quiet so long that I figured he'd fallen asleep.

"Leah," he said, startling me.

I steadied my nerves and turned back to him. "What?"

"You need to know that it doesn't matter to me," he said, his eyes open and honest. "Well, it matters because it hurt you, shaped you. But the rest of it? None of it matters. I hope one day you'll tell me so that I understand *you* better, but that's the only reason. I read one article that gave vague details, and then I shut it down. I wasn't digging for gory details, or voyeurism. I just wanted to know about you."

"Okay," I said, nodding my head because I was too drained to argue anymore. I wanted to hide away in private and lick my wounds, both the ones he'd inflicted, and the ones I'd caused with my own very public reaction.

He tipped my chin toward his. "And I don't care about whatever physical damage you're hiding."

I almost laughed. "You have the body of a Greek god."

A wry smile lifted the corners of his perfect lips. "I have more scars than you can count. More broken bones than could ever mend. You are far more perfect than I will ever be. I shouldn't have looked, but I did. And now I know, and you know that I know, and the whole plane knows, too."

I rolled my eyes. "And what are you going to do with this knowledge?"

"Understand you better. Learn what makes you tick, what

makes you pull away when I get too close, what it's going to take to break down those walls of yours."

"They're pretty thick," I admitted, knowing they were damn near unscalable.

"Good news for me is that I'm exceptionally good at defying...well, everything."

Our eyes locked—anger, fear, regret, and a new understanding passing between us with a simple glance. He kept me tethered with nothing more than a thought, unable to move or pull away. Then he lowered his head slowly, giving me ample time to pull away if I wanted to.

I didn't.

He brushed his lips over mine in a kiss so tender that my eyes watered all over again. "Nothing matters to me except how you feel about it now. How it affects you now. What you choose to do about it *now*."

"I'm doing the best I can," I answered truthfully.

He nodded. "I get that. But I need you to understand something. To know it in your bones."

"What?"

That devilishly sexy look flickered across his features. "My number one goal is still to get into your pants—and stay there as long as possible."

I almost snorted, but his comment gave me back the one thing his knowledge had stripped away—my confidence.

CHAPTER SEVENTEEN

PAXTON

MYKONOS

Leah's excitement was palpable as we headed out of the airport. It bubbled around her like a living, breathing thing as she took in every detail around us.

"You know this is just the airport, right?" I asked, reaching out my hand for her backpack. How funny that it had only been meant to last us the day trip in Istanbul and now it was our sole piece of luggage for days.

"But it's Mykonos," she said, her smile brilliant as she handed me the bag.

I swung it over my shoulder, glad she was talking to me. I'd been nervous the rest of the flight until she'd taken my hand during landing.

"Pink is definitely your color," she joked as we left the shade of the awning and stepped into the sunshine.

"Men who *don't* wear pink have masculinity issues," I argued.

She laughed, the sound peeling away another one of my layers. If I didn't watch it, this girl was going to have my soul bare. After my confession on the plane, I felt like I'd already stripped.

"Okay, so where are we going?" she asked as I led her through the parking lot.

"Right about…" I pointed toward the usual place. "There."

She looked from the bright blue Jeep Wrangler to me and back again as we came up to it. "And what are we going to do with this?"

I squatted down in front of the left wheel and pulled out the key that had been taped there, dangling it from my fingers. "I figured we'd drive it?"

She crossed her arms under her breasts, the lace of her bra clearly defined against the silk of her shirt. "You cannot steal someone's car."

Oh, this was too much damn fun. I opened her door, popped the glove box open, and handed her the registration. Without waiting for her to read, I started unzipping the top.

"Wait…" She shook her head as I was finishing up. "I don't read Greek, but…that's your name. How is that your name?"

"Because I own it."

Her beautiful forehead puckered. "I don't understand."

"No, but you will," I promised as I motioned for her to climb in.

Once she was buckled, I took off, my turns extra careful and my speed beneath the limit. As we made our way up along the side of the terraced hill, I kept near the middle of the road unless there was someone coming in our direction.

"Whoa," she said as we crested the first hill.

"Yeah," I agreed. The port was spread out beneath us, the waters of the Aegean the greenish blue I missed every day that I wasn't here. Against the backdrop of the shoreline, the white houses, and that little windmill I was fond of, it was gorgeous. Sitting next to Leah, her hair coming loose from its bun, the wisps flying in the breeze, and the top of the Jeep off, it was perfection.

She turned in her seat, trying to keep the view as we headed inland.

"Don't worry. I'll bring you back later. You've never seen anything until you see the sunsets here."

"You've been here," she said, her little eyebrows drawn together.

"Yes," I answered, keeping my hands on the wheel and off her. As the streets narrowed, I slowed to almost a crawl. A branch of pink flowers overhung the gate above us, and I quickly snagged one of the flowers, tucking it behind her ear as I brought my hand back into the Jeep.

"A lot?" she asked, her fingers tracing the outline of the flower.

"Yes."

She rolled her eyes. "Are you going to explain yourself?"

I couldn't stop my grin. "In about ten minutes."

"You owe me," she muttered.

"Anything you want," I promised, picking up her hand and kissing the soft skin on the back of it.

When I lowered our hands to the console between us, she didn't let go.

I knew we were on tentative ground, where our relationship had no definition, but that also meant it had no boundaries—no limits. In that moment, holding her hand in mine was everything.

I wasn't even going to stop to examine how frightening that thought was. No. I was just going to enjoy it.

We neared the other side of the island, where we pulled off onto a dirt road that led to a large white arched gate. "I keep telling her that she needs more security than this," I muttered as we drove straight through.

The house itself was white and fairly large by Mykonos standards, single-level until it followed the terrace of the natural landscape down the hill behind it toward the beach.

We pulled into the circular driveway, and I kissed Leah's hand again. "I need you to know something before we go in there."

"Okay?" she said, her eyes darting between me and the woman who had run out of the front door, her arms wide open.

"I've never brought another woman here." Because no one had meant anything to me. Because I didn't want to give the wrong impression. Because this was my haven, my safety, the one place I could get the hell off the grid, and I didn't want some ex-girlfriend knowing about it.

Because maybe...maybe I had been saving it for Leah.

She gave me a shaky smile, and I nodded before letting her go and jumping out of the Jeep.

"Honey, I'm home!" I called as a petite figure raced into my arms. She was still too damn thin, and I lifted her off her feet, spinning her in a circle.

"Put me down and let me see you!" She laughed in my ear.

I did, my smile uncontrollable. God, I'd missed her—missed everything about her, but nothing more than the way she made me feel, like I was something precious. "I look the same as I did six months ago."

"Liar," she accused me, her eyes a familiar shade of blue. "And who did you bring to meet me?" She took my hand and turned us to where Leah stood outside the Jeep, her knuckles white where she gripped her little backpack.

I moved toward Leah until she took my outstretched hand, her eyes wide and all the more captivating for her nervousness.

"Leah, I'd like you to meet my mother. Mom, this is Eleanor Baxter, the woman in charge of keeping me on the straight and narrow this year."

"Your mom?" Leah said softly.

"Leah!" Mom crushed Leah to her in a hug that would have crippled larger men. Then she pulled back and put her hands on either side of Leah's face as she'd done to mine. "What a natural beauty."

"Our boat left us behind in Istanbul and kind of sailed away with my makeup," Leah said with a grimace.

"Well, you wouldn't know it," Mom reassured her. "How are your grades? What are you doing with your future?"

Leah's eyes widened into huge pools of panic. "I'm near the top of my class at Dartmouth, majoring in international relations, and I'm applying to graduate programs once we're back stateside."

Mom nodded. "What do you like about my son?"

Leah's eyes flickered toward me then back to Mom. "He's true to his word, and his reckless streak is a little addictive."

Mom nodded thoughtfully. "What don't you like about my son?"

Leah relaxed, arching an eyebrow. "His reckless streak runs a little too wide."

Mom laughed. "That is far too true." She dropped her hands, clapping them together. "Are you two together?"

"No," she answered.

"Yes," I said at the same time.

Mom gave me *the* look, and I closed my mouth.

"Maybe," Leah conceded. I nearly cheered. Hell, I'd take an inch as progress with her. "It's complicated."

Mom nodded. "It always is with Wilder men, dear. I like

you. Now, let's get you settled."

She turned to walk into the house, and Leah just about sagged in relief.

I took her backpack and put my arm around her shoulders.

"You could have warned me," she accused.

"And miss that? Never." I tucked her closer to me, loving the feel of her curves against my frame.

"Did I at least pass the test?" she asked quietly.

"You passed it when he brought you here, dear," Mom answered ahead of us, opening the door. I rushed ahead to hold it for them. "That was just for fun."

"I see where you get it from," Leah said with a shake of her head as we all walked inside.

Home. That was the only word that fit whenever I walked into this house. The open floor plan made the floor-to-ceiling windows, and therefore the sea, the main attraction, all the furnishings in the house comfortably minimalist.

It was the one property out of dozens that she'd asked for during the divorce.

"Paxton, why don't you take her down the hall to the bedrooms. You take the blue one and give her the white one with the ocean view. Leah, it's right across the hall from Paxton's just in case that maybe turns into a yes." She threw Leah a wink and headed toward the other end of the house where her room was.

Leah was quiet as I walked her to her room. Well, my room. But I didn't mind giving it to her, knowing it meant she'd be in my bed—the bed she immediately sat on when we walked in.

She gazed out the window, where there was an unencumbered view of the beach below. "It's beautiful here."

"Yeah," I answered, watching the way a slight smile tugged

at her lips. "It is." I'd had those lips on mine, tasted her tongue, felt the way she came apart under my hands. She was every bit the firework I'd known she would be, and I couldn't touch her. Not until she'd made the decision to trust me with everything she was. "You know, I'm going to get settled. There's a computer there if you want to log in to eCampus. I know you're dying to." I pointed to the desk on the opposite side of the bed. "There are some of my clothes in that dresser. They'll be too big for you, but they might work to sleep in tonight." With each word I backed up a little more, until I was standing in the doorframe.

"Are you running away?" she asked.

"Yep," I answered truthfully. "It's that, or I start persuading you to take off your clothes."

She gave me a purely incredulous look. "Seriously?"

"Seriously." Now I was standing in the hall, but I wasn't sure the distance was safe enough, not as tightly strung as I was over her. "Okay, well, I have a practice area here, so I'm going to go check everything out."

"I'll wave a red flag if I get turned on," she answered with a smile.

Fuck it. I crossed the distance between us, taking her mouth in a kiss that was blatantly sexual, my tongue moving inside her mouth the way I craved moving inside the rest of her body. I kissed her like I'd left a piece of my soul with her and I needed to explore every line of her mouth to find it.

She groaned, her fingers digging into my shirt, kissing me back with her own fierce demands.

I'd never felt such a primal need in my life. Not just to fuck her, or even make love to her, but to brand her in a way that she'd never doubt that she was mine, that I was hers.

I broke the kiss and backed away with my hands in the air.

"Yeah, red flag. Good idea."

Then I walked away from her as fast as I could. *You fucking ran, admit it.*

"Paxton, you need to eat something before you head out to that track," Mom called from the kitchen in Greek.

"I'm fine," I answered, but I still pulled out a stool and sat at the bar, the white granite cool beneath my fingers. There was no point arguing with Mom when food was involved.

She put a grilled cheese in front of me and then rested her palms on the counter as I devoured it in about five bites. "God, I miss these," I said, my mouth full.

"What are you doing with the girl, Paxton?" she asked.

"Or we can cut right to it," I said before taking a long sip of iced tea. She still made it sweet—the way Dad liked it.

"She's not your usual type."

I looked away, knowing she'd cut straight through my bullshit. "You don't like her?"

"On the contrary. I might like her too much. At least, too much to let you crush her if you're only interested in the chase."

"That's not fair. She's not like anyone else. She's...she's special to me."

Her eyes softened. "I knew that the moment you showed up with her. You and I have always been birds of the same feather. Nothing ties us down for long. But, Paxton, not everyone is built like us, and you need to keep that in mind before you turn that young woman's maybe into a yes. The life you lead..."

"I can have a relationship, too. I deserve to try." I hated that she saw every problem at its base, every fire at its point of origin.

"You deserve love, Paxton. You deserve a woman who is going to stand by you and support the wild things you do, because it's part of who you are. You deserve to watch yourself through her eyes, to grow into who you can become simply because she deserves your best. But that also means that you have to be willing to change."

Leah's face ran through my mind. How she looked when I first saw her on the balcony, the way her lips slightly swelled when I kissed her, the way I hadn't been tempted by any other girl since I met her. "Maybe I am. Maybe I'm ready."

She squeezed my hand, her eyes lit with a fire I hadn't seen in years. "Maybe you are. Now go tune up your bike—I know you want to—and I should take Leah shopping so she's not stuck wearing your old clothes while she's here."

Leah. Wearing my boxers and a white tank top. Or my pajama pants so loose that I could slide them over her ass. I nearly groaned at the thought. "That would be great. Use my credit card."

She scoffed. "I have more money than I know what to do with."

I leaned over the counter and kissed her cheek. "I know. I just like spending mine on Leah."

She waved me off, and I headed out back, savoring the warmth of the sun as it soaked into my skin. This place had always healed my soul, even when I was a kid. Through the fights and the inevitable divorce, Mykonos had always given me a safe haven.

I hoped it could do the same for Leah.

CHAPTER EIGHTEEN

LEAH

MYKONOS

I messed with my hair for the hundredth time and finally settled on leaving it down. Down said I hadn't messed with it that many times, right? It said that I wasn't nervous. Was I seriously depending on my hair to lie for me?

The minute Paxton had told me to be ready at five o'clock, I'd broken into a sweat. Thank God I'd picked up deodorant, makeup, and a few new outfits to tide me over until the ship came in a few days.

His mom had been amazing, the perfect amount of distance and intrusion—enough to let me know she was interested in me, but not enough to make me feel like I was being inspected. Plus, she had great taste in clothing.

My gaze darted to the white halter dress that hung from the closet door. It was tight on top with spaghetti straps around the neck and then flared out to just above my knees in a breezy flow of fabric. It felt like freedom, flirtation, sex appeal, and Greece, so I bought it on impulse after I tried it on. But it left my legs bare.

He already knows.

I sighed. If I was going to try to be anything real with Paxton, he was inevitably going to see the train wreck of scars down my legs. He said he wouldn't care, and I trusted him. For God's sake, he'd brought me home and introduced me to his mother. If he could open up a piece of his soul, I could handle a couple awkward looks from strangers.

Five minutes later, I'd traded my linen pants for the sundress, slipping into the little wedge heels his mom had insisted on. I backed up enough to see my full reflection in the dresser mirror. The scars were straight, thick lines that ran from my knee to my ankle along the front of my shin, with smaller marks that ran along both sides. Maybe they wouldn't have been that thick if that infection hadn't set in...or if I'd gotten out of the car sooner...

If. If. If.

I shook my head and blew out a long breath. None of that mattered—not anymore.

A quick touch of lip gloss and then I walked out of the bedroom and down the hallway to the kitchen, where I heard Paxton laughing at something his mother said. He was different here—lighter, all Paxton and no Wilder.

All mine. My jaw nearly dropped when I saw him casually leaning up over the counters to put away groceries for his mom. It wasn't just the cut of his button-up shirt, or the way it was loosely rolled on his arms to reveal his colorful tattoos, or even the way his cargo shorts hung on him. It was the domesticity of the moment, seeing him truly relaxed and at peace.

It made my heart lurch, reaching for a future where he'd put the cereal into the cabinet, or sneak in way too much junk food. A future where we shared a kitchen, a home...a life. It was a dream I had no right to even think about, and one I didn't realize how desperately I wanted until this moment.

I was falling for Paxton so fast that I wasn't sure even one of his parachutes could save me.

"Hey, you ready?" I asked, my voice shakier than I intended.

He glanced over and then did a double-take, his mouth slack-jawed. My heart pounded as he came closer, his quick strides eating the distance between us. His eyes drifted from head to toe and back up again, and the air stilled in my chest as the world paused.

"You look amazing," he told me, but it was his eyes that let me breathe again. They darkened with want as he leaned in, his mouth brushing my ear. "You make that dress sexy as hell, and if my mother wasn't across the room, my hands would already be under it."

My eyes fluttered shut, relief washing over me with the same force as the desire pounding through me at the mention of his hands. I knew what they could do, how they could set my body on fire, and I wanted it again—wanted him. "You look good, too."

Lame compliment compared to what the sight of him did to me, but it earned me a smile as he backed up a step.

"You two have fun. I have plans for the evening," his mom called, rattling her keys as she walked out the front door.

"You ready to say yes yet?" he asked, his eyes bright.

"Yes to what? To sex? To being official? To what…going steady?" Nerves crept up my spine, sending chills down my limbs.

"Yes to all," he answered, tucking his thumbs in his pockets. "I mean, sex is optional, but given the pretty intense chemistry between us, I'd say it's a safe bet that it would follow pretty shortly after the other yeses. As for going steady, I'm sure I could find my letterman jacket from high school or something if you want it."

"This isn't funny," I said, panic pitching my voice higher. I felt like we were on the edge of something, and I was either going to gloriously fly or die in the fall.

"I'm not laughing."

"What's the purpose? We'll go our separate ways in eight more months, if we can even last that long. You're not exactly known as Mr. Long-term Relationship."

"Do you always skip to the last page of the book, Leah? Feel us. Feel what we can be like together. I do, and it's nothing like I've ever known. You're right. I've never been a relationship guy, but I'm ready to take that risk."

He reached for me, but I backed away, knowing what those hands, those lips, could do to me. He took risks for a living, of course he was ready to jump headfirst. "Maybe I do skip to the last page. It's safer to know how it ends."

He was merciless, backing me against the wall and threading his fingers through my hair as he lowered his lips to hover above mine. "Well then, maybe it's time you realized that the best part isn't the end. It's what happens in between."

"We'd better get going," I said, chickening out. Heat rushed my cheeks.

His thumbs caressed my cheekbones. "As long as you know that I'm going to keep asking. I'll try to wait another few minutes before giving another run at the gauntlet. You're worth it." He pressed a kiss to my forehead.

I melted, sagging against the wall, relieved and annoyed with myself at the same time.

"You coming?" he asked, offering me his outstretched hand.

"I wish," I muttered, thinking that we were wasting a perfectly empty house. He was right. My head might be holding my heart back to the best of its ability, but my body was fully on the Paxton-train.

"I heard that," he said as he walked me to the Jeep.

The sun caressed my skin, warming it through the open top as we drove off the property and back onto the main road.

He squeezed my knee, then moved his hand up my leg until it rested under the fabric of my dress. Maybe it was that no one had touched me there in years, but it felt incredible. "I like you in dresses," he said, tossing me a grin. "Easy access."

"Neanderthal," I joked.

"Only for you," he replied, and I actually believed him.

"No other girls?" I asked, needing to hear the words.

"Not since we boarded. You thinking of turning that maybe into a yes?" He glanced at me quickly, trying to keep his attention on the road.

"Maybe," I said softly, but he heard me.

"Making progress. I'll take it."

"Where are we headed anyway?"

He picked up my hand and kissed the back of it. "You'll see."

"You know, normally that would make my blood boil."

He glanced over in mock surprise. "No. Not you, Miss Control Freak. No way."

I thought about my file folder back on board, the itinerary I kept meticulously noted and scheduled, and then I laughed. "Of everything I planned for this trip, I can tell you this is not how I pictured things going."

"Disappointed?" he asked as we turned down another road that led to the bluest water I'd ever seen.

I reached over and ran my fingers through his hair as we wound down the hillside. He leaned in to my touch, and everything in me, body and soul, seemed to wake up and stretch, to take notice of how perfect this moment was. "It's even better."

He turned into a parking lot, parked in the first spot he saw, and killed the engine. Then he twisted, and before I could think, his mouth was on mine, taking me in the kind of kiss fairy tales were made of. And his tongue—okay, maybe it was a dirty fairy tale—moved against mine in ways that screamed sex, and passion, and warm nights. Warm nights like this one.

He pulled away before I was ready, then kissed me lightly. "I've been dying for that since I saw you in this dress."

"Me, too," I admitted. I looked through the windshield and found a gorgeous beach dotted with umbrellas to our left, and bare except for a few swimmers directly in front of us. The sun glinted off the water, which met the sand with gentle waves. "Is this…?"

"Kalafatis Beach," he answered. "I remembered you said that you wanted to see it, right?"

I'd thought the moment was perfect before, but this…there were no words for this. Paxton helped me down from the Jeep, and we walked onto the beach. "It's exactly like I imagined it. Just like their pictures." I couldn't look enough, memorize enough, take in enough detail from the pebbled sand under my shoes to the various colors in the water where the blues faded to greens.

"Whose pictures?" he asked.

"My parents'. This is where they got engaged." I pulled my wallet from the bag I'd brought and tugged the worn picture free from the credit-card slot I'd jammed it into. In the photo, my father had lifted my mother above his head, her hair falling to one side so their smiles were revealed, love tangible in every line of their bodies, their eyes. I held it out so Paxton could see, trying to match it with the shoreline.

"That's incredible. My mother grew up here."

"Talk about coincidence," I joked.

"Or fate," he said, taking the picture from my fingers. He walked us down the beach a ways, stopping toward the middle and tilting his head, his narrowed eyes examining the space. "There," he said, pointing directly in front of us as he held up the picture. "They were standing there."

Waves of emotion washed over me in rhythm with the water. "I've always loved that picture," I said, looking at it matched with our surroundings. "My parents have this amazing marriage, and every time I look at this picture I feel how much they love each other. Like I can touch love itself, feel that kind of happiness. It gave me faith that one day I would be able to let someone love me like that." I caught him staring at me. I shook my head. "Silly, I know. I just wanted to be here once, to stand where they stood." *I wanted to see if I could let go of fear and touch love.*

"It's not silly. It's beautiful," he said. "Stay here."

He walked over to one of the beachgoers and spoke in rapid Greek, motioning from the picture to me and then pulling a camera—of course he had one—from his pocket. The young woman nodded and followed him back to where I stood.

"Okay, let's go," he said with a smile and led me near the water.

The woman motioned us to the right, and we moved a little until she held up her hand.

"Oh, one thing." Paxton dropped to his knees in front of

me, his fingers deftly undoing the straps of my shoes. "Hers were off."

He was recreating the photograph. How could I defend myself against him? Steel my heart when he was everything I never knew I'd needed? I expected to hear warning bells in my brain, some kind of mechanism to snap me out of the rabbit hole I was eagerly jumping into, but there was nothing but a feeling of peace, of rightness.

He took off my shoes one at a time, the moment so surreal that I could barely breathe, yet I'd never felt more awake—more alive.

Leaning forward, he placed a reverent kiss on one of my scars, then gave the same attention to my other leg, and my heart threatened to burst. Too much—he was too perfect, too gentle, too close, and yet not close enough. He rose before me and filled every one of my senses until the world around me narrowed to just him. Then he swept my hair behind my neck and over my shoulder.

"Ready?"

I couldn't speak, only nod.

"You are incredible, Leah," he said, and kissed me, the soft caress of his lips breaking past the last of my barriers until I was left bare, my emotions stripped raw in the best way.

Joy filled every ounce of my body, radiating through my smile as he lifted me above his head. He never looked away, his grin playful, sexy, intense, and a touch wicked...just like he was.

In that breath of eternity, it didn't matter that our time was limited, or that our close quarters were intensifying every emotion. It didn't matter that he was everything I swore I'd never want, or that he took risks on a daily basis that scared the shit out of me. And it didn't matter that I'd only known him for five weeks. Anything that could have mattered had fled with all logic and reason, leaving the purest of feelings coursing through my veins, singing along every nerve.

In that moment, I fell in love with Paxton Wilder.

I cupped his face in my hands, savoring the slight scratch of scruff against my palms, and said the only thing I could. "Yes. I'm saying yes."

His grin morphed into the most beautiful smile I could have ever imagined, and the air of possibility charged between us, held us in an electric current more powerful than any I'd ever experienced. "You won't be sorry."

I was too high on love to look past this moment, to look further into our future, or question it. I'd taken the leap and was already mid-fall, too far gone to wonder if he'd catch me, but already knowing he would. Under the sun of Mykonos, with the sand of Kalafatis Beach under us, I gave in to the adventure of my life.

What a way to fall.

CHAPTER NINETEEN

LEAH

MYKONOS

"Are you sure this is okay?" I asked Paxton's mom as she opened the last shade on the guesthouse.

"Absolutely. The rest of his little club gets here in a couple days, and they'll invade the house. Once that happens, there's no peace to be found. Trust me."

I looked around at the beautiful open space. With three of the walls made up of windows, it was as if the house was part of the landscape itself, looking out over the Aegean. It had a bathroom, kitchenette, eating area...and a huge king-size bed.

"Then you should take it," I offered.

She waved me off, her eyes taking that same sparkle Paxton's did. "Oh, no. I won't be here. Once that zoo crew pulls in I'm headed to Paris for the week. I love my son dearly, but he's always done better when left to his own devices. And I promised Brandon I'd visit while he's there on business."

I dropped my bag at the foot of the bed and walked over to where she stood at the wall of windows. "Pax and Brandon... they don't get along very well, do they?" I asked, knowing I was stepping a toe over the line.

She shook her head. "Brandon is their father. Straight-edged and business-minded. Paxton...well, he's me. If you bought them a sailboat, Brandon would assess its worth and where it belongs in his portfolio. Paxton would see how fast he could race it. Neither of them take the time to examine the other's world. Ironically, that's why their father and I aren't married anymore. Even all the love in the world can't stitch together souls that are too stubborn to bend. I'm afraid that's all Paxton has seen when it comes to relationships...to love." She sighed. "Are your parents still married?"

"Yes, ma'am. Nauseatingly happy." A stab of longing ripped into me. What was it about knowing I couldn't go home until Christmas that made me miss them a little more?

"None of that 'ma'am' stuff. It's Athena." Mrs. Wilder shook her finger at me.

I blinked. "Wow. The same as our ship. Talk about coincidences."

She looked out over the Aegean with a wistful look. "As I said, all the love in the world."

Before I could ask her what she meant, Paxton walked in with his bag and dropped it next to mine. "You sure you don't mind the take-over, Mom?"

She smiled at him. "Not at all. I'm glad they're coming."

"Already here!" I heard through the open door and turned to see Little John standing with his arms open.

I fought my immediate urge to dive behind the bed to hide my shorts-clad legs and held my ground. If he asked, then I'd simply have to answer.

Paxton hugged him, the sounds of vigorous backslapping echoing in the tile-floored guesthouse. "Good to see you!"

"Me? What about you two? So busy heating up Istanbul that you couldn't get your asses to the ship on time?"

"And so the invasion begins," Mrs. Wilder said with a conspiratorial wink in my direction. "John, it's good to see you."

"You, too, Mrs. Wilder." He swiped his ball cap off his head. "Thank you for having us."

"It's my pleasure. Also, the crane should be functional in the next hour or so." She kissed Paxton's cheek on her way out. "Keep the foam in the pit, dear. It was a bitch to clean up last time."

"Crane? Foam?" I asked. "Do I even want to know?"

Paxton wrapped his arms around me despite the fact that John was there. *Guess we're public.* "You'll want to watch."

"Oh really?" I looped my arms around his neck, energy humming through me from the simple contact of his body against mine. Last night I'd only gotten a chaste good-night kiss, which had played in my head all day.

He nodded. "Oh yeah. And you know if you get—"

I pushed him back with a laugh. "Yeah, yeah. I know. Red flag."

He gave me a panty-dropping smile. "Exactly." Then he moved in close enough to whisper in my ear, "And your ass is incredible in those shorts. See you down there, Firecracker."

I watched them walk toward the track, grateful that it was only Little John here. At least I didn't have to worry about someone trying to sabotage or hurt Paxton. I tied back my hair with a bandana before I followed. One thing I'd learned about Paxton? If he said I'd want to watch...

Then he was about to do something worth watching.

• • •

I wasn't sure I could watch it again. Yet I still sat there, my ass growing more numb by the second. But how the hell was I going to walk away?

Paxton repeatedly drove his freestyle bike at dizzying speeds from the back of the track until he hit the tallest ramp I'd ever seen, flying off it and flipping.

Every time he jumped the ramp. Every time the metal thing at the end of the ramp allowed him to fling himself into the air so he could flip forward. Every time my world slowed as he rotated, bringing the bike around with him until he came crashing back to earth, landing in the giant foam pit. Sometimes he landed vertically, almost nailing the rotation. Other times the bike came down on top of him.

My breath held. Every. Single. Time.

I only started breathing again when he gave me the thumbs-up from the pit. Then he latched the bike onto the hook of the crane and Little John lifted it out.

They talked about what went right or wrong. Then it started all over again.

They paused for lunch, then dinner, then kept at it until the sun went down. If I was this sore from watching him, I couldn't imagine how his body felt.

He swore, punched at the foam, yelled out his frustration, but he never quit, never gave up. He was incredible. I'd known it all along, but that had been watching him twist and turn, completing impossible tricks. But now that I watched what it took for him to be the best, I was awestruck.

All through the day he'd told me to head down to the beach, that he didn't want me wasting my entire day watching him work. But I was glued in place, unable to move for the fear that I'd miss the first time he did it, or the inevitable hospital trip if things went wrong.

I was amazed by the growing understanding of what it meant to love someone as extraordinary as Paxton, knowing that the risks he took were something he'd never change because they were an integral part of him. And like his tattoos, I might occasionally forget they were there, but it was only because I already saw them as part of his skin.

He would always be a daredevil.

That realization was as terrifying as it was sexy, watching this man I loved pushing his body to the limit of what it could endure.

This was the reason every muscle of his body was defined with purpose, why he looked like the Greek god he was when he took off his shirt.

Speaking of which.

He unclipped his chest protector, leaving him in a tight black Under Armour shirt. "I'm calling it. I can't see far enough ahead of me to make this safe," he said, motioning to the darkening sky. "If we were home I'd turn on the stadium lights, but we don't have them here."

I stumbled to my feet, feeling rushing to the parts of my body that had fallen asleep. "Good. It forces you to break for the night."

"I can't believe you sat here all day and watched." He brushed his hand over my cheek. The look on his face wasn't quite defeat, but it wasn't victory, either. It was a weary, bone-deep exhaustion.

"I heard it was the best show on the island," I said, leaning up on my tiptoes to brush my lips against his. "Paxton?" I looked up at him under my lashes and ran my hands along the waistline of his pants dampened with sweat.

"Leah?" His lids lowered, taking on that look that sent heat spiraling through me, electrifying my nerves.

"You smell."

He laughed, and my world righted, bringing back my Paxton from the world of Wilder. "Yeah, I think I should do something about that."

"I agree, especially since it's just the two of us in that small house."

"With one big bed," he added, running his tongue over his lower lip.

One line and my body was practically singing with anticipation.

"Hey, Pax, your gear is stowed. I'm thinking about watching a movie. Anything you're in the mood for?" Little John said as he walked over.

"Nah. Leah, you choose. I'll be up after I shower."

But ten minutes later, as I thumbed through Mrs. Wilder's DVDs, all I could think about was Paxton's naked body in the shower. Wet. Warm. I bet the water even traveled down those carved fuck-me lines.

I reached the end of the row and nearly fell over, distracted.

"I got my hands on the new Warren Miller. I bet he'd love that," Little John said, coming from the hallway with a DVD case in hand.

"Yeah, I'll go ask him," I offered, and then nearly ran out the back door before he could say anything.

What the hell was wrong with me? I'd never been this distracted over a guy before. Sure, I liked sex...or what I remembered of it, but I'd never been the girl to jump a guy. *You've never had orgasms like the one he gave you in Istanbul, either.*

Well, there was that.

The shower was still running as I opened the door to the guesthouse. Paxton had lowered all the shades but the ones that looked out over the water, making the house feel like a warm, steamy cocoon.

I walked over to the bed and kicked off my sandals, then took the bandana from my hair, twisting the fabric in my hands. What was I going to do? Say, "Hey, maybe you could...I don't know...do me?"

You even sound awkward to yourself.

Was this what I wanted? *Yes.* I wanted to feel him on top of me, to see the blue in his eyes darken with want, with need...for me. I wanted to be the sole focus of all that intense energy, to be the one who brought him to his knees.

I wanted Paxton because he was mine and I loved him.

That love didn't scare me like I thought it would. No, it gave me wings, made me bold, ready to grasp every sensation I could, because I never imagined I'd be able to feel it again.

Yet here it was, and so much stronger than the first time.

Forgive me, Brian, but I know you would have wanted me to be happy.

The water stopped, but my pulse sped up. The shower door opened and closed, and my chest tightened. This would be easy. I could tell him that I was ready, and then we'd go watch the movie, and our good-night kiss wouldn't end with a kiss.

It sounded so simple, so why was I such a bundle of oversensitive nerves? Even my soft V-neck tee felt scratchy against my skin.

Oh God, he didn't know I was here. What if he came out naked?

I spun, turning my back to him when I saw movement in the doorway. "Hey, I'm in here," I called out. *So not sexy.* Why couldn't I have an ounce of Rachel's sex appeal, her complete ease around guys? Or just her advice?

Because you're here...on Mykonos, with the hottest guy you've ever laid eyes on.

"Hey," Paxton called out behind me.

"Are..." I took a deep breath and tried again. "Are you naked?"

"No, but I can be," he answered.

I pivoted, turning slowly to face him.

Oh fuck me, he may as well have been. A single white towel hung off his lean hips, held in place by a pesky little knot. His hair was damp, and tiny droplets of water clung to his tattooed skin, traveling the lines of his muscles as gravity commanded.

Every single cell in my body screamed with wanting him.

He was every fantasy. Every bad boy I'd been warned against. Every athlete I'd ever admired. Every prom king and every outlaw at the same time. He was the untouchable, the answer to every love letter I'd never gotten, and the only cure for the ache that was steadily growing, unfurling in my stomach. And for some reason I'd never understand, Paxton Wilder was looking at me like I was dessert.

"Leah?" He lifted his hands above his head, grasping the doorframe.

Every single muscle in his abs flexed. Every. One.

Was he even human?

"Firecracker, is everything okay?"

I nodded, trying to find my voice. "I wanted to see you."

"Okay." His voice dropped, but his hands stayed where they were.

"I just... I wanted to..." I shook my head. "Last night you kissed me."

A smirk danced across his face. "Yeah, and this morning. I plan on doing that a lot."

I twisted the bandana in my hands. "Right. But is that all?"

"Is that bothering you? I didn't move in here with you expecting sex, Leah. I didn't ask you to be with me so I could screw you." His face tightened.

"No, no. That's not what I'm thinking." Why was this so hard? "I'm asking if you want to do more than kiss me."

Now every muscle in his torso strained. "Is that what you want?"

He sounded so damn calm, and I was a huge wreck. How fair was that? And he hadn't even moved from the doorframe. A shred of self-doubt crept in. "Only if you do."

His eyes went almost comically big. "Only if *I* do? Are you kidding me? The memory of how you feel under my hands goes through my head about every fifteen seconds. There's no question there."

"But you're not moving." I tried to swallow past the lump in my throat, but it wouldn't budge.

Again, his upper body tensed, the muscles in his forearms rippling where he held on to the doorframe. "I'm over here because I don't trust myself to get any closer to you without stripping those clothes off your tight, perfect body."

"Oh."

"So if you're telling me that you're ready, I need you to be damn sure, Leah. Because I have wanted you since the first time I saw you, and I have been so fucking good about keeping my hands to myself. You have no clue what you do to me, how much self-control I have to use to keep from pressuring you."

"Oh." That giant knot in my throat drifted lower, lodging in my stomach as my core started to simmer.

"So now all I get is one word?" he asked.

I wasn't sure I was capable of more. All my brain cells were currently scrambling to form a coherent thought that wasn't *now.*

His eyes dropped to where my hands wrung my bandana.

My red bandana.

It wasn't a flag, but it would do. I lifted it with one hand and waved it twice before letting it flutter to the floor. His eyes darkened, and I was surprised he hadn't broken through the doorframe from how hard he pushed against it.

"Say the words. I need to hear them. No misunderstandings between us, ever."

My entire body was damn near humming, and he hadn't even touched me yet. "I want you, Paxton."

He lowered his arms slowly and, keeping my eyes locked with his, stalked me with lethal grace. I held my ground, my heart pounding harder with each step he took, like my body had Paxton radar, and it was blaring the sweetest alarm.

He didn't stop until his mouth was on mine, kissing me breathless, turning my mind—and my knees—to mush. My hands tunneled through his hair, and he grabbed my ass, lifting me against his chest. His grip shifted to my thighs as he ran his lips down my neck, and I locked my ankles around his waist.

And shit...there went his towel.

Paxton was naked, gloriously, fully naked, and I wasn't even in a position to appreciate it. I settled for second best, running my hands down his sculpted back—until I found myself on mine, sinking into the soft bed with his delicious weight on top of me.

"You lost your towel," I told him as he nibbled at my collarbone.

"I did," he answered, his hands squeezing my thighs with

just the right amount of pressure. His thumbs snuck under my shorts, so high on my upper thigh that he brushed my panties.

"We... We have to..." There was something, I knew it, but I just didn't care. Not when he ran his hands to my waist and then under my shirt, dragging the fabric up.

"We have to what?" he asked, his mouth at my ear. His tongue traced the shell, and I groaned. He had a way of finding spots I never even realized were so sensitive.

"Movie. We're supposed to watch a movie," I managed to get out.

He slid down my body, trailing kisses up my bare stomach, leaving chills in his wake as he reached where my shirt pooled at my bra line. "I'd rather watch you come a few times."

A few? "Feeling ambitious tonight, are we?" I asked, my hips moving of their own accord. I nearly groaned when they brushed his erection.

He hissed at the contact. "Just stating the truth."

"Should we do this later?" My body nearly cried at the thought of not finishing what we'd started. "I don't want Little John to come looking."

He kissed the underside of my jaw. "He's not going to come looking, I promise. And if you think I honestly give a fuck that we're missing the movie, you're sorely mistaken. I'd miss every movie for the rest of my life if it meant I got to touch you. Unless you've changed your mind?" He tensed above me.

"No," I reassured him. "Never."

Without looking away, he raised my shirt over my head, and I eagerly lifted my arms to help. "Thank God," he whispered, and then kissed me.

He consumed me, taking over every thought with each stroke of his tongue, each angle he used to deepen the caress.

He kissed me like I was the answer to every question he'd ever had, and in turn, I held nothing back.

He unhooked my bra with a snap of his fingers, and then he slipped it down my arms so it could join my shirt on the floor. When he lowered himself to kiss me again, we were skin-to-skin, and the contact was enough to send flames licking down my body, pooling the heat between my thighs.

He groaned. "You feel incredible," he said with one last pull at my lower lip. Then his lips trailed a path to my breasts, where he took one hardened nipple into his warm mouth.

I sucked in a breath and arched against his mouth, craving more and knowing he could deliver it.

My hands found his hair, his shoulders, anything that could anchor me as pure sensation took over. There was nothing but Paxton, and that was perfection in itself. He moved to the other breast, his hands never ceasing their movement between my waistline and neck, bringing every nerve ending to life with his touch.

He made me feel worshipped, adored, and I loved him all the more for it.

I pulled gently on his hair, and he looked into my eyes, dragging his tongue over my nipple. Pleasure rushed through me. He made it so easy to want him.

I twisted my legs, and he gave in to my silent demand, rolling over so I knelt on top of him, his hips between my knees. His hands flexed on my thighs, subtly digging in to the muscle as I traced the line of his dragon tattoo, looking up to watch his eyes darken as I reached the tip of its tail.

Then I used both hands to explore the lines of his chest, his abs, leaving no inch of skin untouched. He had various tattoos running the length of his arm, some down his abdomen, and tiny scars peppered his otherwise perfect skin.

"What are you thinking?" he asked, his voice low.

"That you are pretty much every fantasy come to life," I answered. "I can't believe I get to touch you."

He ran his hands up my rib cage until he cupped my breasts. "I was thinking pretty much the same thing. Except dirtier. You're way too good for me."

"Good?" I asked, raising my hips and sliding down to his thighs so his erection sprung between us. Then I took hold of it at the base with one hand and caressed the length with the other.

"Fuck," he moaned, arching his hips into my hands. He grasped my hips, his fingers tightening on me. "Leah," he warned.

I ran my thumb over the head of his dick, and he groaned, his stomach muscles tensing. Having him under me, losing his control because of me, was intoxicating. I moved him again through my grip, reveling in the juxtaposition of soft skin and the steel underneath. That thought sent another ache shooting straight through me. He was beautiful, his throat working, neck arching, face tight with restraint...and he was mine.

As if he sensed me watching him, his eyes snapped open. "Enough," he growled, and flipped me to my back, rising above me before kissing every rational thought from my head. "You push me closer to the edge than anyone I've ever met," he said against my mouth.

"Good," I fired back. I didn't want to think about every other girl he'd taken to bed, every woman who'd put her hands on him, felt the power flexing beneath his surface, but that didn't mean I wasn't well aware of how many there had been.

I closed my eyes against the unwelcome thoughts, wanting

this minute to be special, to be different. *You're the only one he's claimed as his*, I reminded myself, but that sliver was under my skin, stealing some of my joy.

"You enjoy testing me?" he asked between kisses, one of his hands weaving through my hair while the other caressed my side, stoking the fire that was already burning within me.

"Yes," I admitted. His fingers flirted with the waist of my shorts. And I was almost ready to tear them off myself before he flicked open the button.

"Why?" he asked, licking and sucking the sensitive skin at the base of my neck.

I arched my hips, hoping he'd get the message that I wanted his hands, and I wanted them now. "Paxton," I pleaded when he didn't move.

He met my eyes as he slid the shorts down my legs, and I was more than happy to help. Then his hands stroked back up, his thumbs lightly tracing my scars, but he still didn't look away. Even when his thumbs stroked along the *V* of my panties, he held my gaze, that look hotter than any caress could have been.

Until he ran his thumb over my core, nothing but a scrap of lace between us. "Damn, you're soaking wet," he said, his eyes momentarily closing as he took a deep breath. I wasn't embarrassed—I was desperate, and if he didn't put his hands on me soon, I was going to combust. "Do you want me to touch you?"

"Yes," I said instantly.

"Tell me why you like to test me," he prodded, using his thumb to press on my clit through the material.

My hips bucked. "Paxton, please," I begged.

He pressed again, dragging the material across the sensitive nerves. "Tell me."

I hated how much control he had over me in bed as much as

I loved his ability to turn me molten with a simple movement. "Why?"

He licked a path between my breasts until he ended at my mouth, kissing me deeply. My hips rocked against his hand, but he moved with me, unwilling to give me the friction I needed. "Because I don't like whatever thought crept into your eyes a minute ago. Because I want this—want you—too badly to let anything else into this bed besides the two of us."

My fingers flexed on the muscles of his shoulders. "Because I want you to remember this—remember me." *Because I want to be the one you don't forget when this is over.*

His hands found my ass, and he jerked me against him, his dick rubbing right where I wanted him, and I whimpered. "I will always remember this." His thumbs tucked into the straps of my panties, and he dragged them down my legs, leaving me utterly bare in front of him. His breath was ragged as his eyes followed the reverse path back up. "You are so fucking exquisite." He stroked my hips, then dipped to my waist before reaching my breasts and cupping them. "You're curved everywhere that drives me wild, and that little gasp you make"—he thrust against me while rolling my nipples and I drew a quick breath—"yeah, that one—makes me desperate to bury myself inside you so I can hear it again and again."

His words were enough to have me writhing beneath him. "Pax, I want you," I said, knowing he loved the words.

"And I want you," he promised, kissing me gently while rocking against my core, sending another shock of electricity through me, winding that spiral in my belly tighter. "But you need to know that I don't need to remember you, Leah. Not when I have zero intention of ever letting you go."

His mouth conquered mine, wiping away my doubt, my

insecurities. He was mine now, and that was enough. He broke the kiss only to slide down my body, bending my knees to spread my legs wider. "Now turn off that beautiful brain of yours, Firecracker, and just feel."

He gave me a wicked smile, then held me apart with his fingers and licked through my core.

My back came off the bed and my fingers flew to his head to push him away...to pull him closer. "Holy shit."

His tongue swirled around my clit as one of his fingers slipped inside me, and I was a whirlwind of pleasure. "You taste even better than I imagined," he said against my flesh. "How do you want it?"

My chest heaved, the tension in me so tight that I was afraid I'd snap. "I...I don't know," I answered.

"Tell me," he ordered with another long stroke of his tongue.

Sparks flew behind my eyes. "I don't know! God, that's amazing."

He lifted his head, his gorgeous eyes slightly wide. "You've never had someone go down on you."

My teeth sank into my lower lip, and I shook my head.

A fierce look of possessiveness washed over his face. "Even better. Hold on to the sheets, Firecracker."

My hands gripped the sheets, twisting them between my fingers as he set his mouth back on me, licking, sucking, exploring me with his fingers, lips, and tongue. He pressed where I gasped, lingered where I moaned, thrust his tongue inside me when my hips bucked against him.

My legs shook, the tension within me so tight it was a blissful torture. Then he whispered, "Let go, baby," and with one more stroke of my clit, I was flying, waves of euphoria washing over me, through me, as I came, his name on my lips.

He ran his tongue over his lower lip, and I nearly came again. How the hell was someone that sexy? *How am I ever going to look at you again without remembering what you can do with that mouth?*

"That's the general point," he said.

"Shit, I said that out loud." I grimaced.

He grinned, but it was strained. "And much appreciated."

Every line of his body was strained to the max, his muscles nearly locked, tiny beads of sweat dotting his forehead, telling me that he needed to be inside me as badly as I needed him there.

"Condom?" I asked.

He leaned over the bed, grabbing one from his bag.

I laughed at how prepared he was. "Planned this, did you?"

He ripped the foil packet open and rolled it over his erection, the sight sending another wave of want through me even though I should be sated. But my body was more than ready for what was next.

"Hey, a guy's allowed to dream," he said, his weight settling on me as I brought my knees up to cradle his hips.

"You dreamed this?" I asked, kissing the stubble along his jaw.

"I fantasized this, and I promise the reality is even better. But you..." He cupped my face as his erection nudged my entrance. "You're the dream."

He kissed me, and I melted into him, into what we could be. His thumbs stroked over my nipples, and that fire was kindled in my belly again. I rocked against him, letting him know that I was ready, and he simply tugged on my lower lip with his teeth. "Patience."

Fuck patience, I wanted him *now*.

Then his hand reached between us, his fingers lightly

petting me, stroking the hypersensitive flesh, and I arched up against him, taking his breaths in my gasps as he worked me over, brought me back to the brink while restraining himself.

"Paxton, please. I want you inside me. I need you."

He groaned. "God, you kill me."

I reached between us and guided him to me. With one hand he gripped the back of my head, looking deeply into my eyes. "You're everything," he promised as he thrust home.

We both cried out.

I burned a tiny bit from the stretch, but he held still, kissing every other thought from my head as I adjusted to having him inside me.

When I moved my hips against his, he groaned and then began to move with sure, steady strokes, lingering inside me before beginning again, like he couldn't bear to leave but couldn't wait to come back.

Each stroke hit exactly where I needed, filled and moved me, fed the fire that was dying to be set free. His hips kept perfect rhythm, never breaking pace as he made love to me, his eyes never leaving mine except during his kisses.

Even when I thought he'd be spent, his muscles locked, he kept moving, kept stroking me higher and higher until I felt that edge approaching, but I needed more.

"Pax," I whimpered, "I need—"

"Yeah, I know," he agreed, cradling my ass to rock into me harder, faster. I wrapped my legs around his hips, and his eyes squeezed shut. "You're so fucking perfect. So tight. Wet. Hot. God, Leah. I want to live here."

That mouth of his pushed me higher, and I rocked against him, meeting his thrusts until he was pistoning within me, rubbing over every nerve I had, then using one thumb to press against my clit and kissing me. "Let me feel you come around me." His eyes begged, and I was powerless against the intensity of that look, the way he saw through to my soul as he worshipped my body. "Leah."

He rubbed his thumb in a circle over me as he switched angles, hitting a spot so perfect that I had no choice but to let go, allowing the orgasm to take me to the stars while he kept me anchored to the earth. I felt him tense above me, within me, and he growled my name as he came, shuddering with exertion.

I'd never felt so exhausted or so alive in my life.

He held me until our breathing calmed, then cleaned us both up before pulling me into the shelter of his body, settling the covers over us.

Out of everything he'd done to my body, it had been the way he'd looked at me that had sent me spiraling, and I had to laugh.

"Are you giggling?" he asked, a smile in his voice as he rolled me under him.

"Maybe."

"So sleeping with me is funny? Because I didn't hear you laughing a few minutes ago. Do you need a refresher?" He bit his lip, and I nearly went limp. I wasn't sure my body could handle another round.

"I realized that my first impression of you was dead-on," I said, stroking my hands over the dampened skin of his back.

"And what was that?" His eyes were bright but more relaxed than I'd ever seen them.

"That you could make me come with just a look."

He arched an eyebrow. "Challenge accepted."

It turned out my body was more than capable of another round...

And another after that.

CHAPTER TWENTY

Paxton

Mykonos

I slid the last of the eggs onto the plate and then added the toast next to the bacon. Two glasses of orange juice and two forks later, I balanced the tray on my way to the guesthouse, carefully navigating the stone path.

It had to be about ten o'clock. I should've been on the bike already, but John was still sleeping, and Leah was in my bed. If I hadn't been carrying her breakfast, I would have jumped into the air and heel-clicked.

Instead, I took extra caution as I opened the door to the guesthouse. She'd need the calories after last night, that was for damn sure. I'd never been with someone like her before, so open, honest in her reactions, so addictive that if I wasn't worried about wearing her down to exhaustion I'd already be inside her again.

She was perfection.

Leah slept in our bed, her hair tangled around her shoulders, her hand tucked under her pillow and the other reaching for the empty place where I'd slept. The white sheets twisted across her body, and her cheeks still wore a flush—or was that whisker burn? I probably needed to shave.

Shit, I hoped her inner thighs were okay.

A fierce feeling of protectiveness swept over me as I sat on the edge of the bed, setting the tray on the mattress. She was mine. She'd not only said yes on that beach, she'd literally thrown the red flag and trusted me with everything she was. Talk about humbling.

She was mine to protect, to care for.

And I wasn't going to let that scare me—at least that's what I told myself as I brushed a strand of hair off her beautiful face. Sure, the last time I did this, officially staked a claim on a woman...well, Leah wasn't *her*, and I wasn't going to make the same mistakes again.

And I still had a month before that whole situation bit me in the ass.

Tell her, she'll understand, my conscience screamed at me. Maybe I should. Leah wasn't the kind of girl to cut and run because of my past. Maybe if I came clean now—

Her eyes opened slowly, and she blinked a few times before giving me a sleepy, sexy smile. "Is that bacon?"

I laughed. "That's exactly what every guy wants to hear the morning after. Forget the 'how was it for you' awkwardness and let's go for the bacon."

She sat up, covering her magnificent breasts with the sheet. I'd never seen a woman look so good in the morning, especially after I'd kept her up almost all night. "Pretty sure you already know it was good for me," she said, plucking a piece of bacon from the plate. "I lost count of the orgasms." She moaned as she chewed, then swallowed. "So good."

My dick hardened. *Down, boy.* If I'd thought that spending

one night with her would kill my obsession with getting her naked, well...it had done the opposite. Now I knew how she tasted, how tight she was surrounding me, knew how it felt to watch her fly apart and surrender myself in return. She'd gone from an obsession to an addiction overnight.

"I'm sorry, did you need to have the 'how was it for you' conversation?" she asked, her head tilted.

"Not really, I already know both sides. Do you?" Now I was the one stealing bacon, reveling in the comfortable domesticity of breakfast in bed with Leah.

"No," she said, her tone adamant as she sipped orange juice.

"Really?" I'd always been asked, every girl wanting to know where she compared.

"Really. I'm well aware that your numbers are scary high, and I'd rather you not lie to me. So instead, how are we doing for a morning-after in your ranking?"

"First place," I answered truthfully. "And second, and third, and every place, really."

Her eyes lit up, and I realized how badly she needed words, needed to be shown that she was wanted. "Really?"

"Really," I said, grinning and wondering how many times we could say *really* before it didn't sound like a word anymore. "This is definitely first place. Second would be waking up next to you in Istanbul. Third was watching you come out of my bedroom yesterday morning, and the rest are ties for every morning since I've met you."

"Those don't count," she said, fighting her smile and failing.

"Sure they do. Because every morning since we've set sail, I've woken up and wondered when I'd get to see you."

Her lips parted slightly, and I leaned forward, bracing my hands on either side of her hips, and kissed her sweetly. Then

I pulled back so she could see my eyes, hoping she'd see the truth. "Last night was the best night of my life, Leah. Hands down. Being with you is unlike anything I've ever known."

Her eyes were huge, the deep pools reflecting the hope I felt in my own heart. "Even better than winning your X Games?" she challenged with a sparkle.

I nodded slowly, the truth catching me by surprise. "You put your faith in me, which isn't something that happens often. I don't take that lightly."

She leaned forward, running her fingers through my hair. "Everyone has faith in you, Paxton. You have an entire entourage that believes in you."

I shook my head. "Not everything is as simple as what you see. Sure, the Originals, Landon, Penna...Nick." I closed my eyes against the pain of saying his name before opening them again. "We're a family—the four of us—but everyone else is just along for the ride. And those cameras? Don't be fooled. They want to film spectacular stunts for the money, the views, but the outcome works for them either way. People aren't around us just to watch the tricks, they're there to see the one time we don't make it. I get a hell of a lot more hits on a video where I crash than when I pull something off, because fans love their heroes, but they're always waiting for them to fall. But you... you want to be with me in spite of what I do, not because of it. You put your faith in me as Paxton, not Wilder, and that means more to me than you'll ever know."

She kissed me, tasting as sweet as her orange juice. Our lips clung, savored, but never pressed for more; that simple caress was enough.

The door flew open behind us.

"And the cavalry has arrived— Whoa, there's a girl in your

bed!" Bobby's voice burst my bubble of happiness.

I flung the rest of the sheet around Leah, pulling her into my chest to shield her. Thank God my back was to the door. Shit. The crew was here a day early, and I'd lost any chance of talking to Little John about the stunt "accidents" without everyone else overhearing.

"That's no girl, that's Leah," Landon answered, "and if I know Pax, he's about to tell you to—"

"Get the fuck out!" I yelled over my shoulder. "And so help me God, if you have a goddamn camera in here I will crush it, Bobby. Do you understand?"

Bobby threw up his hands and backed out of the room, blocking the entrance from the camera that waited outside and leaving just Landon and Penna in the room.

"Ummm...surprise?" Penna said, her face more grimace than smile. "Sorry, we honestly thought you'd love an extra day to practice with the whole crew, so we bribed the captain and pulled in a day early."

"Great," I growled, then looked directly at Landon, "now get the fuck out."

He nodded once, and I felt the scar we'd long since laid to rest rip open. Leah was mine, and I wouldn't share so much as a glimpse of her bare skin, yet this one precious moment had been trampled on. Landon turned and walked out without another word. Smart man.

"Well, it's good to see you, or rather, not see you, Leah!" Penna called out.

"You, too, Penna." Leah's head dug farther in to my chest, muffling her voice, but she raised a naked arm, waving.

Once I saw the door close behind Penna, I steeled myself for the mess I'd made with Leah. For someone as private as she was, that had to be horrifying. She shook against my chest, and I cringed. Tears were the last thing I wanted to cause her. I tilted her face up to mine and gaped.

She wasn't sobbing, she was laughing.

"Are you okay? I can't believe that just happened."

She wiped away a tear and kept giggling. "Of course nothing with you would be normal. But hey, I guess now we don't have to worry about having the whole 'hey guys, we're together now,' convo with your crew."

Her laughter was contagious, and I found myself chuckling with her. "Shortest honeymoon in history, right?"

She kissed my cheek and climbed out of bed, our sheet covering her in the sexiest toga I'd ever seen. "Don't worry, you have another seven or so months to make up for it." With a wink, she took her bag and slipped into the bathroom.

Seven months.

Yesterday the time we had left on the cruise seemed like forever, but with one sentence, it suddenly wasn't long enough.

Not by a long shot.

"Man, I am so fucking sorry," Landon said as I walked over to him at the end of the ramp. "Little John said you were in the guesthouse. He never mentioned Leah."

"I'd love to say that it's okay, but it's not," I answered honestly. We hadn't lied to each other in years, and I wasn't going to start that shit back up again.

He looked away and nodded. "Yeah, I get that."

I saw the cameras walking in the distance and took advantage. "Listen, I have to ask you about something, and it's not going to be pleasant."

He immediately met my eyes. "Anything."

"The rigs from the first zip-line. Did you store them? Put them away?"

His forehead wrinkled. "No. But if you're looking for them, the production crew has been stashing most of the stuff under my bed and in my closet. I didn't want any of the gear getting lost."

I nodded. "Yeah, we found them the day we were looking for your pack."

"Oh, okay. Then what's the deal?" He looked confused, maybe worried, but not guilty.

I let go of the breath I'd subconsciously held. "The brakes had been tampered with."

His eyes flew wide. "No fucking way. Seriously?"

I nodded.

"Pax, I would never do anything to hurt you. You know that, right? No matter what's gone down with us in the past."

"Yeah. I do. I didn't even want to ask, but it wasn't just my life at stake on that thing. Leah was with me." It was one thing to risk my life following my passion, but another to put hers on the line.

"Okay, well, who else had access to the rigs after you assembled them?"

"I don't know. I had the crew take them. They were only out of my sight for maybe ten minutes, but I've never been worried about this shit."

"Son of a bitch."

"Yeah. And there's more. My chest plate from Rome has a clean break. The damn thing is straight. Someone fucked with it."

"Who knows?"

"Just you and Leah. I was going to bring Little John and Penna in, too. We need all eyes open."

He nodded. "Yeah. Little John's been with us the longest, since we were what—seventeen? I'd bring Brooke in, too. She's family."

"You don't think it would be too much after what happened with Nick?" She'd been devastated, and no one could blame her.

"I think she'd kill us if there was a danger to Penna and we kept it from her. Plus, she's working on a problem that came up while you were cuddled up to Leah. Some of our videos are being hacked on the site. Nothing big, but in combination…"

My stomach tightened. "We're under attack."

"It looks like it, and Brooke will know that something's up." He motioned behind me where Penna walked down the hill with Leah. The cameras would be coming soon, and it would be game on.

"How's that going, by the way?" he asked quietly.

"Great until you assholes showed up."

He clutched his chest. "You wound me."

"She's not a fan of all this, and she's been freaked out since Rome."

Landon smacked my back. "You found a good one. Try not to fuck it up."

I bit back the urge to say something that would do more harm than good. Along with being protective of Leah, I was realizing that I was possessive, too. Great if this were the Middle Ages, not so great while filming a documentary where my fuckups could send this brand-new relationship down in flames.

"Is that the kicker he designed?" Penna asked, looking up at the metal piece that dipped down at the end of the ramp.

"Yeah," I answered as I wrapped my arm around Leah's shoulders. "He shipped it here. It's working great. I just can't seem to nail the full rotation."

"How's it going?" she asked, studying the ramp with a practiced eye. Penna was the only one close to keeping up with me on a bike.

"I'm coming down vertical in the third rotation."

She sighed and rubbed her hand over her eyes. I didn't need to be a mind reader to know where her head was, because mine was there every time I hit the ramp. "I'm consistent, Penna. I always make it that far."

"Yeah, until you don't," she muttered. "Look, the live exhibition is in what, seven weeks?"

"Somewhere around there," Landon chimed in.

"We haven't announced what you're doing. Let's kill it. Pick something else." A shot of fear raced through Penna's eyes. "We're not losing both of you to this fucking trick. It's not worth it."

My muscles tensed, and I glanced at Leah's slightly widened eyes. *Damn it, Penna, I wasn't ready to tell her yet.* "No. We all had one thing we wanted to nail on this trip, one trick that would make the documentary phenomenal. This is mine, and it's the least I can do for him."

A look passed between the three of us, and they each nodded. "Okay. Then let's see how to get you there," Penna offered begrudgingly.

The cameras caught up to us, Bobby looking unapologetic, since he no doubt got the shot he wanted this morning. I needed to call in legal to see how much of the documentary I could cut Leah out of. She didn't need to be exposed like that, especially not on my account, especially since we hadn't discussed officially going public.

"Hey, guys, why don't we show you the ramp?" Penna offered, flashing her mega-watt smile that usually distracted anyone with a dick.

Landon rolled his eyes in my direction but got on board. "Yeah, you'll probably want to see where he has to start from to build momentum," he said, guiding the cameras back toward the track and away from Leah and me.

"Tell me now," Leah demanded once they were out of earshot.

"Leah..." Her name was a sigh on my lips as she moved to stand directly in front of me.

"No one's ever done this before, right? Completed it? Look at me, Paxton."

I did, taking in the slight look of panic in her eyes, the stiff way she held herself away from me. "No. No one's completed it."

She crossed her arms over her chest, but not in stubbornness. It looked more like she was trying to hold herself together. "Okay. Who's attempted it?"

My jaw flexed. I didn't want to answer. I wanted to drag her back to our room and make love to her until she forgot the question. Until we both forgot what was waiting out here.

"Paxton."

"I only know one other person in the world who's tried it."

"Okay, and where is he? Is he still trying to do it, too?"

"I highly doubt it."

"Why?" Her eyes pleaded with me for the truth.

I gave it to her, breaking the vow of secrecy I'd sworn to him, because I couldn't bear to lie to her.

"Because he's in a fucking wheelchair. He couldn't land the

rotation, and the crash paralyzed him." There it was.

I expected her reaction to be nuclear. It was more of an electromagnetic pulse. There was no explosion, but the light in her eyes, the happy energy she'd had radiating around her all morning, died in a split second.

I would have rather seen her rage than watch those damn walls go back up.

She didn't say a word, simply kissed me, the press of her lips heavy with fear and a touch of desperation. Then she turned toward where she'd sat all yesterday and walked away.

Yeah. I definitely would have rather had a yelling Leah than a silent one.

When I finally had my gear on, ready to hit the ramp for the first time that day, I looked to where her seat was, expecting to see an empty space.

She sat, her outstretched legs covered in white, gauzy pants, reading one of the literature books Penna had brought with her from our assigned homework.

It didn't matter to her that what I was doing was dangerous, that any minute she could be sitting in the hospital with me— she was there.

Damn it, that pressure was back in my chest, ten times what it had been, burning with an intensity that only Leah could soothe, because she was the balm to everything that was broken inside me.

I prayed that I didn't break her, too.

CHAPTER TWENTY-ONE

LEAH

MYKONOS

He had no self-preservation instinct. That was the only reason I could come up with for why he would do this to himself. Any one of these people could have messed with the zip-line rigs, or weakened his chest protector, and he was putting his life in their hands. Again. Watching him yesterday was hard enough, but this was torturous. He started his umpteenth run at the ramp—I'd lost count of how many it had been—and I held my breath as he went flying, tumbling through space, until he landed closer to the full rotation in the foam pit. Thank God the sun would be going down soon, because I wasn't sure how much more of this he could take, let alone how much more I could stomach.

Penna leaned over the foam pit, analyzing what had worked, as Little John moved the crane to lift him out.

Paralyzed. The only other person was paralyzed.

Over a stupid trick.

I flipped another page in Kahlil Gibran's *The Prophet* and tried to pay attention, but it was useless. We'd already missed a couple of each class, and I didn't even want to think about what it was going to take to catch us both up, but I was going to have to.

Paxton couldn't afford to have anything else on his mind while he was hunting death.

Paralyzed. Ugh. I slammed the book and threw it on the blanket. All over a stupid documentary that he said was the least they could do for *someone else*. What would even possess him to want to try something that had done that to someone else...unless...

I sat up, watching the dynamic between the three of them, Landon, Paxton, and Penna. There was an empty space between them, like someone was missing from the conversation— because he was.

Because the fourth Original wasn't taking time off. Nick had to have been the one hurt. He was the one paralyzed.

That's why Paxton was so hell-bent on getting the trick down. Was he doing it to show up the friend who'd stolen the only girl he'd ever cared about? I doubted it. Paxton wasn't that petty.

But the evidence suggested otherwise.

Add to all of that the nagging feeling in my stomach that not everyone here had Paxton's safety as a priority, and I was a bundle of nausea.

When he blew me a kiss, I wrapped my arms around my knees and forced a smile. This was the last place I wanted to be, waiting for disaster to strike, but if I left it would distract him, and possibly bring on said disaster. I was damned if I did and damned if I didn't.

So I stayed.

My breath froze in my chest as he came barreling down

the track, driving at the ramp faster than I'd ever seen him go before. He launched higher, and my teeth sank into my lower lip, as he flipped once...twice...three times...

And landed on both wheels in the foam pit.

The celebration began at once, the crew all whooping with arms raised. Paxton didn't wait for the crane, just climbed out of the pit, jumping to the ground and ripping off his helmet mid-run.

Exhilaration burst through me like a joyful shock to the heart. He'd done it!

I was in his arms before I even realized that I'd stood. His mouth found mine, kissing me with both of his hands tangled in my hair. My arms were around his neck, and I held on for dear life, well aware of how dangerous everything was around him, knowing I had to savor each kiss, never waste any of them.

"You did it!" I yelled as he swung me around in his arms.

"Not quite, but almost," he said, laughing, punctuating his comment with another kiss.

"What do you mean?" I asked.

"He has to actually land it on the dirt and ride off, now," Landon answered, smacking him on the back. "That was amazing!"

Yeah, I was right.

No self-preservation.

...

Fuck. This.

How long was he going to keep this up?

Day two of watch-Paxton-try-to-kill-himself, and our last day on Mykonos, had me camped out on a separate area of the track. They'd moved the ramp, which had taken hours, and packed dirt higher on the mound Paxton was supposed to land on.

Except he'd skidded out more than he'd landed it.

Every time he hit the dirt, I felt the crash in my bones, the scrapes on my own skin. I rubbed my hands over my bare arms as he picked up the bike again, giving me the thumbs-up.

When the hell did I get to give the thumbs-down?

Selfishly, I was exhausted. My eyes tracked every motion around Paxton, watching to see if someone messed with him, the bike, the ramp, the crane...all of it. It had to be someone close to him, someone familiar with the gear and his routines. We'd ruled out Little John last night over a quiet dinner—after all, the rigs had been found on board, and Little John hadn't been on the ship since Miami.

That only left every other Renegade to question.

"It's not easy to watch, is it?" Brooke said, sitting down next to me.

"Hey, when did you get here?" I asked.

She shielded her eyes from the sun with her hand. "This morning. I had to do some tech work on the website and the channel. We've been hacked a few times since we set sail, and a bunch of the videos were taken down."

"Do they know?" I motioned to where Paxton was discussing the last jump with Landon and Penna.

"Yeah, Penna's the one who asked me to look at it. I used to run all their site stuff before they blew up big, and she's not quick to trust people, even if she's paying them to maintain the site."

A sick feeling settled in my stomach. "Do you think it's malicious? The videos coming down?"

She shrugged. "I'm not skilled enough to tell you that. I

don't know. But I can say that there are a ton of worse things they could have done in there than just take down some videos."

As a single incident, the site hacking didn't seem too bad, but when combined with the mishaps with Paxton, it was adding up to something that had my stomach twisted in knots. Plus, if Pax knew, why hadn't he told me? *Because you would have screamed until he shut down the practice.* "Right."

I was going to hand his ass to him later.

"It's probably some stupid hacker kids out for bragging rights or something. I wouldn't worry too much about it," she finished. "Are they done for the day?"

"They shouldn't be, it's not even lunch—" The words died on my tongue as Paxton stripped off his chest protector and then the Under Armour beneath it, leaving his torso deliciously bare. Sweat ran down the carved lines, making his tan skin glisten in the sunlight. The nasty bruise along the side of his rib cage was turning green, but even that didn't detract from his appeal. He could probably radiate sex in a full body cast.

All it took was one look in my direction and my body was humming, despite the fact that he'd made love to me before breakfast.

Or rather...I'd been breakfast.

He grinned as he walked up to us. His blue eyes held me captive as he bent to kiss me. "You look good enough to eat."

I raised an eyebrow, and he laughed. Apparently I wasn't the only one who had this morning on the brain. "Well, I think we should probably get you some lunch, don't you?" I asked.

His eyes dropped to my lips, and he lifted me out of my chair by my waist, pulling me against his chest. "Are you offering?"

Yes. "No. I meant food. Real food. The kind that fuels that body you're torturing out there."

"Oh, you fuel me, Firecracker." He kissed me again, and I nearly forgot where we were.

"You two are nauseating. Cute, but vomit-worthy," Penna said from behind him. "Let's get going; our reservation is in about thirty minutes."

"Reservation?" I asked.

"I'm taking you to lunch," Paxton answered. "So if you'll go with Penna, I'll hop in the shower real fast."

"It's a group date," Landon added.

"A group date," I parroted. "I didn't realize anyone else was seeing anyone," I mused out loud.

"Oh, well, you date one of us, you kind of get us all," Penna said with a grin.

"That's a show I'd pay to watch," Landon said with a wiggle of his eyebrows in our direction...until he caught Paxton's death glare. "You know... I think I'll go wait on the plane."

"Plane?" I looked up at my boyfriend. *Boyfriend. How amazing is that?*

"I didn't want our first official date to be ordinary," he said with a soft kiss on my forehead.

"Oh, nothing with you could ever be ordinary." I laughed.

"Thank you."

I tilted my head. "I'm not sure that was a compliment."

He held my face in his hands and kissed me softly. "Wait and see what I have planned for us."

...

"Y ou want me to what?" I asked a few hours later, standing on a hilltop in Zakynthos, over three hundred miles away from Mykonos.

"BASE jump," Paxton said, positively giddy.

"You want me to jump off a thousand-foot cliff? Are you out of your mind? I don't even know how to operate a parachute." No way. No freaking way.

He brought my hands up to his heart, as if the beat would reassure me. Damn it, he was right. "First, it's actually only nine hundred feet, and we'd go tandem—together. I'll work everything, and you'll just enjoy the ride."

All around us, the Renegades were strapping on their harnesses and parachutes. Little John was even helping Brooke into one.

"You're doing this?" I asked her.

"Hell yes. This is Navagio Beach—one of the most epic sites ever. I'll never get an opportunity to try this again. Besides, I'll pull the cord so fast that there won't be much free fall, just the view."

I was at a loss for words.

"I told you this was a bad idea, that it wasn't fair to make her do this," Penna said quietly enough that only Paxton and I could hear. "Leah, if you want to walk down, I'm with you all the way."

Paxton shot her a look. "Point noted. I'd never *make* her jump."

I shook my head. "This feels like a death wish."

"I'll second that," Little John said as he brought our harnesses over. "Bobby is going to kill you when he realizes you ditched the cameras on this one."

"Why would you do that?" I asked. "This is exactly the kind of epic stuff you need for the documentary."

His features softened, and he kissed me. "Because a beautiful girl once told me that not everything epic was meant for a worldwide audience."

Okay, that was good. "Well, an insanely hot guy argued that."

His heart-stopping smile stole my breath. "He still does. Epic stunts are meant to be seen by the world."

"Then why leave the cameras?"

His knuckles brushed the underside of my jaw. "Because my whole world is already right here, watching."

Excuse me while I reform from the puddle I melted into. I sighed and looked around at everyone snapping on their helmets.

"Okay, if I were to agree to this, what would happen?"

I swore to God that I nearly saw him fist-pump.

"I packed our parachute and put together our harnesses, so everything is as safe as can be."

"When did you have time to do that?"

"Last night after you fell asleep. You know...after round two."

Landon snorted next to us, and I smacked Paxton's chest with the back of my hand. "Seriously?"

He shrugged. "Hey, you asked. Anyway, you'll be strapped to my chest, and we'll jump off. As soon as we're clear of the rocks, I'll pull the chute. The winds are great today, so they'll carry us straight down to the beach."

I peeked over the side of the cliff. "And that giant shipwreck down there?"

"We'll miss it. Trust me, Leah. I'm really good at this. Ridiculously good at this, as a matter of fact."

"Well, you don't need your ego stroked," I said, my nerves kicking into high gear.

"I can think of other things that like to be stroked," he whispered into my ear.

"Not funny," I spat back. "Parasailing is one thing, but you're asking me to jump off a cliff, Pax. Think about it."

He led me away from the group. "I know. This is what runs through your nightmares, right? Because I've seen a couple of them now."

I stiffened. Shit, I guess the one last night hadn't been as quiet as I'd hoped. "I'm s—"

"Don't you dare apologize. We're in this together now, you and I. You asked me to help you get over your fear, and that's what I'm trying to do. That's why the cameras aren't here."

My heart jumped, then pounded, beating an obnoxious rhythm in my temples. "What if I can't do this?"

He pulled me against his chest, one arm wrapped around my back and the other stroking my face. "I'll be with you. All you have to do is find the courage to say yes. I'll do the rest. And if you can't do it, then we'll walk back down and meet the others on the boat."

"But you'd miss your chance to do it."

"For this trip, sure. But the beach isn't going anywhere. You have to know that you're more important to me than this. Whatever you decide, I'll be okay with."

"We wouldn't fall for long?" Was I actually considering this? Crap, I guess I was. After all, hadn't I asked him to help me? The whole purpose of this trip had been to step outside my comfort zone—to live—and this was definitely living...if it didn't kill me.

"No, just long enough to clear the rocks."

"One in twenty BASE jumpers dies. That's according to a 2014 study by—"

His mouth stopped my rambling, kissing me soundly. It wasn't overly passionate or sexual, it was more comforting, reassuring, but it still set a deep vibration running through me.

"That won't be us," he promised. "I will never let anything hurt you. Not if it's within my power. Do you believe me?"

I nodded slowly, pulled into the force of his words, the expression in his Mediterranean-blue eyes. "I do."

"Do you trust me enough to do this?"

Wasn't that what this was all about? Did I trust Paxton enough to push my fear to the side? Logically, I knew his history with jumps, knew that if I was going to do this, there was literally no one on the planet better to do it with.

Emotionally…the guy wanted me to hurl myself off a cliff.

Laughter bubbled up, shaking my shoulders and bringing out an embarrassing snort.

"Leah?"

"I was thinking that jumping off a cliff is one way to fall for someone." Ludicrous, but so fitting.

"You falling for me, Firecracker?" he asked softly, an unnamable emotion passing over his face.

Jumping off the cliff was definitely preferable to this conversation. I wasn't ready to reveal any of my feelings, and I knew he wasn't nearly ready to hear them. Throwing the *L* word into our relationship was the most surefire way to kill it.

Sure, I'll date you.

Oh, by the way, I'm in love with you, too.

Yeah. No.

"I kind of like you," I said instead.

Now he was the one laughing. "Yeah, I kind of like you, too."

"Wilder!" Landon called from where they were all lined up at the cliff's edge. "You coming, or what?"

Paxton looked to me. "Well, do you choose the jump? Or

the 'or what'?"

I was torn. What if I got up there and chickened out? What if something happened on the way down? What if I broke my ankle on the landing, or I puked all over Paxton?

But what if I didn't do it?

Brooke was right, I'd never get this chance again. And besides, Rachel would have already harnessed up.

Paxton would keep me safe.

"Let's jump." The words came out of my mouth before I could think.

His face lit up. "Let's jump."

A few minutes later, Paxton knelt, putting me into the harness he'd double- and triple-checked, sliding the straps up over the leggings I'd changed into. "I like these," he said with a smirk as he ran his hands up my thighs.

"Yeah, yeah," I muttered, my eyes fixed on the edge of the cliff, where Penna and Brooke had already jumped. "Don't you want to watch them?" I asked.

He shook his head, adjusting my straps. "Nope, they're not my priority at the moment."

"You sure know how to make a girl feel protected."

He rose up before me, adjusting the shoulder straps with a quirk of his lips. "Hang around. In a few minutes I'll sweep you off your feet."

Only he could make me laugh right before I was about to endanger my life.

Once our helmets were snapped and I was clicked into Paxton's harness, we stepped to the edge. The view was unparalleled. The half-moon beach below was only accessible by the boat waiting offshore, the white sand meeting the greens and blues of the water in stunning contrast. In the middle lay a shipwreck, and I couldn't help but wonder how many jumpers it had seen.

"You ready?" Paxton asked behind me.

My heart lurched into my throat, and I had that same feeling as I did before the zip-line, knowing that something terrifying but amazing was about to happen. "You'll keep me safe?" I couldn't help but ask.

"Always," he answered, our helmets bumping as he leaned forward to kiss my cheek.

"Let's go."

"On three," he said.

"Okay." *Dear God, please don't let me die doing something as stupid as this. I'll be a good person. I'll go to church, and rescue a dog from a shelter, and call my parents every Saturday, just don't let me die.*

"One."

I'll volunteer at homeless shelters.

"Two."

I'll tutor kids in every subject. Or do my best to broker world peace. Yeah. Both of those.

"Three."

In perfect rhythm, we jumped.

My stomach dropped as we did, adrenaline flooding my veins. With each heartbeat, I cut another piece of my fear free, let it fall, and hoped I never caught up with it again.

The chute rippled out behind us, and our descent instantly slowed. The warm breeze caressed my face, and I took in gulping breaths as the sheer perfection of the moment overwhelmed me. It was beautiful—the view, the jump, the fearlessness, and Paxton behind me, steadily guiding us.

"What do you think?" he asked.

"There are no words," I answered.

"Exactly," he said, wonder in his voice. "Remember to bend your knees when we land. I'll try to do most of the work."

A few seconds later we hit the beach. The whole thing took less time than I'd spent debating actually doing it. But it was something I'd never forget, something that could never be taken away from me.

Paxton cut our chute loose and unhooked me. "You okay?" he asked as I spun in his arms.

I raised up, kissing him, slipping my tongue past his teeth and hoping he'd taste the euphoria running through me, the gratitude I had that he'd pushed me but hadn't pressured me.

Unlike Barcelona, this time he responded, tilting his head to get past our helmets and wrapping me in his arms.

"Thank you," I said, my smile uncontrollable.

"No, thank you," he said, kissing me again. "Your trust means the world to me."

"Leah!" Penna yelled, running over to us and hugging me. I was swamped by Brooke, Landon, and a couple of the other Renegades until secure in Paxton's arms, I was the center of a group hug.

"Welcome to the Renegades, Firecracker," he whispered in my ear.

Nothing had ever sounded more like home.

CHAPTER TWENTY-TWO

PAXTON

AT SEA

Leah was going to kill me.

I was officially ten minutes late for the before-class conference Dr. Westwick had requested, because the production meeting ran late. Physics wasn't anything I was worried about, but his email had sounded anything but friendly.

My hand paused on the door when I heard Leah's voice from inside the classroom.

"I'll get knocked down an entire grade if you do that," she said, sounding more worried than when I'd stuck her on the zip-line.

"It's not me doing anything, Miss Baxter. You missed the quiz because you failed to return to the ship in time. There are consequences to your actions."

Asshole.

I walked into the classroom, Leah's immediate look of relief transforming to annoyance when she checked her watch.

"Production meeting ran late," I said as way of explanation as I leaned against the desk she stood next to.

"Not even an apology, Mr. Wilder?" Dr. Douchebag snapped.

"Apologizing would mean that I wish it hadn't happened and I'd do my best to not let it happen again. Seeing as we were discussing the safety of our upcoming stunt, I'm not sorry that it took longer than expected, and as for intending to never be late...well, I know myself better than to make that kind of promise."

Leah sighed.

"Well, be that as it may"—he looked at me over his glasses—"when you neglected to get back to the *Athena* on time, you missed two of my classes, including a quiz."

"Yes," I agreed.

"Seeing as you chose not to be where you were supposed to, I'm under no obligation to let you take the quiz, and I see no reason to let you."

"But, sir, every other professor has agreed to let us turn in all the work due in the next few days," Leah said, her voice calm and rational, but her fingers rubbed her shirt. She was nervous as hell.

"Well, I'm not any of the other professors, am I? Every other student made it back to the ship. Every other student is here for their education, not for some adrenaline-fueled vacation."

"That's hardly fair," Leah started.

"That's bullshit," I finished.

"Excuse me?" Dr. Westwick turned his wrath on me, where I'd rather it have been in the first place.

"Miss Baxter is on board for her education. She's stuck tutoring me to keep her scholarship, and it's not fair to punish her because she was assigned to me. None of this was her fault. I'm the one who caused us to be late returning to the ship. It was my fault, and if she wasn't a work-study student, she wouldn't have been there with me. It's hugely unjust to punish her for something she had no control over—something she has to endure because she wants this education."

His narrowed gaze jumped between Leah and me. "And I'm supposed to cut you a break because your father owns this ship?"

Leah sucked in her breath, and I cringed. Shit. I was going to have to dig out of that hole as soon as we were alone. Meanwhile, I could set this asshole straight and salvage Leah's grade. "No. I don't expect any leniency. I knew the rules. I'm just asking that you not punish someone for not being able to afford the education I take completely for granted—for having to work her way through this trip."

He rubbed his fingers on the bridge of his nose, moving his glasses up and down. "Fine. Miss Baxter, you may take the quiz after class today."

Her knuckles whitened on her shirt. We'd only been back on board for a day; there was no way she'd studied. "Can she have a day to study?" I asked.

"Don't press my buttons, Mr. Wilder."

"Paxton, it's fine," she said under her breath as the first of the students filed in for class.

"Good, then I'll be ready for you after class. Mr. Wilder, you do not get afforded the same luxury." He turned, dismissing us as he headed toward his desk.

"He's such an asshole," I said as I sat in the desk I'd been propped on.

"Your dad owns the ship?" she threw back, taking her seat next to me.

Shit. "No. I mean, he owns the company that owns the ship, but—"

"That company isn't public, so yes, your dad owns the ship." She slammed her notebook on the desk.

"My dad owns the ship," I agreed.

"And that's why you can build a half-pipe in the theater and no one blinks. Why you have the biggest suite, and a work-study kid like me gets into the second biggest suite. Because it's your ship."

"My dad's company's ship."

She glared at me.

"Yeah. All of that."

She flipped through her binder, scanning her detailed notes from previous classes. "What are we going to do?"

"What do you mean?"

She looked over at me, exasperation written on every line of her gorgeous features. "I'm going to fail this quiz, but at least it's more points than I would have gotten if he didn't let me take it. What are we going to do about you? Or did you forget that my fate is tied to yours?"

If the desk hadn't been between us, I would have kissed the look off her face. Partly because I hated the worry lines between her eyebrows, and mostly because I loved kissing her. "Don't worry about me. This is the one class I can afford to take the hit."

"How? I'm struggling to keep a ninety-one in this class."

"I have a hundred. I think that's why Dr. Douche hates me so much. That, and I'm an entitled bastard."

"You have a hundred? How?" Her mouth dropped. Now I really wanted to kiss her, and that familiar stirring in my shorts was damn inconvenient.

"It's Application of Physics. A two-hundred level class. I'm a senior with four-hundred level physics classes. Not to

mention…it's physics. It's literally what my life depends on."
Physics was easy. Laws, mathematics, rules that all made sense.
It was the liberal arts that screwed me. I hated when shit was
left up to interpretation.

"Then why are you even taking this class?" she asked, her
mouth still agape.

"I had room for an elective," I said with a shrug.

She shook her head at me.

Fuck it. I leaned across the desk, grabbed the back of her
neck, and pulled her into a quick, hard kiss, uncaring that I'd
just gone ship-wide public with our relationship. *That's right,
guys. The gorgeous, smart girl is mine.* I broke the kiss before
she could respond, and grinned. "I took the class because you
did."

"Oh." She nodded slowly.

"Are we okay about the ship thing?" I had to know.

"Exactly how much money do you have?" she asked,
incredulous.

"Would it matter if I didn't have any?"

She shook her head.

"Then it doesn't matter how much I do have, right?"

"It doesn't matter. I just wish you'd told me. I hate finding
out stuff secondhand, especially about you, and you know how
important honesty is to me."

My gut twisted. She didn't even know the half of it.

"That's fair. What are you thinking?"

She sighed wistfully. "The *Athena*. Your dad still loves your
mom."

I swallowed and looked forward as Dr. Douche took the
podium. "Love. Yeah, well, it's never done either of them any
good, has it?"

She winced, but the lecture started before I could ask her why.

But there was something in the way she leaned slightly away that made me wish I'd kept my mouth shut.

That was a first.

"At least pretend to have a good time," Bobby instructed before walking away. Landon rolled his eyes and downed the rest of his beer.

The pounding bassline in the ship's club was usually enough to distract me, but this was the last place I wanted to be. Now the challenge would be if I could make it look like I felt the opposite.

"He's still pissed that we had to cancel the Istanbul shoot when you bruised your ribs."

"Yeah, well, not as pissed as I was." I polished off my Newcastle, and when Landon ordered another, I opted for water. I only had to sit here another hour or so before I could spend the rest of my evening worshipping Leah's body, and that deserved my full concentration.

Landon's was on the two sorority girls eyeing us. I wanted to say something to him about not fucking every girl on the ship, about not trying to feed the emptiness with meaningless hookups, but considering I was the one who put him in that situation, it wasn't my... *You know what? Fuck it.*

"So have you thought about slowing it down on that track?" I asked, motioning to where one of the girls giggled at his come-get-me grin.

He shrugged and started peeling the label on his empty bottle. "Not really."

"I know we don't talk about it"—his eyes flashed in my direction—"but I'm going to say this once and let it hang there. You're not going to find the answer to missing her underneath that girl's dress, or the one after her, or the one right after her."

"I don't know what the fuck you're talking about. I'm fine." The hard I-will-kill-you look he threw at me said otherwise.

"Right. Well—"

"Drop it," he growled. A second later his Casanova smile was in place, ready to woo another Band-Aid for his still-hemorrhaging heart.

"You're Wilder, aren't you?" sorority girl number one asked me, leaning close to be heard over the pounding bass in the ship's club.

"I am," I answered with my expected grin.

Mischief Lounge was full because it was a Friday night, which meant no classes tomorrow. It was our only day in Athens, and I'd promised Leah we'd do all the artsy stuff she wanted, as long as we could pause to play a game of human Zorb Ball bowling in the Olympic Stadium for the cameras. And then, of course, we'd be holed up the rest of the weekend to get the massive amount of make-up work done that we'd missed while in Mykonos. *Worth it.*

But for now, I was on Wilder duty, playing the bad-boy card so Bobby could get his shots in.

"I'm Candy," she said with a dentist-white smile and fuck-me eyes, then motioned over her shoulder. "And this is my friend, Jules."

"Nice to meet you," I answered. On the opposite side of the booth, Landon was looking at Jules like he'd discovered his weekend. Typical.

"Do you mind?" she asked as she sat on the spare three

inches between me and the edge.

I moved over so she didn't fall on her ass. "Not at all," I answered, because that's what I was supposed to do, especially given the microphones right behind us in the fake-as-hell lotus flowers.

Jules made herself at home on Landon's lap.

If Candy thought she'd pull the same shit, she was sorely mistaken. Damn it, I should have had the talk with Leah today, but she'd been freaking out over academics. I couldn't exactly go documentary-public without her saying yes. Everything they'd caught in Mykonos I could have edited out with the right amount of leverage.

"Ooh!" Candy exclaimed, her boobs bouncing in her tight pink tank top as she flagged the waitress down. "Can we get shots?" She sent me a sideways glance. "Maybe some Sex on the Beach?"

Fucking spare me. It wasn't like I could turn her down on camera.

"Sounds good," I said with a nod to the waitress. "Thank you."

"So why do they call you Wilder?" Candy asked, her hand disturbingly close to my thigh. Usually I'd be all for it. Why not spend a night with a gorgeous woman and no strings attached?

But now I had Leah, and Candy was no Leah.

"It's my last name," I answered.

She pouted. "Is that really all there is?"

"Because he's always up for any trick or any challenge. He's got a wild streak a mile wide," Landon answered.

"I like wild," Candy said, moving even closer.

I slid another six inches away.

"And why are you Nova?" her friend asked.

"Casanova has a way with the ladies," I helped him out. Not that Landon needed any help. Hell, he needed someone to yank back the leash and remind him who he was underneath the man-whore. It just sucked that the reminder was going to come at the cost of my own relationship.

She'll understand if you tell her, one part of me argued.

You blew past the honesty door, bud. Enjoy this while it lasts, the other added.

But losing Leah... God, I couldn't even think about it. A feeling between vomit-worthy nausea and midnight-black sorrow possessed my body every time the reminder crept in that I'd already fucked up the best thing I'd ever had.

"So I can see," Candy said while her friend giggled.

I ran my thumb down my glass of ice water, wiping away a streak of condensation. Was this really how I'd spent my nights before coming on the *Athena*? Is this what had made me happy?

Hell, had I actually *been* happy?

Busy, yes. Challenged, sure. My life was demanding, and awesome at times, but I couldn't remember feeling...happy. Not in the way I had been these last few days.

"...don't you think?" Candy asked, looking at me for a response to a question I hadn't heard.

And that's what I got for not listening.

"I think Wilder might disagree," Landon answered, bailing me out with a discreet nod. "Sure, Bermuda was great, but I think he liked Mykonos the best."

I took the cue. "Yeah, there is something to be said for the beaches there."

"Speaking of sex," Candy said as the waitress delivered our shots.

Nice segue.

"To making unforgettable memories with no regrets," Candy said, raising her shot, "and no strings." She turned her blue eyes on me, and I nodded, slamming back the sickly sweet shot while I prayed for patience.

"Well, you two look like your dance cards are full," Penna said as she reached the table, decked out in club wear that screamed, "look, but touch and I'll throat-punch you." It was her specialty.

"Penna," I said, trying to keep the relief out of my voice. She'd always been good at fending off attention when I wanted to be left alone.

"Well, maybe he saved room for one," Leah said as she stepped out from behind Penna, and my mouth dropped.

Her hair was down, framing her heart-shaped face, and Penna had done something to her eye makeup to bring out the gold flecks in her eyes. Given the plunge of that black halter neckline, I would have said she dressed her, too.

Leah glanced between Candy and me. "Or maybe you are full up?"

Shit. I was not going to get into a fight with Leah over this superficial bullshit. Before I could toss Candy out of the booth—cameras be damned—Leah gave me a smile that hit me a hell of a lot harder than that shot.

She arched an eyebrow at me in flirtatious challenge, and I took it. "I think I can squeeze you in," I said with a serious nod. "If you'll excuse me?" I said to Candy.

She huffed but moved so I could get out of the booth. Even with the stuffy, heated air of the club, I instantly breathed easier.

"Hey, have you met Justin?" Penna asked Candy, steering her toward one of the new Renegades. God bless her.

I turned back to Leah, who looked up at me and laughed. "I

leave you alone for five minutes…"

"This is not what it looks like," I started.

"You're not putting on a Wilder act for Bobby?" she asked.

My mouth opened and shut a couple times. "Yeah, that's exactly what I was doing."

"Then it *is* what it looks like to me." She fingered the rolled-up sleeves of the collared shirt I wore. "But you do look ridiculously good doing it."

I glanced to Bobby, who was shooting me a death glare from where he was set up against the wall. Guess we'd ruined that shot. "You're not mad?" I asked.

"Not at all." She moved her hands to play with the buttons on my shirt.

The woman was a saint.

"It's not like I didn't know who you were when I agreed to whatever we're doing."

What. The. Fuck? "I'm sorry?" I asked her.

She looked up at me. "We never agreed to exclusivity, and if you're supposed to keep up your image, there's nothing I can do about it." Her eyes lowered, and her forehead puckered. "I mean, I'm hoping it wouldn't go past that booth—"

"We never…?" I shook my head then gave Bobby the "cut" sign. "We're dancing."

"We are?" she asked, but I was already leading her by the hand to the floor.

I pulled her into my arms as the slow song played, my hands a hell of a lot gentler than my tone. "What the hell do you mean we never agreed to be exclusive?"

Her fingers played with the hair at the top of my neck. "Did we?"

White-hot jealousy set my chest on fire when I thought

about another guy coming within an inch of her. Touching her. Kissing those soft lips. *Over my dead body.* "We're agreeing to it now."

"Okay," she said, like it was the simplest answer on the planet.

"Good," I said a little harshly. "Did you honestly think I was going to see other women after what happened on Mykonos?"

Okay, maybe a whine crept in there.

She shrugged, but the wince clued me in that her defense mechanisms were in control. "No, but when Penna suggested we come down, and then you were snuggled up with Blondie... I don't know. It's like you're two different people—Wilder for the cameras, and Paxton for me—and I thought maybe Wilder needed to appear available."

The way she saw me, cut through every layer I'd built up, was downright scary. "I am both, and I can tell you that both sides of me are wild for you." Her lips parted, and it took all of my restraint not to kiss her. "Bobby needed some party shots to layer in, and I agreed. But you and I have never talked about going public for the camera. Everything on Mykonos I can put a lid on, and even what happened in class wasn't filmed. I wasn't going to make that choice without you."

"Oh," she said, her voice all breathy.

"This is your choice. I would never force it on you—the cameras, the publicity, the press—but I can tell you that no matter what you decide, things will never go further than having a few drinks on camera with fans. I'm with *you*. If you want to go public, I'm all for it. Nothing would make me happier than not having to look for cameras before I kiss you."

"Really?"

I absolutely loathed the surprise in her voice. "Really."

What was with us and that word? "If you want to keep our relationship private, I'll respect that, too. I'll hate it, but I never want you to be uncomfortable. I can watch my hands in public," I promised, making sure they were currently north of her ass. "Probably not my eyes, but I could try."

The few heartbeats it took her to answer felt like years. Of course I wanted to go public. I wanted everything about us on film, so when she eventually realized what an asshole I was—and left me—I'd have something of her to hold on to. I wanted everyone on this ship—hell, the world—to know that Eleanor Baxter was mine...for as long as she'd have me.

"Okay," she whispered. "We can go public."

"Really?" I asked, ready to crow.

"Really," she said with a smile I couldn't wait to kiss off her face.

And she'd given me permission to.

I moved one hand to her ass and gripped the base of her neck with the other, then took her mouth. Deepening the kiss, I used every skill I had to publicly claim her—and lost myself in the process. The dance floor and everyone around us disappeared, until there was only Leah in my arms, her sweet mouth under mine, her whimpers in my ear.

Kissing her got better, hotter, every time, like giving in to the unreal chemistry between us only let the fire burn brighter—and that fire was about to burn us both alive in the middle of the dance floor if I didn't get a grip.

"Take me to bed," she whispered in my ear, then ran her tongue along the shell.

"Your wish is my command," I answered, steering my girlfriend toward the door. I waved Bobby off when I heard him calling my name and kept going.

I didn't stop until I had Leah naked, under me, then on top, screaming my name as she came. I kept going until I had explored every inch of her skin with my hands and tongue, committed every curve and hollow to memory again. Once I found my own release and tucked her in against me, our skin sweaty and our breathing calmed, my body finally stopped moving.

But knowing what was coming for us…well, my mind was a completely different matter.

CHAPTER TWENTY-THREE

LEAH

MOROCCO

It wasn't natural to be this happy. Even when I'd been with Brian for a year, I'd never felt this contentment or the giddy need to see him the way I did Paxton.

On the one hand, it made me feel like utter shit. I'd loved Brian. Maybe not a desperate, soul-consuming love, but a softer version—one that was blurring at the edges with time.

But on the other hand, it gave me the sense that maybe I was finally moving past it in a way therapy hadn't pulled me through.

I felt free, lifted, and for the first time in forever, morning brought an incredible sense of excitement to see what my day would bring, instead of dread. I especially loved days like today where I woke up in Paxton's arms, tracing the lines of his tattoos until he opened his eyes.

"You ready?" Penna called from our living room.

"You look good in everything, so let's go," Paxton joined in.

I rolled my eyes and looked in the mirror one more time. It was day number two in Morocco, and we'd been anchored at

Casablanca for two days. After yesterday's sweat-fest while we were on the World Religion excursion to the Hassan Mosque and subsequent churches, there was zero chance I was going back out there in pants. When Paxton told me to wear a swimsuit under my clothes, he'd unknowingly solidified my choice.

Well, semi-solidified, otherwise I wouldn't have been there debating the thigh-length black shorts I'd bought in Mykonos.

"You know, mornings would be so much easier if you'd agree to move into my place," Paxton said.

I grabbed my floppy sun hat, oversize glasses, and travel wallet before leaving the safety of my room. "As I recall, this whole ship is your place, so really, I already did."

His eyes swept my frame, the usual heat sparking there, and when they caught my shorts, he looked up, blazing with pride. "You look amazing."

"Let's go. I'm not holding up our trip so that you can make out, and the last time someone left you two to your own devices, you ended up off the ship for five days." Penna pointed to the door.

"It was a good five days," I argued as Paxton's arm wrapped around my waist.

"Worth every second, and all that fucking make-up work," Paxton swore with a kiss on the top of my head.

"Yeah, well, you still took the hit in Physics," I said as we walked into the hallway.

"A ninety-two is hardly a hit. I've got two other solid Bs, so I think we're okay."

"We'll see what happens when your Lit paper's graded," I fired back, leaning into him as we entered the elevator.

"I'd have gotten an A if you would have written it for me," he muttered.

I elbowed him. "Not happening."

"I was joking." He laughed, wrapping me in his arms.

"I wasn't aware that we'd gone from ESPN to Lifetime," Zoe spat when she got on, rolling her eyes.

"Sheathe your claws before it becomes *Jerry Springer*," Penna snapped.

"We made it!" Brooke yelled as she pulled Landon in behind her.

I did a few calculations on the weight allowance when Little John squeezed in the elevator next, but sighed in relief when he told the rest of the crew they'd have to catch the next one.

I took the ramp off the ship without breaking a sweat, and we met up with the others at the bus. And by bus...well, at one point it *had* been a bus, I just wasn't sure that's what it qualified as now. The top had been sheared off so it looked more like a giant flatbed with benches.

"Mr. Wilder!" the guide driver called out.

"Mr. Mantoui?" Paxton shook the man's hand. "Nice to meet you."

"I am a big fan! It's my pleasure to take you to Paradise Valley. It is one of the most beautiful places in our country." He motioned for us to board the contraption.

"We're all excited," Paxton promised, then posed for a picture with Landon and Penna before we climbed on.

The twenty or so seats were all taken by camera crew and Renegades, and I walked down the aisle behind Paxton to find a seat.

"Hey, what happened to your legs?" Zoe asked, stopping me with her arm and openly staring.

I met her stare unflinchingly. "Car accident," I answered. It was the CliffsNotes version of the truth, but it was all she deserved. Hell, I mostly said it for myself, anyway.

"Nice," Landon answered across the aisle, lifting his board shorts and knocking Zoe's arm out of the way as he bared his thigh and the jagged scar that ran from knee to the hemline. "This was the summer I was obsessed with BMX."

Penna stood behind her and lifted her shirt over her stomach. "This was my first attempt at a backflip," she said, pointing to the hand-length scar that ran down her left side.

"And you've already seen every single one of mine," Paxton said, turning around. He didn't shoot Zoe a death glare or even look at her, simply bent, grabbing my upper thighs and lifting me up against him. "But I'll be happy to give you another show," he whispered into my ear as he backed us into our seat a few rows away.

He sat in the middle and nudged my legs to straddle him, which I did happily. *I love you.* It was on the tip of my tongue, screaming from my heart, but I couldn't form the words. It was still too soon, too raw.

"All of us have scars. You fit right in," he promised. "But I will tell you that these shorts are going to distract me all damn day."

I kissed him, uncaring that we were on display. He tasted like the mint of his toothpaste, all tangy and fresh, and I couldn't help but press deeper. His grip was tight on my thighs, his hands warming my skin as his tongue set a fire inside me.

He groaned, pulling away and resting his forehead against mine. "If we keep that up, I'm hauling you back inside."

"Not this time," Bobby interjected, taking the seat behind us, his nose covered in a thick layer of zinc. "Your sexcapades are not ruining this. It's going to be epic. This is one of the primo places to cliff dive in the world."

"Hey, Bobby," Paxton called over his shoulder. "Who do you work for?"

"What?" He let that sink in a second and then rolled his eyes. "You."

"Just checking," Paxton finished, and I laughed as I slid off his lap, taking the seat next to him.

"Welcome Renegades," Mr. Mantoui called into the microphone as we pulled out of the port. The breeze nearly stole my hat, and I took it off, turning my face up to the sunshine as the group gave a cheer. "I cannot wait to show you more of my country. Tell me, are you ready for an adventure?" he asked, and Paxton snorted at the use of his line.

Looking up at the strong lines of Pax's face, feeling my hand safely encased in his, I honestly was.

"Okay, maybe the hike was worth it," Brooke said as we sat on the edge of one of the pools of Paradise Valley.

"It's spectacular," I agreed. Sure, my muscles were on fire from the hike, but the price was small compared to the view. The aquamarine pools ran the length of the valley, and ours boasted a waterfall that broke through halfway down the cliff walls that were freakishly tall on one side and terraced on the other, cocooning us in a tiny piece of heaven.

Especially when Paxton stripped off his shirt and dove in. Exactly when was this attraction going to mellow? Knowing I could touch him, kiss him, strip him naked at my whim should have tempered the ridiculous amount of lust that pounded through me when I saw him. Instead it made me want to jump him. Repeatedly.

It made our study sessions way more difficult, yet so much

more rewarding. It also helped that he'd made it to all of his classes in the two weeks that we'd been back on board.

"Is it as deep as the reports said?" Penna, already stripped down to her tankini with boy shorts, asked from the shore that had been hollowed out by water about five feet beneath us. Brooke and I waited on the ledge above her, laying out our towels.

"We should be good. It's definitely a ways down. We need to watch these rocks here." Paxton pointed to the shelf of boulders that lined the shore on that side. "Landon?"

"Let's test it!" Landon yelled from another rock ledge about twenty feet in the air, not even midway up the cliff wall. Then he jumped, yelling something as he fell to the water below, landing with a huge splash.

One by one, the Renegades took the skinny path to that ledge and jumped, each one getting braver than the last, flipping, twisting, and landing while the cameras rolled.

"Ready to head up?" Penna asked Paxton.

"Up to where?" I looked down at where he stood on the strip of beach below us.

"We're jumping from up there," he said, pointing to the top of the cliff.

My eyes went up...and up. "What? How tall is that?"

"About a hundred feet," he answered, shielding his eyes from the sun with his hand so he could see me.

"Is that safe?" I asked as he climbed his way up to me, his feet sure on the smooth stone surface.

"Eh," Landon answered, his hands making the so-so motion. "Only those of us who have jumped from pretty high before are trying it."

"And this isn't one of your 'let's get Leah to do something

wild' things, is it?"

Paxton shook his head, reaching for me and dripping water onto my thighs as he caged me in with his arms. "Hell no. This is something that could actually hurt you, that I can't protect you from."

I wiped a drop of water from his cheek. "Could it hurt you?"

He shook his head. "Nah. I did a jump from about a hundred and twenty feet once. While drunk. Which is probably the only reason I did it. Stupid, but I've got this. You could walk up with me, though."

"Need some courage?" I asked with a grin.

His brow furrowed. "I was more hoping that you'd bring down my shoes."

I outright laughed. "One of your minions can't do that?"

"Maybe I just like you being the only one to handle my junk." He gave me puppy dog eyes.

"Nice. What'll you give me?"

"Orgasms."

I arched an eyebrow. "What will you give me that I can't already have?"

"I will dedicate all of tomorrow to studying. No tricks, no practice, no gym time. Just you, and me, and books. Boring books. Not even *Kama Sutra* books."

Ugh. Those eyes got me every time. "Promise?"

"I promise." He leaned in, brushing his lips over mine. "Honestly, though. I heard the view up there is unparalleled. Figured you might like to see it."

"Well, I guess you're only in Morocco once, right?"

"Absolutely." He got up and put on his shoes for the hike.

"Want to come?" I asked Brooke.

"Hell no," she answered, spreading sunscreen on her skin.

"I'm not hiking all the way up there just to hike all the way back down. I'll cheer you on, though."

We took off, following a gently worn path to the top of the cliff, scrambling over rocks in a few places that had Paxton giving me a push...more likely giving him an excuse to get his hands on my ass, but I wasn't complaining.

My breathing was heavy once we reached the top, but he was right, the view was astounding. The falls from the tip of the valley were visible from here, breathtaking and slightly dangerous-looking. I could make out the lower-walled pools from here, too, all the same aqua color that begged for a dip.

"What are you thinking?" Paxton asked, holding my hand as we stepped closer to the edge. He paused before we got too far, knowing there was no way I was willingly looking over the side. Even the pebbled ground felt unstable up here.

"That I should go for a swim when I get down there. Want to go with me?"

"Hell yes. I'll wait for you at the bottom. He motioned to a member of the camera crew, the others already stationed along the pool. "He'll walk you back down. Okay?"

"No problem," I answered as he strapped on his helmet with the GoPro camera for the Wilder view of the jump.

"I'm obsessed with you," he said before he kissed me. "You know that, right?"

I love you. "You're not too bad yourself," I answered. "Now go have a good day at work, dear."

He kissed me again and went to stand with the others. Paxton, Landon, Penna, and two of the junior members all stood at the edge, ready for their turn.

I sent up a prayer that they'd all make it safely, but I had to have faith that they knew what they were doing.

"Remember to jump out. If you go straight down you'll bust open on those rocks below," Paxton ordered, and my nerves crept up a level.

"See you at the bottom!" Landon called out, taking a few steps backward and then running off the cliff face and disappearing.

I heard a splash a few seconds later, and the Renegades cheered. My curiosity got the better of me, and I took a step forward, but not too much. What was the fun if I didn't see them do it? The two junior Renegades went next, one giving off a high-pitched scream that reminded me of an angry toddler.

Then Penna jumped, and I held my breath until I heard the splash, and then her voice as she surfaced in victory.

"Kind of a rush, isn't it?" the camera guy asked me. "You should come look from up here. It's completely safe."

I inched forward, my stomach dropping when the pool came into view below. I needed to see that he hit the water, that was all.

Paxton winked at me with a Wilder grin, backed up a few steps, and ran for the edge, soaring into the air with a triumphant yell as he flipped once and landed in the water feetfirst, missing the rocks by a good fifteen feet.

Thank you, God.

Landon cheered from the shore, but I couldn't breathe until Pax surfaced, inhaling at the same moment he did.

"Let's head back down," the camera guy said, and I nodded as he turned to leave.

"I'll be right behind you," I said, looking back to Paxton. "You okay?"

"Absolutely! Get your gorgeous ass down here so I can get you wet!"

"Paxton!" I laughed.

"Water, of course. Only water," he promised, but I could see that smile from here.

"Right," I said with a sarcastic nod. "I'll be down in a second." I backed up a couple feet and blew him a kiss, poised to turn.

The rocks rustled behind me—no doubt the camera guy was getting tired of waiting. "Better jump." A sinister whisper hit me at the same time the blow came to my upper back.

All I heard was the blood rushing through my head, the pebbles skidding beneath my sneakers as I slid toward the cliff's edge. It was over before I even realized it had started, my momentum carrying me past the point of no return.

I grabbed for the bush at the edge, making contact as I fell over the side. My right hand closed around the branch, screaming in protest from the wood cutting away at my skin as it slid down my palm.

"Leah!" Paxton's yell sounded like it was miles away.

My shoulder jerked as it caught my weight, the rest of me slamming into the cliff face. Pain exploded in my cheek, but I didn't let go.

"Leah!" Paxton screamed again, but I couldn't force sound through my throat, not even to scream. "Baby, you have to reach up with your other hand. Somebody get to her!"

"Landon's already running!" Penna answered.

Using all of my strength, I swung my left arm up enough to grab the branch. It was barely as thick as a curtain rod. There was no way this thing was strong enough to hold my weight. My toes scrambled to find purchase against the rock face, but there was nothing big enough for my foot.

"Firecracker, talk to me!" It was only the sheer terror in

Paxton's voice that broke through the lump in my throat.

"Pax!" Was that even my voice? Something wet ran down my arm, and my hands felt slick against the branch. Blood. I had to find a foothold.

I slipped, catching myself at the tip of the branch, but my foot found a tiny outcropping that my toes might fit on. My right toes made contact, and I breathed a slight sigh of relief. "I...I think I found something."

"Hold on!" Pax yelled. "Landon's coming."

"Don't leave me!" I cried out.

"I'm staying right here, baby."

He sounded so far away—because he was.

It had taken us ten minutes to hike up here. There was no way Landon was going to make it faster than five. I just had to hold on for five minutes.

I moved my left foot over, hoping to find another toehold to take some of my weight off the branch, and off my ruined hands. The weight on the tiny ledge was too much—it gave way.

A primal scream ripped from my throat as my feet kicked, but my hands held steady, my grip slick but still firm on the wood. My breath came in giant gulps, and I kept my eyes focused on the wood.

Don't look down. That had been what kept me alive after the accident.

How the hell did I end up here again?

The wood at the base of the branch creaked.

My head snapped up, and my eyes darted to the bush. *No. No. No.* "Pax, it's gonna give!"

"Just hold on!" he yelled again. "Damn it! Why the hell don't we have an emergency crew here? Something?"

The branch tore at the base, and I slid another foot down

the cliff wall with a shriek, but it didn't snap completely.

At the same moment, my toes grazed another outcropping just beneath me. Maybe it could bear my weight, maybe—

It ripped clean through, the sound tearing apart the tiniest hope I'd had of surviving this. *God, Mom. Dad. And Paxton's going to see it.*

This time the branch didn't stop me, coming clean out of the ground. I let go and dug my fingertips and toes into the rock as I fell.

Paxton screamed my name.

My hands caught the outcropping my toes had been aiming for, my muscles locking as the impact jarred every molecule in my body. Another scream bubbled out of my throat as agony lit up my arms like flames, protesting every damn thing about this situation.

The pounding in my heart grew increasingly loud until I realized that it wasn't my heart at all—it was footsteps.

"Leah!" Landon's face came into view at least ten feet above me, sweat-soaked and beet red. "It's okay," he said between heavy breaths.

"This is not okay!" I yelled back. "I can't hold on much longer."

"No, but you're a fighter, and we're going to get you out of this, you understand?"

I nodded the tiniest fraction, scared to move any muscle. Landon surveyed my surroundings, leaning way too far out over the edge.

"There's a foothold above your right foot if you raise it a few inches," he said.

Slowly, I did as he suggested, and found it. My muscles screamed, but I pulled up enough to stand on the small ledge, bringing my left foot, too. It took my weight and held it, but given the way pieces crumbled, I couldn't depend on it. "I don't know how long this will hold."

I didn't know how long *I* would hold.

"Can we get a fucking rope up here?" Landon asked.

"It's coming!" Penna yelled.

"Hold on, Leah!" Brooke added, the sound echoing around me.

I focused on the rocks directly in front of my face, but they morphed in my mind, changing colors, texture, until I wasn't on a cliff in Morocco, I was back above the car crash with Brian's body burning beneath me.

Just let go, my memory called to me. *No one is coming for you. You can't hold on. Just let go and it will all be over, the pain, the fear, all of it. He's already dead.*

But it wasn't Brian beneath me, it was Paxton—whom I loved—who was very much alive. Still, my choice remained the same. I wasn't strong enough to hold on indefinitely, and I wasn't brave enough to let go, so I hung in limbo like I did then.

"Leah, with the angle you're at, I can't get to you. You have the only foothold, and if I come down, I'll crush your fingers, which would be pretty detrimental to the goal, don't you think?" Landon asked.

"It could put a damper on things," I said, my voice shaking with my gulping breaths. I couldn't get my breathing to slow, or my heart rate to calm. "Landon," I said quietly enough so only he could hear me. "My hands. They're bleeding, and I'm going to slip. I'm going to fall." Every second my muscles grew weaker, my grip less firm.

"Yes."

He said it so calmly that I didn't panic when I looked up at him, even when more of the rock crumbled beneath my feet. "I'm not going to last until the rope gets here."

"No." His eyes were soft, steady.

"Leah, you're doing great. Just hold on, baby!" Paxton yelled up.

"Am I going to die?" I asked Landon, like he held the answers to the universe.

"No." He shook his head. "But this is going to take everything you've got. Are you ready?"

"Paxton shouldn't see," I said. "He shouldn't have to watch."

"He's not leaving you. That's why I'm here and he's still down there, waiting for you. We're going to have to be quick, before you lose too much strength to do this." He turned his head and spoke over his shoulder before looking back to me. "The crew made it back up. There's no rope, Leah. This is all about to be on you."

I didn't know what he had in mind, but I could barely hold myself here, let alone do any acrobatic feats. And Paxton...he was going to see me fall. He'd be the first one to my mangled body.

"Paxton," I said quietly. "I love him. I never told him, but I love him."

"He knows. He might not admit it, but he knows. We all do. It shines out of you two the minute you're in the same room— anyone can see it."

"I don't want him to watch."

"Leah, listen to me," Landon snapped. "You're not going to die. I forbid it. I'm not going to lose my best friend's girl on some jump in Morocco. This is not how your story ends, and it's not how his ends, either. Do you understand? He'll be destroyed if anything happens to you, so if you can't fight for you, then you fight for him. Got it?"

I swallowed as my arms started to shake from exhaustion.

"Pax!" Landon yelled down.

"Yeah?" he answered. "Is my girl okay?"

"I need her to jump, Pax." Landon kept his eyes locked with mine as he said it.

"You have to be fucking kidding me!" I yelled.

"Okay!" Pax called out at the same time.

"It's gotta be quick, brother, she's weakening fast!"

"Firecracker, you okay with this?" Pax asked me.

"No!" I shouted as more rock gave way beneath my feet. My arms would never hold me if I lost my foothold.

"Concentrate on my voice, Leah. You can do this. You're going to have to jump backward to clear the rocks beneath you. Do you understand?" Landon asked, never looking away.

"Rocks equal kersplat?" I questioned softly.

"And water equals safe. Water equals Paxton. Got it?" Landon asked, a trace of fear seeping into his eyes when my fingers slipped another centimeter.

"What do I do?" I called out.

"You push off with your feet as hard as you can and let go, baby. You have to come down as straight as possible, okay? Hitting the water is going to hurt, but it's going to be okay," Pax called up.

Let go. Just let go and it will all be over. But this time, letting go meant giving it everything I had. This time letting go could kill me...or it could save me.

"No one can do this for you—God, I wish I could—but I'm here, Leah. I'm not going anywhere, do you understand? You can do this," Landon promised, his voice steady and even.

For the first time I looked down.

Fuck. Shit. God, I'm going to die. The distance may as well have been a mile. Panic crept up my spine and my vision narrowed, blackening at the edges.

"LEAH!" Paxton screamed. "Listen to my voice. Push with your feet and jump now!"

I sucked in a full breath, and my vision returned to normal as I whipped my head back to the rock face. I was not going to give in, to pass out and die by default. I would choose my fate. Either I made it, or I didn't, but it would be of my own making.

And I wasn't about to become Paxton's tragedy.

"Okay," I called out, my voice stronger than my failing arms.

"You've got this, and he's got you," Landon promised.

I nodded, pulled my body as close to the cliff as humanly possible, said a prayer, and then pushed off with every ounce of strength I had left.

My stomach dropped out as I plummeted, my arms flailing in circles as if I could slow the descent. The ground rose at a dizzying speed, the canyon wall flying by me in a blur.

Pain shot through my legs, vibrating up my spine to my head when I hit, then sank into the water. *You cleared the rocks.*

Water rushed up my nose as it rose over my head, and I started kicking with every spare ounce of energy I had, stopping my descent. As I started to rise, strong arms looped around my waist, propelling me upward.

We broke the surface, and I gasped, pulling sweet oxygen into my lungs and coughing out the water that had invaded my nostrils.

"I've got you, baby. I've got you," Paxton whispered over and over as he pulled me to the shore, my back to his chest. The sheer relief of being held in his arms, of having survived the fall hit me, and my muscles simply quit, going slack.

Hands lifted me away from Paxton, laying me on something soft for a moment before he hovered above me again, his eyes bluer than the sky behind him. I'd almost lost him, almost lost myself.

I heard a splash in the background and the soft sound of Brooke crying to my right.

"Leah, Leah, Leah," Paxton chanted my name as his hands ran over my face, my lips, my arms, all of my extremities. "God, Leah. I thought... But you're okay. You're okay." He looked in my eyes, searching for something I couldn't name but desperately wanted to give him to soothe the panic in his eyes.

"I love you, Paxton," I blurted, needing to say it, needing him to know what he meant to me and honestly not caring what he thought about it.

"Leah." My name sounded like the most reverent prayer on his lips, and he gathered me in his arms, holding me tight when my body couldn't return his trembling embrace. "I can't lose you. You're everything."

"She okay?" Landon asked, climbing out of the water at my feet.

"Yeah, thanks to you, she is," he answered, still cradling me against his heartbeat.

"She did all the work, man. Leah, you really are a firecracker," Landon said, taking a dry towel from Penna and wrapping it around my back. "Not many people could have caught themselves the way you did, or hung on like that. Talk about a trip."

Trip? I looked up at the top of the cliff, which seemed even higher from this angle. They wouldn't have seen what happened from this angle—not until I was already falling.

"Paxton," I said softly.

He lowered his head to mine, brushing a tender kiss across my lips. "Leah?"

"I didn't trip. I was pushed," I whispered as quietly as I could.

A look befitting his last name passed over his eyes, and I knew this time he couldn't deny it. There was a traitor among us.

CHAPTER TWENTY-FOUR

LEAH

AT SEA

Paxton held me, my back to his chest, wrapped around me like a cocoon in his bed that night. He hadn't taken no for an answer, simply carried me to his room, dressed me in his boxers and a T-shirt, and crawled in behind me.

It was after midnight, and despite his body heat and my utter exhaustion, I still couldn't sleep.

"Are you hungry? Do you want me to order more food? Get a sleeping pill from the nurse? Bring the doctor back?" he offered, his arm tightening over my chest, careful not to brush my bandaged hands.

I shook my head. "I don't want to sleep."

"You need to." His chin rubbed against the top of my head. "Your body is wrecked and needs the rest."

"I don't want to have the nightmare," I whispered.

He pressed a kiss to my hair. "I want you to tell me about it. You don't have to, but I want to know. Watching you up there today, and knowing I couldn't get to you... God, Leah. I was so fucking scared. And I saw it, that moment you almost gave in."

I took a deep breath, steadying my nerves and savoring the scent of him. "We were coming home after a party. Brian had probably had a couple beers, but it wasn't like he was drunk." His face flashed in front of my eyes, how beautiful his smile had been, how easy it had been around him. "He wanted to take the canyon road home, even though it was longer. He loved his damn car, and he'd just gotten new tires on it, but the roads were slick from the rain earlier." I reached up, my forearms tightening over where Paxton held me, safe and secure. "I told him to slow down, but he smiled and said he could handle it. To trust him, and I did. We'd been together all of senior year. But he didn't slow for the curve in time, and there was skidding, and we busted right through the guardrail."

I closed my eyes, but the images were only more vivid in my imagination, so I opened them again, turning over so I could see Paxton's face instead of Brian's. I concentrated on the curve of his chin, the line of his mouth, afraid that if I saw his eyes, I couldn't continue. "The first impact was rough. I only remember the drop in my stomach as we fell, and then the jarring stop. Then nothing until I woke up hours later."

Paxton brushed the hair back behind my ears but stayed silent, simply listening. "When I came to, Brian's body was pinned to his seat by this branch as thick as my arm. There was blood…so much blood. And he was already gone. I don't know how long I cried, suspended there by my seat belt, but it felt like an eternity. Once I got myself under control, I saw that my door was jammed shut, but I could get out of Brian's…but I couldn't climb over him. I couldn't use him like a step stool to live while he'd died.

"My phone had been flung out of my hand, and when I heard it ringing from the hatch in the back, I thought it would be easier, better for him, if I unbuckled, and got to it. I could get help. But the shift in weight—"

My eyes squeezed shut, feeling it all over again. Paxton kissed my eyelids, grounding me, keeping me with him instead of in the past.

"The shift in weight caused the car to fall again, this time farther, until we hit a massive boulder, and I was a ping-pong ball in the car, hitting…everything. My legs…they went through the windshield."

Paxton hissed and pressed a kiss to my forehead like that would take away the pain, and oddly enough, it slightly did.

"Once…once I got myself back into the car, I knew I had to get to the ledge next to us. The car was balanced so precariously. I wanted to take Brian, I did. But that branch had broken off inside the car—he was still pinned to the seat."

I opened my eyes but kept them on Paxton's chin, my gaze unfocused. "I don't know how long I sat there debating. Probably hours. Every time I shifted my weight, the car moved, so by the time I found the courage to climb out—to go over Brian— I got out just before the car fell. There was no time to even try to get him. I couldn't even give his body to his mother."

"That is not your fault," he said softly, anchoring me in the now, pulling me back from where the memories didn't want to let go.

I ignored his absolution. There were some wounds that time scabbed but never truly healed. "The ledge was big enough for me to pull myself onto, but barely big enough for my butt, and my legs were useless, so I held on to the rocks and the vegetation, and I prayed that I wouldn't black out from the pain. The car fell one last time and burst into flames about five hours later, and I was about ready to let go when the rescue crews arrived."

"Oh, baby," he whispered against my skin, his arms tightening around me.

"There were so many times I thought about letting go, giving in. I'd spent all my life preparing for these huge life struggles—for college, and morals, and what I would do with my life. In six hours, that ledge taught me more about life than I had learned in the previous eighteen years. The hardest battles—the most meaningful ones—they're fought against ourselves. Against our own fears, our own weaknesses, our own shattered expectations of what we thought this life would be. I'd almost forgotten that until today, when I had to make that same choice."

He didn't say anything, just kept stroking my hair, letting me take my time.

"My legs…the infection set in and caused all sorts of issues with the draining and setting the bones, and well… They are what they are—a constant reminder that I didn't have the courage to get out of the car when I should have, a reminder that I lived but Brian didn't."

"A testament to how strong you are," he added.

I shrugged. "That's how I met Rachel. We were both in the orthopedist's office, me for my legs, her for a broken arm. When we realized that we were both headed to Dartmouth in the fall, we clicked. She's my polar opposite, the wild to my safe, the impulsive to my logic. She pulled me through. That first year…the grief was so deep, the nightmares way too realistic, the panic attacks cruelly frequent… I know she kept me alive. I honestly can't believe I actually came here without her."

Paxton tilted my head, wearing an expression I couldn't read. "I'm glad you did. I couldn't imagine spending these last months without you. Every single second has been amazing."

"Even today?" I joked.

He kissed me gently, but with a touch of desperation that hadn't been there before. "Especially today."

I somehow felt naked, exposed. "Paxton, will you tell me about Nick? He's the one who's paralyzed, isn't he?"

His eyes widened momentarily, but he nodded. "The triple front was always the trick he wanted to master, to nail first. And like a jackass, I jokingly challenged him, told him I'd nail it first. He wasn't ready, and neither was I, honestly. After the accident, he wouldn't see anyone, even Brooke."

"Brooke?" I asked.

"Yeah, they'd been together for years. He shut everyone out, and we kept it quiet out of respect for him. He finally reached out when he heard about the documentary, which was the whole point, and he's been a godsend."

"Really? How?"

"All the equipment design has been him, that kicker I'm using for the front? It's his. But he figured out why we're doing this whole thing, and he wanted to be a part of it."

"Why are you doing it? You're risking a hell of a lot."

"Nick wasn't as well-off as the rest of us. We met up at a skate park when we were kids and became the Original Renegades, and this lifestyle, it doesn't come easy...or cheap. With his accident, even though we kept it quiet, he missed shows, lost sponsors, then started losing everything. Landon and I, we can easily keep him afloat financially, but we can't touch his depression, or how he feels about his future. But this can give him a future in the arena he loves, that will allow him to not only support himself but build his life again. I know you don't know him, but Nick is as much my brother as Landon, as much my friend as Penna. This started as the four of us, and we can't sit back and watch while he implodes any more than he already has. And we've seen a huge difference since he came back on board. He'll call now, he gets excited about the gear—the stunts. He has equal production credit in the movie, equal billing. That was the secret deal we struck with my father, why he's the one who's producing the movie...and consequently holding my leash."

"Who knows?"

"Just my dad, Penna, Landon, and I. He still won't talk to anyone else, especially Brooke."

I nodded, snuggling closer into his chest. His warmth was delicious, and he smelled incredible, like ocean, and Paxton... and home. "That's why you can't shut it down." He'd been muttering about killing the project all evening.

He shook his head. "No. I love Nick, but you—"

"I'll live." I took a steadying breath. "I understand guilt, even if it isn't warranted. If I had a chance to help Brian... I don't, and you do for Nick. If you want to keep going, I'll support you. But I am honestly terrified of something happening to you, so we have to find out who is after us, who benefits the most from shutting you down."

"Leah, while we're alone, I need to ask. When you fell, who did you see at the bottom? We have to rule people out."

I closed my eyes and let the memory in that I'd been pushing out all afternoon. "You," I answered. "Landon was already on the shore, but I saw him there next to Penna. Bobby, I think? Some of the camera crew? I know I left Brooke on the blanket, and Little John was standing there, too."

"Okay. What about Zoe?"

I stiffened. Had that voice been female? It was gruff, but it could have been forced. "I don't remember. I mean, she could have been down there. I don't want you to accuse her of doing something because I didn't call roll while falling to my near death."

"Near death, indeed. Okay. Not a word of this outside us, Landon, and Penna, okay? They're the only ones I trust anymore. And you're moving in here. No argument."

I knew I should fight that, stand on my own, but being held by him felt so good, so safe. "Okay." The pain meds were finally kicking in; everything was blurring at the edges.

He pushed my hair back off my forehead. "Sleep, Firecracker."

My eyelids grew heavy. "The night of the accident, I held on because I knew if I let go, I'd end up with Brian."

"Right." He didn't stop running his fingers through my hair, the massage soothing, lulling me to sleep.

"Today, I let go because I knew I'd end up with you."

His breath was ragged as he pulled me closer. As I drifted off to the rhythm of his heart, I realized it was the first night we'd slept in the same bed without having sex, and yet it was the most intimate we'd ever been.

"It wasn't just a moment today," I whispered. "I do really, truly love you."

I fell asleep before he could respond, but not without realizing that he hadn't said it back.

CHAPTER TWENTY-FIVE

PAXTON

AT SEA

"How is she?" Penna asked as we gathered on the deck. It was nearing three o'clock in the morning, but none of us could sleep. Landon leaned back against the railing, his arms folded across his chest, and I stood on the empty side, the three sides of our triangle that used to be a square.

"She's finally asleep," I said, running my hands over my hair. "Who the fuck pushed her?"

"I don't know, but we need to figure it out," Penna said. "Who else knows she was pushed?"

"Just us," Landon answered. "She said it pretty quietly."

"Us and the person who pushed her," I corrected him. Barely contained rage rolled through my body, stretching through my limbs, begging to be let out to cause destruction, to pulverize the person who had hurt her.

"Right. Okay. I was on the shore, you were in the water, Landon was right next to me," Penna said, rubbing the skin between her eyes. "I remember Little John yelling for help, and that was behind me. He was next to Brooke, I think. We could ask her, but she's still pretty shaken up. I think it reminded her too much of when Nick crashed."

Landon nodded. "Makes sense. Some of the CTDs were back there, too, but I wasn't paying much attention."

"Did you pass anyone when you ran up?" I asked.

He nodded. "Some of the camera crew—the ones who'd gone up with us—were about halfway when I reached them, but they'd heard the screaming and were headed back up. I honestly ran right past them."

"I need their names, even if we have to line them up. Who else do you guys remember?"

Penna's forehead puckered. "I don't remember where Zoe was...or Bobby, for that matter, but I know they didn't make the initial hike up."

"Bobby called for support," Landon said. "I heard his voice, but I don't remember when."

"Who are we missing?" I asked.

Penna shook her head. "I don't know. There were so many people there."

"Whoever pushed her could have hidden off the trail," Landon said. "I ran so fast that I didn't look on either side of me. Shit, they probably could have made it back down before Leah hit the water."

"Okay. Well, that's way too many people to narrow it down. Fuck. What do you guys want to do? You want to kill the movie?"

"No," they answered in tandem.

"We said we'd see it through for Nick," Penna said.

"I'm not letting this take anything else away from him," Landon added.

I knew that would be their answer and sighed. "Right, but

you guys haven't been the targets. I don't care about me as much, but they went after Leah. She's…" I swallowed, trying to get past the lump that formed in my throat. "I can't let anything happen to her."

"They used her against you. That's the only explanation. Leah hasn't hurt a fly."

"Yeah," I answered, unable to get out another word. I knew it the minute she said she'd been pushed.

Landon nodded and looked at Penna. "If they went after Leah to get to Paxton, you need to keep an eye on Brooke. She could be a target to get to you. Everyone knows how close you are."

A slight panic rose in Penna's eyes. "Who the hell would want to do this to us?"

"I don't know," I answered. "But we'll run two practice sessions from here on out. CTDs can have their own—we're closing our practices to everyone but Originals and Little John. Fuck the cameras. Fuck Bobby. We'll still do the stunts, but everyone handles their own gear, and we keep everything contained as much as possible. And guys, I don't care how much we love Nick—the next incident and we have to call it. This isn't worth any of our lives, and he'd be the first to agree."

They both nodded and headed off to their rooms.

I crawled back into my bed, wrapped a sleeping Leah in my arms, and let her breathing calm me down. She was okay. Her wounds would heal. She would recover.

I wasn't sure if I would. It was one thing to risk my life, but never hers. Not after I'd found her. I had to keep her safe.

Tell her why she's really here, and she'll leave.

My entire body tensed, my stomach rolling at the thought of what her face would look like when she realized what I'd done, what I'd kept from her. But the safest place for her to be was next to me, so I'd have to keep my secret a little longer.

Fear like I'd never known iced my veins, stopped my breath. Even if I could keep her safe—and I would—she'd leave eventually. I'd lose this peace, her arms, her love...everything she was.

It was ironic really. I'd finally found the one person I wasn't willing to risk in my pursuit of landing a trick, and I was going to lose her anyway.

I pulled her closer and breathed in the scent of her hair, tried to infuse her into my lungs, my very being, and practiced every apology I could think of that might keep her with me when everything eventually hit the fan.

But for right now...I just needed to keep her alive.

"If you skid out one more time you're going to lose pieces of your skin," Penna lectured as I righted the bike again. The South African track was deserted except for a few of us. After the shit in Morocco, I'd gone through with our agreement and banned everyone from the training sessions the Originals were a part of, and I didn't give a fuck if they were calling me a diva behind my back. Keeping the people I cared about safe was all that mattered.

"I've landed most of them," I argued, ripping off my helmet. Sweat trickled down the back of my neck. It wasn't too hot in Cape Town, but the protective gear was baking me.

"Most isn't all," Landon said, siding with Penna in both words and stance, their arms across their chests.

"Well, this is the last ramp we have before Abu Dhabi, so what the hell do you two recommend?"

"Call it off. Pull a less difficult trick," Penna answered.

"We need it for the movie."

"We don't need another Renegade in a wheelchair," she snapped, then rubbed her temples.

"All right, what do you guys want to do?" Little John asked as he walked over, Leah by his side. She'd given up a two-day safari to stay with me while I trained during our field time, and I hated that she'd done it as much as I adored her for it.

She put her hand on my arm and looked up at me with concern in those whiskey eyes.

"I don't know," I told him. "I've got it, but I don't, and I won't get another chance to practice until we're in Abu Dhabi. What do you think?" I asked Leah.

Her lips parted, and she blew out a long, slow breath. "I think that I'm the last person who should be offering you advice on this. But I do know that you're exhausted, and sleepy people are sloppy people. Seeing that you don't exactly have the kind of job where sloppy is an option, I think you need to rest."

"I hate it when you use logic."

Her smile sped up my heart. "Well, one of us has to."

"I think she's right," Landon said. "You've landed enough that the two days of practice we can sneak in at Abu Dhabi should solidify the trick for the show."

"We still sure about a live broadcast?" Penna asked.

"I am if you are," I answered. "Look, we're risking a lot this year. We don't even know if the program will give us the extra week we need for the X Games in January. We need this to be big. A canned recording of us jumping around isn't going to do it. We need the synchronized stunts we've been practicing, and all the other tricks to make this work. We need the triple front."

First Landon nodded, then Penna. "Okay," she said.

"Can you get in any time in Madagascar?" Leah asked.

I shook my head. "The first day is all school trips, and the second is for the skydive. We don't even have access to the equipment there that we'd need."

"Then it looks like rest up and don't break anything on the skydive," she said with school-teacher seriousness, looking down at her watch. The bandages were off her hands, but there were still healing cuts on her palms from the branches she'd clung to. "Okay, put your toys away. We have to study tonight for the World Religions quiz tomorrow. Plus I need some extra Physics time."

I internally winced. Having her with me at practice was phenomenal, and I could take the hit, but I hated that I was stealing her time, too—hated the feeling of dragging her down. "Why doesn't Landon take you back? I need another few minutes here with the bike. That way you can get in your work, too."

"I don't need an escort."

I picked up her hand and kissed one of the pink lines that marked her skin. "I beg to differ. Please give me this? Take Landon?"

She softened. "Fine. Hurry, okay?"

My hands cradled her face, and I kissed her soundly. "Absolutely. Put on something sexy, and I'll be there even faster."

She huffed. "Uh-huh, as long as you think yoga pants and a hoodie are sexy. Bye, Pax." She waved her fingers at me and walked toward the door with Landon.

"I love yoga pants," I called after her. "Easy to pull off!" Just the thought of sliding them over her ass had me ready to chase after her.

"Only if you study!" she yelled back and disappeared.

A little of my sunshine went with her.

"Does she know?" Penna asked as we walked toward the bikes.

"Know what?"

She rolled her eyes. "You damn well know what."

"No. She doesn't. It would ruin everything." I popped the lid to one of our gear boxes and started packing stuff away.

"So, what, you're not going to tell her? That's pretty messed up, even for you."

I stopped, looking up at her. "She'll leave me. We both know it. And if she's not talking to me, I can't protect her from whatever is out there gunning for us."

She canted her head. "Pax—"

"No. I don't want to hear it. I'm aware of the giant fucking mess I've made. I've only got a couple weeks with her before the shit will most definitely hit the fan, and I'm not giving them up. I don't care if it makes me more of an asshole, and maybe if I get these weeks with her I can convince her not to kick my ass when it all comes out."

"Guilt much?" she asked.

"What?"

"First, I wasn't talking about *that*. But yes, she's going to kick your ass, and she should. But she loves you, so you've got a fighting chance that you can pull through it."

"Then what the hell are you talking about?" I asked, running my hands over my hair. The closer we got to second trimester, the more paranoid I was becoming, the more desperate I was to hold on to Leah. "When am I going to tell her what?"

"That you're in love with her, you ass."

I blinked, then swallowed. "I'm not..." Wait. Wasn't I?

The incredibly sweet pressure in my chest, the way I couldn't breathe fully unless I was touching her, the constant longing to make her smile… "Shit."

"It's about time you caught up," Penna said.

I glared at my oldest friend.

"What? The rest of us knew pretty damn quickly. Probably by Barcelona and definitely by Mykonos. There's a reason you suck at poker. And it's not our fault that you're kinda slow on the emotional uptake." She stared me down.

"What the hell am I supposed to do now?" I asked, lacing my fingers behind my neck. Love. The one emotion I never chased. The one high I'd never wanted to experience. God, it felt great, which would only turn to horrible when I lost her.

"Tell her. Kiss her. Pray to God you can make it through the storm you're headed for, then marry her and make pretty little Wilder babies."

"Yeah, and I'll turn a pumpkin into a carriage and shit while I'm at it." Fuck, why the hell had I fallen in love with Leah? Love was bullshit. It warped the world, made you promise things like forever and then apologize to everyone around you when forever turned into "well it was a great decade, right?" Love led to lawyers, separate houses, custody agreements, and screwed-up lives. Love was a temporary frenzy that resulted in lifelong consequences.

"You're supposed to be the prince, not the fairy godmother. But I bet you'd look stellar in a dress," Penna joked. When she caught wind of how much I was *not* joking, she sighed. "It's love, Pax. It's what some people spend their whole life searching for. Do you know what a miracle it is to love someone and actually have them love you back? You have a chance at something epic."

"Not when I'm going to lose her!" I shouted. I rocked

forward, covering my eyes with my hands. "I never thought this would happen. I never thought she would be...her, but she is, Penna. She's so fucking exquisite that I can barely believe that she lets me touch her, lets me share her time, her bed, her heart. What the hell am I going to do?"

I couldn't tell her. That would only rip her apart more, rip us both apart when it didn't work out, when she realized what I'd done, when she realized that I lived a life that was fun to hang around for nine months, not a lifetime. No, telling her opened doors I couldn't close, left them ajar just enough to let in the fire that would ultimately burn my ass to the ground. Love never worked out. Not for my parents, not for Landon, or Brooke, and it definitely wouldn't stick around for me. She'd already told me how important honesty was to her, and I'd already blown it.

Hell, I'd ruined us before I met her.

Penna gently tugged my arms down and then wrapped hers around me like we were five again. "Tell her. Kiss her. Pray to God you can make it through the storm you're headed for, then marry her and make pretty little Wilder babies," she repeated. "The answer to that question will always be the same no matter what stage you're in. You are the strongest man I have ever known. So you dig in, you take the rain, and you fight like hell, because that's what you're about to go through."

I nodded, but I knew the truth: out of everyone in my life, Leah was the angel...and they didn't exactly hang around in hell.

• • •

I loved her. About a billion different swear words went through my head as I opened the door to the suite. Was she going to know when she looked at me? *Maybe I should just tell her.*

Yeah, and then what the hell would I do when she walked out?

No. I was keeping this to myself.

Besides, we didn't need words for what I had planned.

"Honey, I'm home," I called out when I saw Landon lounged on the sofa, a copy of *Les Miserables* in his hand.

"She's in your room," he answered without looking up. "Did you finish reading?"

"Yes, Mom," I said, already headed up the flight of stairs to our room. At least now I wouldn't have to find an excuse to get her up there.

"Good, because I don't think CliffsNotes is going to cut it on the final."

"You, too? I already have one hard-ass riding me." Or she would be soon.

He laughed. "Just reminding you that your grades affect us all, my man."

"Yeah, I never forget that," I tossed back as I opened the door to my room. I threw my equipment bag on the bed after locking our bedroom and walked out the sliding glass door, which was already open to the private balcony.

My chest swelled with that inconvenient love when I saw Leah in the lounge chair, Physics book in her face, her eyes squinting to read in the dying light. "Hey, Firecracker," I said softly, and she dropped the book.

"Hey, you." She stretched, her shirt riding up over her smooth stomach. "Man, it feels like I've been sitting here for hours. What happened to you?"

"Sorry, I went for a workout," I said in lame excuse. I had, but it had been more for my tangled mind than my body.

"Okay, well, I brought you takeout from the cafeteria since you missed dinner." She motioned back inside our room.

I crossed the distance in a few strides, my ass hitting the cushioned lounge chair at the same moment my lips found her belly.

"Hmm..." she hummed, her fingers tangling in my hair as I kissed my way up her rib cage. "I'm guessing you're not hungry?"

"Not for dinner," I answered. I raised her shirt over her red lace bra and, just like that, my body screamed for her, the need that had built since I'd realized that I was in love with her finally overtaking every other logical thought in my head.

She arched into my mouth when I ran my tongue over her lace-covered nipple, my name the sweetest whisper on her lips. Damn, I loved when she did that, like it was instinctual. Like to her, my name was synonymous with pleasure.

She raised her arms, and I tugged the shirt off, sending it to the deck. "Pax...we're outside," she said as I pulled her yoga pants off her long, beautiful legs.

"Surrounded waist-high by steel on three sides. No one can see us," I promised. I'd never let anyone see her naked. All of this was mine, and mine alone. Including—fuck me—those matching red lace panties. "Red," I whispered, nearly swallowing my tongue.

"The closest I could get to a flag," she said with a sexy smile.

I ripped off my shirt and slid up her body so I could feel her against my skin. She was perfect under me, her knees coming up to cradle my hips. "Noted," I said with an answering grin, thankful I'd snagged a quick shower at the gym.

Then I kissed her, and she met me full-on, until we were a flurry of roaming hands, tongues, teeth, and soft moans. Everything about her intoxicated me, demanded every ounce of my focus. When I had her in my hands, everything disappeared, and it may as well have only been us on the ship—on the earth.

Her hands slipped into my shorts, and I slid them down my legs, kicking them off until we were both naked. When she reached for me, I took her hands and pinned her wrists over her head. "Let me worship you," I whispered in her ear before taking the lobe gently between my teeth.

If I couldn't say that I loved her in words, I would do it with my hands, my mouth, my every single movement. I showed her my love with each kiss, lingering where she gasped, sucking on the sensitive patches of skin under her perfect breasts.

I kissed her mouth softly, then took her deeper, until I couldn't tell where her mouth began and mine ended. Her legs moved restlessly, locking around my back, and I groaned at the sublime feeling of her, wet and ready against me.

"Paxton," she moaned as my fingers tested how ready she was. Of course she was already slippery, our bodies were always magically in sync. I loved that about her, too, loved how the sex only got hotter and yet somehow reached me on emotional levels no one else ever had.

I leaned over, taking a condom out of my wallet and, in quick motions, protected us both. "Is out here okay?" I asked. It was hot as hell to have her on our balcony, but there was zero chance I would make her do something she didn't want 100 percent.

She nodded, her eyes half-lidded and drunk on lust. "I trust you."

Her words shot through me like nothing else could have.

"You're everything," I said with a kiss as I slid inside her. *I love you.* The words were in my head, my heart, my thrusts as I found a slow, deep rhythm within her perfection. She was heaven, squeezing me tight every time I withdrew and moaning softly when I drove back in.

I love you, I thought, barely stopping the words from tripping out of my mouth as I memorized the way she looked, the way her neck arched as she met each of my movements, drove me to soar with every kiss, every time her fingernails scraped across the skin of my back. I didn't say it aloud, but it coursed through me all the same, bringing me higher than I'd ever been with no chute to break the inevitable fall. But for just this moment, I let my love for her consume me, move me, drive me—and her—toward the kind of heaven I only knew in her arms.

Even as I felt that pressure—the tingle at the base of my spine—and I knew I was close, I couldn't stop. I would never get enough of this, of her. There would never be anyone else who fit as perfectly against me, who drove me to the brink with a simple smile.

She was it.

I moved my hand between us and stroked her clit, pressing where she liked, quickening my thrusts to match my hands and her moans.

"Pax!" she cried out, and I surged forward, capturing her mouth and muffling her next shout when she came, clenching around me so tightly that I couldn't help but let go and let the waves of my orgasm wash over me.

I pulled the beach towel she'd brought out around us and tucked her into my chest, holding her as close as I could. I understood it now—why people gave up logic for love. If Leah had asked me to quit riding, quit boarding, I would have done it in a heartbeat if it meant keeping her.

She was better than the hit of adrenaline I craved, took me higher than any rush of endorphins at a victory. She'd become more than the thrill, she'd become the air, the only thing I absolutely needed to live.

As she looked up at me with those expressive eyes, sleepy in satisfaction, I'd never felt so alive...or so terrified.

"You sure you don't want some dinner?" she asked, always thinking about me first.

"I'm good. I'm sorry for missing it. Was it busy?"

She shrugged. "Pretty empty. I think half the students went on the safari trip."

"I'm sorry you didn't get to go."

"I'm not. I don't regret any of the time I spend with you."

God, I loved her—and not a little kind of love. My heart was practically glowing. I probably looked like a warped glowworm or something. "I'll take you sometime," I promised. "One day, we'll come back so we can go look at the lions."

Her eyes widened. "Paxton..."

"Yeah, I know what I said. I implied that we'd be together long after this cruise is over. You need to know that this isn't a fling to me, or some distraction. I've never felt anything this real in my life, and I'm not going to let it go—let you go—just because this trip comes to an end."

"I go to school on the East Coast—"

I leaned in, kissing her quiet. "I know how to use planes. Look, I'm not saying let's figure this out tonight. We have months. But I am promising that I will bring you back here, and we'll look at lions, and elephants—"

"And giraffes?" Her eyes lit up.

"Anything you want."

As long as you still want me.

CHAPTER TWENTY-SIX

PAXTON

MADAGASCAR

"Did you get it turned in?" Leah asked, the noise from the airfield making her shout.

"I'm about to attempt one of the riskiest skydive landings ever, and you want to know about my English paper?" I retorted, unable to keep the grin off my face. Of course she did.

"Well…yeah. I have zero control of what happens once you decide to bail out of that perfectly good airplane, but your grades are pretty much my responsibility, so yeah, I'm asking if you turned in your paper." There was a slight panic in her eyes, in the tense line of her mouth.

I took her in my arms and kissed the worry off her face, tasting her fear, her love, and taking them both for my own. It had been so long since I'd been scared for myself.

"Yes, I turned it in," I assured her. "I can tell you all about the themes of love and loss in *Les Miserables*, of redemption and penance. I nailed it, I promise."

"Good." She sighed, as if that had been the real reason for her worry. "I should have looked at it."

"No, you needed to study, too. It does me no good to pass all my classes if you can't rock some physics."

"Speaking of physics," she said as she grasped the shoulder straps of my harness. "You sure about this? I've done a ton of research into Tsingy de Bemaraha, and if you so much as miss the drop zone..." She shook her head.

I cupped her face in my hands, running my thumbs over her porcelain skin. "I know what I'm doing, and I'm really, ridiculously good at this. Maybe not as good as Landon, but hey, we all have our strengths, right?"

"Not everyone can be perfect," Landon said, smacking my back as he walked by close enough to hear us, apparently. "Now kiss the girl good-bye and let's blow this gin joint."

"You know that would have gone over better in Casablanca, right?" I asked over my shoulder.

"Get on the plane, smart-ass," he threw back.

"Okay, you go with Little John. Be careful on the trip in, and I'll meet you at the drop."

"You're sure this is...safe?" Her eyes widened.

I glanced over her shoulder, where Little John stood with Brooke at the car, far enough away that they couldn't hear us. "Yeah. It's just Penna, Landon, and me on the plane. No other Renegades. We all packed our own chutes, and I'm the one who paid the pilot. We're okay. And nothing has happened since Morocco. Maybe..."

"Maybe almost killing me scared whoever is screwing with you?" she asked with a quirked eyebrow.

"Yeah, well...I wasn't going to put it that way, but maybe. I'm not taking any chances with you, though. Stay close to Little John and Brooke, okay?" They were the only ones who had been with us from the beginning, the only ones with a vested interest in us, and the only ones outside Penna and Landon I could trust with Leah's life.

"Okay," she agreed. "And you...you know, don't die or anything."

I ran my hands down her hair, tendrils whipping free from both the breeze and the aircraft behind us. "I won't. And you wait with a red flag in case it turns you on."

She laughed, and my heart lit up like the Fourth of July. God, I loved this woman. Loved her laugh, her worry, her anger. Loved when she sharpened her claws on me, and when she tucked them away. I loved how she pushed me, not just in sports like everyone else, and not with her own gain in mind, but genuinely wanted me to better myself as a person. I loved the way I wanted to be that better person *for* her—to be exactly what she needed in her life.

"You're my everything," I said to her, hoping she could hear what I meant to say. She needed the words, I knew it, but I couldn't say them, not when letting them past my lips demolished every wall I'd built. There wasn't any piece of protective gear that could guard me from Leah, or the way she could mangle my heart if she left.

The way I knew she eventually would leave when she realized I hadn't been honest with her. But no matter.

"I love you," she answered, her heart open and shining through her eyes, as if I could physically see the glow of her emotions.

I kissed her one last time, pouring everything I had into it— my love, my hope, my need for her. I held her close and hoped that each stroke of my tongue made up for the words I couldn't say, every motion reaching for more of her soul, because she already owned mine.

I was wholly, deeply, irreversibly in love with a woman who was way braver than I could ever be.

"I'll see you in a few," I promised as I pulled away from her lips.

"Be safe."

"Always."

I boarded the plane as the SUV carried Leah off to the drop zone.

"You tell her?" Penna asked as we strapped on our helmets.

"No."

She shook her head. "Never took you for a chicken, Pax."

"Maybe it's kinder to her."

"Or maybe it's the one thing that could keep her with you," she spat back.

"What are we talking about?" Landon asked as he came from the back of the plane.

"Paxton's an ass," Penna answered, her eyes never leaving my face.

"Oh, I thought maybe we were talking about stuff I didn't already know." He laughed.

Penna's eyes met mine across the cabin, her expression hardening, because we both knew that there was way too much Landon didn't know, that I was being dishonest with two of the people who meant the most to me.

But the wheels were already in motion, and this late in the game, I was powerless to stop them. Problem was, those were the same wheels that were going to crush me.

• • •

Adrenaline rushed through me, spiking every sense, feeding me the kind of high that only came in moments like these. The best part? I glimpsed Leah across the drop zone.

Now this moment was perfect.

Shit. The breeze shifted, blowing me near one of the sharp limestone formations of Tsingy de Bemaraha, the gray rocks reaching up from the earth like daggers waiting to catch my chute.

Pay attention, jackass.

I successfully steered away from the rocks and hit the drop zone, one of the only clear sites in the entire park. The ground rushed up to meet me, and I bent my knees to absorb the impact, running so I didn't fall on my ass. Then I cut my chute away, unsnapping the latches, and watched Landon execute a perfect landing.

He shouted in victory as Penna landed next.

"Last as always, Rebel!" Landon yelled out, aware that the cameras were on us.

"Someone has to make sure you losers jump," she countered, cutting away her chute.

We met in a cheesy group hug that made the moment perfect, except we didn't have Nick. We would never jump with Nick again, and in moments like this I missed the arrogant son of a bitch.

"We did it," Landon said quietly, and we all bowed our heads to meet in a triangle, each taking a moment to thank God we'd been allowed to survive our stupidity.

"One for the books," Penna agreed.

"For Nick," I said.

"For Nick," they agreed softly.

Then we broke, and I caught Leah in my arms mid-run, crushing her to my chest and winding my fingers through her thick hair. This was heaven.

"I'm glad you didn't die," she said into my neck.

"I'm sad there's no red flag," I joked, but squeezed her tighter.

She kissed me, her relief evident. The tension was gone from her body, the worry erased from her eyes. "I'll show you some red later," she promised.

"Is that so?" I asked. My eyes darted over her tight jeans and short-sleeved shirt, wondering what she had underneath.

"See, I told you the weather would hold off," Little John said, high fiving me.

"You were right," I admitted, scoping out the gray clouds coming in.

"Badass jump, my friend."

"It was worth it. We've got some great footage," I said as Bobby walked over with the crew.

"We do, too. That was phenomenal, Wilder. I did worry toward the end there, but you pulled it off."

"It definitely isn't easy. The winds are a bitch around here, and those rocks aren't exactly rolling out the welcome mat."

"Neither are they," Landon said, pointing to two SUVs marked with the symbols of the local authorities as they pulled into the clearing.

"We're fine," I assured him as I pulled off my helmet, storing it in the bag Leah handed me. "Everything's in order?" I asked Bobby.

He nodded. "Absolutely. We pulled the permits out of your desk this morning. Though I wish you'd let me hold on to them for the whole trip."

I shook my head. "No way. No offense, Bobby, but it's my ass on the line for half this stuff, not yours."

Leah threaded her fingers through mine as the officers

approached. By the looks on their faces, they were not pleased.

"You are the jumpers?" one asked in English, barely controlling his shout.

"We are," I confirmed. "Is there a problem?"

"This is protected land. Many endangered animals live here." They didn't stop until they were only feet away from us. Penna sidestepped toward me, and Landon did the same, so at least we were more of a unit.

"Do you have your passports?" he asked.

I balked. "What? We're with the *Athena*."

"Yes," Leah answered, taking out that travel wallet of hers and presenting him with four passports.

I looked at her in question as Bobby and the crew presented theirs.

"Madagascar law. We have to carry them," she explained simply.

"Thank you," I answered, thankful that the woman I loved was a hell of a lot smarter than I was, and that she majored in International Relations.

She gave me a tight-lipped but sincere smile as the officers looked over our passports.

"Well, Paxton Wilder, do you have permits for destroying the peace of our park?" the officer asked, speaking for the other three.

"We do," I assured him and glanced to Bobby who already had a manila folder out. "Every legal *T* has been crossed and *I* dotted, I promise."

"We'll see about that," the officer said, thumbing through the papers.

Leah's hand tightened in mine, and I drew her closer. It was one thing to be all reckless and ignorant by myself in a foreign country, and quite another to put Leah in danger when I had zero clue where the nearest embassy was, or even a basic understanding of Madagascar law. It didn't help that these guys were not playing around.

They talked amongst themselves, and a sick feeling settled in my stomach, growing every time they glanced up at us. "Everything is legal," I promised, unable to take the silent appraisal.

"Yes, your jump was sanctioned, though I don't know how much you had to pay to see that one get through for a permit."

Bobby looked away briefly and then shrugged at me.

"So we're fine, right?" I asked, more than ready to get Leah into our SUV and get her the hell out of there. Little John already had the doors open and Brooke tucked away. Good. Now we just needed to get Penna and Leah in.

"Yes, it appears that everything you did was legal," the officer said with a puckered brow.

"Excellent. Then if you won't be needing us..." I guided Penna with a hand on her lower back, and Landon took her hand as I took Leah's again.

We circled around the officers, and I breathed a hell of a lot easier when they didn't stop us.

"Oh, Mr. Wilder?" the officer called out.

Fuck. So close.

"No fucking way!" Bobby yelled, and I turned to see the camera wrestled away from one of the crew.

"What the hell?" I questioned the officer.

"Everything you did was legal, yes, but there was no permit for photography within the special bounds of the park," the officer said with a shrug. "We'll need to take any film you took."

"The hell you will!" I roared. "We have every permission.

We've seen to every permit, and you're not taking our tape." We'd just completed the toughest landing of my life, and there was zero chance in hell that they were taking the film.

"You have nothing to say about this, Mr. Wilder," he said with a tight smile. "And you don't want to fight us on this." His voice was deceptively smooth.

The crew lost their battles as three cameras were confiscated. Landon and I locked eyes above Penna's head. They hadn't touched the GoPros attached to our helmets, which were all stored.

"This is bullshit," I said.

"Be careful with your words, Mr. Wilder. You're not in the United States, and we take these matters quite seriously, I assure you."

"Now if you'll hand us the cameras from your helmets, we can call this a day."

"Over my dead body," Landon bellowed, putting Penna behind him when they reached for her bag. "Don't even try."

I stepped in front of Leah. "Look, we have the permit. If it's not there, it's on our ship. If you would like to follow us back to the *Athena*, we can clear this up. If we can't locate the permit there, or through your legal channels, we'll hand over the footage." My brain scrambled for anything that would keep this from escalating.

"There should be a record in your office," Leah offered. "If we have the paperwork, then so do you."

The officer didn't even look at her. "You do not have the permits with you, now hand over the bags."

"No." I shook my head.

"Paxton, this isn't the U.S.," Leah whispered into my back. "You don't have the same rights here, so be careful."

I squeezed her hand to let her know that I'd heard her. Of course I knew that, but at the moment, they wanted what I'd busted my ass for—what our documentary desperately needed—and there was no chance I was giving it to them when I'd gone through hell for all that fucking paperwork.

"You do not get to tell us no," the officer said, his eyes flickering over my right shoulder.

"Pax!" Leah screamed, her hand ripped away from me.

I spun around, a cold rage settling over me when I saw an officer wrench the bag away from Leah, shoving her to the ground in the process. Two steps and my fist was in his face, knocking him back. "Don't fucking touch her!"

"No!" Leah yelled as two of the officers tackled me from the side, pinning me into the hard ground, tiny rocks cutting into my skin.

They yanked my arms behind my back as Landon picked Leah up off the ground, putting her behind him with Penna. Little John ran toward us while Bobby yelled at the men, but I heard nothing, simply saw the wide fear in Leah's eyes as the same officer I punched walked over, flipped me to my back, and slammed his fist into my face.

"Paxton!" Her voice was the ringing in my ears as another blow fell.

I vaguely saw Landon holding her back, then Little John lifting her over his shoulder. They had to get her out of here. She had to be safe. They could take the fucking cameras as long as they kept their hands off Leah.

"I think one more to learn his lesson," the biggest officer said, and the third punch was delivered.

Then I saw nothing.

CHAPTER TWENTY-SEVEN

LEAH

MADAGASCAR

"Where the fuck is it?" I screamed at Bobby, tearing apart the file in Paxton's room—our room. He was anal about one thing, the freaking permits, so I knew it had to be here.

"Leah, we've looked everywhere," Bobby said softly.

"How is that possible? Where are the permits for the rest of the trip?" I asked.

Landon leaned against the wall, his arms folded against his chest. "He keeps the permits in his fire safe, and only puts out the ones for the next stunt. You watched me check the box, and it's not in there."

"What are we going to do?" They'd picked up Pax's unconscious body, and when Landon had moved toward the officers, one had pulled a weapon on him, which I knew was the only reason he'd calmly handed over the other cameras.

There was no chance he'd endanger Penna's life, or—as I was learning—mine.

But they had Paxton, God-knows-where, doing God-knows-what to him. I didn't know what the punishment was here for hitting a police officer. Or what we could do to help him. "Do we call the embassy?"

"The ship is on it," Penna promised, her knees tucked into her chest. "I hate feeling so goddamned useless."

Brooke put her arm around Penna. "He's going to be okay. He's Paxton Wilder. They'd be foolish to do anything to hurt him—not with who his dad is. When can we get in to see him? We've got to find that permit, and then all of this will be cleared up."

"Until then, we're dead in the water," Landon said.

"We have until tomorrow night," I added quietly.

"What do you mean?" Penna asked.

"Finals are during this leg between Madagascar and Abu Dhabi. If Pax isn't back on board, he'll miss finals, fail this term, and your funding is terminated." I almost laughed. "The funny thing is that his grades are just another problem. I don't honestly care about my scholarship. I'll go home tomorrow if that would keep him safe."

Landon wrapped his arm around my shoulders and pulled me into a hug, his taller, lankier frame comforting but only driving home how much I wanted Pax's arms around me, his heartbeat against my ear.

"We're going to do everything we can, Leah. There's nothing we won't do, no line we won't cross to get him out of there. Okay?"

I nodded, the gears in my brain turning, looking for any solution, even the quasi-legal ones. He was Paxton Wilder, for crying out loud! His father was the head of a multibillion-dollar media company.

His father was going to kill him when he found out.

"You know...I think I'm going to lay down for a bit," I said, forcing a smile.

"Yeah, of course," Landon said, giving me a final squeeze before leaving, ushering everyone out but Penna.

"He's going to be okay," she promised. "You should see some of the stuff we've gotten into before."

"In foreign countries?" I asked.

"Well, maybe it's never been quite this bad."

"I can't imagine anything happening to him. I love him." My voice broke.

Her eyes softened. "You know he feels the same, right?"

Did he? Even though he'd never said the words, I felt it every time he touched me, the way he told me that I was his everything. "Yeah, I think so. He's never said it or anything. I'm not sure he's capable of saying it."

She nodded. "His parents' divorce...what happened..." she trailed off.

"I know about the girl. About what happened the last time he tried to have a real relationship."

Penna's eyes flared in surprise and then she smiled. "I know he's not perfect, but he cares about you in a way I've never seen him with anyone."

"He loves me," I said quietly. "He loves me." I repeated with more conviction. "He doesn't have to say the words for them to be true."

"Just don't give up on him, okay? Not in any sense."

I forced a smile, knowing what I had to do, and what it might cost me. "We'll figure it out. All of it."

She hugged me. "I'm so glad he found you."

I nodded, unable to say anything else for fear I'd tell her what I was about to do. With one final squeeze, she left me alone, closing the door behind her as she left.

Without hesitation, I opened Pax's nightstand drawer first, pulling out his international cell phone, and then dug through my flex file of cruise papers to find the number I'd hidden. The card felt heavier now than it had when I'd taken it.

The bed sank under my weight as I sat down. My hand smoothed Paxton's side, wishing he were here to leave the bed an unmade, rumpled mess, wishing I'd handed over the camera without a fight, done something to stop him from flying at the officer.

He might hate me for this, but like Landon said, there wasn't a line they wouldn't cross.

This was my line, Paxton's line, and I crossed it with a simple press of my fingers to the numbers on the phone.

It rang twice before he picked up. "To what do I owe this honor?"

His voice...they were so similar, yet different enough to make my heart hurt.

"It's Leah Baxter... You gave me your number—"

"I know who you are, Leah. What's wrong?"

"Are you still in Paris? We're in Madagascar, and Paxton's in trouble. Big, scary trouble, and I don't know how to get him out of it."

"I'll be there in fifteen hours, give or take the time it takes to locate the flight crew."

A huge sigh of relief escaped me. In this, Paxton's name could protect him. "Thank you, Brandon."

"Don't thank me, Leah. I can assure you that Paxton won't."

• • •

I dropped my bag on our bed the next day after spending the morning on the field-study trip for World Religion. Not that it had done me any good. My brain had been with Paxton, but at least the presence of my body gave me a check mark in the participation box for my grades.

There was a knock on the door and a two-second lull before it swung open, like it was a warning, not a request for entrance. "Good, you're here," Brandon said as he walked in, his suit ditched for jeans and a Henley, which made him look way more approachable, attractive, even.

"I'm so sorry, Leah," Little John said from behind him.

"It's okay, I called him," I answered.

Little John's eyes widened right before Brandon shut the door in his face.

"Okay, he keeps the permits in a fire-safe box..." Brandon muttered, throwing the cushion off the love seat by the window. "Here." He lifted the box out of a cutout in the frame. "Paranoid son of a bitch, but I guess it's working out in his favor."

"We already checked the box, but how did you know about it?" I asked, walking over to where he placed it on the desk, working on opening it. Landon had been pretty clear that only the Originals knew where Paxton kept the permits, and Brandon didn't seem the daredevil type.

"Because he told me when I saw him this morning," Brandon answered as he popped the combination lock.

"Wait, you saw him?" I asked.

He looked up from the stack of manila envelopes. "Yeah. They let me in a few hours ago."

"How does he look? Is he okay?" A thousand questions raced through my mind, but those were the most important.

"He looks like his face went a few rounds with an MMA

fighter, but he's okay. And funny, he asked me those exact questions about you."

"They wouldn't even tell me where they took him." A surge of unwanted jealousy turned my words harsh.

"Well, your last name isn't Wilder, and that changes things," he said. "He's going to be okay, Leah. We just have to find this permit. They'll release him either way, our lawyers are seeing to that, but if he wants to keep his film, we have to find it."

"We already looked through the box."

His phone rang, and he cursed. "Shit. Looks like Dad knows. Leah, look through those files again and see if he stuck it in the wrong folder. He swears it was in there. I have to take this."

He stepped out onto the balcony with his phone, and I pulled out the box, emptying its contents onto the dark blue comforter. There were files for each of our locations that looked exactly like the one Bobby had held while we were in the park yesterday, the same files I'd watched Landon search through earlier. I looked through every one from the start of the trip up through Abu Dhabi. One marked "Personal" caught my eye, so I opened the flap.

Please let him have misfiled it.

I pulled out the stack of papers and thumbed through. His birth certificate, his enrollment papers for Study at Sea, his contract with his father. For being as reckless as he was, Paxton had a better sense of organization than I gave him credit for. A smile ghosted my lips when I ran my thumb over his tutor assignment, my name standing in stark relief against the white paper.

Something so small as this sheet of paper had grown into this incredible love that pulsed so powerfully in my veins that my heart actually ached with the perfect weight of it.

A torn picture fell out of the stack as I lifted it, landing in my lap, photo-side down. On the back in Paxton's handwriting was etched, "Don't lose sight of the endgame."

I flipped it over, and my stomach sank, my throat burning with bile as it rose.

No. No. No way. Not possible.

But that was Rachel. My Rachel...

Paxton's Rachel.

His thumb brushed the tattoo of three ravens in flight under her right ear, and his mouth was on hers, the two smiling even mid-kiss.

He looked happy, adoring, like the woman he held was the sun in the sky.

He looked at her like he looked at me.

My heart cracked, the feeling so consuming that I could almost hear the rending, the strain as it finally snapped and broke apart.

I barely registered the sound of the sliding glass door opening and closing. "Okay, good news and bad. Good that the lawyers tracked down the permit in the appropriate system, so Pax's cameras will be released. Also good that Dad got the charges dropped and they're releasing Paxton now. Bad that my father knows— Hey, are you okay?" Brandon asked when I finally looked up to meet his eyes.

If they were as dead as I felt inside, he had every reason to worry. "Yeah, I'm fine," I lied.

With a crease between his eyes, he walked over, gently taking the photo from my hand. "Rachel. Man, it's been years."

"They were together?" My voice sounded foreign to me.

"Yeah. She was always over at the house that summer after

I graduated with my MBA," he said.

"She's my best friend," I whispered.

His Paxton-like eyes widened, drifting between mine and the picture. "Oh, shit. That's why..."

"Why what?" I demanded.

"Look, he cares for you. I knew that the minute I saw him with you in Barcelona, and I know you have feelings for him. Don't do something irrational."

"Why what?" I repeated, my voice louder, the ugly cry echoed in my hollow heart.

"Why he chose you as his tutor," he said softly, damning Paxton with each word.

Every muscle in my body locked, unwilling to see how far the rabbit hole went. "I don't understand."

Brandon sighed, the asshole-ish look completely wiped off his face. "Why he had us offer a second full ride if you agreed to tutor him."

So he could get Rachel on board.

"I'm going to be sick," I said, bringing my knees to my chest.

"I'm going to get him. Do you want to come? Talk this out? I know there's more to this. Like I said, Pax really cares about you."

He cared about me, but I was wholeheartedly in love with him, and suddenly that difference, which hadn't meant as much this morning, meant the world now.

My gaze dropped to the sheet I'd just been all swoony over, the tutor assignment, but this time, my eyes caught the sentence it had missed before.

"Dear Mr. Wilder, we're happy to say that your request has been granted."

I stumbled to my feet. All of it had been to get Rachel on

board. Even my suite, which he'd been so adamant that I keep, was to keep her closer to him.

It was all for Rachel.

I was just the placeholder until she got here.

Barely making it to the toilet, I heaved up lunch, wishing the acid in my throat would burn the rest of me into ashes—wishing the hurt would simply cease. But I loved him, my whole heart was in, and now it felt like that heart was rebelling in the only way it could.

I wiped my mouth with the back of my hand and leaned against the cabinet. Rachel.

Just the thought of Paxton kissing my best friend was enough to send my stomach into convulsions again.

She loved reckless boys, and Pax was the definition of reckless. God, it all fit together. I met her a few months after that picture had been taken—and she'd told me how wounded her soul had been by a guy she wouldn't name.

The same way I couldn't name him.

What lengths had he gone to get her on board? *Screwing you,* my shattered heart answered. He'd kept me close, tried to keep me happy to show me the trip of my life so I wouldn't leave before she got here. He must have known that she wouldn't come if I left.

Every moment had been carefully calculated to get my best friend here—to get her back into his arms.

I was nothing more than the means to his end.

My head rested against the smooth wood, and I closed my eyes against the bright bathroom lights that made everything all too clear.

I loved him.

He still clearly loved her if he'd gone through all of this to get her back. But he loved me, too, didn't he? That look in his eyes, the way he touched me, how careful he was with me...that was love, whether or not he'd admit it. Or was I making that all up in my head, too?

What a fucking mess.

What was I going to do? Stand around and watch when Rachel showed up next week? Watch them fall back together while I slept in the room next door? I loved Rachel, I wanted the best for her, to see some spark of happiness in her eyes, but this...could I give up Paxton?

Was Paxton even mine to give up?

Stupid. I was so stupid. I'd let myself fall into him, his touch, his words...everything. Even our first kiss had been my initiation. Of course he'd gone for it, kept me happy. Kept me close. I'd slept with him, given him everything I had, while he what...pined for Rachel?

He'd used me, and it felt so dirty, so wrong, so opposite of how I'd felt when he touched me. Had he been thinking of her, his endgame, while he'd been with me? Kissing me? Inside *me*?

My stomach rolled again, and I heaved into the toilet.

"Leah..." Brandon said from the doorway.

"Just go," I said.

I wanted nothing to do with any Wilder men. I was done, as empty as my stomach finally was.

"Is there anything you want me to tell him?"

"Take that picture with you. He'll get the point."

CHAPTER TWENTY-EIGHT

LEAH

"Hey, this is Rachel. If I'm not answering it's because I didn't hear the phone, or maybe I just don't feel like talking. Leave a message, and I'll eventually return it."

I hung up and cursed.

Why couldn't this be like the movies, where the other character answered the damn phone so you could have the emotional moment? Where she told me that everything I'd learned was wrong, that she'd never been with Paxton, that there was some evil twin out there with an identical tattoo. Where everything he'd done for me hadn't been only to get closer to my best friend. Where I was actually the main character and not relegated to secondary bullshit.

Real life sucked.

I looked around my room, my unpacked bags thrown haphazardly into the tiny space. I'd only been in Paxton's room for a couple of weeks, but it was long enough for this space to feel unfamiliar, even though it was technically mine. I wasn't sure even my heart was technically mine at the moment.

My gaze drifted to the clock.

Twenty minutes until the *Athena* was set to sail. The others waited on the pier for Paxton to make it back, but I couldn't leave my room, couldn't see a space beyond the door, or a time beyond the next breath, the next heartbeat.

Nausea twisted my stomach, but at least it kept me physically grounded to reality. Besides, the pain that registered in my brain was nothing compared to the agony my soul demanded be felt. Everything hurt, ached both with the need to see Paxton and the overwhelming urge to smack the shit out of him for what he'd done—what he'd kept from me.

God, had he thought about her when he was touching me? My chest constricted, my throat closing around tears I refused to shed.

I curled up on my bed, hugging my knees to my chest like it would help me hold myself together, and counted through my breaths, focusing on the numbers, forcing air through my lungs.

I'd come so far only to go right back to where I'd been two years ago, fighting to make it through the next minute.

Grief had taken me when Brian died, but this heartbreak felt so much sharper, like every nerve in my body had been sliced clean through and was screaming. After all, Brian had never chosen to leave me. Paxton had made the choice all along.

And if I could finally be honest, the way I'd loved Brian at eighteen was nothing compared to the way my entire soul belonged to Pax.

Or at least it did.

As the horns blew and we pushed off for sail, there was a knock at my door. I clutched my pillow to my chest and walked barefoot to the front of the cabin. "Who is it?" I asked.

"Leah, please." Paxton's voice came through the door, and I leaned back against the wall of the hallway, fighting every instinct to open the door. How could I even look at him, knowing what I did? Still loving him like the complete and utter fool I was?

"Go away," I said.

"No. And if you don't let me in to explain myself, I will sit out here all night. I will play obnoxious eighties hair ballads and scream your name until the captain is on us both."

"I don't care," I lied. That would be quite possibly the most embarrassing thing he could do, not to mention that he'd wind up on-camera, my heartbreak fodder for a worldwide audience.

"You're lying."

Fuck.

I reached out and unlocked the door, turning the handle enough for him to push it open. Then I sucked in a breath and tried to find the willpower that had kept me clinging to a canyon wall two years ago, the strength I'd had to finally let go and save my own life a few weeks ago.

I walked into my living room, knowing that he'd follow. Then I pulled out the bottle of vodka Penna left in our freezer and downed a shot, hoping it was cold enough and high enough proof to numb the bleeding edges of my soul.

Then I turned around, my breath sucking in at the battered lines of Paxton's face. "Are you okay?" I asked, hating how beautiful he was, even with the purple shading of his cheekbone and the cuts on his face.

He touched the swollen, discolored cheek. "Yeah. Doc already checked me out. Nothing is broken, just bruised and a little cut up."

"Is it true? Rachel? All of it?" I spit out with my usual

verbal grace.

He ran his tongue over his abused lip and looked away. "Yeah."

I tried to ignore the way the tiny shred of hope inside me screamed out in agony as it died. "Everything you did...my scholarship, my tutoring assignment, this suite down the hall from yours...was that just to get Rachel on board?"

"Yes," he whispered, a tortured look in his eyes that had no right to be there.

"Rachel was your endgame," I said, remembering the words on the picture.

"At one time, yes, but not anymore. I promise," he said, reaching for me.

I sidestepped him, putting the couch between us. "Explain," I ordered, my voice as flat as my spirit.

"Everything I did at the start was to get Rachel here, yes. Everything you listed, and more."

"Asshole." What more could there possibly be?

"You always knew I was," he countered before ripping his hands through his hair. "God, this is not going how I had planned."

I crossed my arms over my chest. "Please, do tell me what you had planned." *Was it breaking my heart? Playing with me until you could have her?*

"Yes, I used you to get to Rachel, but it wasn't for me, I swear."

I laughed, the sound evil to my own ears. "Really."

"Really."

My nails bit into my palms at the use of what I had begun to think was our word. How junior-high immature was I? How blind had I been? "You're just kissing her in that picture, that's all."

"First, I have no clue how that picture got here. I haven't seen it since I ripped Landon's face out of it two years ago and shoved it in a box. Whoever put it there obviously knows where I keep private shit at my house, and apparently how to get into my fire box here."

"Landon?" What the hell?

"Yeah. Landon. He was the one who fell for my girlfriend, who was sleeping with her while I was trying to be respectful and keep it in my pants."

"Landon?" I repeated, trying to let it sink in. "I thought it was Nick."

"Nick? He would never do that. He loved Brooke so much I figured they'd have three kids by now. It was Landon. I wrote the endgame comment on the picture before I showed it to him, because he was on the side, looking like a love-struck puppy. That's when the pieces started to click and I figured it out. No guy looks at his best friend's girl like that. That's when he came clean and told me they'd been together since the spring. Then he started spouting the 'we never meant to hurt you' and 'we didn't want to break up the team, but we're in love' crap." His laugh came out self-deprecating and sarcastic. "How *in love* are you if you're still making out with your boyfriend and getting a side piece? If that's love, I want no part of it."

"Okay," I said, mostly to fill the space, not knowing what the hell to say to that kind of comment. He wanted no part of my love? Or any love? "And the endgame comment?"

"I told him to remember our endgame, which had always been the Renegades, to remember what we were working so hard for—what he was screwing up. And then I made one of the worst decisions in my life, and I gave him an ultimatum. It was her or us."

"You didn't fight for her?" I asked. Was he going to fight for me? Did I even want him to?

"I didn't love her. I thought I did at the time, but now I know better. At first, he chose her. He left the Renegades, and I ripped him out of the picture and shoved it into a box under my bed to remind me that this was what love does, it destroys everything around you, makes you give up the people you care about most because of some temporary, hormonal surge that inevitably wanes with time. At least...that's what I thought then. Watching them leave—the betrayal I felt—that was all from Landon. Sure, Rachel hurt me, but Landon wrecked me, destroyed everything I depended on."

"You wanted him to prove his loyalty, and he failed," I guessed, remembering how he'd told me that was the one quality he had to have in a friend.

Paxton nodded. "He couldn't live without the team, and a month later begged me to reconsider, but I was too pissed and too immature to see the bigger picture. So my ego won, and he lost the only woman he's ever loved. It's something that I've paid for since that day, watching him fuck every girl we come in contact with and connect with no one, watching that light in him die. I did that."

"*He* did that," I countered. "He could have chosen Rachel." *The same way you could choose me.* God, even when I was this utterly destroyed, I still looked for his excuse.

"I'm trying to give him that choice now. That's what all of this was about—getting her on board so he'd have a chance with her. Yes, I used you, and that is unforgiveable, but I had the best intentions."

"Well, you know what they say. The road to hell is paved with good intentions. So you did it for Rachel, and for Landon, you say. But you still lied to me every day, every moment since I met you. Is that why you got so close? To make sure I'd stay when she didn't show up? To keep me happy? Did you ever honestly care about me, because I feel like some pawn in this huge chess game, and you're just moving the pieces around like none of us are real people with real feelings."

"Of course I care about you!" His brow puckered. "It's complicated."

"Yeah, well, it's pretty fucking clear from where I stand. Was sleeping with me part of it? Getting me so wrapped up in you that Rachel would have to agree to stay when she got here? When she realized that you'd caged her on a ship with the one guy who broke her heart so badly that she can't speak his name?" My mind raced. "I remember her saying there was someone who destroyed her, who dropped her and never looked back, and I can tell you that Rachel isn't a forgiving person. There's no way she would have agreed if she'd known he was here...if she'd known you were here."

"I know."

"Damn it, Paxton!" I cried, my eyes blurring for the first time. "You didn't just use me, you manipulated me to get to Rachel. She's my best friend!"

"And he's mine!" he countered. He took a stuttered breath. "The first moment I saw you, I thought you were the most refreshingly beautiful woman I'd ever seen. Then I found out you were...well, you, and I knew I couldn't touch you, that I had to put that instant connection somewhere far away before we ended up here. Yes, at first I wanted you to understand us, like us, want to help us so that you wouldn't run when Rachel couldn't make it, and I prayed you'd be the one who would convince her to stay when she showed up. But I never expected *you*. You had me from the first moment you hooked onto that zip-line with me. Hell, maybe even before that."

"It doesn't matter." I shook my head. "None of it matters now. How am I supposed to believe anything you say? It was all a lie."

"No," he said, coming around the couch. "Not my feelings for you. Not what happens the moment I look into your eyes, or I touch you. I swear to God that none of that is a lie. All of it is real—way too real."

"What am I supposed to do with that?" I asked, backing away when he stepped closer. "Are you seriously pulling the it-started-as-a-game-but-then-I-fell-for-you line?"

"It was never a game, I swear. Yes, I wanted to keep you happy, at first because I needed Rachel to get here, and then because I love to see you smile. I kept you close because I needed you to feel invested in me, my grades, the Renegades, all of it—and then because I couldn't bear to not be around you. I don't know what you're supposed to do. I can only tell you what I hope you'll do. I hope you'll forgive me. I hope you'll look at me and see that the only truth that matters is that what we are is extraordinary and epic, and worth the shit we're going through. That someone planted that picture so you'd see it, so you'd walk away from me. That this is another way to sabotage us. Please see it, Leah."

"Why would I?" I threw in his face.

"Because you love me!" he shouted back.

God, I did. I loved him so much that I wanted to believe him. I wanted to believe that the picture meant nothing, or that someone had planted it. Wanted to believe that it was out of love for his friend that he did this to me, love between Landon and Rachel. But it wasn't enough. Not when he'd used me, lied to me, manipulated me, and even when things had "gotten real," had never clued me in. "It's not enough," I replied. Not when he still needed me to keep Rachel from leaving the minute she got here. Not when he knew with one phone call I could destroy his plans. He still needed me. That's why he was doing this.

His eyes went wild for a moment before he seemed to gather himself. "Because I'm in love with you."

Everything stilled, as if the second hand agreed not to move, or all thousand people on the *Athena* stopped breathing. He'd finally said it, but now I couldn't trust him, couldn't believe what he was saying. "No," I replied. "Love doesn't lie, manipulate, or use people to get what it wants. If you loved me, you would have told me about Rachel. If not at the start, then at least in Istanbul, or before I gave myself to you in Mykonos. Love means that you put someone else above yourself, above what you want, and you never did that. Rachel was your endgame—for Landon or not— and I was never above that consideration. You never once put my feelings, my trust, my love, above your need to get Rachel on board. Love doesn't do that."

God, I'd given him everything. Not just my body but my past, my soul, everything I kept locked so deep that even I forgot it was there. And he'd only been after Rachel.

"Maybe your love doesn't, because it's perfect. You are basically perfect, Leah. But my love is messy, imperfect, makes mistakes, and is overwhelmingly selfish, because I need you. I need you more than air in my lungs or even the Renegades. So yes, I'm in love with you, and maybe you don't like that because you can't control it, but it's the truth. You can choose not to forgive me for this—I'd understand—but you can't stop me from loving you."

I wavered, and not a slight sway, an earthquake kind of

waver. "You haven't even apologized. When you're sorry, you're supposed to apologize."

He grimaced. "I can't apologize for this because I'm not sorry. I'm not sorry about how I got you here, or for putting you in this suite. I'm not sorry about getting you to tutor me, or even putting you on the zip-line. I can't regret a single thing that brought us here, brought me to you."

As he walked toward me, I stopped retreating until he stood a breath away, his hands on my face. "But that doesn't mean I don't have regrets. I'm sorry for every time you were hurt on my watch. I'm sorry for every time you doubted yourself, every time I tried to hold back from you, because we could have had so much more time. I'm sorry for making fun of your travel wallet when it saved my ass. I'm sorry that I didn't find you when we lived miles apart, before either of us became so jaded that neither of us believed love like this was possible. But mostly I'm sorry I didn't tell you that I loved you from the moment I realized it, the moment my chest thought it might burst from it. The moment I thought I almost lost you on the ramp, or the way you called me out on my bullshit in Istanbul. I'm sorry I didn't tell you in Mykonos when I found that missing piece of my soul inside you. But mostly, I'm sorry I didn't say it back when you were brave enough to tell me that you loved me, because I wasn't. Because I knew that the minute I let myself feel this"—he pulled my hand over his heart—"and you realized what I'd done, that you'd leave, and I'd be destroyed. All I have are shitty examples of how love turns out. Please forgive me. Show me there's another outcome."

"Paxton," I whispered, unable to say anything else. Maybe it was enough. Maybe the circumstances that brought us together meant nothing in the long haul, and that what counted was the way we loved each other now. Maybe Rachel didn't matter, the lies could be forgiven, and it was...possible. But I'd never know if he truly wanted me, or if he saw me as the lynchpin to Landon's happiness.

A knock sounded at my door.

"Don't answer it," Paxton begged. "Whoever it is can wait until we get this settled."

But I needed the breather, the space to think. I broke our quasi embrace and walked down the hall, Paxton on my heels, like he was scared I'd walk out before we finished.

The knob twisted in my hand, and I opened the door.

I gawked.

"Well, that's some hello, nice to see you," Rachel said before flinging her arms around my neck and pulling me into her familiar hug. "Thank God I found you. I saw this video on Instagram last week, and I knew I had to get here. Do you have any idea how many calls I had to make to get on the ship a week early? Or how many flights, for that matter? They only let me do it because second term starts at the next port and I told them I needed the same adjustment time the other students had gotten. I have to talk to you."

She pulled back, cupping my face in her hands, concern lancing through her beautiful brown eyes as she saw tears in mine. "I'm too late, aren't I?"

"I don't...I don't know," I answered, unable to string anything else together. Instead, I stepped back enough to open the door full width. She was beautiful, average height, but always toned, her body the kind of perfection that Paxton was surrounded by daily. Her black hair had new highlights in it, just the tip of the iceberg when it came to the no-holds-barred way she expressed herself. She was my polar opposite in so many ways, which was why we were such great friends, why I could see why both Landon and Paxton had wanted her. I'd always admired her, but never felt inferior to my best friend, and this sucked.

"It's okay," she promised, but then her mouth dropped as she looked behind me.

I sidestepped and braced my back against the wall. Then I watched every nuance of Paxton's face change from shock to cringe-worthy acceptance. "Rachel."

"Wilder," she said, swallowing. She looked between us. "Oh...oh God no. No, Leah, no. He'll eat you alive. I'd hoped the video was wrong. Why didn't you tell me?"

Her glare whipped toward Paxton. "You made her sign an NDA, you fucking asshole."

A wry grin twisted his lips. "As I recall it wasn't me fu—"

"Paxton!" I snapped, throwing my hand over his mouth. The asshole kissed the palm and gently pulled my hand away, refusing to let go when I yanked.

Rachel's eyes hit the floor before she composed herself. "Let me know when you'd like your biggest mistakes thrown in your face, Wilder. I'm happy to oblige."

"I'm kind of living that moment right now, but thanks for the offer. It's always good of you to fuck up my life at opportune moments, but hey, at least the X Games don't start next week."

Rachel flinched. Oh God, he'd found out right before the X Games? *And he'd still medaled.* I couldn't decide if I was impressed that he'd kicked ass even after having his heart broken, or if he had a heart to break. *You know that's not true.*

I silenced my conscience. "This is getting us nowhere. Rachel, I'm so sorry but I'm a little off. I just found out about you two." I shook my head. "You three. Whatever. Of course I'm glad to see you. I don't think I've ever been happier to see anyone." Then I looked up at Paxton. "I need you to leave."

"Yes, please leave. I think you've done enough damage," Rachel snapped.

"Leah," he begged, his blues going all soft and buttery, ignoring Rachel.

"No. You've had months to come to terms with what you've done, what you set me up for—us up for. I've had all of four hours. You owe me time. That's the least you can give me."

He searched my face, no doubt looking for a weakness. "Okay," he finally said. "But I love you. I'm not giving you up."

Rachel snorted. "What do you know about love, Wilder?"

"What you taught me," he fired back before recoiling and sucking in a deep breath. "Why do you even think you're here?"

"What? Studying abroad?" Realization dawned, her eyes growing huge and her hand covering her mouth. "You didn't."

"I did. Because you two deserve the chance you never got. He doesn't know you're here—I'm not a masochist—so it's up to you when you tell him. If you tell him." He looked at me, his heart in his eyes. "Firecracker?"

"Go study," I whispered. "We have finals the day after tomorrow, and you tied our fates, remember?"

"Can you forgive me?"

"I don't know, but if you press me for that answer right now, it'll be no. I need some time."

He nodded. "Okay. I can give you that. But I need you to believe that I love you. If you trust nothing else, trust that."

"This guy I know told me once that anyone can claim they can do something. It's what you show the world that matters, right?" I said.

"Yeah. Something like that." He gave in. "I'll see you in class." As he passed Rachel, who looked ready to fly at him with claws bared, he said, "I know you're pissed. But we're at sea for the next five days, so you can't exactly get off the boat anyway. Take your time and think. Don't run. I just ask that you think of everything Leah has done for you, and for once, think of someone else, too...and if you choose to leave, please don't take her with you. Don't take her chance the way I stupidly took yours."

Paxton dodged the luggage cart that arrived at the same moment, Hugo nearly jumping out of his way. As Hugo brought the cart in, Rachel pulled me into the first open bedroom—it happened to be mine.

"What happened?" she asked, her voice nearly a squeak. "I leave you alone for three months and you fall into my old life. I'm cruising Instagram last week and a Renegade video popped up that showed you, and I just about peed myself. Tell me he didn't get to you."

I burst into tears. "I fell for him, and all he wanted was to get to you. Oh God, Rach. I'm so fucking stupid."

"No," she soothed with a heavy sigh, pulling my head to her shoulder. "You have a heart bigger than this ocean, Leah. It's not stupidity, it's love."

"I hate love," I said, hiccupping.

"Yeah. It sucks, and I know more than I should about loving a Renegade," she agreed. "Well, since I'm too damn late to save you from yourself, what do you want to do?"

"I don't know. Is that okay? I know he's your ex, and this must be the weirdest thing ever, but you're my best friend."

"Don't do that. I don't factor into this, not with Wilder. He's an ass, but he's your ass. It's between the two of you."

"Why can't it be easy?" I asked.

"It never is. But I can tell you one thing. There was a reason I left him. Why I...cheated with Landon." Her breath caught on Landon's name, something that never happened when she talked about guys.

"What was it?" I asked, genuinely needing to know what would make someone walk away from someone as all-consuming as Paxton.

She forced a smile. "Because he never looked at me the way he did you right now."

I shook my head. "How?"

"Like you were air and he was on the verge of suffocating. Like you were literally the only thing that could save his life or give it meaning."

"Oh."

"Yeah. I found that with someone else, and Wilder took it away. I can't tell you what to do, but you deserve to know the facts."

I loved him. I could never deny that, and maybe—just maybe—he loved me, too. But could I ever know if he really did? Or would I always wonder if he just wanted to keep Rachel close?

I wasn't sure I'd ever know—or if I could love under those terms.

"What about you? You came all this way knowing that Landon was here?"

She gave me a tight, forced smile. "You are my best friend. You held me together when it felt like everything else was ripping me in ten thousand directions. Landon... He took enough from me; I'm not letting him take this trip, too. And this is about you. I would do anything for you. If you want to go, we'll go. If you want to stay, we'll stay."

She pulled me into a hug, and I let myself sink into the familiarity of my best friend. But part of me died, too. Paxton's plan had worked. Whether or not Rachel stayed, and Landon got his chance, was all up to me...and everything revolved around my feelings for Pax.

As far as I would go to secure Rachel's happiness, how was I ever going to know if being with me was a price Paxton would pay for Landon's?

CHAPTER TWENTY-NINE

PAXTON

AT SEA

I poured another shot of tequila and sighed as it burned down my throat. Numbness, blessed numbness—that was all that I wanted. I think that was my sixth...wait...seventh...no...sixth. Fuck it. I gave up.

There wasn't enough alcohol to burn this pain away. I'd once foolishly thought that the Rachel/Landon shit was the worst I'd ever feel. But on the pain scale, that was a stubbed toe. This was the decimation of my fucking heart.

She had to believe me, didn't she? She had to see how much I loved her, that she wasn't just some tool to get Landon and Rachel back together. She knew me, right? Hadn't I let her in? Let her see how much she meant to me? But she was right, I'd put Landon's happiness above my own, and that meant I'd put it above hers, too.

Now that Rachel was here, was there a way to prove my love to Leah? To show her that she—and not the love life of my best friend—was my priority? I couldn't even tell Landon that Rachel was here, not until she'd made her choice. I wasn't going to fuck with his head just to have her tuck tail and run. God, I only wanted everyone to have it all, for everyone to be happy.

This isn't a fucking sitcom.

"So are you going to tell me what this fight with Leah is about, or are you going to make me guess?" Landon asked, pouring himself a shot.

"None of your business."

He threw the shot back and leaned against the bar, no doubt judging my unshaved face and general lack of hygiene. "You ready for finals tomorrow?"

I shrugged. I'd studied all day, gone to every class in preparation, sat next to Leah, unable to touch her and hating every single second of it. She'd been polite but hadn't even met my eyes. Ironic, since that's the relationship we should have had in the first place.

I'd had my bones broken, joints ripped apart, hundreds of stitches through my skin, but nothing had ever felt like Leah breaking my heart.

Fuck that. I broke my own heart. Maybe that's why it hurt even more.

"Okay, well this has been a nice talk. Guess I should get some sleep," Landon said. There was a knock at the door. "Saved by the knock...or whatever."

I headed outside, bracing my weight on the deck railing.

"You look like shit," Brandon said, leaning against the rail next to me.

"Thank you, Captain Obvious."

"I like your ship," he said, looking out over the water. "I've been exploring during my mini-cruise. Thanks for letting me stay until Abu Dhabi."

"It's Dad's ship," I countered. "And you're welcome. You

saved my ass, remember?"

He shook his head. "Leah saved your ass. If she'd waited to call me you'd have been left behind. She's quite a woman."

"She is."

"It's your ship, Pax. Dad signed it over to you."

"What?"

He shrugged. "He divested certain assets before he submitted the paperwork to take the company public. This, and the house in Aspen, they're yours. He figured you'd need them for this extreme life you lead. Well, the ship was more an income source. The house was his indulgence."

"I own the ship," I said slowly, trying to wrap my head around it.

"Yep," Brandon popped the P. "I tried to talk him out of it. Let's face it, you fuck up pretty much everything you touch, but he'd already done it. The papers are in your fire safe."

"Wow."

"Yeah, I said the same thing."

"Did you…?" I started, but couldn't finish.

He half smiled. "We were gifted equally, don't get your panties in a wad on my account. Look, that shit you pulled—hitting the cop…" He put up his hands when I glared at him. "Whether or not he deserved it for putting his hands on Leah, the arrest nullified your contract with Dad to fund the documentary."

"What?" I nearly shouted. "So you come down here saying you're going to save my ass, and then instead stab me in the back?"

He shook his head. "You stabbed yourself. That temper of yours could jeopardize everything Dad is working for."

"And he said that he's pulling the funding? It's primarily his decision, isn't it?"

"He has final say, but I think it should be brought to the board. I love you, brother, but you're anything but a sound investment while we're going through this right now. If it was at any other time, I wouldn't press it, but your reach is down, you're not posting as much to your channel, and what you are posting isn't getting the hits that you're used to. You gave up the tour for this year, so your sponsors aren't hanging around, and you don't know if you'll be allowed to compete in the X Games if your program here says no. You've got too much going against you to be a sure bet."

"I've never been a sure bet, Brandon. That's why I win the medals. You don't get those things by sitting on the sidelines waiting for the safe time. You do it by grabbing your balls and going for it, but I'd never expect you to understand." Anger overtook every other emotion except fear, which was running neck and neck to keep up.

"You have always had an edge I didn't get, Pax. I think you're a reckless, stupid son of a... Well, that's our mother, so I won't finish that." He sighed. "But you are so much of Mom, and I envy that. I always have. Do you think you could promo the documentary with what you have?"

I thought through the footage we'd gathered since boarding. "Not the full film, but I could put together a kick-ass trailer."

"I need something concrete for the board. Numbers."

"What kind of numbers?" I asked, hating that, as usual, Brandon's pound of flesh might be more than I could give.

"You have six days until the live expo?"

"Yeah. Three more days at sea, and then two days to practice."

"How long to cut the trailer?"

My mind scrambled, calculating who we had on board. "At least a day."

"That leaves you five days to get a million hits."

I damn near choked on air. "That's impossible."

"Every pop star pulls it off fairly quickly."

"Right, well, I'll let you know when we have Adele jumping a motocross bike, okay? Shit like that is harder than it sounds."

"I know exactly how hard it is. And I'm talking legit views, Paxton. Not paid subscriber crap."

"How would you even—?"

"You're my little brother. No matter what happens between us at home, out here we're on the same team. I know exactly what it takes to make your business go. I want you to succeed. I just don't want you taking Wilder Enterprises down while you're doing it. You hit one million views by the time you take the stage at the live expo, or the board will vote to yank your funding. Hell, even with the million hits, they might vote to yank it."

"Fucking great," I said. The six—or seven—shots hadn't been nearly enough.

"It will be." He slapped me on the back. "Good luck. I think you might need it."

I stayed out there long after he left, mentally going over what footage we had, what would be sensational enough to warrant getting one million views. At least we had the jump footage, but what would make the best highlight reel?

I came back inside, flopping onto the couch, my head telling me I was still moving long after I stopped.

"What did the grim reaper want?"

"We have to edit a trailer in the next twenty-four hours and hit a million views before the live expo in Abu Dhabi."

"Or we could call up Santa Claus and have him deliver early. I mean, we're only five weeks or so out, right?"

I grunted in response, my mind trying to fight through the haze of alcohol to function.

"I guess you're right, most of the people around us are just waiting to watch us fall," he said, pouring another shot.

It was the same thing I said to Leah, ironically as I was falling...for her.

Falling.

"Wake up Bobby and tell him to get the production crew in here," I ordered.

"Pax, you're pretty drunk. Do you think this is the time to call a production meeting?"

"With this kind of idea? If this works, we'll serve shots at the production meetings," I answered as Penna came in with a suitcase. I'd almost forgotten how much she and Rachel hadn't gotten along.

"Were you going to tell me?" she snapped at me, tossing her bag on the floor.

"What?" Landon asked.

"Oh, Leah's roommate showed up a week early, so I'm back in here with the boys," she answered.

"It's okay," I said to her. "I think I've figured out how to get Leah back."

It might cost me my documentary, but it would be worth it.

She was worth everything.

CHAPTER THIRTY

LEAH

ABU DHABI

"Fuck, could it be any hotter here?" Rachel asked as she fanned herself on the deck.

"You know Landon can see you out there," I said through the open door.

"He's at the expo site, practicing with Wilder," she answered.

"How do you even know that?" I asked as I packed up my books from this trimester. Our last final had been this morning, and I'd actually managed to keep my attention on the test instead of on Paxton sitting next to me. English and our verbal examinations and defense of our thesis hadn't been so easy. Especially not when Paxton stood in front of me and answered the class's interrogation on his thesis on the theory of love and redemption in *Les Miserables*. It was like he'd directed every answer at me.

"I may have paid off Hugo to let me know," Rachel responded, reminding me that I'd asked her a question.

"Well, if that wasn't slightly unethical. You've been here three days and you've got the staff on payroll?" I finished as I leaned on the doorframe.

She shrugged.

"Do you want to talk about him? Landon?" I clarified.

"I'd rather rebreak every bone I've ever mangled. It would probably feel the same." She pulled her sunglasses down and dismissed the topic like only Rachel could. "So, have you seen this trailer?"

"What trailer?" I asked.

"I guess they cut a trailer for the documentary, and they're trying to get it to a million hits before the expo tomorrow."

"Oh." I hated being out of the Renegade loop as much as I desperately needed the space. "No. I haven't seen it. I promised Penna I'd go over and watch the rehearsal, though. I'm guessing you don't want to go?"

"No, thank you. How are you doing with all this? I mean, you've been swamped with finals, and I know you love to hide under schoolwork, but really?"

I sat on her lounge chair and fingered the hemline of my black shorts. I used to be scared to put my legs into the sun because the scarring would only stand out more with a tan, but now it simply was what it was—another part of me like the freckles on my nose or the color of my eyes.

"I don't know," I answered honestly. "And I don't know how to talk to you about it. You're my best friend, but you're his ex, and that's really freaking weird. I can't think about you two without wanting to vomit."

She slid her sunglasses up into her black hair. "Leah, I love you like a sister. What Wilder and I had was so long ago, two and a half years, and if I had to rate that relationship in importance in my life, it's probably somewhere around a four, and that's only because it led me to Landon." She winced, like even his name was painful. "Landon, I loved...and I thought he loved me, especially after he walked away from the Renegades for me. But that was the month of the X Games, and it was just too much, and when Wilder dropped the ultimatum, Landon chose them. I didn't think I'd be able to breathe for the longest time. He was my ten, and then he was my zero. What is Wilder to you?"

"He's an eleven," I admitted. "He probably shouldn't be. The guy isn't exactly known for monogamy."

"Has he looked at anyone since you've been together?"

"No. He's always made me feel like I'm the only one he notices." My eyes slid shut. "But I don't know how much of that was real and how much was just keeping me happy to make sure I wouldn't leave before you got here. When I think of everything he did, how deep the plan went to get you on board, and then I think that maybe to him, I'm only a cog in that plan...I can't breathe."

"I saw him with you, you're not just a cog. Maybe you were at first, but the way he begged you? If you were just a part of his plan, he wouldn't still be after you. Wilder never gets attached, he never begs, and he never apologizes—all of which he did for you. His plan worked. I'm here, and I'm going to stay."

"You're willing to stay? You're sure?" My voice pitched in excitement. She'd offered already, but I had to be certain.

"Yeah. If you're in, I'm in. Once upon a time I let Landon ruin me. I'm not letting him ruin this, too. If that means I have to duck him in the hallways, then fine."

I hugged her, careless of her suntan oil seeping into my shirt. "I've missed you so much."

Her arms closed around me. "Same here. I was kind of lost without you, and you were halfway across the world, getting lost." She laughed.

"Yeah, but as ridiculous as this sounds, I feel kind of found, too. And I know it was Paxton, pushing me, accepting me, loving me. Rach, what am I going to do?"

"I can't answer that. You've done pretty damn well on your own, and honestly, if I'd been here to start with, I would have done everything in my power to keep you away from Wilder, and look what a huge mistake that would have been. You know him in a way I never did, and you"—she gestured to my bare legs—"the changes he's brought in you are amazing. I hated you being here without me, but I'm so glad it happened this way."

"Me, too," I said. "I just don't know how to trust him."

"That's going to be something you have to decide. No one else—not even Wilder—can make that choice for you. But you and I both know how rare love is, and if you two have it, then fight for it. Figure out the rest as you go along."

"And don't look where it's taking us? What happens after this trip is over?"

She smiled. "I kinda feel like it should take you to your bedroom, and then to the expo site. After that it's all up to you."

"Bedroom?"

She smiled and shrugged, then went back to sunbathing.

I walked to my room and found a red package on the bed with red tissue paper and a red card. *Subtle, Pax.*

My hands shook as I opened the card, ripping through the paper. It was from one of the tourist sites on Mykonos, with a glossy picture of the shoreline. When I opened it, my eyes prickled.

> *"This is my endgame. You said you wanted to touch love, and you did. You do with every breath. I know I messed up. I know you don't think you can trust me. But you wondered if you'd ever be able to let go and let someone love you... Let go, Leah, because I already do."*

I closed the card and gently put it down on the bed before I unwrapped the frame inside the bag. It was the picture from Mykonos. When had he had it developed?

My fingers traced our lines, my breath caught at not only the look on my face but on Paxton's—the complete devotion I saw in his eyes as he held me above his head. A guy couldn't fake that kind of look.

Could he?

I wanted to say no. Everything in my body cried out that he was real, that our love was genuine. But what if it wasn't? What if I was making a fool out of myself, when I should be bailing, getting out of this relationship when I needed to?

What if I hadn't learned my lesson from Brian's death, and I was still hanging on to something that I needed to run from— destined to break more and more the longer I stayed?

But what if my fear was what I was clinging to, and Pax was the one I should be running toward?

I closed the door behind me and checked my watch. Practice was still going—I could make it. I would have been even faster, but I'd changed into pants and a breezy shirt so I didn't stick out like a sore thumb here in Abu Dhabi.

Paxton's door opened, and my heart stuttered, even though I logically knew he was already at the expo site. Little John came out shaking his head until he saw me. "Oh thank God, Leah. Are you headed to the site?"

"Yeah, I promised Penna I'd stop by."

"Good. Paxton is a wreck out there, all jumpy about damn near everything. Rebel's bike broke, and it's a hot mess. You'll calm him down."

Don't count on it. "You going back?"

He nodded. "Yep, as soon as I can find Rebel's pink bandana. She says it's lucky or something, and I didn't see it in her room."

"Where did she say it was?" I asked. I hadn't seen it at our place, either.

"In the purple backpack?" He looked at me for the answer.

Luckily I had it. "That backpack is Brooke's. I bet it's in her room, not Penna's. Do you have her key, too?"

He nodded, and in a few seconds had her door open. "Do you mind?"

"Not at all," I answered, hurrying in. Her suite was smaller than ours but gorgeous. I checked the closet, the bedroom, and the living room, finally heading back into the bedroom and looking under the bed.

"Bingo," I said, pulling it out. It caught on the bed frame, and I yanked it clear, but as I did something fell from the frame. Shit, I hoped I hadn't broken the bed.

It was a piece of folded paper, and I tossed it onto the made bed before standing up with the backpack. I plopped the bag onto the bedspread and opened it, digging through until I found the pink bandana Penna loved. As I zipped the pack up, feeling pretty darn victorious, the seal on the top of the paper next to me caught my attention.

It was an official-looking document to be kept in a bed frame, but it was none of my business. After I stored the backpack, my morals wavered...then fell. I snatched the paper off the bed and opened it.

What the fuck?

It was the photography permit from Madagascar.

Brooke. No way. It wasn't possible.

Chills raced up my limbs, pooling at the base of my neck. She was the one helping to admin the site when the videos were being hacked. She had access to Paxton's gear, to his fire box. She'd been the one to push me on the ramp that day, and Morocco...

Damn it. I'd heard her voice, but only Little John had been standing on the shore when I'd been pushed. In the confusion, she could have called out from anywhere, and I wouldn't have noticed.

But why would she do it all when her own sister was a Renegade?

I looked up over the paper and Brooke's nightstand came into view, a framed picture of a handsome blond guy with one arm wrapped around her and the other braced on a motocross bike. *Nick.*

I didn't have all the pieces, but I had enough.

My feet flew as I ran from the room, clutching the bandana and the permit. "Where is Brooke?" I asked Little John as I almost fell into the hallway.

"At the expo with Penna. Why?"

"We have to get there, now!" I shouted, already running for the elevator. "How fast can you drive?"

"I'm a Renegade," he answered, as if that was enough. It was. "But Wilder gave us explicit orders that we're supposed to go slowly if you're in the car."

Of course he did.

I stabbed the elevator button. "Forget what Paxton said. We have to get there as fast as possible."

"What's going on, Leah?"

"I know who's sabotaging the stunts."

· · ·

I closed my eyes and held on to the door handle while we skidded around another corner. "Just make sure we don't get arrested. Our group doesn't have the best track record with foreign authorities."

Little John nodded but kept his full attention on the road, weaving us in and out of cars with the ease of a professional stunt driver...because he was. That didn't help the nausea crippling me, or the heart-stopping fear.

"It's kind of like being in your own action movie," he explained as we flew through a red light.

"Overrated," I answered in a high pitch.

"Yet effective."

We skidded to a halt in front of the expo site—a huge arena—and we both abandoned the car while the engine still ran. Little John threw open the doors, and we sprinted inside.

"Damn, this place is huge."

"Get Paxton," I ordered. "Page him on the intercom, or whatever. I'm going to find Brooke."

He nodded, and we split directions. I ran past the concession stands to the entrance of the arena. The floor had been covered in yards of dirt, Paxton's huge ramp center stage with others flanking it and a stunt track bordering it all. I made out the bright blue stripes on Paxton's bike on the smaller ramps. At least Little John would be able to find him.

Each section was in use, and the noise was deafening as motocross bikes revved their engines, then drove full throttle. I scanned the stands, looking for any of the Originals.

Security had done a good job, and the stands were nearly empty, but there was no sign of Brooke.

A flash of white caught my attention, and I looked up to the Jumbotron that hung in the middle of the arena. "Shit," I whispered, seeing Brooke on the catwalk, her hands on the wires that held the huge monitor. Whatever she was doing—it wasn't good.

"Brooke!" I yelled, but there was too much noise.

Paxton couldn't hear me, but Little John would be there soon. I just had to keep her distracted. I traced the path of the catwalk and ran to where it intersected with the wall, then climbed two flights of stairs as quickly as I could until I reached that level, sprinting to the ladder.

A fucking ladder.

You got this. Hand over hand, and one step at a time, I hurried up the deathtrap, keeping Paxton's face in my mind as I climbed higher than I ever thought I'd be able to, finally coming out at the catwalk.

"Don't look down," I whispered to myself. Instead I locked my eyes on where Brooke fumbled on her stomach, her hands beneath the catwalk. She had hold of one of the giant light fixtures, but the way the catwalk wobbled when I stepped onto it told me she'd loosened that, too.

The motion also alerted her to my presence, and her head swiveled, a wild look in her eyes I'd never seen before. "Stay back!" she yelled. "I don't want you to get hurt, Leah."

She had the light already loose, hanging by what looked like a single screw. Shit.

"Whatever you're doing, Brooke, don't. Please. Someone could die."

She turned and stood, her hands locked around the railing like mine were. "He should! That stupid fucking trick took Nick! Someone should be punished! Instead they're making a movie. A *movie*! While he's confined to a wheelchair for the rest of his life, so ruined that he won't even let me see him, they're here, doing what he loved. Paxton shouldn't be the first to do this trick. It was never his, it was Nick's, and they've all forgotten him!"

"I know it feels that way," I said, taking another step on the swaying catwalk. "What was your plan? Drop the whole catwalk? Have you lost it? Your sister is down there!"

She hesitated, looking down briefly.

"I disabled Penna's bike. She's fixing it in the back. I'd rather die than hurt her. I don't want to hurt you, either."

"And that's why you pushed me off a cliff in Morocco?" I glanced down and saw Paxton still riding the circuit, and I silently cursed Little John. I didn't know how long I could keep her occupied before I was the one she threw off the catwalk.

"That was unfortunate," she admitted. "But the cameraman walked away, and you were alone. I thought you'd jump, land in the water. I hoped you'd be scared enough that Pax would stop the movie, or you'd just leave, and he'd fail his classes. I never meant for you to get hurt."

"I could have died!" My brain was misfiring, trying to reconcile the angry woman in front of me with the friend I'd made the first morning on board.

"You didn't, but you might if you stay up here. Now, go!" She bounced slightly, and the metal creaked, then descended a couple inches.

"I can't let you hurt Paxton or anyone else," I said, clinging to the railing.

"They need to understand that what they're doing ruins lives. It ruined Nick's life, and it destroyed mine! And they don't care! They just keep on going, keep pushing. It's not fair! I only want them to stop!"

My hands tightened on the rails, my knuckles turning white. "Let's get down, Brooke. We can talk about this on the ground."

She shook her head. "I've come too far, especially now that

you know. Then again, I could blame it all on you. Nothing bad started happening until you showed up that first day."

Another bounce and the angle deepened. I looked down to see Paxton at the start of the center ramp. The one we were directly above. God, this was the moment she'd been waiting for. "Don't do it," I begged.

"For what it's worth," she said, looking down at Paxton before she glanced back up to me. "I think he loves you. Even if you were just a tool to get Rachel on board."

My eyes widened.

"Of course I know. Don't be stupid. I've known since Penna ran the background check on you when you both applied to the program. That's why I grabbed that picture before we left L.A. The only one who doesn't know is Landon. Which is kind of fitting, seeing as Paxton was the only one who didn't catch on when Rachel and Landon were fucking around behind his back. It hurts to turn the tables, doesn't it?"

"So you planted the picture so I'd find it?"

Keep her talking. He hasn't started yet. Distract her.

In fact, he wasn't there at all. I breathed a sigh of relief.

"Don't get excited, he's just backing up to get enough speed to hit the ramp. This will be the jump of a lifetime," she said with a smile that didn't even look like hers. She was losing it right in front of me, and if I couldn't stop her, someone was going to get hurt...or die. "The one Nick would have made if he'd been here. But Paxton always has to have it all, doesn't he? The tricks, the girls...even you. It was hard to watch you fall for him, knowing he was just using you. I really like you, and I thought you'd be smarter, that I wouldn't have to involve you, but then I saw how badly he wanted you, needed you, and I knew you were the key to everything. If you were hurt, if you quit, the movie would fail.

They'd go home and reassess. After Madagascar, I figured if you saw the picture, you'd leave him to rot in that jail cell. Movie over. Mission accomplished and no one gets hurt...other than Nick, not that they care. But no, you had to call Brandon. You had to fix everything for the guy who only wanted you for your best friend. Where is your self-worth?"

I heard the bike rev, then come flying out of the tunnel. As the bike hit the ramp, Brooke jumped as hard as she could, then ran, the catwalk falling as she raced toward me. When I tried to grab her, she pushed me back, and I fell along the catwalk as it turned into a giant slide. I saw the camera break loose at the last second before I gripped the support beam, catching my weight as the catwalk fell to a full ninety-degree angle.

"Paxton!" I screamed as the camera hit the dirt of the landing ramp right before his bike did. The front tire impacted, the bike flipping and flinging him off, where he tumbled over the side of the dirt ramp, falling twenty feet to the ground.

"No!" The sound was nearly inhuman as it ripped from my throat, seeing his leg at an unnatural angle as people rushed to him, the motors suddenly quiet. "Paxton!"

"I'm here, baby," he said from above me. "Hold on!"

My head swiveled between my arms to see him on the supported length of catwalk, not in a crumpled mess beneath me. "Pax." He was alive. He was okay.

My fingers slipped a fraction of an inch, but it was enough to send my heart into overdrive, beating out a panicked rhythm.

"No!" Brooke shrieked. "This can't be for nothing! You're supposed to be on your bike!"

"Yeah, well, Penna is!" he yelled as he gripped her forearms, yanking her onto the platform.

"No!" she yelled. "Penna!"

I wanted to look down, but my hold was too precarious. *Let her be okay. God, please.*

The metal creaked as he leaned back over. "Brooke?" I questioned.

"Security has her," he said calmly as he headed toward me, Little John lowering him by his feet. "Firecracker, I'm going to ask this time that you not let go."

"Smart-ass," I said, my breath shaky. "Is Penna okay?"

"I hope so," he answered. "Just hold on." His hands gripped my wrists. "Now let go. I've got you."

We locked eyes, and I knew with utter certainty that if he dropped me, I would die. Without another thought, I let go of the railing, trusting my weight to him.

"Pull us up!" he yelled, and we started to rise, the metal creaking and groaning as the screws began to give way. I wanted to close my eyes and wait for the inevitable fall, but I didn't look away from him.

"Move!" I heard the ground crew screaming.

Paxton and I slid onto the catwalk, and as he gathered me into the safety of his arms, the last of the supports gave way, and the catwalk crashed to the now-empty ramp below.

So close. It had been so close.

"Is she okay?" he called down, his arms firmly wrapped around me. I rested my head on his chest, listening to his heart and trying to match mine to its steady beat. For every ounce of bravery that had somehow surfaced, I felt that much weaker lying in Paxton's embrace, like my body was completely depleted of adrenaline, energy, whatever it was that had kept me on that catwalk.

Landon hovered over Penna, his hands running the length of her body.

"Landon!" Paxton yelled, but still didn't move when Landon threw him the universal one-fingered wait sign.

"She's breathing! Give us a second!"

I felt the war within Paxton rage, the need to be with his friends versus the need to stay with me.

"You can go," I whispered.

"Not until you're okay," he responded, resting his chin on my head. "God, when I saw you up here, I didn't know if I could get to you in time. I've never been that scared in my life."

"Me, either," I admitted. "Thank you for coming for me."

"God, Leah," he said, tipping my face up to his, "all I wanted was to trade places with you. There is nothing I wouldn't do to keep you safe."

Now my heart was racing again.

"Pax!" Landon shouted. "I think just her leg is fucked up."

We both sagged in relief. "Are you okay?" Paxton asked.

"Let's get down there," I said.

"It was supposed to be you!" Brooke shrieked from behind us, where she was held by two huge security guards. "She's supposed to be fixing her bike!"

"She wanted to use mine instead, you traitor! You could have fucking killed her!" Paxton railed. "You nearly killed Leah, you had me tossed in jail, and you messed with our equipment? I know you've had a hard time, Brooke, but she's your sister! We're your family!"

"It was supposed to be you! How could you leave him behind? How could you do his trick? How could you use everything he built and just step over him, forget him, knowing what you did to him?"

Paxton helped me to stand, keeping my hand tucked in his. "Because he's helping me!"

Brooke stilled, her eyes blinking rapidly, realization coming back into them. "What?"

"That's his design, Brooke. That's his ramp technique. That's his kicker. Who do you think mapped out the drop zone in Madagascar? Helped design the pipe layout in Barcelona?"

"I don't believe you," she said, panic creeping over her features.

"Then ask him yourself," he snapped and pointed to the end of the motocross track, where a young man sat in a wheelchair, looking up at us.

"Nick," she gasped.

He simply shook his head at her.

"Take her," Paxton ordered the guards.

We all descended as quickly as possible, Paxton and I both breaking into a run to get to Penna. Never once did he let go of my hand after we hit the ground. My lungs burned by the time we reached the main level, where Penna had been neck-braced and placed on a stretcher.

"I need to deal with the arena, but I need to go with Penna, too," Paxton said, ripping his free hand through his hair.

"Go with Penna. I'll stay," Nick said, coming up behind us.

He was devastatingly handsome with thick blond hair that was given to curl, bright blue eyes, and a Paul Walker mouth. "You must be Leah. I'm sorry it's under these circumstances, but I'm glad to meet the woman who's tamed Wilder."

"It's nice to meet you, too, Nick. I've heard a ton of great things about you."

"None of them are true," he said with a grimace. "Seriously. Take Landon and go. I've got it here."

"I'll stay, too," I told Paxton as they loaded Penna into the back of the ambulance. "Between the two of us, we'll take care of it."

Paxton nodded once, then pulled me against him, kissing me fiercely. "I thought I almost lost you."

"You almost did," I said, and we both knew I meant more than what had just happened.

"I love you, Leah. If that means you need me to stop riding, stop filming, stop...anything, I will. Everything is empty without you. I'm empty."

I kissed him gently. "I love you, too. Now go."

"Does this mean...?"

"It means we'll talk later. Get your ass in the ambulance and keep me updated."

"I know what it took for you to trust me with your life up there. I'm just asking for you to trust me with your heart."

"I know," I whispered, needing a little more time for my brain to catch up to what my heart, body, and soul already knew: I was always going to be his.

He stole one more kiss and then jumped into the back of the ambulance. As they pulled out, Brooke was being lowered into a police car, her eyes locked on Nick.

"I'm so sorry," I said to him, unable to process the thought that it had been Brooke all this time, laughing with me, guiding me, and plotting against Paxton. But I knew that my feelings had to be nothing compared to Nick's.

"Me, too," he answered, his eyes saddened with a loss I could only imagine. "Me, too."

CHAPTER THIRTY-ONE

PAXTON

ABU DHABI

"And how do you feel your lack of training time has impacted your preparation for today?" Martin Sykes asked, thrusting his ESPN microphone in my face.

"It hasn't been easy," I answered honestly. "The Renegades put a priority on college this year, which is something we're proud of, but we've had to balance schoolwork, field studies, and general fun with as strenuous a training schedule as we could handle."

"How has training on board a cruise ship challenged you?"

"The boat moves."

Sykes laughed, and I didn't bother to tell him that I wasn't joking.

"We found that when we were at sea, we were focused on our studies and physical training. We had limited facilities in port, but we had some great friends open their tracks and ramps to us, for which we are eternally grateful."

I glanced to my left, where Landon was taking his own questions, and farther down, where Penna sat with a bevy of reporters, her leg, casted in bright pink from the hip down, propped on a chair.

"And the loss of Rebel after yesterday's training accident?" Sykes asked, following my line of sight.

I forced a wry smile. "As you can see, she's not lost, she's healing."

"Right. Bad choice of words. Do you think the priority on school is what caused that accident?"

He waited easily, unknowing that he'd just ripped open the still congealing wound.

"I think there are a lot of factors that led to Rebel's accident, but I can assure you that we've taken protective measures to make sure nothing like that will happen again." And it wouldn't. If I ever had to sit in another hospital for one of my friends, it wasn't going to be because I'd been too ignorant to see what was really happening.

"Right. And that trailer? You took a big risk going with that angle to draw in views."

This time my smile was genuine, especially when I saw Leah coming through the doors behind him, wearing that flirty sundress she'd bought in Mykonos. I couldn't wait to slide my hands up those smooth thighs— *Concentrate!* "Right, the trailer. That motive was purely selfish, but I wanted everyone to see that what makes life extreme isn't always just pushing your body to the limit, it's also about opening yourself to new experiences, whether they're physical or emotional."

"Has she seen it yet?" he asked with a sly smile.

"You know, I'm not sure. But I think I'm going to go ask her, if you don't mind," I answered.

Sykes laughed. "Ah, young love. For ESPN, this is Martin Sykes with the X Games Gold medalist Paxton Wilder, leader of the famed Renegades."

I gave the camera a sharp wave and a grin and then headed toward Leah without asking if he'd want to talk again after. If I succeeded, they all would. If I failed...they all would. Either way, I wasn't getting out of here today without a ton of cameras shoved in my face.

"Hey. I didn't want to bug you, I just wanted to say good luck before I found my seat," she said, nervously tucking her hair behind her ear. "Plus, our grades came out," she added nonchalantly, like our entire future wasn't riding on them.

My stomach dropped. "Okay?"

A slow smile spread across her face. "You passed with a 3.4. That physics class pulled up your GPA. Well, and your Lit final."

"It was good," I bragged.

"Yeah, like your ego isn't big enough already."

"How did you do?" She'd kept a 4.0 since freshman year, and the last thing I wanted was to be the one who pulled her down.

"All As! Physics was so close I could have taken a wrong breath and gotten a B, but I kept my 4.0."

Thank you, God. I swept her into my arms, lifting her up so her lips were level with mine. "What should we do to celebrate?"

"I figured you'd go do that triple front you've been busting your butt for, and then deal with the media."

"Maybe we could grab dinner? Talk about us?" I asked, her feet still dangling above the floor.

She looped her arms around my neck. "I think you might be the first man in existence to want to sit around and talk about our feelings."

"Well, if some other man wants to talk about our feelings, I might have a problem with that."

"You know what I meant."

"I did, and I do. I want this settled between us so we can move on."

Her face fell, and I immediately regretted my word choice.

"Have you seen the trailer yet?" I asked.

She shook her head, and I lowered her slowly to her feet, letting our bodies press against each other but denying her the kiss she was staring at my lips for.

"We'll talk after," she promised, but nothing more.

"Okay."

It killed me to let her walk away, but I had to prep. The show was starting in ten minutes.

"Hey, I need a second," Brandon said from behind me, shocking the hell out of me. He wasn't even in a suit; instead he was dressed down to look almost normal.

"Whoa, what are you doing here?"

"You're our investment."

I gave him a what-the-fuck look.

"Okay, you're my baby brother, and I wanted to be here when you pull off the triple front flip, okay? Maybe I'm a fanboy at heart." He shrugged. "Besides, after what happened yesterday, I wasn't leaving."

I nodded. "First, never say fanboy again. Brooke is in custody—psychologists have been called in—and so is the worker she paid to loosen the catwalk. If she hadn't almost killed my girlfriend and her own sister, I'd almost applaud the genius of her planning."

He nodded slowly. "Penna will recover?"

"Yeah. She's heartbroken, but you'd never guess it the way she's putting on a face for the cameras. She's stuck in that cast for three months, but knowing her, she'll be on the ramp in that wheelchair."

"Okay. And speaking of wheelchairs…"

"Nick is here, but he's sticking to the background. He's not ready to deal with press yet, and I'm okay with it." I canted my head. "You brought him, didn't you?"

Brandon shrugged. "I may have told him that there was a seat on the jet if he wanted it. And then I may have sent that jet for him."

I sucked in deep breaths, trying to get my emotions under control, and then I mentally said "fuck it" and threw my arms around my brother, slapping his back. "Thank you."

He returned the gesture. "Don't mention it."

I pulled away. "I guess we'd better get up there. How many views are we at?" We'd been a thousand shy about an hour ago, and I knew Brandon—he was an asshole about numbers.

"You're close, but you're not there," he answered.

I nodded. "Yeah. I figured. We took a gamble with the trailer, but she's worth it."

"What are you going to do?" Brandon asked.

"Use the ship."

"What?"

"If we don't make it, I'm going to the board. As in put my ass in a suit, fly to L.A., and use the ship as collateral against the cost of funding the movie. We both know the ship is worth a hell of a lot more than the production costs."

"There's an idea." A spark flashed in his eyes that I almost called pride.

"I know Dad will be pissed. It's Mom's ship."

"Yeah, well, Dad's in Mykonos right now…if you catch my drift."

My mouth dropped. "No fucking way."

Brandon nodded. "Why do you think he's been working so hard to hand over everything? He told me that there's a difference between making a living and making a life."

"Holy shit." That was incredibly unlike our type-A father.

"Then he told me that watching you is what taught him that."

Okay, now I was speechless. "I don't...I don't know what to say."

"Say you'll use the ship. Dad spent your entire life investing in you. Now it's time for you to invest in yourself, and I honestly think he'll be excited that you're making a business decision for once. You've got this. Now go jump through the air." He slapped me on the back again and walked off, passing Landon. "Break your leg, asshole," he called out, flipping him off.

"Nice to see you, too, Brandon," Landon answered. "Damn, that guy has a memory like an elephant. Is he ever going to let that go?"

"Steal a guy's girlfriend once, and his brother hates you for life," Penna answered, wheeling over to us.

Landon winced. If he'd known what had gone down the last week with Rachel here, he'd be doing a hell of a lot more than wincing. "Come on. That's ancient history."

"Not as ancient as you might think," I said with a grimace, then pushed Penna away before he could ask what I meant.

All three of us made our way along the plywood path that had been set down for Penna until we reached the ramp that led to the raised dais. I glanced up at the Jumbotron. We were still a hundred or so views away from a million. So incredibly close, but not close enough.

"No regrets," Landon said.

"None," Penna agreed, squeezing my hand. I glanced down

at her, but she already had her Rebel smile in place, and I hated that while we might be at the end of our crucible, hers was just beginning.

I found where Leah sat next to Brandon in the VIP box. No regrets. Well, unless she still didn't want me after this trailer played. Then I would have basically laid my heart out on top of mortgaging my ship. Yeah.

The announcer did his thing, but I wasn't listening. I only had eyes for Leah, and the way she fidgeted with the skirt of her dress that bared her legs.

Then I found the microphone in my face and slipped into being Wilder. "What's going on?" I asked the crowd, and they roared.

"We're the Renegades, and we thought we'd put on a show for you guys! I'm Wilder, this is Nova, and Rebel, of course, had a little mishap, so she'll literally be sitting things out until her bones can catch up to the level of badass that she is."

The crowd booed, but cheered when Penna took the mic. "Sorry, guys, I said go, and the bike disagreed. Don't worry, it's three months, tops. And if you're nice, I'll let you sign my cast," she added with the flirtatious grin she was known for.

Then she handed the mic back. Damn, I was proud of her.

"Right, so how many of you have seen the trailer about what we've been up to these last three months?" I asked. The crowd went wild.

"At least they like it," Landon said quietly.

True, but there was only one reaction I was interested in. I met Leah's gaze and spoke only to her...well, and the fourteen thousand other people here. "We were asked to cut a trailer that would give you guys a glimpse at the stunts we've been pulling, and I realized something. If you hang around the Renegades

WILDER

long enough, chances are you're going to see one of us fall."

The crowd booed, and Penna did a mock salute that turned the crowd to soft laughter.

"The truth is that I fell. Hard." Leah's lips parted. "And I didn't realize just how hard until I was already on my knees, begging for mercy. Love does that to you—breaks you down and then builds you back up into something even better. I can tell you that it's an extreme sport of its own, but it's more dangerous, because the outcome isn't solely in your hands, and there's no parachute once you jump."

Her eyes widened, and it took every ounce of my willpower to stand on that stage instead of going to her.

"So in case you missed it, here's the first glimpse of our new project, *International Waters*."

The arena darkened as the trailer began. Fuck, I couldn't see her face, or watch her reaction. This sucked.

The music started, and I knew by heart what she was watching. It wasn't just the stunts…it was me falling in love with her. It was the moment she'd agreed to zip-line, then when she'd called me an asshole and climbed out of the pool. It was me absorbed in her smile in Bermuda, and the moment I'd pulled her onto my lap when she fell off the ramp while we were at sea. It was me calling her baby, trying to get her to wake up, cradling her to my chest. It was her face watching me skateboard in Barcelona, and the far shot of when she'd kissed me on the beach. It was our kiss in Rome, on the bleachers, and the shots Bobby had snuck through the window as we studied, neither of us able to concentrate much on the books. It was the Mykonos sunlight in her hair, and the GoPro footage I hadn't even realized Penna had taken when we BASE jumped at the shipwreck. It was the slow dance in the club, the way I watched her walk away when I was supposed to be practicing, all interwoven with the Renegades commentary about what experiences they were having on our trip. It went to me begging Leah to let go, and her jumping in Morocco, and landing in the water, and her flying into my arms after the landing in Madagascar.

I'd never in my life been as thankful for Bobby's snooping cameras, or the masterful way he knew how to cut tape. He'd taken three minutes and, instead of putting out an extreme sports trailer, produced a love story punctuated with the adventure of a lifetime.

The crowd cheered as the lights lifted, but I kept my eyes on Leah, who had tears streaming from hers. "So what do you say, Firecracker?" I asked into the microphone. "Are you ready for the adventure of a lifetime? Because I know you're the only rush I need."

I stood immobilized until my play-by-the-rules girl vaulted over the divider and bolted for me. Then I dropped the mic, uncaring as it hit the ground, and jumped from the dais to meet her halfway.

My arms wrapped around her at the same moment her mouth found mine. I angled for a deeper kiss, knowing that I was claiming her not just in front of fourteen thousand fans, but everyone watching live on ESPN—realizing that she was marking me as hers, too, and loving every second.

I broke the kiss before we went to an NC-17 rating, and simply rested my forehead against hers as the crowd went berserk around us, taking in every single nuance of the moment. "I love you," I said to her.

"You're everything," she said, using my own line on me. "Oh, and I love you, too, which is something I don't see changing anytime soon...or ever."

"I like forever."

She smiled. "I said ever."

"Yeah, well, you know me—I have to push everything one step further."

"Forever," she agreed, and kissed me softly, which sent up another raucous cheer. "Now you'd better go jump before the crowd turns on me." Then she ass-smacked me in full view of our audience, and I laughed. "Go get 'em, Wilder."

"Paxton. Always your Paxton."

"Yeah, it's a good thing that I love the other guy, too, even if he is king of all the wild things." Then she flashed me a smile and went back to the wall, Brandon helping her over.

The show went off without a hitch. The junior Renegade crew hit every stunt, nailed their timing, and made the fans drop their jaws. Landon hit spectacular whips and air, pulling all sorts of freestyle shit that had the crowd screaming his name. We pulled off our tandem tricks, moving together with one heartbeat as we always had—brothers in all but blood.

When it was time, Penna kissed my cheek backstage, Nick gave me the thumbs-up, and I gunned it, soaring toward the ramp, hitting the kicker at the exact right moment, and turning once…twice…three times…before landing, my entire body tingling from the adrenaline and the roar of the crowd.

"Paxton Wilder is officially the first to ever complete a triple front!" the announcer called out, his excitement as palpable as mine.

"You did it!" Leah called out as she raced to me, and I lifted her up, spinning us to her laughter. "You flew!"

I stopped as the other Renegades rushed us, the cameras not far behind. "How could I not, when you gave me wings? Besides, I actually kind of like you," I said, remembering the first time she'd told me that she wasn't overly fond of me.

Her smile lit my world. "Good, because I'm head over heels in love with you."

"Now that's a stunt I'd like to see."

"Later," she promised.

And at the end of it, with Leah in my arms, the taste of her in my mouth, I found home, peace, and a victory so sweet that the rush would last me a lifetime...or until I could talk her into making that forever official.

I kissed her again, thankful for the miracle in my arms and the knowledge that we had a forever full of "laters."

Starting today.

ACKNOWLEDGMENTS

First and foremost, thank you to my Heavenly Father for blessing me beyond all measure.

Thank you to my husband, Jason. Babe, a year ago we were in New York, praying for an answer, a way to keep our family together. Now Audrey-Grace is adopted, we're together in Colorado, and all is right with our world. Thank you for being my rock, not just during this last, insane year, but always. Thank you for hopping red-eye flights when I needed you, and for kissing me the same way today as you did when we first started dating. You are my constant. Thank you to our children, who had their lives uprooted, have seen three houses and three schools in one year, and still radiate joy...when you're not plotting against one another. Thank you for cleaning up the Silly-String War of 2016 before I had to use my ugly voice, and giving me a reason to work so hard. The love I have for all six of you knows no bounds. Thank you to our social worker, Kristy Trimper—I think out of everyone in this world, you have seen me at my worst and my best, and we cannot thank you enough for fighting on behalf of our daughter. You're the reason we're home, complete, and thriving.

Thank you to my parents, who adapted to five little kids in their house while we moved from NY. Thank you to my sister, Kate, for giving me a reason to put down our roots here, and not rolling your eyes too hard as we struggled to find where we belong. Thank you to my brothers...you guys rock. You should come home more often...seriously. Thank you to Em and Christina for knowing that I always mean to call you back.

Thank you to my editor, Karen Grove. Karen...I love you, and I don't say that lightly. Thank you for digging through a book I wrote in the month we unpacked our house and using your magic to make it shine. Thank you for taking a chance on the Renegades, the Flyboys...and me. I'll do my best to never let you down. Thank you to the insanely talented staff at Entangled: Liz, Melanie, Debbie, Brittany, Candy, and Curtis, you guys make my dream come true on a daily basis. Also... I'm never going on the Ferris wheel of death again, so don't ask. Thank you to my PR team, Melissa—you hold my sanity in your hands on just about a daily basis. Thank you for always giving me a safe place. Linda—squirrel-chaser extraordinaire, thank you for being my bestie, my cheerleader, and always remembering extra bobby pins when I inevitably forget mine at any of our various signings. Allison—thank you for being not just a fantastic PA, but an amazing friend. Thank you to my phenomenal agent, Louise Fury, for believing in me, cheering me, grounding me, and pushing me to be better. I'm grateful for you every single day.

Thank you to the incredible authors who keep me sane. Rachel, Cindy, Mindy, Molly, I'll zip-line with you anytime. Gina-freaking-Maxwell, thank you for being my spirit-sister and keeping vampire hours with me. Kristy, Lauren, Laurelin, Alessandra, Christine, Corinne, Claire, and Rose, thank you for answering every insane question I could ever ask and giving me a place where anything goes. FYW ladies...thank you for giving me a reason to wear pink on Wednesdays. You ladies are such a class act. Mandi, Heidi, Isabelle, and the rest of the TBR group, thank you for amazing chat sessions that constantly allow me to procrastinate. Katrina, Lizzy, Michelle, Jenn, Kennedy, thank you for being awesome—no seriously—there's nothing like being surrounded by brilliant, empowering women. The bloggers who work so hard to promote, review, and support authors. You guys are my rock stars: Aestas, Natasha T., Natasha M., Jenn, Kimberly, my love—Jillian Stein, Jen, Reanell, Lisa and Milasy, Angie, Beth and Ashley, and the countless others I can't fit here. I could fill up an entire book with how much I adore you and how grateful I am for the work you do! Liz Berry, thank you for taking a chance on me, and always making me feel extraordinary.

My Flygirls...you guys...you're everything.

Lastly, thank you again to my husband. Because you close out every day of my life with so much love that I can't help but write swoon-worthy book boyfriends...after all, I'm married to the original Flyboy. God, I love you.

Wilder is a thrilling story of death-defying stunts and heart-stopping romance. However, the story includes elements that might not be suitable for all readers. PTSD, paralysis and physical injury, grief and loss, night terrors, motor vehicle accidents, high-risk stunts and tense situations, scars, mentions of hospitalization and imprisonment, conflicts with police, and graphic sex are shown in the novel. Readers who may be sensitive to these elements, please take note.

*Don't miss the exciting new books
Entangled has to offer.*

Follow us!

f @EntangledPublishing

◉ @Entangled_Publishing

♩ @EntangledPub

AMARA
an imprint of Entangled Publishing LLC